ANGELA

Another Kind of Cinderella

Easy Silence

Also by Angela Huth

FICTION

Nowhere Girl
Virginia Fly is Drowning
Sun Child
South of the Lights
Monday Lunch in Fairyland and other stories
Such Visitors and other stories
Invitation to the Married Life
Land Girls
Wives of the Fisherman
Wanting

NON-FICTION

The English Woman's Wardrobe

FOR CHILDREN

Eugenie in Cloud Cuckoo Land
Island of the Children (ed)
Casting a Spell (ed)

PLAYS

The Understanding
The Trouble with Old Lovers

ANGELA HUTH OMNIBUS

Another Kind of Cinderella
Easy Silence

ANGELA HUTH

An *Abacus* Book

This omnibus edition first published in Great Britain by
Abacus Books in 2002
Angela Huth Omnibus Copyright © Angela Huth 2002

Previously published separately:
Another Kind of Cinderella first published in Great Britain in 1996 by Little, Brown
Published by Abacus in 1997
Reprinted 1999, 2000
Copyright © Angela Huth 1996

The following stories have previously been published:
'Another Kind of Cinderella' in *Winter's Tales*; 'Dressing Up' in the *Daily Telegraph*;
'Mothers and Fathers' on *BBC Morning Story*; 'To Re-Arrange a Room' in *Marie Claire*;
'The Wife Trap' in *Raconteur*, 'Squirrels' in *Winter's Tales*; 'Mistral' in the *New Yorker*;
'Men Friends' on *BBC Morning Story*.

Easy Silence first published in Great Britain in 1999 by Little, Brown and Company
Copyright © Angela Huth 1999

A CIP catalogue record for this book is available from the British Library.

ISBN 0 349 11527 3

Typeset by M Rules
Printed and bound in Great Britain by Clays Ltd, St Ives plc

Abacus
An imprint of
Time Warner Books UK
Brettenham House
Lancaster Place
London WC2E 7EN

www.TimeWarnerBooks.co.uk

Another Kind of Cinderella

For my mother

Contents

Another Kind of Cinderella   1

Dressing Up   27

The Day of the QE2   41

Mothers and Fathers   63

Laughter in the Willows   79

To Re-Arrange a Room   115

Alternative Behaviour   125

The Wife Trap   153

Squirrels   179

Mistral   203

Men Friends   223

Another Kind

of Cinderella

'Now come along, gentlemen, *if* you please,' urged Lewis Crone, waving his baton. 'What we want is a little more *up*lift in the last bar, don't we? Up, up and *away*.'

'Stuff it, Lew,' murmured Reginald Breen, second violinist, under his breath.

He dabbed at the sweat on his forehead with a large white handkerchief. It was bloody hot down here in the pit, even in winter. And he was damned if he'd give the last bar a lift. It wasn't exactly Beethoven the Winterstown Concert Orchestra was struggling to bring some life to, after all. Just wallpaper music to fill the gap where the Fairy bloom-ing Godmother turned the mice into ponies. They hadn't half had some trouble with the ponies this year, what's more – doing their business just at the wrong moment, and so on. Reginald sniffed.

'So once again, gentlemen,' the mighty Lewis, conductor with airs above his station, was saying. 'We'll take it once again, *if* you please.'

What's the point, Reginald wondered, being this partic-ular for this kind of show? Not a soul in the audience would notice whether or not there was a wretched uplift in the last bar. Half of them would be under twelve. The other half, pensioners' outings, were plugged into hearing aids.

For them a pantomime was no different from a silent film. He tucked his instrument under his chin, and turned with an exaggerated look of scorn to his friend, Tom, first violin.

'Better give it the works,' whispered Tom, 'or he'll keep us into the dinner hour.'

'Righty-ho. Last time. Up, up and *away*.' Reginald had perfected his mimicry over the years.

He and Tom lifted their bows in unison. Tom caught the conductor's agitated eye. The orchestra crashed once more into the last few lines of forgettable music. Their sudden energy came from indignation. Lewis Crone had kept them at it since ten this morning. They were now hungry, bored and fed up with his absurd attention to detail. Trouble was, Lewis had once seen André Previn rehearsing an orchestra on television. Since then he had applied his own version of Previn's methods to the WCO, causing much suffering and discontent. In the old days they'd played through the score a couple of times at the beginning of the season – *Jack and the Beanstalk, Aladdin, Mother Goose,* whatever – and that was it. Now, all this pernickety fussing was driving them to near rebellion. Most of the players – weary, professional men – had considered resigning, but none actually did so. There were not many openings for their class of musician on the south coast. Tom was the most vociferous in his complaints. Reginald encouraged him in his discontent, for Tom's resignation would be to Reginald's own benefit. Once Tom had gone he, Reginald, would surely become first violin. He had waited some thirty years for this position. Over and over again others, outrageously, had been placed above him – incompetent musicians, mostly, from outside the orchestra. And once, worst of all, a very junior 'talented' violinist from the WCO itself. He hadn't lasted long: no stamina. Many times Reginald had suffered the humiliation of being passed over, and had kept his silence and his hope. He could not afford to resign.

The morning's rehearsal over, Tom and Reginald made their way along the front. They exchanged few words: music was their only common interest. Proper music. Tom carried his violin case under his arm. Home, this afternoon, Tom would be practising the Mozart concerto. Reginald would be attending to his mother.

The sea breeze on their faces was good after the stuffiness of the orchestra pit. Reginald always enjoyed the short walk home. It refreshed him, gave him strength for the tasks ahead.

'Still haven't got the coach finished, I hear,' said Tom.

'Coach and beanstalk, it's the same every year, always late.' Reginald smiled at the thought of the familiar incompetence.

'At least we'll see Valerie in her spangles, tomorrow.' Tom was something of a woman's man, keenly sensitive to the potential of leading ladies.

'She's as good a Cinderella as I can remember, I'll say that.' Reginald himself had been quite taken with her – what he could see from the pit – during the past month of rehearsals.

As the men parted, Tom paused for a last look out to sea. There was a small fishing boat on the horizon.

'Give anything to be out there,' he muttered, more to himself than to his friend. 'Always fancied playing on the deck of a boat, up and down in time with the waves.' He gave a small, helpless laugh. Reginald smiled in reply. He, too, had known fantasies that would never materialise.

He slowed his pace, once Tom had gone. He was always reluctant to return home and face *that* kind of music: but face it he must, as he told himself every day. If he didn't hurry and buy his mother her paper there would be more to answer for.

'Is that you, Reginald?'

The familiar peevish tone bit into his ears as soon as he was through the door. Who the hell do you think it is, he wanted to shout back. Who else would let themselves in at twelve fifty-five precisely, as he did five days a week?

'It's me, mother, all right,' he called, and clenched his fists, taking a grip on himself before going in to the front room.

Mrs Breen sat in an armchair in the bow window. Her vastly swollen legs hung from widely parted knees, slippered feet not quite touching the floor. A mustard crochet cardigan – made in the days when she still bothered to sew the crochet squares together – covered a bosom so cumbersome she was unable to see her own hands in its shade. But the fingers (the worst kind of sausages, Reginald thought, among other savage thoughts) worked skilfully on their own, crocheting away, square after square, hour after hour. The furious, pale eyes, scowling on their ledge of fat purple cheek, were attending to some cooking programme on the television. Mrs Breen had not moved since Reginald had left her that morning. She was not able to move on her own. Her illness meant she was almost completely immobile, though Reginald had reason to think that on secret occasions, when she wanted something badly enough, she was able to reach it. Chocolates in the tin on the bookshelf, for instance. Their unaccountable disappearance, observed by Reginald on many occasions when his mother was in bed, could only mean one thing. But the time had not yet come to challenge her.

Her mauvish bulk backlit by the netted light from the window, Mrs Breen made no effort to drag her eyes from the television.

'I fancy the Ambrosia today, Reginald,' she said, 'with that tin of plums you got last Friday.'

Incapable of shopping herself, her recall of exactly what her son had bought, when, was extraordinary. She would plan the life of half a pound of cheddar down to the last slice, insistent that only an ounce should be used for the sauce for the macaroni, and the merest scrapings for the Tuesday cheese supper with biscuits and tomatoes. Should Reginald miscalculate, and the cheese be finished before its allotted time, Mrs Breen would be moved to one of her famous rages when every blood vessel in her body enlarged, darkened, and threatened to burst through her glowering skin.

'Anything else?'

'Tin of curried spaghetti still there, is it?'

'It is.'

Reginald's heart pounded in relief. Last night he had had half a mind to eat it, but had resisted on the ground that he had had no energy to ask his mother's permission.

'Then I'll have that.'

Reginald went to the kitchen to set about opening tins and preparing the tray. The room faced north. Any light that managed to challenge the old curtain at the window was diffused by the coarse-grained and very dirty net. A smell of disinfectant clashed with the smells of years of frugal meals. Opening the window was forbidden, so the air was never cleared. The kitchen gave Reginald a headache every day. He dreaded it. But there was no escape. How many years, now? Eight? Almost nine. And how many more . . .?

When he had placed his mother's tray of lunch beside her, he returned to the kitchen. But he could not face either washing up last night's supper dishes and the breakfast, or making himself a sandwich. Instead, he went out into the strip of ill-kept grass that was the back garden. When his father had been alive, herbaceous borders ran down both sides – borders that kept the old man's every spare moment fully occupied. From the thin earth, he had managed to persuade a magnificent show of hollyhocks, tulips, dahlias (his speciality) – the lot. But Reginald could never be bothered with gardening. Everything had gone to seed, died off years ago. Now the lawn was bordered with weeds. But the apple tree, the single tree in the Breen family possession, still blossomed. And the blackbird still lived there. Reginald listened to its song now – vibrant, optimistic notes that gave him the courage to go on, sometimes. He lit a cigarette. Into his mind came a picture of Valerie, who in tomorrow's dress rehearsal would be in all her finery at the ball. He looked forward to that. He found himself pecking quite fast at the cigarette, then grinding its stub under his heel with a force that surprised him. Valerie was the sort of girl, had things been different, Reginald might well have approached. He had no great ambitions concerning her, of course, even in his imagination. With the difference in their ages, marriage was naturally out of the question. No: all he wanted, or told himself he wanted, was a friend. Her funny crooked smile and short bouncy hair inspired him with exciting ideas of friendship. Perhaps one day he would summon the courage to speak to her, see how things went.

'Reg! It's time.'

Reginald allowed himself a moment's more reflection, then returned to his mother. It was time for the dreaded visit to the bathroom, the ungainly negotiating of the dim passage, the old woman's entire weight on his arm, her invective spewing in his ear. Then, the long afternoon. He would have liked to go to his room, have another go at the Tchaikovsky. But his mother could hear, she said, however quietly he played. It hurt her ears, all that screeching, she said – she had always wanted Reginald to go into insurance, like his father. The violin was forbidden in the house.

Instead of music, it would be shopping at the Co-op, hoovering the stairs, two hours of bad-tempered Scrabble, another tray for high tea, television, and the terrible ritual of putting Mrs Breen to bed. By the time Reginald went to his own room he was exhausted. Like a disobedient child, he would play his radio under the bedclothes for a while, very loud. This was the part of the day he most looked forward to. Much though he enjoyed his nightly blast of illicit music, it put him to sleep almost at once.

*

On the noticeboard at the stage door it was announced that the transformation scene was the first to be rehearsed. Reginald felt a slight pricking of anticipation as he undid his violin case, took out the instrument and wiped its bow. The awkward notes of his fellow musicians, tuning up, usually filled him with gloom and unease as he faced the long morning of indifferent music ahead. Today the squawks of striving notes could not touch him. He tried out a few notes himself, tightened a couple of strings. He scarcely noticed Lewis Crone blundering up on the podium, cocky, grinning, one hand fingering a yellow tie.

'Making a statement, what?' whispered Tom, who was using a duster to polish his violin – a very superior instrument which could not have been better cared for had it been a Stradivarius.

'Won't get anywhere,' replied Reginald. He had no idea why he made this comment, or if there was any truth in his speculation.

The stage lights were switched on, bringing life to the Ugly Sisters' grim kitchen.

'Idiot,' yelled a voice from off-stage. 'That's the ballroom effing light.'

The peach light was dimmed, replaced by the kind of light usually glowing in the front room at Reginald's house. No wonder Cinderella, shortly to be sitting by the giant fireplace, needed a Fairy Godmother. Reginald could have done with one most days himself.

Bev Birley, in fishnet tights and a short satin tunic, came striding on to the stage. Bev was Prince Charming. Last year she had been Jack, the year before Aladdin. Beginning to show her years, too, thought Reginald, noting the definite thickness of her hips. He had never liked Bev – not that he had ever had occasion to talk to her. But she was stuck-up, haughty, tongue like a whiplash to junior members of the cast, though all agreeable smiles to visiting stars. Between seasons, Reginald saw her sometimes in the town walking a terrier. Once, he recognised her picture in the window of an optician. She was wearing flyaway blue-tinted glasses and her hair had been stuck down with grease. She still did not look very nice. Presumably, not being in national demand, she had to do any job she could to keep herself going between seasons.

'Anyone wanting me this morning?' Bev shouted into the darkness of the auditorium, legs spread wide, hands on hips, her annual stance in every proposal scene. There was a slight titter in the orchestra pit. Tom nodded towards Reginald. Bev scowled.

'No one wanting you till two, darling,' the director called from the back of the stalls. 'See you then.'

Bev stomped off.

'Stuck-up bit, know what I'd like to do to her,' whispered Tom.

Reginald had no time to imagine what this might be because Cinderella came on to the stage just then, wrapped in a large cloak. She wore a great deal of scarlet lipstick which made her crooked smile look very grown up. As Bev passed her, she whispered something that made them both smile, and ruffled her hair.

'Cheek,' said Tom.

'Taking liberties, sucking up, usual thing,' agreed Reginald.

'Quiet now.' Paddy Ever, the director – or Ever Anxious, as he was known – had moved forward to take command. He leaned over the pit and shouted up at the stage.

'Why are we wearing a cloak, darling, in the kitchen?'

Cinderella, Reginald could see, looked confused.

'Wardrobe said it was a cloak for this scene. Suppose I'm cold in this bloody great kitchen, no central heating.'

The musicians smiled among themselves. At the beginning of the day they were ready to respond to any kind of joke, no matter how feeble.

Paddy scratched his head. 'I mean, *would* Cinderella suddenly be in a cloak? *Why* would she be in a cloak, now, but only in a dress in the last scene? Is it viable, is all I'm asking. Is it *rational*?'

Paddy's worries were known to hold up proceedings, sometimes for ages. The musicians flicked their music, rested their instruments. They could be in for a long spell of problem-thrashing before Lewis requested their first chord.

'Don't be daft, Pad: cloak on, amazing quick change in the dark. Stands to reason.'

Paddy's face briefly relaxed. Reginald did not envy him his job. 'Balldress under . . . point taken, darling. But why the sudden lipstick?'

They could hear Cinderella sigh. 'Can't put lipstick on in the dark, can I?'

'Righty-ho, lipstick on. Let's go.'

The Winterstown pantomime was all a very different kettle of fish to the Palladium, Reginald thought, as he did every year.

The rehearsal began. Cinderella and the Fairy Godmother, a dear old thing who had been in panto for years and whose underarms, these days, swung as the wand waved, played the scene too far downstage for Reginald to see anything. He could only just hear Valerie's sweet voice and strange emphasis. 'Oh, god*mother* . . .' He liked such original rendering.

It wasn't till after the mid-morning coffee break that the musicians were required to play the few high notes whose purpose, as Lewis so often explained, was to convey excitement. There was drama with the ponies, as usual: two nasty little Shetlands, hired at great expense from an animal psychiatrist, but who had minds of their own just the same. They refused to stand still, and laid back their ears warning what would happen should they be pressed to act against their will. One of them nipped young Andrew, the coachman. A part-time actor mostly out of work, Andrew proudly admitted he started off at the bottom year after year, but remained convinced that one day his moment would come. Trouble was, as he once confided to Reg, he was so nervous of the ponies, despite their small size, that it was all he could do to keep holding their reins, let alone think himself deeply into the part of the coachman. A lamp fell off the coach as soon as Andrew returned from being bandaged, and then the door wouldn't open. 'Bloody useless wand,' snapped the old godmother, longing for her lunchtime Guinness as the carpenter hammered away at the door.

It was a morning full of laughs – the kind of morning that made up for so much of the aching boredom of the job. And at last Cinderella appeared alone in the spotlight, cloakless, dazzling in a dress of sequins splattered on to net. Reginald still could not see her properly: he would have to wait for her upstage number, *I'm going to the ball*, for that. As it was, the wolf-whistles and laughs from the stagehands – an old tradition at any leading lady's first dress rehearsal – made him uncomfortable. For all its good humour, Reginald did not like the idea of Valerie in all her finery being laughed at.

At the lunch break, Reginald hurried out alone from the pit. He had to break the news to his mother – whose dinner was, thank God, provided by Meals on Wheels today – that there was to be an unscheduled rehearsal this after-noon, due to delays this morning caused by the coach and ponies. Her outrage was predictable. He would have to lis-ten to ten minutes of abuse and insult – 'If you were Sir Thomas blinking Beecham I might understand' – before providing her with a calming glass of brandy and making his escape. Dreading the scene ahead, he barged clumsily round the corner that led to the stage door, and bumped into Valerie herself. She was still in her balldress. The sequins, in the poor winter light, looked asleep.

'Excuse me, I'm so sorry . . .'

'Reg, isn't it?' Cinderella gave him a wonderful smile. Her grasp of every name in the company endeared her to all.

'I have to let my mother know . . .'

'Like the dress? Isn't it gross?' She laughed. 'See you later.'

Reginald spun home, weightless. His mother's fury, the

cold sausage for his lunch, the smell of the kitchen, the jibes at his general uselessness, meant nothing to him. Impervious to everything but the extraordinary thumping of his heart, inspired by Cinderella's smile, he was in and out of the house with astonishing speed. As he hurried back up the garden path, almost enjoying his mother's wailing in his ears, Reginald knew he was in love with Cinderella, and was to spend the afternoon playing for her alone while she danced above him at the ball.

In the next two weeks of rehearsal, Reginald did not run into Valerie backstage again. But in his new state of love he was quite happy to be patient, to hear her sweet voice above him, hear the tapping of her feet, and to catch the occasional glimpse of her when she was upstage. Her prancing little body and enchanting smile were particularly appealing in her ragged dress, though he saw her best at the ball: the choreographer had naturally arranged for the prince to waltz with his Cinderella as far upstage as possible. Reginald, putting his soul into every note of the banal waltz, followed her steps as Bev swung her about. They gazed into each other's eyes, the woman and the girl, acting the kind of happiness which was so convincing it caused Reginald a jealous stab. Fact was, they were much better actors than he had ever given them credit for. The audience would believe this was Prince Charming – not Bev the part-time optician's model – in love with Cinderella, not Valerie who, Reginald knew, sometimes sang in a pub to make ends meet.

He longed for an event that he knew would never happen: waltzing *himself* with Cinderella in some posh hotel ballroom with chandeliers, far from Winterstown. Then on the balcony of their suite, the moonlight and roses bit: he would play a little tune – one of his own compositions, maybe, while she sipped champagne. Next, he would kiss her. So hard she could no longer smile. After that . . . but there his fantasies stalled. He could only imagine a paling dawn sky.

None of that would ever happen. It was some consolation, watching her, to know that at least *this* was all make-believe. What Reginald could not have borne would have been Val (she had become Val in his mind) dancing, in real life, with another man. He closed his eyes as he pulled the final note from his violin. He longed.

At the first performance of *Cinderella*, as always, there was a full house. The audience, mostly pensioners and school-children, loved it. Val, taking many bows, had never looked so appealing. She and Prince Charming held hands and smiled copiously at each other. Reginald would have liked to have gone round to her dressing-room and joined the crowd of admirers he presumed would be there, tell her she was wonderful. As it was, he had to hurry. His mother would be furious at his lateness caused by the prolonged applause.

Once again, he ran into Valerie, surprisingly, in the passage that led to the dressing-rooms. She was still in her balldress, an old cardigan slung around her shoulders.

'Good first house, wasn't it?'

Reginald nodded. The compliments rose, then withered in his throat.

'Bev and I are just off for a hamburger. See you.'

She was gone.

On his way home, Reginald decided what to do – for now, he believed, he should waste no more time, act fast. He would send her flowers. Huge great bunch in cellophane, small card in the envelope saying *From a secret admirer*. The thought of this plan went some way to dispelling his fury with himself for not speaking to her. She must think him a useless old man. But time would change all that. Plans beginning to crowd his head, he opened the front door.

'Is that you, Reg?' His mother's shriek was more than usually annoyed.

Protected from her by his inner strategies, Reginald went calmly to deal with her cocoa, the wearying process of putting her to bed, and all the arrows of her fury.

Reginald dreamed that night of himself and Cinderella at a princely ball, but he never sent the flowers. He managed to leave early enough, next morning, to get to the florist before rehearsals for a concert. But he was so confused by the scents and colours and prices, he left without buying. He'd had in mind pure white lilies, or cream old-fashioned roses mixed with cornflowers – the kind of thing his father had been so proud of in his border. The florist seemed to have only crude red or rust flowers on stiff stems, leaves unbending as swords. Nothing worthy of Cinderella.

Then, just as he was coming out of the shop – the assistant's eyes contemptuous on his back – he observed Val and Bev walking down the other side of the High Street. Both wore jeans and anoraks. For a moment it was quite hard to recognise them. They paused, kissed each other on the cheek, and Bev disappeared into Boots. Valerie, turning to continue on her way, saw Reginald. She waved, smiled her glorious smile, arming him for the day against all adversities.

There were plenty of those. At the rehearsal for a concert in the Winterstown Hall, Lewis was at his most waspish and petulant, quibbling with Tom's tone and Reg's high C, and sneering so hard at poor old Jim Reed on the drums it was a wonder the man did not resign on the spot. But as his bow soared through the *Enigma Variations*, transporting him to the English countryside in May, walking in meadowlands with Cinderella, it came to Reginald that the only way to make any progress with her was to *do* something. Like ask her out for a drink.

At the lunch break that day the other members of the orchestra left for an hour in the pub. Reginald could not be persuaded to join them. He wanted to be on his own: Meals on Wheels was dealing with his mother. There was no reason to move.

He sat, violin across his knees, in the forest of empty chairs on the stage. The music played on in his ears, not disturbing the real silence. Down in the vast hall, chairs were stacked against the walls ready to be regimented for the next concert. A thin rain pattered against high windows. The light on the bare walls was dull as old stone, and it was cold. But Reginald spent an undisturbed lunch hour, oblivious of everything around him, walking with Valerie in Herefordshire (a place he had always longed to visit). He was, for once, at peace.

After the performance that night he hurried to the stage

door, and then out into the alleyway at the back of the theatre. It was still raining, a cold hard rain that damply spotted his mackintosh. He stood, eyes on the square light of the glass door, violin case under one arm, heart pumping audibly. Members of the cast and orchestra came out in groups, and singly. Once a show was under way, nobody planned much of a social life after performances. They were all keen to get home.

Almost last, Valerie emerged. She wore a scarf wound high round her neck, but no hat. In the rain, and the light from within, the frizzy mop of her hair glittered like a swarm of fireflies. Behind her, Bev was talking to the porter at the stage door. She wore her imitation leopardskin coat and seemed to be cross about something. Val saw Reg.

'What's up, darling?' she asked.

Reg moved his free hand on to the solid, familiar curves of his violin case.

'I was wondering,' he said, 'if you'd care for a quick drink on your way home?'

He deliberately said quick because there was not much time. He had taken the precaution of making up some story to his mother about having to see the manager, but her credulity would not stretch far. Half an hour's grace, at the most.

Val laughed. It was not the friendly laugh. But perhaps sound was distorted here, out in the rain.

'Why not?' she said. 'Bev and I and some of the others are going down to the Drake. Want to join us?'

Reg paused for a second. Val's idea did not fit in with his plan at all. The last thing he wanted was to be with her in a crowd, perhaps unable to exchange a word. He wanted her to himself, just a small table, somewhere, between them. He wanted her full attention while he told her some of the things that had been piling within for as long as he could remember, and had never been spoken. His violin had been the sole recipient of his feelings, the music his only consolation. But man cannot live by music alone, as Tom, who had many an eager woman on his arm, so often said.

'I don't think I will, thanks. My mother . . .'

'Very well. Another time.' Val was not interested. But then something of the approaching Christmas spirit, Reginald supposed it was, entered her funny little head. She decided to be kind. 'But tell you what: tomorrow after the matinee? Bev's going to the dentist so we can't go over to her mum as per usual. We could have a coffee.'

'A coffee?'

A kaleidoscope of difficulties swooped through Reg's brain. More excuses to his mother would have to be thought up, and where would be a suitable place to go?

'Very well,' he said.

'Meet you here after the show, then. Bev!'

Bev hurried out, glanced at Reg. Val was all smiles.

'Blimey, what a night.' Bev snapped up an umbrella, put her arm round Val, drawing her beneath it. 'Cheers, Reg,' Bev said, and Reginald watched Val slip her arm into the crook of the nylon leopardskin one.

They moved away, in step, huddled snugly under the umbrella, confident of its shelter, like those people in the advertisement for a life insurance company. Reginald waited till they were out of sight. Then, hugging his violin case, he turned into the full blast of the rain, in the direction of home.

Reginald and Val sat at a small table in the window of the Wimpy Bar - nearest eating place to the theatre. Reginald had suggested they go to the tearooms further down the High Street, altogether a more comfortable place, but Val had insisted she fancied chips in the Wimpy.

Two cups of thin coffee sat between them. Val covered her chips with spurts of ketchup from a plastic tomato. Reginald kept one hand on his violin case, propped up beside him. His head was empty from lack of sleep. He was drained, exhausted, by his imaginings. He didn't know where to begin. Ten minutes of their half-hour had passed, and all he had done was to make a disparaging remark about Lewis Crone. Val had disagreed. She said far as she was concerned he was a good sport.

'It must be boring down in the pit,' she said eventually, 'not seeing anything.'

'You can see enough. I get a good view of you dancing in the ball scene.'

'That!' Val laughed, more friendly than last night. 'See Bev treading on my toes? She's a horrible dancer.'

She laid one hand flat on the Formica tabletop, examined her nails with great interest as she slightly lifted each finger in turn. Reginald wanted to cover her hand with his.

'You're a lovely dancer, though,' he said.

Val gave him a teasing look. 'Reg! Haven't you got a wife, a woman? Someone? You always look so down in the dumps.'

'There's my mother to be looked after.' Reg suppressed a sigh and tapped his violin case. 'There's my music. I'm all right, just not one of life's jokers.'

'No.'

The speech Reg had rehearsed most of the night, inspired by Bach under the bedclothes, welled. It was now or never, he thought.

'But I'd like to get to know you – nothing . . . out of line. Cup of tea sometimes. Talk. You know. I haven't much of a life socially. What with my mother. Drink with Tom, Saturdays. End of a concert drink with the boys. Not occasions to talk . . .'

Reg petered out, aware he had lost the thread of his message. The rubbish he was talking sounded close to self-pity. He didn't want Val's pity: last thing he wanted. And she had stopped picking at her chips. She pushed her empty cup away, stiff-handed. Gave a tight little smile, as if she decided she must get through this little scene as graciously as possible, but it was boring.

'Poor old Reg. Well, it's fine by me if we have another coffee some time. Though I'm leaving Winterstown, March. Doing three months in Manchester, an Agatha Christie.'

Reginald's heart contracted. He would have to think about that later: the bleakness of the spring.

'Anyway,' she smiled, nicely this time, 'you must be fifteen years older than me, Reg.'

'Probably.'

It was dark outside now. The pair of them made awkward shapes reflected in the plate-glass window. Madness seized Reg so fast he was unable to control it, to reason with himself.

'But I'm over the moon about you, see. Nothing bothersome, mind. Just, watching you dancing away, Cinderella in her ballgown, I fancied your pretty smile was for me. Daft, I know.' He saw her look of alarm, tried to slow himself. 'All I want is to talk to you, don't I? To tell you things, give you a good time, spend my savings on you. I've a fair bit put on one side – nothing to spend my wages on all these years. What do you think, Val? Would you let me, sometimes?'

Val gave a small laugh, perturbed. 'I don't want anything like that, nice though you are.'

'No. Well. I didn't rate my chances high.'

'It's not that I'd mind a chat from time to time. But Bev wouldn't like it. There'd be trouble. I've had enough trouble.'

'Trouble with Bev?'

'Bev's my friend.'

'I know Bev's your friend. But she can't order your life about. A woman.'

Val sighed. 'Have to be going,' she said. 'Meeting her at six.'

'Meeting Bev? What's she got, this Bev?'

In his confusion, Reg could not be sure of anything. But for a moment – so short he might have imagined it – he thought Val looked scared.

'A nasty temper if things don't go her way.'

'You shouldn't put up with her. I mean, do you *like* her?' Later, Reg reflected, his boldness may have been impertinent.

Val shrugged. 'Thanks for the coffee 'n' chips.' She stood up, swirling the scarf round her neck.

'Cinderella,' said Reg. 'Cinderella.'

She bent briefly towards him. He could smell her breath: ketchup, chips, coffee. She patted his shoulder.

'Chin up, Reg.'

'I want you to know' – her hand fled from his shoulder – 'that every performance it's you I'm playing for, Val, down there, all that rubbishy music. One day I could play you Brahms, on a beach somewhere, tide coming in, never go back to the orchestra. They'll never make me first violin is what I'm afraid of, not even when Tom goes. You could, you could come with—'

Val turned from his jibbering, impatient. Reg could tell from her eyes she thought he was a silly old fool, letting go.

'What you must remember is this, Reg.' Her voice was harsh as flint now, cutting the quick of him. 'You're a nice guy, but I'm another kind of Cinderella.'

She was gone. Striding through the purplish light, the ketchup tables, the bleak landscape of Formica and burgers. Reginald remained standing, clutching his violin case, peering through the window. In the late-night shopping crowds he thought he glimpsed a leopardskin coat, but of Val he could see nothing.

That night he kept his eyes on the music, did not look up to see Cinderella in her balldress dancing with Bev the prince. Reg had always known she was not for him, any more than was the position of first violin. But who was she for? What did she mean, another kind of Cinderella?

After the performance he hurried off to avoid an accidental meeting. It was a night full of ironic stars. Just twenty-four hours ago, in the rain, she had given him some hope. He didn't know why he bothered with hope, anymore.

'Is that you, Reg?' Furious voice. Usual thing.

Reg made his way slowly across the small, stuffy hall and into the front room. He opened the door, surveyed the familiar picture of the monstrous old woman who was his mother: the mother who had messed up his entire life. Plumped up with indignation, she sat upright in her chair, accusation flaring across her purple cheeks, obscene legs swinging. If it hadn't been for his binding duty to her, things would have been different. If he had been a worse son he would have had a better chance.

'What kept you then? Dancing with Cinderella?'

She gave a sneering laugh, thumping one swollen hand into the soft mess of crochet on her knee. Reginald swung his violin case above his head, and moved towards her in silence before they both screamed.

Dressing Up

'Please, just one more chance,' cooed Prunella in her most persuasive voice. 'Just lunch and the afternoon.'

There was a long silence while her daughter Audrey, on the other end of the line, struggled to weigh up the pros and cons of her mother's request.

Prunella, although dreading this call, was fed up with watching time flood by with no sight of her grandchildren. It was over two months, now, since the unfortunate incident. Surely enough time for anyone to find forgiveness. But Audrey had never been rich in charity. Even as a small child she had shown signs of her father's hardness. She was vigorous in her condemnation, ungenerous in her understanding. Prunella had always been a dutiful mother, and hoped she always would be. But she couldn't like Audrey.

And how beastly she had been about the incident. A very minor mishap: no ill effects on the children. They had had *fun*, as they always did have when they came to their grandmother. More than they had at home, for the most part. It wasn't Prunella's fault Audrey had been held up in traffic, so arrived late to collect them on that particular day. Well, by six, half an hour later than her usual time for the first one, Prunella was exhausted, in need of something. She must have had two gins and tonics before Audrey arrived. Having started late, perhaps she had drunk them faster than usual. What with one thing and another, on the way down the path to Audrey's car she had stumbled, cut her knee, felt dizzy. There had been quite a palaver, Audrey pulling her up, grumbling away, telling the children to buzz off and find a plaster. 'You're irresponsible, Mother,' she had hissed when the children, all sympathy for their grandmother, had run off. 'How do you expect me to feel about leaving them with someone who *drinks*? Anything could happen. I shan't let them come again.'

Prunella hadn't felt like arguing. She had sat on a kitchen chair, one stocking an ignominious roll beneath her knee, watching Audrey savagely dab the bloody patch. The children hugged her goodbye, said they hoped they would see her soon. She had given them a box of chocolates, which afforded Audrey the opportunity for a familiar lecture on children's teeth before hurrying them away. Prunella hadn't seen them since then. Audrey was carrying out her threat. This was her punishment. Drink: and no grandchildren. Deprivation of the two people who gave her most pleasure on earth, these days. She was a callous monster, Audrey. How could she have given birth to one of so little compassion?

But this silly feud had gone on long enough, Prunella thought, at dawn the autumn day of the call she eventually forced herself to make. She must put an end to it. She must swallow pride and anger, apologise, make promises not to touch a drop before the children arrived or while they were there: promise anything. She must compromise herself in a disgraceful way. But any form of humiliation was worth it to see the grandchildren.

At eleven o'clock she drank two cups of coffee without their usual addition of brandy. This daily booster, she had found, gave the necessary strength for the rest of the day. Unfortunately, Audrey's antennae were so acute she seemed able to tell if her mother had put so much as a dash of sherry in her trifle, just by her voice over the telephone. So this morning, wanting to take no risks, Prunella had denied herself fortification. Without it she was feeling very shaky. The receiver of the telephone danced at her ear. Sweat frosted the back of her neck. Her heart was leaping like a young lamb.

'One more chance, then,' said Audrey at last, in her tight little voice. 'You know the conditions.'

'I know the conditions. Of course I—'

'Just lunch and the afternoon. I'll drop them at twelve. And no chocolates either, please.'

'Poor mites! Very well, no chocolates. I've missed them so much. They must wonder why they haven't been for so long.'

'They haven't said anything.'

Prunella knew Audrey was lying. She was able to detect her daughter's lies on the telephone every bit as distinctly as Audrey could detect her own small indulgence of alcohol. But this morning she didn't care. The main thing was she had won the battle. The horrible waiting, the isolation, was over. She would see the children in just two days. Dear George, gallant beyond his years: Anna of the laughing eyes. Prunella poured herself a third cup of coffee, laced it with a fierce shot of brandy.

She was determined to take no risks. After breakfast on

the day of the children's visit, she put the bottle of brandy in the dining-room cupboard – a cold, deserted room she scarcely visited – and locked it. She put the key in the pocket of her apron, hoping she would forget where it was. Back in the warmth of the kitchen she placed a tea cosy over the bottle of gin. The smile of its white label stretching across its elegant green shoulders was the temptation evenings, afternoons, that she could not resist So long as it was hidden, she would be quite safe.

The hours passed so fast in busy preparation of the children's food that Prunella did not stop for her usual cup of coffee, let alone brandy. At twelve, everything ready, the table laid, Ribena poured, she remembered this and smiled to herself. Sometimes, it was so easy. When you were happy, there was no need for a booster. Maybe she'd leave the brandy in the cupboard. Not touch it tomorrow, either. Make a real effort. Sling out the grinning gin. *Reform*, as Audrey would say. Though what would Audrey know about the near-impossibility of such a thing?

The bell rang on the dot of twelve-thirty. Audrey was always punctual, and superior with it. She gave a hurried smile, trying to disguise the twitching of her nostrils, the mean detection of drink on her mother's breath. Hoping to catch me out, the bitch, thought Prunella. But it didn't matter. With George and Anna wriggling under each arm, she felt bold, strong.

'Do I pass the breath test?'

'Don't be stupid, Mother. I'll be back at five.'

Once Audrey had gone the children burst from strait-jackets of polite demeanour – always worn in the shadow of their mother – and hugged their grandmother so hard she was almost knocked over. She managed to brush aside any answers to their questions about why they had not seen her for so long with the promise of small presents awaiting them in the kitchen. She produced shiny black pencils with their names engraved in gold, with notebooks to match – 'For your secret thoughts,' she said. The children laughed. They were always delighted by the quaintness of their grandmother's presents, so carefully chosen. At home, they were rich in computer games, Walkmans, miniature televisions – quick, easy, expensive presents which could be bought with no trouble. Spoiled in this respect, they still appreciated real worth: their grandmother's presents were of especial value.

Prunella's kitchen, where she spent most of her time, blazed with signals of her life. Old photographs, lists, theatre posters, half-finished pieces of tapestry were either stuck to the walls or piled on the floor or chairs. It was not uncommon to find grated carrot in a pair of satin evening shoes that had lodged by the stove for the past twenty years, or a rusty trinket in the fruit bowl. The children, accustomed to the white Formica sterility of their own kitchen at home, loved the room. It bulged with memories of happy afternoons since their earliest childhood, and was always full of the warm expectation of exciting things to come. Occasionally they would venture into the large, cold, unused rooms of the house, deserted since their grandfather had died. But they thought of them as sad, dead rooms, that made shivers run down their backs, and would quickly hurry back to the life of the kitchen.

As usual, they ate hungrily of their grandmother's food, made promises not to tell about the chocolate pudding. They listened enchanted as she told stories about her intriguing past, which had been a very glamorous time, and indeed she had been very famous. A dancer, a singer, a bit of both – and only twenty years ago some television company had come and persuaded her to talk about her past: they had seen the recording over and over again. She was a star, their grandmother, they could tell from the many photographs of a beautiful face that smiled from the mists of the old photographs on the walls. And even today she was a star, bright red hair – the children didn't believe it when their mother said it was a wig – long gipsy earrings, scarlet nails, silver eye-shadow. But for the wrinkles, she could be mistaken for a rock star, they thought. And underneath her apron she wore velvet dresses of crimson or purple or sapphire that flashed a patchwork of light, and she smelt of face powder from a bygone age.

'And what shall we do today?' she was saying. 'How best shall we pass the afternoon, little ones?'

'Dressing up,' they said.

'I thought so,' said Prunella. Of all the old-fashioned activities she thought up for them, dressing up was the favourite. 'I brought down some new things from the attic.'

In a trice they had leapt upon the huge cardboard box waiting under the window. (It had taken three whiskies, last night, to give Prunella the strength to drag it down from the attic.)

'How did you get this down all by yourself, Gran?'

'Easily!'

'You're brilliant, Gran,' said Anna.

Prunella, dumping dirty plates into the sink to be washed at some future time she had no wish to think about, beamed. She listened to the small cries of amazement and amusement as the children plucked pantomime clothes from the box. They would pull something on, then, more strongly attracted by something else, pull it off before it was in place.

The dishes cleared, Prunella sat at the table giving advice and encouragement. She panted a little, felt a little light-headed. Well, the children's visits were dizzy times, stirring up the stale old quietness till the kitchen became a place she could hardly recognise. Besides, she had worked so hard this morning, never a moment off her feet.

What she wanted was a drink.

The children were ready at last. George was a small laughing cavalier, ostrich feather swooping from his velvet cap right under his chin; Anna was a shepherdess with a laced bodice and yellow silk stockings.

'Wonderful!' Prunella clapped her hands. 'You look real professionals.' This, they knew, was her highest compliment: she had been the most professional professional in her time. 'Now for acting.'

'Not without you, Gran.'

'What, me? Dress up too?'

This moment of mock surprise was a small charade enjoyed every visit. Prunella would feign reluctance, then find herself persuaded.

'Well,' she would say, as she did now, 'if that's what you

want . . .' And they would shower her with myriad things to choose from till she, too, had become a character, a star from some world-famous theatrical show.

Prunella stood up. Knees shaky. She fended off the gust of scarves and jackets they threw at her.

'Just a moment, darlings. Gran just needs a . . . to keep her going. Put on some music, George, why not? Let's begin with our old *Blackbird* to put us in the mood.' She opened the fridge, took out the bottle of white wine. She poured herself a tumbler.

George, child of the technological age, always had some trouble with the workings of the maplewood box his grandmother called the radiogram. But eventually he persuaded the old table to spin the 78 record – *Bye Bye, Blackbird*. They had known all the words for years.

'When somebody says to me
Sugar sweet, so is she
Bye bye, blackbird . . .'

Within moments, Prunella found herself pumping the old power into the song. The once-famous voice trembled poignantly on every note, drowning the thinner voices of the children. She drank a second glass, picked up her skirts, pointed a velvet shoe with a diamanté buckle.

'Now, off we go. Follow the silly old bat, won't you? *Bye, bye, blackbird . . .*'

'You're not a silly old bat, Gran.'

The children knew the rules: copy every movement precisely. This afternoon Prunella was full of invention. They skipped around the table waving their arms as if carrying invisible boughs. They grabbed apples from the bowl and threw them high. They flicked their fingers under a running tap at the sink. They – and this was their favourite part – climbed up a chair on to the table, creaking the old pine top as they twirled between bowls of hyacinths – and then leapt down the other side. Those brief moments high on the table felt like being on a stage.

'Oh, happy chorus line, darlings,' Prunella sang. She downed a third quick glass. 'Up we go again, why not?'

This time, on the table top, she did a few steps of the can-can. Amazed by their grandmother's high kicks, the children gave up trying to copy her. They watched, entranced.

'Not the right music, of course, but I can still kick a leg, can't I? Let's see if I can't find a can-can record.'

Prunella, jumping ambitiously back down on to a chair, missed her footing. There was a crack, a thud and a dignified whimper, all muffled by the music as she flung one fat arm dramatically behind her.

'Gran? – Quick, George,' shouted Anna.

George slithered off the table, laughing. He bent over Prunella on the floor.

'Are you doing your dying scene, Gran?'

Anna prodded a vast velvet hip, its lights twinkling less brightly in the shadow of the table. She could see, so close to Prunella's eyelids, the smudges of silvery blue were thick and uneven. The lids looked like wrinkled blue worms lying side by side. When her eyes were open, you didn't notice this. Anna wished they would open now. The record slurred to the end. Now the only sound was the running tap.

'You can get up now, Gran,' she said.

'Think she's dead?' asked George.

'I suppose I'd better feel her heart.' Anna was top in biology at school. She ran a reluctant finger over the left velvet breast, feeling the warmth but no distinctive heartbeat.

'There's stuff coming out of her mouth,' observed George, 'and isn't she a funny colour? Maybe she's unconscious.'

'I'll ring for an ambulance.' Anna's coolness in a crisis had been rewarded by making her a prefect. All the same, the telephone jittered in her hand.

'Better not say she's dead,' said George, 'or they won't hurry.'

One of the ambulancemen removed the scarlet boa from Prunella's neck and quickly plunged down, locking his mouth on to hers.

'Kiss of life,' Anna explained to George.

'Wouldn't fancy that,' George giggled. The ambulanceman sat back on his heels, frowning. 'You've got lipstick all over you.'

'Pipe down, young chappie. What about you two?'

'Our mother will be here any minute,' said Anna.

'That's good, because we'd best get a move on.' He was helping the second man to attach a drip to Prunella's arm, still stiff in its last flourish.

It was a struggle to lift her on to the stretcher. One of her shoes fell off. The boa left scarlet feathers on the ambulancemen's uniforms. George deplored the sight of his grandmother's knee, suddenly revealed, that only moments ago had been so impressive in its kicks.

'Poor old Gran,' said Anna. She hated the sight of the shock of copper hair tipped sideways, proving her mother was right about a wig. She hoped George would not notice.

'If she's not dead, then it's her best ever dying Juliet.' Tears of admiration ran quietly down George's cheeks.

Audrey, hurrying punctually down the path, found her way impeded by the ambulancemen and stretcher. In the second she paused, she saw the multi-coloured mound of her mother, clown-white face smudged with blue eyebrows, powdery blobs of salmon pink ironic on the old cheeks. She screamed.

From the front door the children watched her livid journey.

'Cool it, Mum. Gran had a fall.' Anna herself felt a strange calm.

Audrey swivelled round at the slamming of the ambulance doors.

'You *idiots*! Of all the stupid . . . Quick, we must follow her.' She ripped off George's hat and threw it nastily to the ground. 'What *happened*?' George retrieved his hat. He had no time to answer before Audrey ran into the kitchen, saw the empty bottle, the up-turned chair. Again the children watched her from the door.

'Christ! I can't believe it. Never, ever again . . .' she shouted, exploding eyes glassy with tears.

Anna hitched up her skirt with pitiless hands.

'No use threatening us,' she said. 'Gran may be dead.'

'On the other hand,' said George, 'it may just be one of her best dying scenes.'

He knew about the sweetness of revenge from his history books, and the power it could engender. With a solemn look he replaced his feathered hat, tilting it in just the way his grandmother had assured him, light years ago, was appropriate for a laughing cavalier.

The Day
of the QE2

Nothing very much ever happens in Ballymorning, a small town of little significance on the Irish coast. While the folk who live there are proud of its tranquillity, they do sometimes wish that a quiver of excitement would bestir the peace that lies flat, heavy, stifling, over its uncrowded streets and shops of unfashionable gentility. Even the pubs afford little gaiety, except on the occasions of a wedding party or a funeral wake.

The young of Ballymorning usually leave for Dublin or Cork as soon as they are able, there being no work and no temptations to keep them at home. If they feel any nostalgia for the town of their birth when they have gone, this is not reflected in the number of occasions they visit their homes. Once departed from Ballymorning, resigned parents know, there is little likelihood of their offspring returning. There is a familiar pattern, discussed by many a mother who has done her best, of contact with grown-up children becoming more infrequent. It is the penalty, perhaps, for such peace and quiet.

Some years ago, a few of Ireland's tourists began to discover the limited attractions of Ballymorning. The view from its harbour is the thing they like best. You can see them standing there in little groups, identifiable by their anoraks the colours of nursery rhymes, polystyrene beakers of coffee in hand, gazing out beyond the curve of the giant harbour wall, allowing their gaze to follow the North Sea to the horizon. Sometimes they sit on the coils of tarred rope. Eyes strained by the abstract contemplation of the sea, which tells them nothing, they seek relief in the seagulls bouncing in the air above them, their orchestrated shrieks making contemporary music that shreds all contemplation. They point their cameras this way and that, these tourists whose delight is to notch up places on film, and go on to somewhere better supplied with amusement.

The older inhabitants of Ballymorning do what they can to take advantage of this new, albeit thin trade. Irene O'Connor, in the Post Office and General Stores, has initiated a sideline in homemade soda bread and scones. She's up half the night baking, but the profit, in the summer season, is worth her effort. Her neighbour Jack Riley, formerly a tinker, applied himself to the renovating of his old pony trap. He spent three months polishing, painting, mending, oiling. Then he clipped his old piebald cob, long since retired from the shafts, and advertised rides in the trap down to the harbour and back. This proved popular with visitors longing to be free of their children for quarter of an hour. One look at Jack and his quaint transport, and trust reared its cautious head. There was no doubt the children would be in safe hands. And they were. Jack made them laugh with stories of his past life on the road. Word of this entertainment travelled. Takings are now good. The pony cart rides cause a seasonal ripple in Jack's retirement. The benefits of initiative have come to him just in time to enliven his old age, and he is able to offer more copious rounds of Guinness in the pub. He feels quite proud.

Tom Deary, retired teacher and part-time barber, is another of Ballymorning's inhabitants to have been inspired by the thought of making profit from the tourists. Tom is a character who commands universal respect in the town: so kindly and mild a man there never was. He is said to have come from some minor aristocratic family, about which he is modestly vague. This belief was strengthened in 1952, when an uncle bequeathed to Tom his almost new Armstrong-Siddeley. A suitable garage was built for the wondrous car, which had only travelled 130 miles in its five years of life. Tom, perhaps inheriting a reservation about mileage in his genes, has only added some eighty-four miles to that number in the last forty-five years. Those miles were most reluctantly agreed to: on one occasion he allowed the Armstrong-Siddeley to be used as a wedding car for his niece Sheila, who then took the further liberty of asking Tom to drive herself and her husband to their hon-eymoon hotel some way to the south. This caused Tom many traumas concerning the lodging of confetti on the carpeted floor, and in the difficult places between the leather seats. The second occasion for the car's outing was a charitable cause. A neighbour's daughter, crippled by an accident, requested a trip in a fairy-coach for a birthday treat. Her desperate mother reckoned Tom's car was the nearest Ballymorning could get to the desired coach, and set about her persuading. Tom found himself in a morally weak position. He could hardly say no to such a request, and wondered at the reluctance of his heart. He agreed with a smile which he hoped would disguise his feelings. And once they were on the road, mother and daughter on the back seat full of praises for his careful driving, his amorphous fears vanished. He had taken the precaution of covering the seat (against what, he could not say, even to himself) with sheets of plastic and several rugs, and in the very slow covering of seven miles, much to Tom's relief, nothing untoward happened.

No: to Tom Deary transport was not the point of the Armstrong-Siddeley. So grand a car, for a start, was not for the modest likes of him. To drive about in a machine of gleaming green paint and sparkling chrome would have been quite out of keeping with his character. It would have looked like pride. It would also have alienated him from his friends who owned lesser cars, or those who could only rely on public transport. To Tom, the car was simply a trophy: a symbol of the best of British craftsmanship, a sample from the days when cars *were* cars, beautifully hand-finished things which, in return for love and care and attention, would remain in pristine condition for more than a century.

Tom, who had once loved but never married, spent all his spare time on the upkeep of his inherited car. Three evenings a week he polished, vacuumed, treated the owl-eyed headlights to doses of Windowlene wiped carefully off with the most expensive chamois leather. Regularly he sent off to Dublin for supplies of superior beeswax polish with which to maintain the gleam of the walnut dashboard, with its irregular pattern of small round windows set in silver frames. Behind these, very simple dials remained unmoving, until the occasional moments when Tom turned the key and pressed the starter button, and the small arrows jumped to life telling him what he knew, but liked to have confirmed: petrol tank full, oil fine. He kept the smart little clock, also inlaid into the walnut, wound. When, at the end of his work, he would sit in the driver's seat, relishing the smell of the fat leather seats the colour of Jersey cows, the comforting silence was scarcely chipped by the discreet tick of this gallant little clock. Garage doors open wide, sun beating on to the dazzling bonnet, stuffy warmth making him drowsy in his stationary Armstrong-Siddeley – this, for Tom Deary, was happiness.

In all probability, nothing would ever have changed his routine had there not been a sudden crisis in the garage roof. A particularly hard wind caused it to let in rain in several places – a tacky construction, the garage, for all its expense, and now presenting real danger to the well-being of the car. Tom lived on a meagre teacher's pension – there was not much barbering these days, and the old wisps of hair he still tidied up were always 'on the house'. So how could he pay for repairs to the garage roof? Tom put the matter to Jack Riley, who in a conspiratorial whisper made mention of the fact that he, Jack, was doing very nicely out of his little business with the pony cart. Tom then recalled that his great-niece, Sheila's daughter, imprisoned in a loveless marriage, had mentioned she was doing well from her own sideline, selling postcards down by the harbour. The tourists were obviously the answer to his prayer, Tom thought. He walked slowly into the night, a sharp fish-wind coming up from the sea, to reflect upon how he himself could take advantage of them.

There was a struggle in his soul all night long, for Tom knew that the single thing he had to offer was the Armstrong-Siddeley. The problem was, the very thought of strangers riding in his car, however exorbitant the fare, cast his spirits so low he could feel a physical sawing in his breast bone, and in all his sobriety he felt the weak dizziness of a drunk man. Why, strangers with no appreciation of fine things would be up to all manner of tricks. They would stuff sweet papers down the arms, spill drinks on the carpet, blot out the sweet smell of the leather upholstery with their own crude scents of sweat and cheap aftershave. Tom could not bear to contemplate such things. Besides, driving them along the lanes he would be so worried about the possible lapses in behaviour that his power of concentration would be at serious risk. He might land them all in a ditch, destroying the car completely. No, there would have to be another way.

It came to him early in the morning: an idea so simple, so watertight, he wondered it had not occurred to him sooner. It was this: on fine days (business would be closed should rain threaten), he would ease the car into the road outside his house and allow any passing visitor to sit in it, for anything up to half an hour, for a small fee. Just to *sit*, mind. Never in the driver's seat, and with the doors open, to make sure any alien smells could not be harboured. Tom himself would pace round the vehicle, keeping a beady eye while he regaled his customers with stories of the car's history. Here, he acknowledged, as the car had led a somewhat dull life mostly in the garage, he would be forced to use his teacher's imagination, and work on a few embellishments.

Should there be any sign of untoward action, such as a sticky sweet being unwrapped, the offender would be politely requested to get out of the car at once.

This, it seemed to Tom, was the perfect solution. Tourists would be only too willing, surely, to pay for such an experience. Though it might lack the predictable excitement of a big dipper, or the charm of listening to Jack Riley's pony's hooves making their olden-days clip-clop on the cobbled streets as they sat in the uncomfortable seats of his cart, this would be something quite different, unimagined. Luxury! What Tom could advertise, in the modern jargon he so despised, but appreciated its uses, was *quality experience*. For how many people had ever seen so beautiful a car as the Armstrong-Siddeley? Let alone sat in one? Oh yes, he was on to a winner. The garage would surely be paid for within weeks.

Tom set about composing his advertisement, which he was to put in the window of the General Stores. He wrote in a fine copperplate hand, but the wording proved difficult. He was not a natural slogan man. Cutting down his description of the Armstrong-Siddeley's attractions to a few compelling words he found very hard. It took some dozen attempts before he was satisfied with the finished advertisement. Meantime, he cleaned the car with extra vigour, and decided on the part of road on which he judged the car would appear to greatest advantage.

Early in the New Year, the first tourists were observed discovering the unusually quiet spot of Ballymorning. The time had come for Tom to launch his business. One morning he opened the garage doors, intent on taking out the car. But somehow he found himself distracted, polishing the back number plate and oiling the ignition key which swung from a tag of real pigskin – the sort of thing not provided by car manufacturers today. On several other occasions, he made serious attempts to begin. It was only a matter of starting the engine, he told himself. But he never quite managed to get the car into the road and, as the weeks, growing warmer, passed by, the Armstrong-Siddeley remained undisturbed in the garage.

One morning in early spring, Tom, like many of the folk of Ballymorning, heard an announcement on the local radio. It seemed that the QE2, on a journey across the Atlantic, was forced to stop, for unspecified technical reasons, just outside Ballymorning's harbour. There it would be anchored, at midday, for some hours. Possibly even the night.

The announcer went on to say that the Mayor of Ballymorning, Clive O'Farell, had lost no time in seizing this opportunity for the people of his town to enjoy the kind of excursion they had never previously imagined. He had arranged for several fishing boats, in return for a small fee, to ferry anyone willing out to the great ship. There, they would be afforded a tour of its amazing decks and staterooms, and given a free cup of tea and plate of luxury cakes (as they were described) before returning home.

Glory be, said Tom Deary to himself, hand shaking badly over his softly boiled egg. How the devil did Clive O'Farell swing that one? Had he simply rung the Captain of the QE2 and put to him the suggestion, claiming it would be a good PR move for Cunard? Tom laughed out loud at the thought. Trust Clive: he'd always been a wily operator. He and Tom had been at school together, sat side by side in class one year. Clive, with his shocking red hair and endearing smile, had been the perpetrator of numerous tricks on teachers. His powerful innocence was always convincing. He was never caught. Tom always knew Clive would go far, and he had certainly accomplished the business with this clever move. The people of Ballymorning would be indebted to him forever – for here, at last, in most unexpected form, was the excitement they had been waiting for, needing, for so long.

Tom hurried off to ring some of his friends, find out how the thinking was going round the town. Even as he picked up the telephone, he knew that his own desire to board the QE2 would have to be sacrificed. Because now, faced with real impetus, crowds drawn to Ballymorning from miles around, he could no longer put off the evil hour. To him, the arrival of the ship was a sign from the Almighty. 'Get up off your backside, Tom Deary,' he could swear he could hear the good Lord saying. And he would. Today would be the launching of the Armstrong-Siddeley. A treat the tourists could never have envisaged. So long as they could find the way to his house (explained at some length at the bottom of his advertisement), Tom had no doubt in his mind that they would find it every bit as rewarding an experience as trudging the long decks of the QE2, and gorging themselves on free cakes.

Others in the town, Tom soon learned, were of his opinion: it would be foolish indeed to waste all the opportunities within reach on this very special day. They had all heard the news at 8 a.m. and again at nine (Tom, polishing the bumpers by then, had missed the repeat). They were all hurrying to prepare for the on-rush of visitors, the like of which they might never see again. Such general astonishment and such delighted shock had not been felt in Ballymorning for as long as anyone could remember.

In the centre of the town it was evident that the radio announcement had caused a considerable flutter. Tom quickly made his way to the General Stores to make sure his advertisement had not been removed from its prominent position in the window. He was pleased to find it still propped between a pyramid of homemade chutney and a basket of early Easter eggs: he was paying 50p a week for the exclusive position. Outside the two pubs, plastic chairs and tables were being dragged on to the pavement by owners who would normally scorn any such niceties. Fruit and vegetables were hastily being arranged in boxes outside the General Stores, a gesture not normally risked due to the changeable nature of the weather. Polly Shaunnessy, in the tobacconist, had come up with the idea of a special offer on dozens of iced lollies she had mistakenly over-ordered some months ago. She had carefully chalked the announcement on her old school slate. In the rush to sell wares, any old wares, several housewives not known for their hospitality now put notices for *Teas* on the front windows and were, Tom presumed with a smile, hastily baking behind their net curtains.

He decided to take a quick look at the harbour, see what was happening down there. After that, he would have to return home, drive the car into the street and be on duty for the rest of the day. In his mind, he saw dozens of visitors, those who preferred the idea of the Armstrong-Siddeley to the QE2, impatiently awaiting their turn to experience its magnificent seats. He might, he felt, have to be quite strict with the visitors: put on his schoolmaster's authoritative voice, insist they wait their turn in orderly fashion.

Five minutes later, he was amazed to see that, already, an unusual amount of cars were parked. Judging from their number plates, they had come from as far afield as Belfast and Cork – why, some of them must have heard the news at six o'clock and started driving towards Ballymorning straight away. Many of them kept to their cars, unspeaking as they took in the stretches of sky and sea before them, drinking tea from flasks. Others, collars up against the breeze, paced back and forth, cameras to the ready, their pleasure at being first, getting the good places, quite evident. None of them was yet drawn to either of the ice-cream vans – there had plainly been an earlier race for the best position. This had been won, by a few yards, by the local lad, Polly Shaunnessy's son Paddy, whose ancient converted van was splashed with wildly spelt promises. *Tuti Gelati! Genuine Italein flavours! Irish-Neapoltan ices!* Paddy's grandmother had come from Naples. His mother had inherited her talent for making ice-cream. Paddy, with his troublesome van that was a familiar sight broken down at the roadside, was one of the few young ones who had used his initiative instead of fleeing to a city, and was making an almost adequate living. Tom was pleased to see Paddy had parked as near as possible to the flight of stone steps that led down from the harbour wall to the fishing boats. He could not have been better placed to catch tourists in the queue to go over to the QE2. Competition, in the shape of a sterile commercial company van plugging 'Softee Ices', had not dared to park so close to the edge of the harbour and the surly-looking salesman within was no match for Paddy Shaunnessy's cheeky charm. It was a grand thing Paddy was the winner in his competition, thought Tom, and bought a chocolate ice to show where his loyalties lay.

'It's a great position you've got yourself here, Paddy . . .' he said. 'You should do well today.'

'I'm hoping so, myself. Are you going over to the big ship?'

Tom shook his head.

'In charge of my own business. Too good an opportunity to miss. It's the car, up there at the house. The Armstrong-Siddeley, all polished fit for the Pope himself. I'm bringing it out for people to sit in. Experience, you know. Should you see anyone fed up with waiting to get over to the QE2, you might oblige me by suggesting there's an alternative treat awaiting them not two streets away.'

'Sure, and I'll do that, Tom. Good luck to you,' said Paddy.

Tom, back to the sea, saw that a great many cars now were crowding into the harbour. There was a traffic jam in the small street that led down to the sea-front. A man was shouting, waving his arms. In the Edwardian houses of dun-coloured stucco and paintwork of long-dead brown, windows were opening, heads appearing. Turning away from this unusual, faintly troubling sight, Tom wandered down the long, narrow arm of the harbour wall that jutted into the sea. He made his way carefully between the nets laid out on the ground to dry. He licked slowly at the superb chocolate ice-cream – there was no commercial firm in the world that could compete with Polly Shaunnessy's ices – and looked over the almost flat grey waters, chipped here and there with sliver shards small as candle flames. There was no sun in the sky, but great braids of light fell vertically from narrow gulfs in the cloud. Tom preferred these subtle colourings of the sea and sky to the more popular blues, sparkling with sun. In the water-colours of Ireland he found a low-key peace. The bright places in travel brochures had never tempted him. The smell of tanning oils made him nauseous. He liked brisk, fresh air. Ice-cream finished, he took a deep breath: smells of salt and fish were plaited into the sea breeze. He had grown up with the constancy of this pungent breeze, and would never desert it to live further inland.

With some reluctance, Tom Deary broke his reflections to turn for home. In truth, he would have liked to stay where he was, eyes fixed on the horizon until the QE2, no more than a white speck the size of a distant gull, cut its way through the distant greys. He would have liked, with the others, to have sailed over to her on one of the rank fishing boats, and enjoyed the few hours contrast sitting like a bloody millionaire in a cushioned chair, chef's cakes and sandwiches on a table beside him . . . Something good to remember, that would have been. The stuff of fantasy. Still, it was more important to launch his own business. Mindful of the exigencies of the garage roof, Tom put wistful thinking to one side and hurried home.

Half an hour later he was gently easing the Armstrong-Siddeley from the garage. He parked it, with all the precision of a chauffeur used to driving such a car, in the road outside his bungalow. Although its high polish and dazzling chrome were as near perfection as anyone could imagine, Tom was of the opinion that it would be a waste of time merely to stand on guard beside the car waiting for customers. So he fetched his box of dusters the colour of marigolds, and the paler, primrose lengths of chamois leather, and made his way round the familiar body of his beloved machine, re-polishing what had already been re-polished a thousand times. He contemplated switching on the wireless. This, like the dials and the clock, was exquisitely incorporated into the dashboard – a few inches of knotty golden fabric, above a couple of handsome switches, was the only indication that the complicated mechanics of a wireless were embedded behind the walnut facia. But then he changed his mind: best not to tax the battery, he thought. Best not to ask too much of an old girl on her first outing for a very long time.

So Tom fetched his small black portable radio from indoors, and listened to it while hand and duster made their balletic circles across the dazzling paintwork. On the local news he heard that the response to the QE2's imminent arrival in Ballymorning had been beyond all expectation. People were arriving from all over. On the main road from Dublin, there was a queue outside the town almost a mile long. Visitors were parking on double yellow lines. The local police force was overwhelmed. Supplementary forces were being rushed in to control the traffic. One pub had reportedly already run out of beer. And down at the harbour the crowds were estimated at five hundred. People were warned, said the newscaster, to keep well away from the edge of the harbour wall, lest in the scrum someone should be pushed over the edge.

Wonderful, thought Tom Deary. That was all wonderful, indeed. Just what Ballymorning needed to give the locals a shot in the arm. He stopped his polishing for a moment to look down the street, see if any of the crowds so keen for the QE2 experience might be making their way towards the Armstrong-Siddeley experience – it could be a way of filling in time till the great ship arrived, he thought. If there were so many of them in the shops, as the newscaster had said, then it was unlikely they would miss his advertisement. But the street was empty. Well, to be realistic, it was more likely folk would plan to see the car on their way home. They would want a good place in the queue for the expedition to the QE2: Tom could understand that. Again, a painful wince went through him: what he would have done to be one of the first on a fishing boat, approaching the great white bows of the ship across the water – vast as an iceberg, it must surely be, vast as a skyscraper, and yet a structure that could still be lightly tossed by an angry sea. The kind of thing that made you think, that.

By midday, Tom reckoned there was not a single speck or smear left visible to the human eye. He put away his dusters. He was hungry but, not daring to leave the car unguarded, decided not to go and make himself a sandwich. Instead, he sat in the driving seat, wound down the window. Carefully, he poured lukewarm tea from a flask into a plastic cup, wiping both utensils with a handkerchief to ascertain no wayward drop would slither on to the leather upholstery. The smell of the beige leather provided its usual sense of pleasure: the thickness of the seat behind his back and under his thighs evoked a security that he could not have explained. Through the open window he could just smell the sea, a smell as frail as fine netting. Once, he'd taken a girl called Patricia to a dance in a dress of pale lilac netting, which she called tulle. For some reason, the delicate smell of the sea, nosing into the stuffy air of the car, put him in mind of Patricia – her smile, in particular.

Tom had forgotten to pick up his portable radio from the pavement. Rather than move from his comfortable position, he switched on one of the shining knobs of the car's wireless. From out of the strip of knotty golden fabric came the newscaster's voice, clear as anything.

'The people of Ballymorning, who were expecting the arrival of the QE2 at midday, have just learned from the Lord Mayor that announcements made earlier this morning were by way of an April Fool . . . Hundreds of visitors who had rushed from miles around to witness this spectacle, and indeed to take the trip out to the great ship itself, are said to be bemused, disappointed and even angry. Over now to our reporter in Ballymorning harbour . . .'

Tom, shocked, switched off the radio. He listened to the hollow silence. An April Fool, for heaven's sake. How could he, along with so many others, have been so gullible? How *could* Clive O'Farell have arranged trips around the ship, come to think of it, for all his cheeky daring? What a lot of idiots they all were . . . Even as he smiled to himself, Tom had to deal with a jolt of disappointment within him. He imagined the scenes down at the harbour, the confusion as hundreds of people tried hastily to leave in their inconsiderately parked cars. No wonder some of them found it no laughing matter. Still, the joke had been no bad thing for Ballymorning's locals. Trade in all areas, for a few hours, had been astonishing. And at least some of the disappointed visitors, surely, would make their way up to the Armstrong-Siddeley.

Brisk with hope, Tom got out of the car. In his excitement, he slammed the door more forcefully than he had meant to, and cursed himself. Then he stood to attention, in readiness for his first customer, waiting for the business to begin. Any minute, he thought, possibly dozens of people would arrive, grateful to be afforded some amusement to make up for the disappointment over the QE2, pleased that their journey to Ballymorning had not been wasted after all.

By four that afternoon, still standing stiff as a ceremonial guard by his car, Tom was dizzy, hungry. But when he saw three figures appear at the end of the street, determinedly approaching the Armstrong-Siddeley, all such sensations vanished. There was a man in the middle, a woman on either side of him. As they came nearer, Tom could see the man wore a tartan anorak, and tracksuit of trousers of a particularly offensive maroon. They were made of some kind of slimy material that caught the light. The women – one middle-aged, one in her twenties – were just as offensively dressed in bright, chemical colours. But they were smiling. Tom smiled back, forcing the stiff muscles around his mouth. They stopped, the potential customers, a few yards from where the car and Tom were parked. Tom deemed it wise to let one of them be the first to break the silence.

'Glory be to God, Holy Jasus,' said the man after a while. 'Quite a car you have here. How does your business operate, then?'

'Do we get a five-mile ride? I shall be waving through the window like the Queen,' said one of the women. She disengaged herself from the man, came perilously close to the car's bonnet. She reached out a finger. Very cautiously, as if to judge the quality of a piece of jewellery, she touched its paintwork. Then she quickly withdrew her finger, as if burnt. '*There's* polish for you,' she said, to no one in particular. Tom's eyes jumped to the tiny imprint her finger had left, indeterminate as a scrap of cobweb. He longed to take a duster to it, restore perfection. But, sensing that might look like rudeness, he remained where he was.

'You don't get an . . . actual ride in the car,' he said. 'As you can see, she's a very fine antique. I would not want to take the risk over our narrow lanes, now, as I'm sure you can understand.'

The man scratched his head, puzzled. He, too, came dangerously near.

'We read your notice in the Stores,' he said. 'We thought seeing as there's no QE2 we might as well get a ride in a limo.'

'Then I'm sorry you misunderstood the wording,' said Tom. 'It was not meant to suggest there would be a ride. Just a sit down in a remarkable old car, to reflect on the craftsmanship of times past, perhaps . . . For the quality experience,' he said, seeing their faces.

A look of sullen disappointment had now taken the place of the man's smile.

'We've come all the way from bleeding Belfast,' he said. He screwed up a fist and banged the car's bonnet. 'What sort of attraction do you think that is? Sitting in a stationary bloody car?'

Tom wanted to punch the man harder than the man had punched the car. But still he controlled himself, made no attempt to answer the rude question. The tension was broken by a squeal from the young woman. She leapt forward, grabbing the man's arm.

'Don't you see, Dad? You know what this is? It's another April Fool! Two in one day.' She smiled lavishly at Tom.

Her father looked at her. Comprehension began slowly to ooze from his pores. His expression of anger gave way to one of good humour, made sluggish by drink. He laughed, a raw, brutish laugh.

'Good heavens, you're right, too, girl. Place is full of April Fools, I'll say that now. Something to remember. Caught twice . . .' He twinkled at Tom. 'You've pulled off a fine trick, sir. Good luck to you.' He laughed. The women joined him, red mouths pulling back from smoker's teeth. They turned away, linking arms again.

All the way down the street they continued to laugh. As Tom got into the driving seat to return the car for the last time to the garage, he could hear them. He placed his hands evenly on the steering wheel, contemplated the trio through the immaculate windscreen. They shifted from side to side of the pavement, the women supporting the man in his unsteadiness. Their ugly noise still reached him. Tom wound up the window, cutting it off.

Silence returned: safety. Tom started the engine. For a moment he listened to its discreet music, then gently steered the great machine towards the garage. It occurred to him that people so foolish to think that his idea was an April Fool were not the sort of people who would have been any good at describing the trip to the QE2, had that not been an April Fool: and he found this thought was of some comfort.

Mothers

and Fathers

*T*hey had been sitting in the room together for a long time, in silence, unknown to each other, surreptitiously reading signs as strangers do.

He saw a woman in her early forties, an arrogant flare of nostril, fading reddish hair, good cheekbones, floppy beige clothes considerably smarter than those of most of the mothers he encountered on school occasions. She saw a man ten years older than herself, once perhaps handsome, now balding, red silk handkerchief in the pocket of his pinstripe suit indicating a certain flashness that did not match his aristocratic shoes. They continued their silence.

The door opened. The secretary, who earlier had shown them to the room to await their appointments, came in. She was clearly flustered.

'The headmaster's just been on the phone,' she said. 'It seems there's been an accident on the M1. He's stuck in a tailback that goes on for miles. Dreadfully sorry, but hopes you're able to wait. He'll ring again in twenty minutes with a progress report . . .' She kneaded embarrassed hands.

'I'll hang on till then,' said the man.

'So will I,' said the woman.

'Can I press you to a drink?' Both parents shook their

heads. 'Very well. Make yourselves comfortable. I'll be back as soon as I get the next call.'

'Jack Johnson,' said the man, as soon as the secretary had gone.

'April Verner.'

They shook hands, looked at each other more pertinently. Jack Johnson sighed, took the handkerchief from his pocket and waved it about like a conjurer before dabbing his completely dry forehead.

'Damn nuisance, this. I've come all the way from Lincoln.'

'I've only come from London.' April smiled sympathetically.

'Almost seven-thirty.' He sighed again, petulantly this time. 'You'd have thought he could have made use of his mobile phone a bit earlier, let us know.'

'Perhaps he wasn't quite sure how to use it.'

Jack saw April smile to herself. She had pretty teeth. He looked at her with more interest.

'How do you mean, doesn't know how to use it? Everyone knows how to use a mobile phone. Any man who doesn't know how to use a mobile phone shouldn't be a headmaster.'

Their eyes met.

'Probably you're right,' she said.

'Son here, have you?' asked Jack after a while.

'Two.'

'I've just one left, B Block. Fourth and last, thank heaven, the fees. Little wretch . . . The others were all in the top stream.' The minuscule twitch of his mouth suggested his pride in their achievement, rather than the disappointment in the present little wretch. He flicked at the strap of a gold watch. 'Up to no good, this last one, little monkey. Thought I'd better come and sort things out, see Smiley face to face. Headmasters can be evasive on the telephone, don't you find? So happened I was on my way to the West Country. Would all have been very convenient if it hadn't been for this hold-up.'

'Both of mine are in trouble. One not working – I mean, really not working. The other caught twice in the City by himself. There without permission.' She smiled again.

'Boys will be, and all that,' said Jack, smiling in return.

Their next spell of silence was interrupted by the return of the secretary.

'It's quite hopeless, I'm sorry. Mr Smiley's just rung again to say there's no telling, it may be hours. You mustn't wait. Would you like to make new appointments now, or shall I ring tomorrow?'

'Tomorrow'll do,' said Jack. 'When I'm with my office diary. Most inconvenient.' He shook his head, making sure the secretary was in no doubt of his feelings, indicating just what he thought of a headmaster who goes away on an afternoon when he has appointments with busy parents in the evening, thereby running the risk of failing to keep those appointments. Smiley should have been in school all afternoon, prepared. He should have made absolutely sure he was there.

The secretary, a-dither with more apologies, showed them to the front door. They walked together out into the road, where Jack Johnson's Bentley was parked in front of April Verner's Volvo.

'I've booked myself into The Old Parsonage for the night, matter of fact. Lovely place, always stop there when I have a chance,' said Jack. 'Why don't you come and have a drink before you go back to London? We could even have a bite to eat.'

April hesitated. She was hungry, tired. It had been a long and busy day at the office. No time for lunch. No time for shopping. Empty fridge at home. Empty house. Martin off somewhere in France, setting up one of his deals that necessitated Marilyn, his personal assistant, being there too.

'Lovely,' she said. 'I'd like that.'

In return for a drink and a sandwich, she was prepared to put up with almost any kind of company, even this tetchy father for whose fourth son she felt instinctive pity.

In the bar of The Old Parsonage, they sat at the small, polished table, previously booked for one, in a corner. April looked round at the hazy colours of the room, with its lively wood fire and myriad pictures on the walls, and a curious sense of luxury possessed her. These days, she was rarely asked out for a drink. Spontaneous adventures, the essence of her youth, had long since ceased. No matter how dreadful Jack Johnson, and she didn't like the way he waved ostentatiously at the waiter with a fat hand, she was determined to enjoy the next hour.

'Bottle of champagne – how about that? We need something to calm us down. Wretched fellow, Smiley, messing us about like this.'

April nodded. She longed for champagne.

'How about bagels and smoked salmon? They do it jolly

well here. Or the lobster ravioli, would you rather? Mind you leave room for the tiramisu.'

It was fun, choosing what to eat, though when she gave herself a moment to analyse the fun April realised it was the nefarious element more than the company that appealed to her. Here she was in Oxford, having supper with a fellow parent because the headmaster had not turned up . . . and Martin had no idea. Not all that wicked, really.

'Let's get through the CV,' Jack was saying, as they sipped the dry champagne. 'I'm a printer. Businesses all over the place. Lot of travelling about. Live in Lincolnshire, one wife, four sons. You?'

April hoped that after two rather large gulps of her drink she could be equally succinct.

'I'm a barrister. Specialise in divorce.' She saw Jack's eyebrows briefly clench. 'Just the two sons, as I said, both still here. My husband's in the import–export business – can't say I know a great deal about it. It means he has to go abroad a lot. He's in Paris at the moment.' With Marilyn, she didn't say.

'That's us, then,' said Jack, filling glasses. 'Jolly good. Now we can get on to something interesting.'

No immediate subject sprang to either of their minds, but halfway through their ravioli they found themselves ruminating on the one topic they had in common – parenthood.

'I suppose we're all bloody awful mothers and fathers, no matter how good our intentions to be otherwise,' ventured Jack. The champagne-induced pinkness of April Verner's cheeks appealed to him. 'Nature of parenthood. Nothing but failure and disappointment. Well, I go too far. When they do well, it's jolly satisfying. And I have to say my eldest three are a bright lot, conscientious. Suppose they got their brains from their mother – she's a scientist. I was never a scholar myself, nothing very brainy about Jack Johnson. Except when it comes to business. I'm a businessman through and through. Love it, the cut and thrust, the money. But young Simon, the little wretch I'd come down to talk about – he's a funny lad. Bit of a flibberty-gibbet, like me. Bit of a depressive . . . Don't know what's got into him these last couple of years. He's a worry, to tell the truth.' Jack paused to fill their glasses. 'Could be, I suppose, not quite ideal conditions at home these days, getting to him. Sheila and I seem to . . . have our disagreements. Think Simon's got it in mind we may be going to get divorced. Well, that's not so, but I'm damned if I know how to convince him. Awkward sort of subject. I'm not much good at that sort of thing.'

'My two are always asking why their father is away so much,' said April, after a while. 'I mean, they know it's business, his work. But it's as if they have their suspicions.'

'And might they be right?'

'No.' Lying to a stranger was better than disloyalty to a husband, for all his unfaithfulness.

'That's good. Ravioli all right?'

'Delicious.'

'You can't hide much from children. They're canny little buggers, see much more than you suppose.'

'True.'

'You're a damn pretty woman, if I may say so.'

'Thank you.'

'Are you on for the tiramisu?'

'Please. I'm something of a chocolate freak.'

'Cream's my undoing. You'll never convert me to this crème fraîche business. Sheila's always saying I'll end up with a heart attack. But a man can't be expected to give up all treats, can he?'

April's silence showed she felt the question to be rhetorical. In fact, her head was so fizzing with small explosions of light that it would have been beyond her to give the silly question a considered answer. Through the scintillating veil before her eyes, she saw her host as he must have been some twenty years ago, before his love of cream had pouched the skin around his jaw and the business lunches had reddened his cheeks. Her thoughts then turned to Martin. He was not a generous man. He would not consider it economically sound to spend money on champagne for his girlfriend. Somewhere in France, Marilyn would be sipping *vin ordinaire*. April felt unusually happy.

With the tiramisu, they had a second bottle of champagne. The chocolate seemed to have a sobering effect on the alcohol.

'What I always wonder,' said April, 'is how much example rubs off on our children? I mean, if they see their parents working hard, does this mean they follow suit, or determine to behave quite differently? Our two are far from stupid – in fact, both are particularly good at maths. But they say that judging by us hard work isn't all that rewarding – what can they mean by that, I wonder? They say it means we're away so much. Or if we're there we're always so preoccupied, not concentrating enough on them. Talk is nothing but plans, they say. There are few peaceful times.' She paused. 'The sad thing is, they're right.'

Jack briefly patted April's hand.

'You'd better have a lot of coffee before driving home.'

'I will.'

'Or, you could stay.' He watched her face, unable to read signals.

April found the idea uninteresting, but she was very tired. She did not like the thought of the drive home. Perhaps Jack meant she should take a room herself . . . though by the look on his face, he didn't.

'I've a charming room. The one, it's said, where Oscar Wilde discovered his proclivities.'

April smiled. If the example of parents rubbed off on to their children, then his four sons must be a pompous lot, she thought. Jack, taking her expression to mean acceptance, pressed her hand rather than patted it this time.

'I don't want to appear presumptuous,' he said. 'That's the last thing I want. Two strangers brought together by the non-appearance of a headmaster . . . very rum, but could just be our good luck. Shall I see if they have a room for you?'

That was rather nice of him, thought April, her head still afloat, her body deliquescent from the warmth of the fire. Considerate. A kind man. Martin far away with Marilyn. Too weary to listen to arguments within her, suddenly the fight went out of her.

'Don't bother,' she said.

April was intrigued by the bedroom, transformed from

the spartan place of Wilde's day. Everything had been thought of: safe, clock, magnificent Italian shower in the marble bathroom, fridge full of drinks, comfortable armchair, interlined curtains, fruit and flowers.

'Amazing,' she said. Exploring the place slowly enabled her to postpone the future imperfect, the awkwardness of making the next move towards the night in the large bed.

'I can see you're not used to hotels, this sort of thing.'

'No.'

'Ah.' Evidently Jack was.

As the champagne began to ebb, giving way to the clarity of mind induced by black coffee, April began to see the scene in all its horror. She had become a mere pawn in what was a normal way of life to Jack Johnson: trips away from home meant automatically picking up any available woman. He sat heavily on the bed.

'I won't lay a finger on you,' he said, 'if that's what you want.'

The horror receded: he was a man of surprises. April now felt she had maligned him. He wasn't simply a ruthless seducer, after all. In fact, he seemed a lonely man. Rather sad. And it had been a very generous dinner. A question, so often struggled with in her youth, came back to April – was he owed payment for such a dinner? What should she do? Even now, there was time to go.

April shut herself in the bathroom to confront herself. Twenty minutes later, she reappeared in the white towelling bathrobe provided by the hotel. Jack was watching the television, drinking whisky. He looked up, appraising.

'Parents,' he said, and laughed a little grimly.

The next morning, Jack Johnson and April Verner took breakfast at the same table, with its comfortable chairs, where they had dined the night before. A new fire was burning, pale bars of sun sloped across the white-clothed tables.

Jack had to be in Bristol at ten. He kept glancing at his watch. April was free until the afternoon, when she had a meeting in Chambers. She felt inclined, on so temperate a day, to linger in Oxford a while, walk through Magdalen deer parks, perhaps. See if the fritillaries were out.

'Well,' said Jack. The inner battle between impatience to be off and the desire to remain polite to the end of this assignation caused sweat to froth on his temples. He signalled for the waiter, the bill, no less ostentatiously than he had the night before. Between them they had eaten a whole basket of warm bread rolls and croissants baked at dawn.

'I must be off.'

'I might stay a while.'

'You do that. Another cappuccino? Read the papers.' He stood up. 'Very nice to have met you.' He leant down, kissed April on the cheek. She felt his dampness, was repelled by the sweetness of his aftershave. 'Could be we'll meet again at our next appointments with Smiley . . .' He put a small white card beside April's plate: business address and numbers. 'Call me if you feel like it, won't you?'

Then Jack Johnson picked up his smart little overnight case with its expensive leather straps and was gone.

April tore the card into minute pieces which she mixed with the crumbs on her plate. Tonight Martin would be home and she would insist, this time, that he came with her to see the headmaster. Tonight he would tell her in jovial detail about his trip to France, only omitting to mention the presence of Marilyn. He would probably forget to ask what the headmaster had said about the boys. It certainly wouldn't occur to him to ask how she had spent her evening. In the same way that trust makes infidelity easy to accomplish, so does lack of interest in a spouse's activities. In Addison Walk, an hour later, April remembered the hopes she had entertained on many such walks as an under-graduate. Love, interest, a liveliness of being as man and wife, the mutual, buoyant pleasure of being parents.

On the journey back to London, April relived the grop-ings of the night and laughed herself to scorn. It was only the second time she had been unfaithful in fifteen years: she should have treated herself, at least, to a better lover. Physically churlish, Jack Johnson had been, and she had had no heart to encourage him in less selfish ways. But, far worse than his ungracious thudding, had been later to see him sleep so quickly beside her, apparently unmoved by a stranger in the bed. He had snored, tossed crudely about in sleep, snatching the sheets from her side. At dawn, April, who had not slept at all, crept out for a bath and dressed. She could not face lying beside his early-morning face, ruddy manifestation of her mistake.

Within days of returning to home and working life, the horrible night disappeared. She could not remember Jack's features, his hands, his voice. And even when she returned to the school some months later, for Sports Day, the sight of him failed at first to re-ignite her guilt.

She saw him in the distance, a cross-looking woman in

skinny spectacles by his side. He still wore the red hand-kerchief: this time it flopped from the pocket of a creased linen suit. Martin, by April's side, followed her gaze.

'Never ceases to fascinate me,' he said. 'You look at the children, then at their parents, and you understand instantly why those children are like they are.' Three plump boys had joined Jack Johnson. They hung about with the important look of old boys returning to their prep school. A small, skinny one clung to the woman. The little wretch, April supposed, her pity renewed. Then they were lost from sight in the crowd.

She next saw Jack lined up for the fathers' race: jacket off, silk shirt darkened with melon slices of sweat under the arms.

'Not much competition there,' said Martin and went to stand beside Jack.

April and her two boys found themselves next to the Johnson wife and children among the spectators. April observed the resigned mouth of Mrs Johnson – the hunched shoulders and bloodless hands, while Martin ran an easy race to beat the rest of the motley field. Jack, she saw, lumbered up second from last.

April, as much as her sons, enjoyed Martin's win (third year running) and found herself laughing, joining the con-gratulations as he put an arm around her shoulders. From the corner of her eye, she saw Jack Johnson dab his face with the red handkerchief and wave. April gave the small-est nod of recognition, dismissing him so entirely in her mind that there was no time to wonder, for the hundredth time, how she could ever have been so unwise.

Martin's arm continued to rest around her shoulders. Since Marilyn had moved to some other company, his infatuation had waned and he was exercising his charms on April, which was often his way between infidelities. At such times, she found forgiveness easy. The love she usually felt it necessary to withhold from her husband she bestowed willingly on him again, hoping it could remain thus for a month or so.

'Tell you what,' Martin was saying to her and the boys, 'I've booked a table for dinner before we drive back, some hotel I heard was the Algonquin of Oxford. All right?' His eyes met April's. She could think of no reason to refuse, and nodded.

The bar of The Old Parsonage was filled with parents and their children that night, celebrating the end of another term, another year. For some, the junction between the end of preparatory school before the step to public school. Around the small polished tables, family life abounded noisily, happily. Martin chose April's favourite white wine without asking. From time to time, her eyes travelled among the very disparate mothers and fathers. The relief she felt that Jack Johnson and his wife were not among them registered lightly as a shadow on her warm skin and, in the kind light of the evening, she liked to think it was only the innocence of her sons that made her want to cry.

Laughter in
the Willows

*I*t was Isabel Loughland's second summer up at Oxford and in her own mind she was a failure. This feeling had come to her within weeks of arriving at New College, and settled more deeply every term. It was nothing to do with her studies. That part of her life, mercifully, was rewarding. She worked hard, taking advantage of hours unoccupied by romantic interest, and the results were encouraging. If she carried on like this, she had been advised, there was a chance she would get a good second-class degree – even a first.

This thought was no compensation for a loveless life. The few girlfriends Isabel had made had paired off with men very soon after they arrived. By now, initial partners had changed and changed again. Keeping up with the shuffle of love affairs was at first entertaining (how Isabel admired their ability to be so positive of their attraction to one, and then so quickly to another). Now it was wearying. She no longer bothered. She had become used to being a lone figure in a coupled society, and reckoned a change in this situation was unlikely. Among the dozens of male undergraduates she had encountered, not a single one had caused her the ungrounding that she knew to be the prime indication of love.

Isabel felt no self-pity: merely, puzzlement. The men who had made advances to her – and even now, when the fear of committing sexual harassment makes for some hesitation, there was no shortage of them – had claimed her as pretty, almost beautiful. Certainly she was a good listener – her mother had taught her there was no aphrodisiac so potent as lending an attentive ear. She could make people laugh. She was the provider of imaginative gestures; she was modest and sympathetic.

The stumbling block, she knew, was the *unfashionable* air that blew off her, awesome as expensive scent. She did not dress like the others, in jeans and grubby layered things, and elephantine boots. She wore long, clean skirts of pure cotton or velvet, and pumps of pale kid. She brushed her hair and, in summer, wore straw hats stuck with real flowers to evensong. Her demeanour gave clues to her limitations. She had no desire to become close to a man after a single drink in The Blue Boar (although she was not averse to a pint of lager), and any suggestions of a kiss on immediate acquaintance were politely turned down. It was not that she was a prude – when the time came, she was convinced she would make love as keenly as her friends. But she was of the outdated belief that the only chance of a lasting relationship was friendship that developed into love and sex: the other way round did not augur well for permanency. While mere lust did not interest her, the height of her ideals caused her disillusion. Several times, her hopes were raised in the direction of a particular figure, only to be crushed by his expectations of instant physical gratification.

She should have been born in a different age, Isabel

reflected, as she did so often. On this fine evening, sitting by herself in New College gardens, she imagined the attraction of life at Jane Austen's pace: the *containing* of realisation. That's what she sought. That was the essence of the romance she believed in.

Isabel picked daisies from the perimeter of her rug. She tried to remember how to make a chain. Various couples walked by, caught up in the kind of rapture which, in her judgement, was too self-conscious to be anything more than temporary. She felt no envy: that was not what she wanted. But disappointment on finding no one of the stuff she imagined, in almost two years at Oxford, was some-times acute. Now, for instance. It was a waste of such an evening, not to be sharing it. Returning to books was sometimes not enough.

The lilacs, nearby, were beginning to unfurl. Blossom snowed down from a cherry tree. Shadows had stretched almost to the edge of the rug. (Isabel was ridiculed for her rug, with its mackintosh backing.) Others, nearby, sat on the grass. Time to go in, she thought. Back to her room. An evening of more study.

She looked up. A single man – a rare sight on a fine summer's evening in college grounds – was coming towards her. He was exceptionally thin, narrow. From a distance, his face was a blade. He wore pale baggy trousers of crushed linen, as if he'd just discovered *Brideshead*. Isabel smiled at the thought. She recognised him. Last week in chapel she had dropped her prayer book. He had picked it up, returned it to her. In the brief moment of the handing over, their eyes had met without interest.

It was evident, in the firmness of his step, that he was not about to pass by. He was intent on speaking.

Isabel shifted slightly, indicating reluctance to be encountered. She wanted to continue with her quiet evening, not have to make the effort to turn down an invitation.

The man was by her now. A concave figure, holding out his hand – an unusual gesture among students. Isabel shook it, surprised by such unaccustomed formality, but good manners instinctive within her.

'Jacques,' he said, 'de Noailles. We met in chapel last Sunday evening. I've been looking for you.'

Isabel suppressed a small sigh. She could not be unbent by flattery.

'Isabel Loughland,' she said reluctantly. 'This is my college.'

Jacques lowered himself, unasked, on to the grass beside the rug. It did not occur to Isabel to invite him to share it.

'I'm at Corpus.' Jacques de Noailles leant back on his elbows, shut his eyes. In the instant that they were shut, Isabel observed a veil of pure evil cross his face. Or perhaps it was a strand of shade extending, now that it was almost eight, from the lilacs. There was something intriguing in the way his narrow chest dipped deeply towards his spine. She liked the cornflower blue of his clean shirt.

He opened his eyes, made no attempt to smile at her.

'Greats,' he said. 'How about you?'

'Mediaeval History.'

'That was an option for me. I would have liked that. But my father said, don't miss your chance of philosophies. He's French. You know what eager philosophers the French are.'

Isabel put down the book she had picked up in readiness to leave before Jacques had arrived.

'Yes,' she said.

'Strange: this is my third year and last Sunday was the first time I've seen you,' said Jacques.

'Not so very strange, so many . . . It's only my second year.'

'Ah.' They talked about their undergraduate lives for a while, and their vacations. Jacques said he divided his time between his mother in Scotland and his father in Provence. After coming down from Oxford, he said, he intended to take a course at the Sorbonne. Isabel told him she lived in Devon. Both her parents were botanists, often away in foreign mountains in search of extraordinary species. She and Jacques did not ask each other many questions. They took it in turns to offer small pieces of information, giving little away.

An hour passed. It had grown cool. Jacques raised himself on to his haunches, made ready to go.

'I was just wondering – is there anything in Oxford that you haven't done in your two years here? That you would like to do? It's difficult to come up with an original invitation. But I'm sorry. Silly question. It was only that I thought a girl like you must have done *everything*.'

Isabel felt herself blush. She let a long moment pass. Dare she tell him? Yes, she decided.

'As a matter of fact, there is one thing. It's so . . . childish. Such a cliché. It's what everyone does in their first summer, but somehow the chance never came. I want to go on a punt . . .'

Jacques did not laugh, as she had expected.

'Well, for that matter, I've never been on one either,' he said. 'It's never occurred to me. *Alors*! We shall go on a punt. I shall make arrangements.'

He stood, very quickly, rubbing his long thin thighs with his long thin hands. He pulled Isabel to her feet.

'Politically incorrect, I dare say.' They both laughed. 'You're taller than I expected.' He swooped down again, as if embarrassed by the intimacy of the spontaneous observation, and picked up the daisy chain. For a moment, Isabel thought he intended to take it: an unlikely romantic gesture. But he gave it back to her, dangling it lightly across her wrist. 'Now, I must go.'

Dusk had covered the grass, thickened the trees.

The next morning, Isabel found a message at the Lodge. *Be at Magdalen Bridge at three p.m. Bring your rug. Jacques.*

Impertinent, the rug bit, she thought. Though not impertinent enough to refuse the invitation.

She lay back in the punt, eyes half closed. All was just as she had imagined. Her rug was spread over cushions supplied by Jacques who tussled, tight-lipped, with the pole. Isabel pretended not to notice his lack of talent as a punter, and did not mind how long it took, the journey down the river. The heat of the sun and plash of water made her sleepy, too sleepy to speak.

At some moment, it might have been an hour after they set off, Jacques announced they had arrived. Isabel, rousing herself, saw they had tied up at the bank beside an enormous willow tree.

'I'd say that was pretty good for someone who's never done it before,' she said, sitting up.

'Thanks. But you were asleep most of the time.'

'Half asleep.'

They lifted out the rug, cushions and a small wicker hamper. This made Isabel laugh.

'Most undergraduate picnics travel in plastic bags,' she said.

'I don't like plastic bags.' Jacques' shirt was dark with sweat. 'If you're going to take a picnic at all, you might as well bother, no? What do you think of this place? Do you like it?'

Isabel looked across the river. The meadows were that bright green of early May with a pointillist covering of cow parsley. Distant woods of new, transparent leaves made delicate fans against the sky.

'Good,' she said.

'And the willow? You like this old tree? It's famous. Lots of people come here. We're lucky to have it to ourselves.'

'You've been here before, then?'

'Oh yes, often. But never by punt. I've always walked.' He answered lightly. A sudden positioning of shadow on his face reminded Isabel of last night's brief illusion of cruelty. He was smiling. Remembering? Who had he come with? With what intent? Questions leapt in Isabel's mind, but they were empty. She wondered slightly at her lack of curiosity.

Jacques parted the thickly-leaved branches of the willow. Isabel followed him into the ribboned vault beneath it. Grass was scant here, worn away by previous visitors.

There were other signs of the popularity of the hiding place, too. An empty crisp bag, a scrunched-up beer can.

'Bastards,' said Jacques. He picked up the rubbish, went back through the branches to bury it. Alone for a moment in this place of gently shifting leaf shadow, Isabel clutched herself with crossed arms. She felt a distant chill. The heat of the sun could not penetrate the walls of the greenery, though it made a million fireflies among the leaves, points of lights that dazzled as they moved with the slight breeze. Isabel wondered if she should suggest they should eat outside.

Jacques returned.

'So hot. This is wonderful, no? The cool.'

They laid out the rug and cushions. The hamper was unpacked. Jacques had *bothered*: there was proper French bread, and *millefeuilles* from the Maison Blanc; pâtés, tiny cheeses in oiled paper tied with twine. Black misted grapes, a bottle of white wine, red gingham napkins and china plates.

'Is all right? Enough?'

'It's fine. It's wonderful. You've gone to such trouble.'

They ate slowly, almost in silence. Isabel revelled in the delicious food, and the way Jacques handed her a piece of baguette with small yellow tomatoes balancing on a wedge of *pâté de campagne*. But she still wished they were outside on the riverbank, despite the heat. The chill beneath the tree continued to strike: the bleak chill of milk bottles on a cold winter doorstep, the dank chill of turgid water – she could not quite place the exact kind of coldness, but it made goose pimples on her bare arms. Isabel pulled on her cardigan. Two glasses of wine had made her sleepy again. She longed to lie back on the cushions, but feared this would look like an untoward invitation. Then, eyes on Jacques' serious profile – he was eating a *millefeuille* with his fingers, forks being the only thing he had forgotten – she realised that no such thought would occur to him. She felt confident of that, though could not explain to herself why . . .

So she lay back, let her eyes trail among the long streamers of leaf that dangled from the branches above her. Focussing more sharply, she could see each one as an individual, with its just visible webbing of veins, its fragile whiplash of spine. There was grey in the various greens, through which the fireflies of sunlight splattered lemony freckles. A sudden gust of breeze made chaotic shadows dance on Jacques' blue shirt.

'Strobe shadows,' said Isabel, more to herself than to him.

Jacques turned to her, one side of curious mouth, awash with *crème patissière*, lifted in agreement.

'Strobe shadows,' he said.

Isabel was grateful for his instant understanding. She fell asleep.

She was woken by laughter. It took her a moment to re-orient herself. Willow tree: picnic: Jacques: that was it. Where was he? The picnic things had been cleared away, the wicker hamper closed and buckled. The neatness pleased her, but she was still cold. The shade under the tree was more intense.

Isabel sat up, looked at her watch. Five o'clock. She must

have slept for at least an hour. A waste, really. But also agreeable. To be able to fall asleep in the presence of a little-known acquaintance who has taken such trouble with a picnic, she was thinking, when she heard the laughter again. A man's, a young woman's. Clashing, chiming. People outside. People seeking shade, perhaps. They would come in, blasting her solitude. There would be awkwardness, embarrassment. Please don't let us disturb you . . . No, no, not at all . . . do come in. Well, how lucky she and Jacques had been for a few hours, Isabel thought. To have had such a popular place to themselves was obviously a piece of good fortune.

She stood up, brushed an insect from her skirt. Head bowed, concentrating, she did not see Jacques return through the branches. When she looked up and saw him before her, she felt surprise. His face, reddened by the sun, was shredded by the straggling shadows of the willow leaves.

'I went for a walk along the tow-path,' he said.

'I'm sorry I slept so long.'

'I'm glad you did. But time to go now. The slow journey back.' He gave a smile that flickered with moving shadow. 'Perhaps I'll do better.'

'Others have arrived, anyway,' said Isabel.

'Didn't see anyone.'

'I heard laughter. Not a moment ago.'

'There was no one out there.'

'Maybe they were just walking by.'

'Well, never mind. We must go.'

Jacques bent to pick up the hamper. A distinct peal of

laughter came from behind Isabel. She jumped round. No one. Nothing.

'There,' she said.

'People playing silly games,' said Jacques. 'Can you manage the rug and the cushions? We'll leave it to them. They can come in now.'

'But the laughter was in here.'

'You're imagining things. People queue up for this place. It's no longer a secret, unfortunately. They come in here to – well, have their fun.'

He led the way through the branches. As Isabel followed him, the long leaves tickled her face with a disagreeable touch. Out on the bank again, she felt relief. A still-hot sun gushed over her: gratifying, comforting warmth that made her shiver pleasantly. The brown water of the river spread taut beneath the waiting punt. A lark sang high above them.

On the way back, Jacques said, 'There's a punting party in a few weeks' time. A whole crowd of us. Would you like to come? It's fancy dress, I'm afraid. Dressing up in Edwardian gear – some silly idea. An awful bother, I think.'

'Nostalgia's so fashionable,' said Isabel. 'Yes, I'd love to.'

'You'll have to find something – some old dress, some fancy hat, put your hair up.'

'I'll rather enjoy that.'

'We'll go together, then.'

By the time they tied up at Magdalen Bridge, the sky was a deep denim blue behind the tower. Crowds of punters were laughing, drinking, eating ice-creams.

*

Isabel found a second-hand shop near the station. She was trying to make her choice. It was dreadfully hot, stuffy. There was a smell of mothballs, old garments, dead starch. The walls were hung with dresses whose heyday was several decades ago, their gold embroidery and lace panels a little battered, but their spirits not extinguished. There was nothing suitable for the punting picnic, the kind of Edwardian tea-gown Isabel had in mind.

'Just got a new bundle in,' said the woman in charge, dumping a pile of twisted clothes on the counter. 'You can see if there's anything you like if you want to look through these.'

Isabel began to rummage through them. They were pale, faded colours, summery stuffs, torn and frayed, some of them, and very crumpled. Within moments, her eyes lighted on a piece of creamy muslin dotted with faint forget-me-nots: she pulled it from the pile. It was exactly what she was after, demure and pretty with small lace Vs that protruded from the long sleeves to cover the back of the hand. All it needed was a sash of palest blue moiré . . . Isabel felt reckless with excitement: the dress was more than she had intended to spend, but she did not care. A picture was beginning to form in her mind – a little hazy, but something to do with seduction, at last, in this dress. Something to do with *possibility*, and Jacques.

Back in her room, she shook out the dress and studied it more carefully: the hand-sewn hems of tiny stitches, the coarse hooks and eyes of the day, the enchanting fabric itself. She hung it over her chair, skirt spread out so that it touched the floor. Then she hurried off to Browns where, for the third time since their expedition on the punt, she was to have tea with Jacques. To date, there had been no invitations for anything later in the day. Things were progressing at just the pace so appreciated by Isabel. With each formal date – snippets of information accumulating – anticipation fizzed a little more: there was reason, Isabel began to think, for hope.

When she returned to her room at about six-thirty in the evening, her immediate impression was of the lack of air. It had been a very hot day, but she had left the window shut, being on the ground floor, for security: it was not unknown for undergraduates to rob each other these days.

On her way to the window Isabel's eyes fell on the dress – of which she had made no mention to Jacques. It was to be a surprise. It was not as she had left it. Slumped considerably to one side, so small a part of the bodice was now propped up against the back of the chair that the slightest movement would have caused it to fall completely.

This was strange. How could this have happened? There was no breath of air in the room. The door had been locked: no one had been in. Isabel's mind raced uneasily before quickly she found an explanation. Someone must have been running in the passage outside . . . the vibration of feet on old boards. All the same, her heart quickened. In the stifling room, the dress looked so desolate she felt a moment's chill. Goose pimples stood up on her bare arms, just as they had when she heard the laughter in the willows.

Scoffing at herself, Isabel picked up the dress with some distaste. She put it on a hanger. The muslin skirt, so soft and dry in the shop, felt slimy against her hands. Almost damp.

Isabel hung it on the outside of the wardrobe. To check that she had been imagining the inexplicable dampness, she forced herself to screw up the frill on the hem with both hands. Obviously, her imagination had been playing tricks. The material was warm, dry, smelling faintly of musty flowers. Cowslips, Isabel thought. She opened the window, took out her books. She sat down at her desk, her back to the dress, wanting to put it from her mind.

But in the next few weeks before the punting party, it caused her some disturbance. She washed it, ironed it, skilfully mended a couple of small tears. All these jobs she found disagreeable: the silly thought came to her that by restoring it to its pristine condition she was somehow intruding. She bought a long blue moiré ribbon which she tied round the waist, a beautiful sash. Then, fearful of crushing it in the crowded wardrobe, she left the dress hanging outside. Each time she returned to her room she was greeted by its hanging presence – a presence more potent than an ordinary piece of clothing on a hanger. Always, she could swear, its position was fractionally changed – she made sure to straighten it before she left, and when she came back it had invariably shifted a little to one side or the other. This change was almost imperceptible, but Isabel's conviction that it *was* a change grew stronger every day. In her alarmed state, she began to imagine that in her absence the garment put up some kind of a struggle. Others, coming to her room, admired it, of course. Handsome symbol of another age, they said: imagine wearing something that prissy today.

Gradually, Isabel herself began to dread coming back to

her room. The greeting from the still dress that moved when she was out became harder to ignore by concentrating on her work. She could not bring herself to try it on: she knew instinctively it would fit. And once the punting party was over, she began to think, she would re-sell the dress, throwing in the expensive sash as an added bonus.

Every few days, Jacques and Isabel met for the same teas – scones and cream and strawberry jam – in Browns, and Jacques unbent a little. One afternoon, he went so far as to suggest Isabel might like to visit his father's house in the Luberon in the vacation. Perhaps, Isabel replied. What she meant was, perhaps the time was coming for things to speed up a little.

'You would like,' he said.

'I expect I would.'

Their conversations were not marked by vitality. Rather, they shifted at a gentle pace, as does the talk of two people, bound by affection, who have known each other well for many years. Isabel found this comforting.

On the day before the punting party, they did not meet. Isabel spent many hours, in her disciplined way, getting ahead with work: she did not want the thought of an essay on Anna Comnena hanging over her as the gathering of punts drifted down the Cherwell . . . Tired by the evening, the essay accomplished, books neatly stacked, she went to bed soon after nine and slept at once.

She woke at three a.m. A thin spear of moonlight through the window had lighted on the waiting dress (re-ironed two days ago), bleaching its creamy colour to a milky whiteness, giving it a cloudy volume as if invisible thighs shifted beneath it. She distinctly saw it move.

Cold, Isabel sat up. Now, as her eyes grew accustomed to the fragile darkness, she could see the bodice and the long limp sleeves that seemed not as limp as the sleeves of an empty dress should be. It was the dress that had woken her, she was quite sure of that, with its sudden, living presence.

Terrified, Isabel switched on the light. At once she saw how foolish she had been: the dress was ordinary again, beautifully ironed, waiting, unmoving. The illusion of moments before must have been the tail-end of a nightmare. She smiled at herself, heart thumping: by now, she thought, she knew Jacques well enough to tell him of the strange experience, and of the odd feelings she had about the dress. Maybe there would be a chance tomorrow. Calmer, but not liking to put out the light, she picked up a book and read till dawn.

The following evening, when the time came to change, Isabel opened her door on to the corridor. In some amorphous way, she wanted the reassurance of others nearby: the scurrying down the corridor, the heads looking in to check on progress. Now Isabel was seen by her friends to be 'in a relationship' too, they treated her with less polite kindness. This evening, finally in the dress, sash bow perfectly tied, muslin underskirt soft against her legs, she was grateful for their crude comments concerning virgin spinsters, and their coarse admiration of her finished appearance. She had piled up her hair in an Edwardian bun: on top of this she put her mother's wedding hat, a period concoction of silk roses clambering over creamy straw, with a tiny veil that half hid her eyes. A velvet ribbon she wore around her throat, to which she had pinned a small star. She was ready.

'You look much more the part than any of us,' said one of her friends. 'But then you've never been of this age.'

Isabel, arranging the Vs of lace over the backs of her hands, blushed. She felt intensely happy. All the misgivings about the dress, the absurd feelings of unease it had caused her, had vanished. She knew it suited her, that she looked well in it. And this was the sort of occasion she had been waiting for so hopelessly for five terms. *This* was the Oxford of her most extravagant imaginings.

It was seven p.m. when she joined a group of girls in long floating dresses to walk to Magdalen Bridge where Jacques, and other dates, would be waiting. Isabel's normal modesty was taxed: she could not help feeling she was the *belle dame* of the group. The others had strived, but somehow failed, in their attempts at Edwardian gear. They wore long shabby dresses with Doc Marten boots beneath. Some of them had piled up their hair, though nothing would disguise the contemporary haughtiness of their expressions, and their language would have been almost incomprehensible to those of the Edwardian era. But they were in high spirits, looking forward to a night of drink and music and love beneath the stars, when their fancy dresses would be ruined on the damp banks of the Cherwell.

At the meeting place there was a huge gathering of yet more girls in long dresses and men, transformed in appearance by striped blazers, cream trousers and boaters stuck with flowers. They bore no resemblance to the seedy, be-jeaned lot of normal day. There was much shrieking and incredulous laughter as food and bottles and ghetto blasters were handed into the punts.

'I thought of bringing my gramophone,' said Jacques, suddenly at Isabel's side, 'but I didn't think it would be appreciated.' His eyes moved politely up and down her dress. He made no comment, but gave her shoulder the briefest squeeze. All around them, others were already greeting each other with greedy kisses on the lips. Jacques had wisely not volunteered to be a punter. This meant he and Isabel could sit side by side, idle passengers, their attention free for the delights of the journey downriver.

By the time the convoy of punts set off, the sky was a deep blue-green, tipped with such refulgent clouds that Isabel imagined a giant peacock, standing on the horizon, had simply raised its fan-shaped tail to the heavens . . . As Magdalen Tower disappeared, and a tunnel of greenery loomed, she found herself sipping pink champagne, Jacques' arm about her. She could feel the boniness of his side. They had never been so close before. Nor had Isabel ever felt such irresponsible deliquescence: no matter what he asked her, tonight, she would agree. They had waited long enough.

Even as the party took place, Isabel was aware of that quality of luminescence that usually touches the memory of things past rather than present reality. She clutched each moment to herself, wanting to preserve it in all its detail. She was not, after all, a girl so used to parties that circumstances had to be particularly vivid to cause the kind of impression that cannot fade. The wonder was increased by the constant presence of Jacques by her side. They shared her rug for the picnic on the bank by the willow, now a familiar place. A half-moon rose in the jade-black sky, its face smeared by unhurried clouds. Someone had brought jars containing candles, which were lighted in random spots, and a man with no apparent girlfriend (Isabel's heart went out to him in 'sublime compassion') sat playing a melancholy tune on his flute.

'This is very mad, very English,' Jacques said. He was folding dismal threads of ham into a piece of bread for Isabel. The food was not of the same standard as the previous picnic, but there was no shortage of pink champagne.

Once seated and eating, the chattering of the undergraduates lost its shrillness. It was as if, awed by the density of the warm night, intoxicated by the smells of ripe hay and damp long grass, they tempered their voices. Such innocence! Jacques replied, when Isabel whispered these thoughts to him. It was just that a good deal of drink and dope has already been consumed, he said. But it seemed to Isabel that the voices were quieter. It was always possible to hear the flute among them.

When the picnic was finished, more cigarettes and joints were lighted. One punt, bearing two couples, set off uncertainly into the darkness. Those left on the bank switched on a tape of rock music and began barefoot to dance. This enraged the others, who thought such crudeness broke the spell of the age they were trying to recreate, and sentimental tunes from the 30s were put on instead.

'Still wrong,' pointed out Jacques, 'but I suppose we can't dance to *The Last Rose of Summer*.'

He helped Isabel to her feet, but not to dance.

'I'm not much good,' he said. 'No sense of rhythm. Let's see what's happening under our tree.'

They stepped from the moody darkness of the riverbank into the thicker gloom beneath its branches. On the ground were more jars of candles, the light not strong enough to turn the long leaves into ribbon shadows, as the fierce sun had managed on their last visit. Several couples were lying together, oblivious of each other, of everyone. Girls squirmed, long skirts thrown back over their knees. They lay on striped blazers, covered by thrusting flannel haunches: mouths locked.

'I told you,' said Jacques.

Isabel was glad of the darkness. She felt herself stiffen, blush. She was suddenly awkward. Jacques took her hand, led her back outside.

'What would you like to do? Dance with someone else?'

'Just watch,' said Isabel.

They took a bottle, the rug and cushions, and made themselves comfortable in one of the moored punts. They watched the dancing and embracing under gently changing patterns of moon and cloud. The music, thin recordings of sad love songs, fluttered down to them. They did not speak.

Isabel, on purpose, had not brought her watch. So she had no idea what precise moment of the night Jacques stirred, and concentrated on rubbing his ankle, which he had bruised some days before.

'I suppose I must admit the impossible has happened,' he said. '*Mon Dieu*: I would never have thought it. I think I have fallen in love. *Je te veux bien*.'

He turned to Isabel, unsmiling. Straightened her hat, lifted the veil. The lace pushed back, she now had an unobstructed view of his face, silvery green, with enquiring eyes.

At about four-thirty a.m. people began to go home. Punts set off alone at intervals, filled with loose-limbed revellers in stained and damaged clothes. When the last punt was about to leave, Jacques suggested he and Isabel should not take it, but walk back a little later. She agreed. She wanted the night to last, not for ever – people who expressed such views were thereby impeding the order of progress – but for a while yet.

So they were left behind. They stood on the bank, waving, the objects of much good-humoured speculation, till the punt rounded the bend, leaving only a few long, sleepy laughs and cries in its wash.

They stood in silence till the voices were finally no more, and then heard bright new laughter behind them. It was distinct, infectious. In the gunmetal light of the dawn sky, Isabel could see Jacques looked annoyed.

'So we're not the only ones, after all. Others are still here.'

He pushed his way through the branches of the willow tree. In a moment he was back.

'No one,' he said. 'I could have sworn I heard . . .'

'So did I.'

'Well, if there's no one, that's good. I wanted you alone.' He patted her shoulder. 'You're cold.'

'Not very.'

Jacques took off his blazer, put it round her.

'I feel,' he said, 'I don't know – restless. Stiff from all the sitting. Do you mind if I stretch my legs for a few yards? Back in ten minutes.'

'Of course.'

Isabel watched him walk away from her. He quickly disappeared into the mist that rose from the ground, a milk-grey mist that matched the paling of the sky.

The place, now everyone had gone, was lonely, the silence oppressive. Isabel longed for birdsong, the dawn chorus, the lowing of cows – anything to cloud the quiet into which the laughter might break again. She felt unsafe without Jacques at her side. Afraid. She wished she had her watch, so that she could time his return.

There it was again: the laughter.

This time it was nearer, but muffled. It was definitely coming from under the willow tree: people hiding, joking, trying to frighten her, was Isabel's immediate thought. Crossly, in her nervousness, she parted the branches and entered the hiding place. On the ground, the candles had burnt out in their jars. A blue suede sandal lay on its side, heel broken. But there was no one there.

Isabel heard herself utter a small cry, clap her hand to her mouth. She turned, ready to hurry outside, when a man appeared through the thickness of the branches.

'Jacques!' she screamed.

As she darted towards him, he backed away, indistinct in the poor light. But she clearly saw a flash of long white hand streaked with black mud, and a recognisable expression of something like evil. Then he was gone, vanished with no word. What terrible game was he playing? Isabel put a hand on the tree trunk to support herself. She was icy, shivering, confused. What had happened? What was this terrifying trick all about? Isabel looked round at the silent jangling shadows of the willow leaves, and knew she could not bear another moment in this horrible place. She must find Jacques, get him to explain . . .

She ran through the branches, hating their touch, and on to the tow-path. It was lighter now: that luminescent moment before real daylight. Isabel looked upriver. No sign of Jacques.

But, some twenty yards ahead, a girl. She was standing with her back to Isabel, looking in the same direction, upriver. Her presence brought relief. Obviously, she was a member of the party who had somehow missed a lift home.

Isabel called out to her. The girl did not move. In the silence between them, Isabel had the curious sensation that she was looking at herself, a mirror image, a reflection that she could not explain. The stranger on the path was the same height. She wore a long, bleached dress, though no detail was clear. Her hair was piled up in the same manner as Isabel's, though she wore no hat. Isabel put her hand to her head and found that her own hat, too, had gone. At the same moment, the reflection touched her hair. Isabel, remembering she had left the hat in the punt, shivered violently.

But, in her usual disciplined way, she called upon every source of common sense to come to her rescue. She was not a great believer in the supernatural: she had never seen a ghost. She did, however, acknowledge that strands of time can be confused, most particularly when some event of great significance has occurred. The complications of such theories were beyond her, and at this moment she gave them no thought. Curious, alarmed, she wondered what trick of the imagination, the light, her eyes, had caused this insubstantial vision of a girl who appeared to be a replica of herself. Perhaps, she thought, it was a mirage. Or even the unaccustomed quantity of pink champagne.

She called again.

This time the girl turned to her. For an infinitesimal moment she could see that she had no face – that is, no face delineated by its features. Instead, beneath the piled-up hair, was a simple disc, silvery transparent as the waning moon. In the second that Isabel was trying to re-adjust her focus, there was a loud crash, a hectic splash in the water. She swerved round to see that two swans had landed. They had set up their positions, cob following swan, in huge swirling necklaces of brown ripples. While the sudden noise had frightened her, the peaceful domesticity of the scene now reassured her. The swans were substantial, safe, not the stuff of illusion. She turned again to see what reaction they had caused in the girl. But she was no longer there.

Jacques was in her place, walking quickly towards Isabel. Happy, judging from his bouncing stride. Isabel ran to him. He waved. From a distance Isabel noticed his hand was streaked with mud. When she reached him, the hand was clean. There was no time for calculations.

Isabel flung herself into his arms. He held her.

'What's all this – hey? What's happened to the happy face of the girl I love?'

The face was buried in the concave chest, feeling the warm dampness of his cotton shirt. Jacques, confused, continued his teasing tone.

'I gave you ten minutes, precisely, to make up your mind. What were you thinking? Do you love me? Or is this heart to be unrequited?' He pushed Isabel away from him. 'Is it something serious? Tell me what's happened. Tell me as we walk back.'

Isabel could not be sure – she could not be sure of anything in this unnerving dawn – but she thought she detected a note of malice in Jacques' concern: the voice was hollow, somehow. Unsoft. Fighting such thoughts, fully aware of her confusion, she took his arm. Pressed together by the narrowness of the tow-path, they began the walk back to Oxford. Long grass each side of them was feathered with dew. Birds had begun to sing. In the security of near daylight, Isabel did her best to describe the hallucinations, knowing how ridiculous they sounded. Jacques made light of her experience – to comfort her, perhaps, she thought. He seemed untroubled, amused by her story: suggested someone could have spiked her drink. But he did agree that he, too, had heard unaccountable laughter.

By the time they arrived at Magdalen Bridge, the sun was up and busses passed to and fro.

'You must not give another thought to all the weird happenings,' Jacques said. 'I put them all down to an unaccustomed drink, and much too much hard work. I'd say you're a little overwrought. You haven't had enough fun at Oxford so far. I mean to change all that. Now you must go back and get some sleep. When you wake, what I ask you to think about is . . . me.'

They parted with a chaste kiss. Isabel, never more grateful for the normality of daylight, hurried back to her room. Her immediate concern was to get rid of the dress. She tore it off, ripping fragile seams, stuffed it into a plastic bag and took it to a dustbin behind the kitchens. Too awake to go to bed, she then sat at her desk, her mind ablaze with a plan. It was only when details of this plan were finalised that she pondered on Jacques' declaration, tried to determine what it meant to her. But rational analysis was elusive, blotted out by image after image of a faceless girl and a terrifying man, both of them familiar.

That afternoon Isabel returned to the second-hand shop near the station. The owner well remembered the bundle of clothes from which Isabel had chosen the dress. They came from a friend, a Mrs Williams, whose husband was a retired lock keeper. She gave Isabel the address.

Two days later, work finished early, Isabel found the Williamses' cottage. It was four miles west of Oxford, an unpretentious detached building on a small lane that ran between two cornfields. The only other habitation in sight was the lock keeper's cottage, presumably where Mr Williams had lived before his retirement. Isabel was hot after the bicycle ride, sweating. She pushed stray wisps of hair under her straw hat, and walked up the cinder path between lavender, rosemary and white tulips.

A large man of about seventy answered the door: rolled-up sleeves, braces, a gardener's hands. He smiled.

'I wonder if you can help me,' Isabel began. She realised she had made no plans for an opening explanation. 'I recently bought a dress from a bundle of clothes you were selling in Oxford. I was interested to know if you could tell me something of its history.'

Mr Williams did not seem averse to the idea of the company of a stranger. He invited her in. 'The wife's just put the kettle on,' he said.

Isabel followed him into a small front room of large polished furniture. Everything was brown – wallpaper, bristling sofa, thick curtains, dull velvet cloth on the table, and the different tones of brown, all burnished by the sunlight, conveyed a low-watt life. How gloomy such a room would be in November, Isabel thought. It was stifling, airless. Windows all shut. She sat on a brown wooden chair at the table, where the only relief was a bowl of orange silk poppies. The wall in front of her was covered in sepia photographs of ancestors in brass frames.

'So what can I do for you?'

Mr Williams' braces were brown, his eyes were brown. Isabel repeated her interest in the dress. Mr Williams gave no indication he thought this an untoward request.

'Can't say I remember it, precisely, the one you describe. There was a whole big bundle – maybe the wife will know the one you mean. All I can tell you is they belonged to my grandmother, Ellen. She was a good woman but she was vain. Always buying herself pretty dresses. We got stacks of them up in the attic, selling them fast. It's quite fashionable, they say, all that sort of old stuff today. We get a good price.'

Mrs Williams came in with a tray of beige cups, tea and brown biscuits. Her husband let out a long sigh. Isabel's heart was beating uncomfortably fast. She felt faint from the lack of air.

'Can you remember a cream dress, Jean, in the last lot that went to Oxford?'

'With forget-me-nots,' added Isabel. 'Muslin. A frill at the hem.'

Mrs Williams poured tea. In the airlessness of the room, it seemed to Isabel, there was a certain reluctance in her action. Her mouth was grim.

'Can't say I can,' she said at last. 'She had so many dresses, much of a muchness.'

She passed a cup of tea to Isabel, then took one of the framed photographs from the wall. 'This is her,' she said. 'Ellen. And Jack.'

Isabel studied the photograph. It was so faded the figures were barely discernible, splattered by milky white splotches. But she could make out the small, thin shape of a woman in a long, tight-waisted dress: impossible to tell if it was *the* dress. Her face was featureless, bleached out, a void beneath her piled-up hair. Beside her stood a tall, thin man, one side of his face too faded to see – in the other, a single eye was fierce, the corner of the mouth turned down. He wore a cricketing blazer, the stripes reduced to almost invisible sepia and cream.

'Can't see much, can you?' said Mrs Williams, a shade of triumph in her voice.

'Funny thing,' said her husband, turning to Isabel and snapping his braces one after the other, 'but you quite put me in mind of Ellen, the pictures I've seen of her. She was pretty all right. Trim.'

'Don't tell me you can tell what folk look like from old snaps, John,' said Mrs Williams. She left the room, taking her cup of tea. Her sharpness made no discernible effect on Mr Williams.

'To tell the truth,' he said at last, 'they were an odd couple, my grandparents. Can't help you much about the particular dress, young lady, but I can tell you they were a very odd couple. Tragic, really.'

Isabel listened to the muffled tick of the brown wooden clock.

'Why?' she asked, still light-headed from the lack of oxygen in the room.

'I shouldn't say this, but she came to a nasty end.' He glanced towards the door, checked there was no sound from his wife. 'The family doesn't like it talked about, but I'll tell you, seeing as how you bought one of Ellen's dresses. It was like this, so my father told me. Young Ellen was a pretty girl, lots of young men keen to court her, but she liked to keep herself to herself. Along came this Jack fellow, a farm labourer. He was tall, thin, but not half strong: could earn more than any of them in overtime during harvest week. Something a bit queer about him, though: wanted to get into the academic world, be a porter at a college, know what I mean? Ideas above his station. But he was the one who changed her mind about going out with a fellow regular, if you understand me.

'They used to do their courting, Jack and Ellen, down

the riverbank, a mile or so from here. He was a strong punter, Jack. Used to take Ellen off in her party dresses, tie up by that big willow – you might know the one I mean – for a picnic and whatever – nothing wrong, I don't suppose, being those days. We've a photo of them somewhere, down there, taken by Jack's sister, my Great Aunt Agnes. Those were the hey-days, I suppose. Then it all went wrong once they were married. There are stories, but no one has the details.'

Mr Williams, even in his wife's absence, lowered his voice.

'Well, Ellen, she refuses Jack first time he proposes. She's quite adamant. She loves him but she doesn't want to be tied down in marriage. So Jack, he bides his time: asks her again. Again, no, says Ellen: she was an independent woman, my grandmother. "Well, I'm not going to give up," says Jack, and the third time he asks her she comes round. Says yes. So they marry and have the one son, my father. Jack stays on the land, no more talk of college work. He slacks off a bit, so the word goes, drinks a bit. Money gets tight. Ellen says she'll go out to work, get a job as a serving maid in one of the colleges. She does, too. Christ Church. That may have been the start of it, the trouble. We can't be sure, but there was a rumour. My father says he remembers as a boy overhearing a row between his parents; something about a steward who'd taken a fancy to Ellen. Maybe she fancied him back. Anyhow, things definitely weren't good at home. Jack was drinking heavily.

'One day, about this time of year, they leave my father

with the next-door neighbour, and go off for the day downriver on a punt. Maybe some kind of celebration – birthday or wedding anniversary. Maybe some sort of patch-up in the place they'd been so happy before they married. Next thing, Ellen's drowned, Jack's taken off for questioning. He swore it was an accident. They'd had a good day, he said, but admitted he'd had too much to drink. His story was they were bounding about in the punt and it had tipped up. Ellen fell over the side – funny story, that, when you think how heavy a punt is. Ellen gets trapped beneath it, can't swim, can she? And those long skirts. You can picture it, her struggle. Jack says he tries to save her, but then he's confused with drink, isn't he? Doesn't try bloody hard enough, is what the family think. He brings her body up, though, dumps it on the bank, gives her the kiss of life, and that's the last kiss he ever gives her. Big trial, all over the papers. People round here still remember the Williams case. Any rate, he gets off. Scot-free. Well, no witnesses, no evidence. Case over: my father gets adopted by a cousin, the lock keeper here: that's how I came into the job. He and Jack never speak again, and I was never allowed to set eyes on Jack. By all accounts he was a nasty piece of work behind the sweet talk, and the funny thing is, he *did* end up in a college. I forget which one, some job in the kitchens.' Mr Williams paused. 'So I can't help you more than that. That's the story of my grandmother Ellen. I bet your dress was pretty . . . she had an eye for nice things, my gran. Sad ending, really. Moral is, as my wife Jean says, you shouldn't say yes when you mean no, however hard you're pressed.'

Isabel left soon after the story ended, apologising for the length of her stay. His wife did not appear again, though Isabel could hear sounds from the kitchen. Outside, butterflies lay spread-eagled on the front path. Isabel guided her bicycle between them, the sun heavy on her bare arms. She began the long ride back to Oxford slowly, for the machine was old and cumbersome, and the warmth of the afternoon sapped her strength.

Jacques' declaration of love spurred a slight change in his pattern of invitations. No more teas at Browns were suggested but, the evening after Isabel's visit to Mr Williams, he invited her there for dinner. They ate gravadlax and ravioli and Jacques asked Isabel, in his naturally formal way, if she would now go out with him. Such were his feelings, he said, he could not imagine any week, any day, without her. He loved her.

Isabel did not answer for a long time. Then she said, 'I think we should just remain friends, nothing formal. For the time being, anyway.'

Jacques' mouth tightened and a wayward shadow ran over his face.

'I don't understand,' he said. 'I've been very careful to take things at your pace. Not to alarm you, not to ask you too soon for any kind of commitment.'

'I know you have, and I appreciate that. I'm afraid I can't explain my reluctance . . . It's just a feeling, an instinct, that you and I would be wrong.' She knew there was no possibility of trying to explain to Jacques the signs, the reasons, that caused her to hesitate to take up his offer. He would observe once again that she was crazed from too much work, and suffered from a fevered imagination.

Jacques laughed.

'While girls less conscientious than you are flayed by love affairs, two years hard study with no light relief has left you haunted by unreal things, visions, illusions fostered by an exhausted mind. The fact is, you're simply *tired*.'

Was that the truth of it?

He sounded arrogant in his conviction. He patted her hand.

'It's not that.' Isabel tried to be patient. 'Honestly. I'm sorry.'

Jacques laughed again, this time a shallow laugh.

'You may think you can get rid of me that easily,' he said. 'But I've waited a long time for the right girl. I'm not going to give up. What do you want – a proposal of marriage? I'd be happy with that. Would that convince you of my love? Will you marry me when you come down next year?'

Isabel, like someone drowning, watched the remembrances unfurl: their first meeting in New College gardens, their first picnic, so many pleasant teas at this very table, Jacques' admirable restraint that exactly matched her own. She pondered, too, on the realisation of her secret love for him, a love still undeclared. Was she a fool to resist, or should she take heed of the tragic Ellen and the strangely familiar Jack?

Jacques could not quite conceal his impatience. 'What is your answer?' he asked.

'The answer is no, Jacques,' she said at last. 'I can't marry you.'

Isabel was aware that the words, even as she said them, did not belong to her. Her refusal of his first proposal was merely an echo, a reflection in time.

Jacques smiled quickly, as if not to alarm her.

'I shall ask you again,' he said, as she knew he would.

To Re-Arrange

a Room

R obert woke first. He glanced at Lisa. Tawny hair, slightly troubled look, even in sleep. He wondered if, when Sarah was back this time tomorrow, the image of Lisa would remain imprinted on the pillow, superimposed on reality.

He knew she had had a disturbed night. She had cried after he had made love to her, and promised it would be the last time he would see her weeping. Then she had turned away from him, restless. After a while, she had said 'Robert?', very quietly, and he had feigned sleep. He was exhausted by their interminable arguments – some calm, some whipped into the slashing words of anguished souls – while they tried to resolve the predicament that had suddenly (suddenly?) appeared six months ago. He did not want to spend their last night in further pointless discussion. There was nothing more to say. It was the end.

'Robert? In exactly five minutes I shall get up.' Lisa managed a smile. Robert touched her cheek. He understood he had five minutes in which he could change his mind, explode their decision. If he pulled her towards him, she could stay for ever.

'Right,' he said.

He tried for a neutral tone – should have been easy

enough, a single word. But it acted upon her like a gunshot. In a second, she was leaping from the bed, cold air splicing the warm scattering of sheets. In one long, continuous movement, she pulled on her jeans and jersey, snapped her hair back into a band, produced her severe, efficient morning face.

'Packing up won't take me long,' she said.

In the huge room that was both their kitchen and sitting-room, Robert poured himself coffee, sat down at the table. Helping her was beyond him.

'There's plenty of time,' he said. In fact, there was not. Sarah had insisted on arriving at two.

'How much?' The depth of Lisa's desperation sang out in the short question. Robert could not tell her she must be finished in an hour, if he was to re-arrange the room before Sarah's arrival. He watched Lisa rip Indian shawls from the sofa. She had put them there the first week she moved in, to hide Sarah's 'hideous' brown corduroy cover. Robert had found them enchanting. When they made love on the sofa, which they often did, they could hear the tinkling of small silver bells sewn to the shawls' fringes.

Lisa flung them into an empty box, where they expired with a few muted chimes. She gathered cushions, brightly coloured, vaguely ethnic. Some were embroidered with squares of glass mirror, angry eyes in the light of the February morning. Lisa kept back one to hug to herself.

'Still smells of the sea,' she said.

They had stopped in an east coast seaside town. Waiting for a shower to pass, they had sheltered in a gift shop, found it among all the ugly things. When the sky cleared, and a white sun came out, they took it to the beach. They spread their macks on wet sand, laid their heads on the cushion and waited till the incoming tide reached their feet.

'Sea lingers,' said Robert. He could see tide marks on the silk. His hand was shaking.

Lisa stretched up for the picture above the fireplace: sentimental watercolour of Edinburgh Castle. They had come across it in a shop behind Princes Street – Robert had slipped out of his conference on World Pollution to join Lisa for lunch. Later that afternoon, silent in front of Van Gogh's turbulent *Olive Trees* in the National Gallery of Scotland, she had cried out that he had never told her he loved her. Robert, startled, though they were alone in the gallery, told her to keep her voice down.

'*Why*,' she had cried, no quieter, not caring. 'Why've you never told me?'

Robert knew his helpless shrug appeared callous. It wasn't the place to explain.

'When you know it's the truth, what need?' he offered.

'That's not good enough.'

'I'm not a man of declarations, you know that. I try to act what I feel.'

'Women need declarations. At least, I do.'

'God, you do. I'm sorry I fail you there.' He gave her his handkerchief, kissed her wet cheek. It had been her first accusation. Their first row. After that, he often observed she tried to contain herself. But she could not stop asking the question.

Eventually, he did bring himself to say the words, in response to the hundredth time of asking. But it was too late. It was no good. Obliging with a response was not the same as a spontaneous declaration, Lisa screamed, just when he thought she would be pleased. He began to lose patience. From that moment, the fragile structure of their affair began to flounder.

She was swiping things from the shelves – ornaments, jars, postcards from mutual friends – throwing them into an empty box, careless of their fate as china and glass clashed against the cardboard. Then it was books, her books. Gaps left in the shelves, boxes full. The room stripped of all her things. Unrecognisable. Robert looked about, horrified.

'What about them?' He glanced at the curtains. Lisa had made them herself, cream linen. She had spent many evenings, at the beginning, sewing – saving money, she said, as her machine buzzed away. When she hung them, a veil of summer sunlight filtered through the folds. At night, the moon diffused itself through the loose weave of the material, making the room a shadow-cave.

'Can't take them. Much too big for my flat. Burn them, why not? *Keep* them, even?' She laughed nastily. 'Can you help me with the boxes?'

Why had he not asked her to be his wife? Why could he not have faced the whole palaver of divorce, Sarah's anger, Sarah's hurt? And spent the rest of his life with this wild, brave, sweet creature whose love for him had never been in any doubt?

'Course I'll help you with the boxes.'

'Then I'll be gone.'

They loaded her small car. She faced him. Snapped off

the band from her hair so that it fell about like it did in the evenings. Thin legs parted, arms folded, defiant.

'I've left the snowdrops,' she said. 'She'll wonder about them, but that's not my problem. You could throw them away, too.'

Robert shrugged. He did not like to speak.

'Well: for three years – thanks.' Lisa shivered. 'At least I'm glad it's February. Most years, after February, things get better.' She gave a fractional smile. They kissed. She drove away.

Robert decided to do all that had to be done very fast. The short time to himself between the departure of his mistress and the return of his wife was inadequate for any internal adjustment. But Sarah had been insistent. (Years ago, he had loved her in her most adamant moods.) It was two o'clock or never, she said. Her lease on the rented flat was up, she had to be out. She had no intention of wandering the streets while her husband, apparently agreeable to her return, indulged in solitary reflection.

It was an awkward job, taking down Lisa's curtains. Robert stuffed them into plastic bags and hid them in the shed. Even more difficult was putting up the old ones. He shook them out, heaved them up the step ladder. Fat blue roses entwined with sour green leaves, clinging to orange trellis. How many evenings had Sarah sat in front of them, garish floral halo behind her, listing reasons why he was a useless husband?

They were in place at last. Terrible. Drawn back as far as they would go, their bunchiness further darkened the room. Robert found the lime and blue velvet cushions, so carefully matched in bad taste, which used to stand on the brown sofa. Sarah liked them to be on tiptoe, Robert remembered: on one point, so that they made diamond shapes against the back of the sofa. He tried. They fell over. He couldn't try again.

What else? The shelf above the fireplace looked naked. He reinstated his father-in-law's picture of a prim galleon on frilly sea. Remembered the candlesticks. Lisa had moved them to the table for *use*, she sensibly said. But had never cleaned them, so their pewter had turned to luminescent black. Robert dumped them at each end of the mantelpiece. He threw away the stumps of candles, finally burnt out last night. Searching for new ones, he came across the photograph. He looked at it. He and Sarah in Paris, late Fifties. Their first illicit weekend. Taken by a student who had joined them for a drink in a café. They had bought the whole film from him, given him a few francs besides.

'God,' Lisa had scoffed when she found it one day, 'your *clothes*. You looked old *then*.' She had tossed the photograph away, no questions, not interested. You look even older now, she meant. Twenty years older than her – and don't forget it. At the time of the photograph, he and Sarah had felt very young. The solemn handbag was no indication of passionate spirits. His love for her had been on a different plane . . . still was.

He remembered that the day Lisa had sneered at the photograph was the day he began to wonder.

It was all done by twelve. Robert sat in the armchair pushed *back* from the fireplace, as Sarah liked it. Shorn of its crumpled shawls, scraped down to the skin of its beige brocade, it felt skinned naked, alien. He would have to ask her for a few changes . . . above all, the curtains.

His hands and feet were frozen. This time last year it had snowed. Lisa and he had walked through the Savernake Forest, snow-quiet, muffled breaking of twigs, arguing about the power of the past – its habit of intrusion. Oh God, what have I done?

Into the silence bit the quiet, menacing crunch of his wife's key. She had refused to give it back – said it would be symbolic of giving up hope. He had thought it impolite to change the locks. She could be trusted not to come round.

He stood, turned. Sarah's eyes were crinkled into a wonderful smile. Perhaps she had just been out shopping, never been away.

'Everything's the same,' she said, looking round.

He saw at once in her ageing body and lively face the woman he had always loved most, despite everything. He went towards her, hoping, dreading. His own smile, unexpectedly easy, responded to her innocence.

They kissed. In the tangle of guilt about her, about Lisa, only one thought occurred: you could spin a whole axis in a single morning. To re-arrange a life, you simply had to re-arrange a room.

Sarah, drawing back from him, had observed the Paris photograph on the mantelpiece.

'My worst nightmare,' she said, 'was that you might have changed things. But you haven't. Once we've had the curtains cleaned, you'll never know I've been away.'

'May it be that easy,' Robert said. Her busy eyes had now reached the table, and Lisa's bowl of snowdrops.

Alternative Behaviour

W here did we go wrong?
      She'll stomp into the kitchen, Meriel, stub out her
roll-up cigarette in a saucer though there's always an ashtray provided. She'll look in the fridge, slam shut its door
with a snort of disapproval no matter how much it holds;
she'll push back my cooking things and sit herself on the
table and swing her skinny legs weighed down with those
horrible great boots. Even before she's said a word, Meriel
brings menace into the house. She shatters our peace. In
truth, we're afraid of her.

What should we have done differently?

We've tossed the question between us so many times
that it's become stale. We can find no solutions and we
can't go on asking ourselves, says Douglas, quite rightly.
We can't go on torturing ourselves, condemning ourselves,
battering ourselves with guilt, exhausting ourselves with
questions that have no answer. Our firm intention is just to
accept, to question no more. But the haunting remains,
the wondering. The constant regret.

Sometimes, when we slip into theories without meaning
to, I suggest to Douglas it's because we're so dull. A dull,
once happy couple. Reluctantly, he agrees. He doesn't like
to think we're dull. To him – to me, we're not. Until all this,

we have had and appreciated our small pleasures in life: security, just enough money, solid house with a nice bit of garden for the roses that are Douglas's hobby, holiday abroad most years, quietly in the same hotel near the Pyrenees where we can walk and gather wild flowers.

By others' standards, our ambitions have been minor ones and we feel no smugness in having achieved them to some extent – Doug a partner in the firm of solicitors after only twenty years. He specialises in divorce and never ceases to be amazed by other people's unhappy marriages. Over the years he's come back with stories of cruelty and violence and calculated unkindness you'd scarcely believe. But he enjoys the job. He's good at it, plainly. Also, his golf has improved as well as his roses – I doubt you'd see a better show of them anywhere in Berkshire.

As for me: well, all I've ever wanted was a quiet life, running the house efficiently, cooking for the family, enjoying the Bridge Club once a week. When Meriel went to weekly boarding school, I admit I did indulge in a few evening classes in pottery, History of Art and botany – things I'd had no chance to study at school and had always hankered after. But whenever Meriel was at home I'd put them to one side. I'd make sure my reading was finished by the time she was back so that I could listen to all her news over a slice of Victoria sponge, drive her over to her friend Lily – whatever she wanted. In all fairness, I don't think she could ever accuse me of neglect, though I suppose, yes, our life to her might seem unexciting. *Dead*, she called it, in one of her rages.

I had three miscarriages before Meriel. The nine months

of pregnancy with her I found hard to believe – hard to believe she wasn't one more life snuffed out before it had a chance. We had always wanted two children, but once Meriel was born, a perfect baby, we decided not to try our luck again. We felt it wouldn't be possible to love another child so much, and all desire to put the matter to the test dissolved. Meriel was enough for us.

'But we must be sure not to suffocate her with love,' I remember Doug saying. We tried very hard to be sensible parents – balanced, understanding but not spoiling, disciplining but not regimenting. We tried to inculcate in her from an early age a curiosity and love of simple things . . .

She'll barge into the house, drinking beer straight from the can and when she's finished it she'll crumple the can up in one hand as if it was so much tissue paper. She has big, manly hands, sinews tough as chains under the hard skin, flat fingers that pry over our things with distaste. Recently she's had her hair shaved round the back and a new earring at the top of her ear. Some years ago, she dyed her hair pink and had it standing up in points, like a clown. I managed not to say anything, and over this new shaved look I'm doing my best not to make any comment. But, I mean: Meriel's twenty-three now. She's no teenager. She's grown up.

By the age of five she knew the names of dozens of wild flowers and was an endearing, rewarding child. Not pretty, exactly: nose a little too prominent, like her father's – eyes a shade too close together, perhaps, but the bright blue that comes from my mother's side of the family. Everyone said she had lovely hair, and she was always turned out neatly – hand-smocked dresses and well-polished shoes. She was a bright little thing: happy, gregarious, loving. She would fling her arms around Doug's neck and ask him for an ice-cream or a story, knowing he would be unlikely to refuse her. From an early age, she would dedicate all her artwork to me, bright pictures of birds, and flowers bigger than the flat houses, *I love you Mum* written in the corner. One of her teachers assured us her draftsmanship was exceptional and she might well be an artist. I was inclined to agree.

At the age of nine, I think it was, Meriel began to show the first small signs of revolt. It was then we noticed that order, so much the norm in our house, seemed to frustrate her. No matter how much I tidied up her room, or persuaded her to do so, it was only a matter of hours before neatness had given way to havoc. She seemed to get a charge from flinging things off shelves on to the floor, rummaging through the neat piles of clothes in her drawers until they looked like a jumble sale, pulling her mattress on to the floor where, she said, she preferred to sleep. Her untidy ways weren't confined to her own room, either. In the kitchen, she spilt things so often it seemed clear it was on purpose. She threw her clothes all over the place, rumpled the cushions, left books and papers on the floor. I think we both felt she was deliberately trying to annoy us, and took some pleasure in our discomfort and unease. Douglas and I hate things out of place: a sense of meticulous order has always been the staff we lean on.

By the time she was twelve, Meriel had given up at school. She was in constant trouble with her teachers and, apparently, no longer interested in any subject, even art.

No more paintings for me. Her father could no longer persuade her to read a book, any book. Her short attention span could accommodate no more than a teenage or music magazine. She spent most of her pocket money on these publications, then flung them down wherever she happened to be.

'Do pick up your magazine, Meriel.'

'Cool it, Mum.'

'Do as your mother says, Meriel.'

'For Christ's sake, stop nagging.'

'Don't adopt that tone with your mother, Meriel, or I shall stop your pocket money.'

'Go ahead and stop it. See if I care.'

'Meriel! Don't be so rude to your father.'

'Oh, piss off, both of you.'

Such language, at twelve. There were variations on this ritual exchange, then Meriel would clump out of the room, stomping the pages of the offending magazines to a mush on the floor in her utter scorn.

In the end, I would always be the one to clear them away.

It was about this time – just before Christmas, I remember – that Meriel chose to rebel against her name.

'What on earth was up with you, giving me such a daft middle-class name? You can imagine how *that* goes down at school.' Surely not too badly, I thought. The school was full of Virginias and Camillas and Emilys, a nice bunch of middle-class girls. 'You can't blame them for sneering,' she added, sloshing her tea aggressively over the side of her mug – a hideous mug, incidentally, orange decorated with black lettering: ***k You, mate. When it was on the shelf, I always hid it behind another mug, turning the lettering away. Time and again I would find it placed back right in the front, its message staring my visitors in the face. It was one of our unspoken battles. Sometimes the mug so enraged me that I vowed I would throw it out, or break it on purpose. But I never went quite that far for fear of Meriel's revenge taking some even more drastic turn . . .

Douglas was concentrating on his *Daily Telegraph*, in one of his best-to-ignore-her moods.

'So anyway, from now on I'm not Meriel, I'm Mog.'

'Meg?' asked Doug, despite himself.

'Not Meg, no thanks. *Mog.*'

'Mog? But Meriel's a lovely name,' I ventured. We had agreed on it within moments of her birth. The small scrunched-up pink face *looked* like a Meriel, I remember saying to Douglas.

'Mog it is. I'm telling you – anyone who doesn't call me Mog won't get an answer. Meriel is *dead*.' She banged down her fist so hard that the Formica table skittered on its thin legs.

'We'll see about that,' said her father, in his most authoritative voice, which sometimes had effect.

'We will,' I agreed. 'Meriel. Mog, indeed!'

She won in the end, of course. Weeks went by when she responded to any question with persistent silence if we called her Meriel. *Mog*, eventually we said, in desperation. We were rewarded with a pleased smile. The triumph of a victory made her more agreeable for a while. And naturally we only called her Mog when we had to. If sometimes we slipped up and said Meriel by mistake, we were regaled with the old fury and rudeness. Our daughter hadn't an ounce of forgiveness in her.

We were prepared for a difficult time during Meriel's teens – that was to be expected. But we never imagined she would push our tolerance quite so far: pierced nose, shaven head, a tattoo on her shoulder – all done without our permission. As for her clothes – in a word, revolting. Why did she always want to make the *worst* of herself? That's what we couldn't understand. Our pretty daughter, at fifteen, was replaced by a brutish, alien creature we scarcely recognised. Drugs were our greatest fear, of course. They seemed the obvious next step. She was in with a bad lot. But when we ventured to have a conversation about the dangers – well, she just laughed, full of scorn. She'd never been into drugs, she said. *Demos* were more her thing.

Indeed, this seemed to be the case, as we discovered to our horror. Most weekends she'd go off with some renta-crowd – anti-students' cuts, anti-blood sports – it didn't seem to matter what it was, if there was a chance of joining a rowdy mob and throwing bricks at the police, Meriel would be there. You'll get arrested, we said. Who cares? she said. You must pay for what you believe in. We despaired. But there was nothing we could do.

Then came the day she walked in with a nasty cut above her eye. Didn't say a word. Dashed up to her room before I could offer to bathe it for her. Shut herself in her room. She wouldn't come down for supper, though she did ask for aspirin. When I asked if I could help, I was told to mind my own business.

After that, as far as we could tell, she went to no more demonstrations. But we noticed other changes. She began to grow her hair back. The fridge was no longer full of cans of beer. She seemed to go out less with her friends. She was working, she said, in her room: and we believed her. So in some ways she became a little easier, though her aggressive feminism and vegetarianism seemed more deeply entrenched than ever. As for her political correctness! We could hardly open our mouths without making some *faux pas* in her eyes. When Douglas complained that an Indian plumber had done a useless job, she threatened to report him for racism. When I said something about the Chairman of the WI, I was blasted with a ten-minute lecture on the necessity of addressing such a figure as a Chair*person*, even though the grey-haired old lady I had referred to had been happy as *Chairman* for the last twenty years. As for the food problem: while I tried my best to cook her things with vegetables and pulses, she sneered at us for our love of the Sunday joint which she, too, once used to enjoy, and our mid-week cottage pie. She managed to make us feel very uncomfortable at meals: always on about the cruelty of killing animals, the dangers of animal fat, and so on. Sometimes I could see Douglas was near to exploding, so goaded by her thoughts. But he managed to keep control, not to shout. It was hard for him just to let her have her say, unchallenged: but easier than the screaming row that would ensue if he tried to reason with her. *Reasoning* was the least of Meriel's abilities.

She did surprisingly well in her exams – no cause for celebration, she said when I baked her a cake she refused to eat because there was 'dangerous' colouring in the icing. Nothing very fancy about getting a few good marks, she said. Just meant it made her way into university that much easier.

Psychology was her subject. Psychology! Douglas raised his eyebrows, signalling only a fraction of the pain he felt. Couldn't she have chosen something better than a trendy, soft-option subject, he asked? With her brains – and he was proud of her brains – history: why not history? She'd done so well in that. Foolish man! He should have learned by then to keep his opinions to himself. Meriel went berserk, screaming at him, banging doors. 'What do you know about what motivates me? When have you ever cared about me as a *person*, not just as your daughter?' Then she slammed out of the house, leaving those cliché questions of modern jargon heavy between us, saying she was going to her friend for the night. (Boy or girl? We did not know). Douglas did not bring up the subject of psychology again.

Once Meriel had gone to university, the house became very quiet. Easier. We were aware of the luxury of peace, of no fear of tantrums or accusations. Surprisingly, she wrote to us several times – ordinary, newsy letters, telling us how she was doing, how she was enjoying university life. She had found a lot of people there who thought like her, she said. Like-minded, was the way she put it. (God forbid, said Douglas.) Once or twice, she even rang us – non-committal, but quite friendly. Then, her third term, we discovered Douglas had cancer.

For some time, he had been complaining about a painful shoulder. He thought it was rheumatism, or arthritis, perhaps. But as it did not improve over the weeks, he agreed to go to the doctor. He was X-rayed. A tumour was found. There were tests. Malignant, it was. A course of immediate chemotherapy was prescribed. I wrote to Meriel, breaking the news as gently as I could.

Twelve hours after receiving my letter she was home. Douglas and I were sitting by the fire with our hot drinks before going to bed, trying to make decisions calmly, in the way that people strive to in a crisis – what would happen about the business, and so on . . . Anyhow, Meriel comes barging in, giving us the fright of our lives. She's red-eyed, shouting, hysterical. Then she's all over her father, hugging him, crying. He has to push her away because, inadvertently, she hurts his shoulder. Then she sits on the floor, hugging her knees (which are poking out of torn jeans) and begins to spew out all this stuff against conventional medicine. The reason she has rushed home so fast, she says, is because she had to stop us deciding in favour of the treatment. Chemotherapy was crap, she said. Had we considered the side effects? Did we know how rarely it was successful? Conventional medicine was for the most part crap. The only way to certain recovery was *alternative*.

There was a long silence. Meriel was staring at her father's doubting face. She shuffled over to him, put an arm around his neck, more gently this time, leant her cheeks against his, just as she used to when she was a small child.

'Believe me, Dad,' she said. 'I've been studying all this sort of thing. It's all to do with positive attitude, freeing the body and soul from all the aggro that's been storing up so many years. Why do you think you've got cancer? Stress, that's why. You're stressed out, Dad.' She glanced at me.

I could see Douglas inwardly wincing at all those jargon words he hates so much, but at the same time he was touched by Meriel's unusual concern. This strange turn of events caught him off-balance. It was a moment, I could see him thinking, which he had to play carefully. If he said the wrong word, off she would stomp again, offended by the spurning of her advice and concern. If he agreed . . . what would we say to our doctor?

'For a start, you've got to get all the anger out of you,' Meriel went on after a while. 'It's got to be released.'

'But I'm not angry,' Douglas said.

'That's what you think. Listen, I know about these things, Dad. Honest, I'm a member of the Healing Society. I'm a Healer. I admit I haven't much experience, hands on, like. But I understand the principles. I believe in it one hundred per cent. When Mum wrote to me with the news, I couldn't help thinking here was a God-given chance to do something worthwhile at last. Make up for my – er, in the past.'

She put her hand on her father's knee, something she hadn't done for more years than I could remember. She looked very young, a child. Douglas seemed to be thinking the same thing. There was a brightness in his eye. He was close to tears.

'You're a good girl,' he said at last. 'I appreciate your concern. I'm not out of sympathy with all the alternative medicine bit myself, as a matter of fact. I've read quite a bit about it – I've been reading everything I can about ruddy cancer in the last few weeks, as you can imagine. But the fact is, this business—' he freed his hand from Meriel's, briefly touched his shoulder— 'could gather speed. I can't afford to hang about. I'd be a fool not to take the experts' advice, start the treatment. We're in very good hands, you know.'

Meriel moved a few feet away from her father. She looked at him with the hard eyes we were used to when she was not immediately able to get her way.

'Do this for me, Dad,' she said. 'Give me a chance. Just a few weeks. It's all a matter of diet, massage, positive thinking. Attitude is everything. Like: there are only another two weeks of term. I won't go back. I'll stay here, organising a programme for you. Starting tomorrow. I'll prepare your food, prepare your soul, Dad. Honest. In fact, not tomorrow – now. No time like the . . . We'll start with a massage, relax you, build up your confidence . . .'

Douglas's eyes moved about, alarmed. Again, he touched his shoulder.

'I'd rather not, a massage,' he said.

'I won't hurt you, stupid. It'll just be temples and toes. You've no idea how much good work on the toes can do.' She gave a confident smile. 'I'll explain it as I go. Now, you lie on the floor, Dad, nice and comfortable, cushion under your head. I'll just get my oils. Let's give it a go. All right?'

Douglas nodded, very weary.

'Very well,' he said.

Half an hour later, I could scarcely believe my own eyes. There was Douglas stretched out on our fluffy carpet, eyes shut, socks off. Meriel, kneeling beside him, was kneading at the furrows on his poor dear brow with her big flat thumbs. She would work them right up into his temples, where once the hair was thick and handsome, and was now so thin. There was an overpowering, claustrophobic smell of lavender oil in the room – a smell, I was later to learn, you can never quite extinguish from a room. A smell I came to associate with the terrible weeks of Meriel's 'cure'. Nothing like the summer smell of lavender bushes, or dried lavender in a muslin bag. In its concentrated form, it is menacing, sickening. I could see Douglas's nostrils twitch, affronted. But he said nothing. He kept his eyes shut, allowing his head to roll with her hands as she kept up a perpetual stream of theories. 'Trouble with you, Dad, is you're suffering from a crisis of identities.'

'I don't think your father is doing any such thing,' I heard myself saying.

'You don't know anything, Mum. That's been one of Dad's problems.'

She moved down to his feet. Watching her at work on them was even more upsetting. The private nature of feet came home to me: no wonder people don't want them exposed. They are not the most attractive part of anyone's body. Douglas's were long and thin, sinewy. The white ridges of bone that stuck up put me in mind of a plucked chicken's wings. As for the nails, well, even the most loving wife would have to admit they were not a pretty sight. Wide, flat, lobster-coloured nails, Douglas had, each one topped with an arc of dense yellow that curved cruelly into the hard flesh of the toes. Sometimes they caused him pain and he would have to go to the chiropodist, who said he had a problem. All this I was familiar with – part of my husband, for better, for worse – a huge blessing he wasn't one of those men who liked to wear open sandals. But it didn't seem right to me, a daughter on familiar terms with her father's feet. There she was, pulling at each toe, prying into the secret places between them, all the time droning on about how each toe sent signals up to wherever. Sounded like a lot of stuff and nonsense to me, but I knew I had to go along with Douglas, do whatever he wanted.

When at last she had finished, Douglas sat up very fast, giving the sudden appearance of a fit man. But he looked dizzied, confused. Meriel sat back on her heels, very pleased with herself. She stretched out her hand, held it a few inches from her father's chest.

'There: I can, like, feel the energy coming off you already, Dad,' she said. 'The anger – can't you feel? It's beginning to make its way out.'

Douglas gave her the faintest smile, patted her on the head. He looked so . . . what was it he looked? I couldn't put a name to it for a moment. Then I suddenly knew what it was: *undignified*. That was it. For the first time I could ever remember, my husband's dignity had been ripped from him. He sat hunched on the floor, oily bare feet ashamed in the fluffy pile of the carpet. His thin hair darkened by the lavender oil, and all askew.

'Go on, tell me you don't feel a difference.'

Meriel gently stroked his feet with a possessive intimacy that gave me the creeps.

'Can't say I feel any benefit *yet*,' he said carefully, 'but then it's early days.' He gave Meriel another smile. She put her arms around his neck. 'Oh my dear, dear girl,' he said, with a kind of exhausted relief, as if this physical contact with his daughter was something he had been hoping for for a very long time.

Upstairs, Douglas had a bath and washed his hair. But nothing would get rid of the smell of the lavender. It came off his skin like some terrible incense, increasing the discomfort of our argument – whether we should agree with Meriel's well-meaning but useless theories – that went on till dawn began to light the familiar things of our room, and the day threatened.

But having lost my argument, I did my best when it came to a show of solidarity. I wore my new red coat, and the gloves Douglas had given me at Christmas, for our visit to the specialist. Douglas put his thoughts to the man with all the articulacy he was capable of when addressing a difficult client. You'd think he'd been an advocate of alternative medicine for years, the way he described the reasons for his decision. He was determined to give it a try, he said. A man had to have faith in his daughter. The specialist listened politely, a sceptical frown on his brow. Then suddenly he shrugged his shoulders, almost as if he thought there was no point wasting precious time on one so obdurate as Douglas, and suggested a compromise. Why not *go along* with Meriel's ideas, he said – after all (and here he allowed himself a small chuckle) they could not do much positive harm. Why not start the course of treatment right away as well? There was a small silence while Douglas considered this reasonable proposal. The specialist looked at his watch.

'In cases like yours, there's no time to be lost,' he said.

With this piece of news, Douglas made up his mind instantly.

'No,' he said. 'I'll give my daughter a chance first. Just for a few weeks.'

'Very well,' said the specialist, and saw us out into the stuffy corridor. I felt as if our lifeline had been snapped. But I kept my fears to myself, and drove Douglas to his office. He was to start arrangements for his deputy to be in charge. Although he intended still to work some days a week, already it was apparent he was not up to a full week in the office. Fatigue hit him every day after lunch. This afternoon, however, he seemed to be full of beans. I secretly wondered, only for a moment, whether there might be something in Meriel's gobbledy-gook after all – some magic, some transference of will. I don't know. I do believe miracles can happen. Though nothing could convince me Meriel could be the perpetrator of the sort of miracle we needed.

I got home late that afternoon, having been shopping at Sainsbury's. I got home to find that Meriel had already been on a spending spree of her own. The kitchen table was entirely covered with fruit, vegetables, and several blue glass bottles of essential oils and many packets of vitamins. In an expensive-looking new liquidiser she was making raw carrot juice – I refrained from asking, but imagine Douglas must have lent her his credit card, or given her cash. A pile of chopped liver with a nasty bluish-purple shine lay on a board. On top of the fridge, propped up in the rude mug, a joss stick was burning. Its sickly smoke curled down over us. The blinds at the kitchen window were half-drawn. Meriel's portable CD player was on the draining board, Indian music mewing forth.

'What's all this?' I asked, lowering my own bags of provisions to the floor.

'Day one of Dad's diet. Starting with supper. Don't put on that face, Mum. Give me some credit.'

Did I put on that face again at supper? I hoped not. But as I watched Douglas struggle with a plateful of raw liver mixed with grated carrot, I could not be sure. Later, Meriel insisted on more pulling of his toes, though she did agree to a scentless oil. I could not bring myself to watch this revolting performance again. I went up early to bed and wept into the pillow.

'Please see some sense, Douglas, and stop all this nonsense. There's no time to lose,' I said, when at last, exhausted, he joined me.

He made an effort to be consoling. He promised me that if Meriel's methods did not result in definite improvements quite soon, he would return to the specialist.

'Don't you see,' he said, 'that she's come to make amends. If we reject her now, we'll lose her for good. As it is, she's back to loving us, wanting us, needing to do something very important for us. It would be madness to reject her. She'd be gone for good. We must give her a chance, whatever the cost.'

What could I do but nod, agree? Whatever feelings a wife may have, she must not add to her ill husband's problems.

In the middle of the night, I heard Douglas get up and go to the bathroom. He was there a long time, terribly sick. I pretended to be asleep.

*

The days go by slowly. Fraught. She'll stomp into the kitchen, Meriel, with bags of fruits and vegetables, pulses and grains and vitamins. There hasn't been any meat in the house – apart from the raw liver – since she came back. Not a thing I fancy, and I can't very well bake a batch of scones just for myself. Never a 'Anything *you'd* like, Mum?' What's more, she's taken over. She's in charge of what goes on in the kitchen. All I'm left with is the clearing up. Still, I suppose I can't complain. She's here, she's all over her father, paying him more attention than she has done for years. Almost an obsessive attention, I might add, as if it's important to her to make her point, to prove her alternative methods are right, superior.

She comes down late – never an early riser. So I do the breakfast, eating half a grapefruit to keep Douglas company, though I can't take the carrot juice. Douglas says its not bad, once you're used to it. He's been a hero, forcing himself to get used to Meriel's diet, I'll say that. Nowadays he only goes to the office twice a week – Meriel packs him a salad and fresh orange juice the night before – and comes back looking ashy in the evenings. But quite cheerful. 'Don't you think Dad's looking better, Mum?' Meriel keeps asking. I can see in his eyes Douglas is hoping for an encouraging answer. So, yes, I say, I believe he is. That's not the truth, of course. I keep the truth from both of them. My private opinion is that he's a bad colour –yellowy skin, a jaundiced colour. Also, he's lost a lot of weight very quickly. Half a stone in a couple of weeks, I'd guess. But that's not surprising, considering the rabbit food Meriel insists he eat. And when he's in her presence, I'm bound to admit he puts on a show of good spirits, swears he's feeling better. That pleases her. She kisses the top of his head and pats him with her big hands. I hate her at those moments. I believe I really hate her.

Evenings, there's a routine. After supper, she and Douglas go next door for another massage session. I really can't abide to watch. They're back on the lavender oil, now: as far as I'm concerned, the sitting room has become un-inhabitable. It stinks. So, after supper, I sit in the kitchen with biscuits and tea – Meriel's vegetarian concoctions aren't exactly filling, and of course I won't touch the raw liver – watching the telly. Every night Meriel tells me, at the end of the session, they're getting somewhere. An inner peace is replacing the old stress, she says. I look at Douglas, but he won't meet my eye.

One night it's one-thirty and they're still in there. I know Douglas needs to go to bed, it's his office day tomorrow. So I tap on the door, poke my head round. Well, it's really spooky. There's dreadful Indian whining music, the smell of joss sticks curdling with the stench of lavender oil. Douglas is laid out on the fluffy carpet, bare yellow feet poking out of the end of his trousers, hands of paler yellow spread out on his thighs, eyes shut. The flesh of his face, was my immediate thought, did not seem to belong to the same man. It was a terrible colour, a sort of thin grey, like the flesh of a snail.

Meriel, kneeling behind him, looks up. Her fingers are twirling about in the air above his chest, as if she is kneading invisible pastry.

'What do you want?' The usual aggression.

'I think it's time for your father to come up to bed.'

Meriel went on with her twirling, as if I had not spoken.

'Here, look at this, Mum,' she said at last. 'You can see what's happening, can't you? The core of his anger. You can see it coming out. It's like smoke, isn't it? It's tangible. You can *feel* it.' She pinched her finger and thumb together as if she was pinching snuff. It struck me she was completely mad. 'Once Dad's free of all this, he'll be well on his way to recovery. Cancer's, like, one hundred per cent caused by stress, anger, rotten feelings that fester into a kind of garbage inside you.' Her chant was familiar by now.

'Not one hundred per cent,' I ventured.

'Listen, I've studied all this. I know what I'm talking about.'

A matter of opinion, my girl, I said to myself. You've only been an undergraduate for under two terms, and you're meant to be studying psychology.

But there again, perhaps all this sort of talk *is* psychology . . .?

Douglas opened his eyes and struggled to get up. He looked very tired, but managed a smile. Both Meriel and I put out a hand to help him up. He had taken off his jacket. I noticed that beneath his shirt his shoulder bones stuck out like wings.

'Thank you, love,' he said to Meriel and I felt myself stung by a terrible feeling. The pain in my chest, the jealousy, was tangible. Then, perhaps aware of my feelings, he put his arm around *my* shoulders, thank God, and leant on me all the way upstairs.

Meriel went back to university at last. Never have I been so relieved. I opened the sitting-room windows wide to try to banish the smell of lavender oil, then set about clearing up my kitchen. She'd left instructions everywhere – pinned to the walls, stuck to the fridge: lists of ingredients I was to buy, how to make a lemon dressing, the importance of carrot juice at all times . . . I don't know. It wearied my head, trying to follow it all. I knew I'd never manage: my heart wasn't in it. In my opinion, what Douglas needed was some nourishing food, something to keep his strength up. I felt like ripping all the bossy little instructions down, throwing them away. Then I thought, better not. Not till I see what Douglas feels. He may want to keep the whole ludicrous routine going. Keep on giving it a chance. Besides, Meriel had left with so many threats. 'If you don't continue the cure scrupulously,' she had said, 'it will be your fault if Dad declines. As you can see, he's *much better* since I've been working on him. He's a different man. Can't wait to get back and tell the Healers about my success.'

I made a small batch of scones that day, put two or three on a plate for tea. When Douglas came home – he comes back much earlier now from his two days at the office – he took one, ate it slowly, relishing every bite.

'Guilty?' I asked with what I hoped was a mischievous smile.

'Just very hungry,' he said.

'What if I made you a steak and kidney pie for supper?'

'I'd eat it,' he said. Well, we hadn't had such a happy evening for weeks.

Douglas made some effort to return to carrot juice and so on for a couple of days, but we both agreed it was time for the experiment to come to an end. It was quite obvious there was no improvement in his condition: in fact, the truth was, as he admitted within a week of Meriel's departure, he felt bloody awful. No energy, much worse pain in his shoulder.

'But no need to worry,' he said. 'Mr Belton was so optimistic, remember? Said I'd probably got a few years, and quite a high chance of full recovery.'

'But you wouldn't start the treatment when he suggested it.'

'Won't have made much difference, six or seven weeks. All the same, I'd like to go back and see him.' I could tell, by that, he was worried. We were sitting on the sofa. It was an overcast afternoon. He'd laid one of his thin hands on my knee. It quivered.

'Why, Douglas?' I asked. 'I'll never understand why you agreed to go along with Meriel's daft theories.'

'Surely you should understand,' he said, so gently. 'I had to win her back. We had to win her back. There've been so many years of alienation. I thought this might be the last chance. I thought it couldn't hurt. Might even be something in it.'

'You mean, you didn't believe in it all, although you kept telling her you did?'

Douglas shrugged.

'I couldn't disappoint her, could I? Here she was, with something *she* really believed in. I haven't seen her so enthusiastic, so involved in something, since she was quite a small child. Besides, I think she was trying to say sorry. Trying to make up for all the difficult years. I wouldn't have had the heart to reject that. You wouldn't, either.'

'She didn't like *me* any better, I noted.'

'One thing at a time. She's not capable of taking on several things at once, remember. She'll come round to you.' This was no time to argue.

'So what do we do about telling her, Doug? About giving up her plan?'

He thought about it for a long time, in silence.

'We don't tell her,' he said at last.

The following week we returned to Mr Belton, the specialist. He interviewed Douglas at length. It was hard to read his thoughts, but I fancied he looked concerned. Douglas, he said, had lost a stone.

'I thought it was worth giving it a go,' Douglas said.

'It was up to you,' Mr Belton said – not unfriendly, exactly. More, a little impatient. He made an appointment for more tests, X-rays. A few days later, Douglas left his office for good. Meriel rang up most evenings.

'How's the routine going?' she kept asking. 'Carrot juice three times a day? You must be getting used to chopping up the raw liver by now, Mum.' We lied to her. We lied and lied, bright voices. She was full of smug pleasure, of course. The story about her father responding so well had been received with much interest, she said. These conversations were very trying. Each time Douglas put down the telephone he looked like a slain man.

'I'd give the world not to be doing this,' he said.

'Let's hope it's not one more of our mistakes,' I said. 'Dear God, where did we go wrong?' The question slipped out before I could stop it.

'We'll never know,' said Douglas.

*

Mr Belton summoned us to tell us about the results of the tests. This time, there's no denying he looked grave. One glance at his face and I knew what the news was going to be.

'The one thing that's certain about this disease,' he said, rubbing his healthy brown hands together, 'is its unpredictability. Sometimes, when all the signs have given little hope, it suddenly becomes almost dormant. Other times, you're pretty sure the patient has months, if not a few years, left, and the tumours multiply with a devastating speed.' He paused. 'I wish you hadn't postponed the treatment,' he said. 'But we'll see what you can do.'

He described it all to us in great and kindly detail, but his words were far away, blowing down through a thin tube in my ears that made an echo. On the way out, Douglas took my arm. I felt its terrible thinness. I felt the sinews tremble, but he was being so cheerful.

'Don't worry,' he said, 'I'm going to lick this thing. I'm a fit man, and whatever Meriel might think, not an angry one.'

We laughed, standing there in the car park, the cars a paintbox of colours flowing into one another. It was the last time I can remember we laughed, and Douglas asked me to drive.

It all gathered such speed after that, there was scarcely a moment to get back to this journal. Besides, I couldn't. I couldn't bring myself to describe the horror of Doug's fast decline: the small spasms of hope always quickly dashed by despair. I looked after him myself for as long as I could, then a nurse came in to give me some relief. His hair fell out. I became fascinated by a small pulse in his temple, beating away, roped in by a swollen blue vein, fat as a worm. Had they always been there, pulse and vein, beneath his hair, all the years of our marriage? It was the sort of thing I began to concentrate on, trying to deflect my thoughts from the reality of the situation. Douglas was dreadfully sick, and new pains began. Terrible stomach pains. It was time for all possible help, things beyond me. He agreed to go into the local hospice, a sunny place with windows on to a nice garden.

The time had come, too, to tell Meriel. I dreaded the call so much. In fact, I gave way to cowardice and wrote to her. I said the switch to conventional medicine had been a mutual decision. It was what Douglas wanted, what we thought would be best. I put it all as gently as I could.

Her first response was at midnight, waking me from a light sleep. A great spewing forth of abuse, anger, tears – all just as I had expected, only worse. Vitriolic. Accusing me of breaking her trust, betraying her. What sort of a mother am I, she asks. What sort of a wife? Giving up *her* way – so successful in just a few weeks, as we had all witnessed – and subjecting Doug to chemotherapy was tantamount to sticking a knife through his heart. When I tried to remonstrate, ask her to listen to reason, she just slammed down the telephone.

She kept on ringing. Whenever I came back from visiting Douglas – and I couldn't worry him with all this, of course – she was on the telephone with her horrible accusations.

This morning was the worst of all. So vicious I can only hope it was the last time she'll ring.

She accused me of killing her father.

'If we hadn't wasted weeks on your stupid methods, your father might not be lying there dying right now,' I shouted back. I was suddenly angrier than I'd ever been in my life, with anyone.

'You bitch,' she screamed. 'Bitch, bitch, bitch.' She disowned me as a mother, she said. I wouldn't see her again, not even at the funeral.

It's late at night now, but I've calmed down a bit. I try to put Meriel from my mind, concentrate only on Douglas. He was very tired this evening, weak. But cheerful as always, holding my hand. He doesn't ask about Meriel any more. He hasn't the strength to hear about disputes. He knows there's only a short time left.

Well, I'm not going to write my journal again after tonight. It's been cathartic in some ways, but nothing can help any more. Besides, I want to spend every moment from now on at Douglas's bedside. Often, sitting there, so quiet, I long to ask him one last time, where did we go wrong? But the time's past. Such a question would be an unfair burden in his pitiful state. Besides, the closeness of death rarely enlightens. Like me, he can have no answers.

The Wife Trap

Seventeen years after their divorce, Peggy Jarrett received a Christmas card from her ex-husband George. She had recognised his writing on the envelope at once, and was puzzled. There had been no word of communication ever since their apathetic farewell in Court, a sleety morning all that time ago. What was he up to now?

Nothing, it seemed. Peggy read the message several times.

Why don't you drop in for a cuppa if ever you're passing this way? Yours ever, George.

Whatever made him think she'd be his way? She had no reason to pass through Lincolnshire, some hundred miles north-east from where she lived. What a daft idea! Besides, in the unlikely event of her being in his direction, what would be the point of dropping in on a man with whom she had had seven years of nothing but boredom, irritation and disappointment? As a husband, George had been nowhere near up to scratch, in Peggy's mind, and she hadn't missed him once since their parting. Indeed, she'd scarcely given him a thought.

Nonetheless, she searched the card for clues. She held it up to the opal wintry light that hung flatly across her small kitchen window, her lips puckered in critical contemplation.

It was a traditional scene: coach and four in front of an olde inn, swirling snowstorm blurring the artist's incompetent draftsmanship. Rubbing her finger over the picture, Peggy could feel the raised paper that had been employed to depict the snow – a porridgy feel that made her shudder. A very low-grade card, she was bound to admit. But then George had never had her instinct for nice things. That had been one of the many life-dividers between them. His obliviousness of quality stuff – curtains, pictures, shoes, ties, anything you could mention – was one of the things that had driven her to despair. What's more, he had shown no inclination to *learn*. Things were just things, as he so often used to say, and as long as they functioned properly that was good enough for him. What do I care if a glass comes free from a garage or for twenty quid from bloody Harrods? he once asked. Funny how she remembered the question. He'd been standing in the kitchen clutching a tin of Quality Street to his stomach at the time. She could hear his sneery voice as if he were shouting at her this very moment. The Christmas card brought it all back to her, the remembrance of all the troubles she'd had with George; the fact that she had married beneath her, and regretted her mistake from day one of the honeymoon.

For a moment, Peggy wondered whether to throw out the card. But then she decided to put it with the rest, in a shoebox on whose lid she had written *Christmas 1995*. Might as well. She had quite a hoard of boxes now, proof that she was in so many friends' thoughts at the festive season. The presence of these cards was a peculiar comfort. Sometimes, even in the heat of July, she would take them out to recount them, and reread the messages of goodwill and cheer. Not that even Jen, her best friend and neighbour, knew anything of this secret ritual. Jen was a great one for Understanding Most Things, as she often reassured Peggy: but instinct told Peggy that there were some things that should not be confided even to a best friend, for fear of misinterpretation.

When she had put the card in the box with the rest of her collection, Peggy almost forgot about it. Although, during the course of the next eight months, her mind did occasionally turn, curiously . . . Once, years ago, she had found a dormouse curled up under a floorboard in deep sleep. She had not disturbed it, but remembering its presence every so often caused a small wick of comfort to flutter in her stomach. George's card acted in the same way.

In August, Peggy's sister Lil suggested Peggy go up for a week to see the new house she and Jack had bought in Alnwick. Peggy didn't much fancy the idea, and knew from experience a week with Lil and Jack would be more like hard work than a holiday. She was driven to distraction by Jack's non-stop boasting about how he was a man for a bargain if ever there was one. In their last tacky little house there was not a single item that had not been a bargain, it was too plain to see. Peggy held no hopes that the knockdown terraced house in Alnwick would be any different. She hated Lil's scarcely disguised sympathy for her own single life – sympathy! That was the last thing she needed, considering her own superiority of judgement was of quite a different class to Lil's; and then the children. They were the sort of children who made Peggy feel glad she had none of her own. Still, despite everything against the idea, Peggy decided she would go, just for a few days.

The visit passed just as she imagined it would, and on the journey home Peggy was aware of an unaccountable weariness. The thought of home, and peace, was cheering, but not all that cheering. As she sat in a motorway café eating her lunch, she reflected on the year ahead of unchanging routine: part-time job at Oxfam, the bridge club, choir practice once a week and dear Jen's interminable visits and enquiries. Nothing to complain about, but nothing to lift her spirits, either. For want of something better to do, she studied the map, thinking that a different way home might relieve the tedium of the next few hours. It was then, by chance, she noticed the small town where George lived, and remembered his card. She measured the distance from her present position with her thumb: some thirty miles, she reckoned. A short visit – cup of tea, exchange of awkward pleasantries – would be under an hour out of her way.

Peggy took but a moment to make up her mind. However unexciting the reunion might be, at least she could make it into a good story for Jen, whose own life always seemed so much more exciting than Peggy's.

An hour and a half later she drew up at an undistinguished house in a suburban street: neat privet hedges and a newly painted wooden gate. She walked up the straight little path feeling nothing at all, and rang the bell. After no response to three rings, she took the liberty of finding her way round to the back of the house. She saw George at the end of a long, narrow garden. The familiarity of his stance – he had his back to her – caused a strange constriction in her chest. He stood there, same as ever, legs apart like a Colossus of suburbia, hosepipe in hands, playing its jet of pale water over a bed of brilliant flowers.

George had worked all his life for a horticultural firm which sold packets of seeds by the million. It had always been his habit to avail himself of free packets, and to furnish the garden so that it looked like pages from the firm's glossy mail order brochures. All too vulgar for Peggy's taste, of course: always had been. Though she had seen the point of free flowers, and in this one matter had conceded to George's determination never to pay for anything in the garden.

She stood quite still, knowing she would have a moment or two to take in his unchanging shape before he turned and saw her. He wore slouching trousers of indeterminate beige, and a polo shirt of a particularly nasty rust that she, Peggy, would never have agreed to. His hair was perhaps a little thinner, and the neat side wings, that curved same as always over his ears, were greying. Had she seen enough? Was this a mad idea? Should she turn and run?

Even as these questions fizzed through her mind, Peggy saw that it was too late. George had spun round and was looking straight at her. He frowned for no more than a second – possibly the strong evening sun was in his eyes. Then he smiled and moved towards her, the water from the hosepipe at his side making a sloppy track across the lawn. He stopped a yard from her – deeper runnels in his cheeks, grey eyebrows, teeth he still had not bothered to have straightened – still smiling.

'Well, I'm blessed, Peg o' my life, I was just about to suss out the hydrangeas,' he said.

The years shot away from Peggy. His news had always been about gardening. Now, after a such a long absence, all he could think to greet her with was his own immediate plan concerning the hydrangeas.

'Were you passing?' he asked after a pause.

'More or less.'

'I knew you would. One day.'

Cocky bastard. All the same, Peggy smiled nicely. 'You've got quite a garden,' she said.

'Not a bad little patch. You should've seen it when I came here. Cup of tea?'

'I wouldn't mind.'

She followed him to the back door. He stopped to turn off the outside tap on the way, and kicked viciously at the green plastic snake of the hose. Once, he had kicked the cat, Pinky, so hard that he had caused a rupture. Peggy remembered Pinky as she looked about George's kitchen: a beautiful marmalade, lovely temperament, everyone said. There wouldn't be any animals here, of course. George loathed animals. Pinky was one of the many things that had come between them.

The kitchen was a room that personified George's view of his surroundings: functional. The walls were a nasty green. There were plastic blinds at the window, a torn shade on the overhead light, a Formica table patterned with ribbons and roses of crude yellow and blue. The smell of stale smoke reminded Peggy of another division of opinion between them, as did the full ashtrays. She had eventually trained George not to smoke in the kitchen, but obviously that rule had lapsed with his freedom.

Peggy drew her angora cardigan tightly round her, and sat on an uncomfortable stool at the table. George, whistling under his breath, switched on the kettle and dumped two mugs on the table. One of them, a souvenir of the Queen's Silver Jubilee, she recognised as theirs. The other was new and ugly. But then in the sharing of things, Peggy remembered, George had been quite generous, allowing Peggy her pick and saying he would not need much stuff just for himself.

Eventually George sat at the other side of the table. A tin pot of tea and a bottle of milk stood between them. Peggy felt some old habit rumbling up through her veins: without asking, she poured the tea. George's first.

'Well, well,' he said. 'What brings you to this part of the world?'

'I've been staying with Jack and Lil. They've got a new place up in Alnwick.'

'Ah, Lil.' George had never shown much affection for his sister-in-law, though once, at a Christmas party, Peggy had found him giving her more than just a polite kiss under the mistletoe.

'You've got a nice place up here, I must say. Very quiet,' she said. Might as well be friendly.

'Quiet! Don't you believe it.' George banged his fist on the table, making the tin pot shudder. 'It's wicked. Break-ins, burglaries, rape, mugging, the lot. Terrible. I organised a local neighbourhood watch, as a matter of fact. I'm what they call the chairman. I'd say things have improved a bit since we put the notices up, but not much. You can't be too careful. Had to spend a fortune on security, I can tell you.'

Peggy followed his glance towards expensive locks on the windows and huge bolts on the door. He'd always had a thing about security, she remembered. But the precautions he had taken here seemed to her a little out of proportion to the value of the contents of the house. No burglar in his right mind would want anything from this kitchen, surely.

'You lock yourself in all right, do you?' George asked.

'Oh, I take good care.'

'Sometimes I've thought, you know – funny thing, but there it is – I've thought, come along, George, send a card to Peg o' my life and tell her to be sure to check her locks. It's a violent world today. But of course I never did. You know me, not much of a writer. So then I sent the Christmas card and lo and behold here you are, so I can warn you in the flesh.'

He smiled. But there was a look in his eye that was new to Peggy. A sort of flinty, manic glare. Possibly it was her imagination. The sun had tinged everything with a glowering orange, making Peggy unsure of her original impression. Perhaps George had changed, in some way she could not put her finger on, which aroused both unease and something vaguely exciting.

They chattered on about the hydrangeas, and George's plans for a new greenhouse, and his addiction to snooker on the television. Two pots of tea were drunk, and then they turned to cans of shandy. These lived on the ledge above the sink and were warm from a long day in the sun:

funny old George, still not much good at looking after himself. Never did remember to put drinks in the fridge.

Some time after eight (amazed, she was, how the time had flown) Peggy remembered the three-hour journey ahead, and said she had better be on her way. The three cans of shandy had made the roses on the table tremble as if through a heat haze. Still, she stood up quite firmly and announced her intention to leave.

'Oh, you don't have to go, surely,' said George. 'You can't drive till all the shandies have settled. It would be irresponsible to let you go. Sit yourself down and I'll get us a sandwich.'

Peggy let herself sink back on to the stool, whose seat had made grooves in her thighs. Suddenly exhilarated by a feeling that time did not matter, she made no protest. With incredulous eyes (in the old days George had never lifted a finger in the kitchen) she watched him open a tin of salmon, spread vegetarian margarine on sliced bread and cut up two homegrown tomatoes.

'Not exactly a feast,' said George, 'but there's plenty of raspberry ripple for afters, and I can probably lay my hands on a bit of cheddar.'

By now Peggy was hungry as well as tired. She ate gratefully, and found herself accepting a glass of homemade elderberry wine. They talked more about the greenhouse, and about who had been promoted in the seed firm in the intervening years (George mentioned a lot of names new to Peggy) and no mention of her own life was made. After they had eaten, they went to the front room – forlornly brown – and sat side by side on the old G-plan sofa that

Peggy, at the time of their parting, had said she would not miss at all. They watched the news, and the snooker, and by the time they turned it off a thin summery darkness had gathered outside the windows.

'Time to be turning in,' said George, as he had said every night of their marriage. 'Have to get up early. Why don't you stay the night, Peg o' my life? It's a bit late to start back now. I've got a perfectly good spare room: never been slept in, as a matter of fact.'

Peggy stifled a yawn. He was quite right, of course: it was no time of night to be setting off cross-country. She sat for a while in easy silence, not thinking about the answer she knew she would give, but wondering why the funny little irritating things about George didn't seem to annoy her as much as they used to. She stood up, stretching in a way she would never consider in front of a stranger: George had never been one to complain of her habit of stretching before bed.

'I'll stay, thanks very much,' she said, arms above her head. 'But no hanky-panky, mind.'

In the dim light she could tell from his amazed expression that no such thought had crossed George's mind.

'Would I ever?' he asked. 'You can trust me. But it's nice seeing you again. Just the same as ever – well, in a way. Let's go and settle you in, sheets and whatnot.'

An hour later, her case unpacked, Peggy sat up in bed wondering at the curious turn of events. Her critical eye took in the ugly maple furniture, the hideous curtains, the central light – she missed a lamp by her bed – and she felt some pity for George. To have stumbled along in such discomfort and ugliness for so long . . . but then he had never been a great observer. Probably none of this affected him in the way it would affect her.

There was a knock on the door. Peggy's hand went to her chest. One of the two nightdresses she had packed to take to Alnwick had a low-cut front. She had chosen to wear this one tonight, for no particular reason.

'Yes?'

'Everything all right?'

'Fine.'

'I'll leave a light on, on the landing.' Pause. 'If I don't see you in the morning, good luck. Drop by again.'

'Thanks.'

Well, blow me down, if he didn't come knocking on my door, Jen. The cheek of it! I told him where to get off. But the fact of the matter is, George is still attracted to me. It was as plain as anything.

Peggy slid down in the bed. Before she could dwell on what could have been, what might have been, she fell asleep, hand still protecting her unassaulted breast.

She woke next morning soon after nine – a most unusual time for her, who was usually up and hoovering at seven-thirty. Hurrying out of bed, Peggy put her lateness down to the thickness of the curtains. No chink of sun slid into the strange room. She pulled them back, annoyed with herself, and looked at a landscape of 1930s suburban villas all staring blankly over their privet hedges. Then she dressed, folded her sheets – one blue, one pink – and packed her case.

Downstairs, there was no sign of George, and no note.

He had plainly left in a hurry. Remains of his breakfast were on the kitchen table. The empty eggshell sat in a cup she had bought on the first anniversary of their marriage. They had been staying in Paignton at the time, and Peggy had been much drawn to this china donkey whose basket on his back served as an eggcup. It was painted with merry yellows and greens, imported from Spain. George, for all his immunity to pretty things, had been taken with it, too, from the start. Nowadays, of course, her taste more refined by the myriad glossy magazines she studied every month, Peggy could see herself rejecting such a donkey with some scorn. But she was touched that George should have kept it, and was still using it. Sentimental old thing, he had always been, in some ways.

Peggy made herself toast and tea, and resumed her uncomfortable position on the stool. In the morning sun the Formica roses of the table were even more dislikable than they had been the evening before, when the shandy had thankfully softened their crude edges. And the old smell of smoke was sickening. But George would never give up smoking, never. He'd die of cancer one day, as she used so often to tell him, and serve him right. Peggy did not hurry over her breakfast: she took her time looking about, memorising every detail so that, tomorrow, she would have the pleasure of describing it all to Jen.

The awfulness of the kitchen, Jen, you can't imagine . . . curtains with a vegetable motif . . .

It was all printed very clearly on her mind.

But despite her uncharitable thoughts, it would not have occurred to Peggy to leave George's house in anything but

a way that would show appreciation for his hospitality. She
washed up – not only their breakfast things, but the dishes
from last night that were piled in the unattractive sink.
She wiped down the Formica surfaces, straightened things
here and there, emptied the ashtrays. Then, finding the
rubbish bin full, she decided her last act of kindness would
be to empty it in the dustbin outside.

I felt I should leave a good impression, if nothing else,
Jen . . .

But the back door was locked. This Peggy discovered
once she had struggled to undo the giant bolts screwed at
top and bottom of the door. There was no key in the lock.
Patiently, she began to search for it – all the obvious places,
the bread bin, under tins, top of the fridge. But no luck. No
key.

Next she tried the small windows over the sink.
Awkwardly leaning over the draining board, she struggled
with locks that were completely unfamiliar to her. So then
she went to the hall. There, the bolts on the stained wood
door were drawn back – but it, too, was locked. Another
search for the key: this took Peggy through all the nooks
and crannies of the stuffy hall, even George's coat pockets
that hung dully from a row of hooks. But again no luck.
Peggy sat on the stairs to think.

I was screaming mad, Jen, I can tell you. The bastard had
locked me in. Imagine! I was his prisoner.

She sat quite calmly for a while, intrigued by a sort of
nefarious peace that seemed to have possessed her. Then,
when the hall clock stirred her with its muffled strokes of
ten, she went to the table on which the old-fashioned,

undusted telephone stood upon an ancient directory. Obviously George's dislike of the telephone had not changed. She looked up the number of his firm in Lincoln, amazed by the weight of the old-fashioned receiver in her hand. She was put straight through to his office. His secretary, an efficient-sounding voice, said Mr Jarrett was out seeing retailers all day and would be going home from his last appointment. No, there was no way he could be contacted. Unlike everyone else, he had always refused to have a mobile telephone. Here, the secretary allowed herself a slight giggle. Was there a message, in the unlikely event of Mr Jarrett ringing in? No, there certainly wasn't, said Peggy briskly – though she had a funny feeling her voice sounded curiously dreamy. And no, she would not be leaving her name.

The bastard, Jen. There I was, stuck. I thought, shall I ring the police?

Peggy returned to the kitchen. There, the overflowing plastic bin sat like an accusation on the threadbare linoleum of George's horrible kitchen floor. Something about it made her look round once more, and this time she saw all the things that could be done by way of improvement. A strange energy and desire to tackle them piped through her. She found an old mop, a balding broom, stiffened cloths, a packet of hardened soap powder, and set to work.

Well, I was dumbfounded. You can imagine. The cheek of it – trapped! Never occurred to me, all these years, poor old Romeo had been wanting me back . . . I just sat there, demented.

Peggy worked hard and efficiently, and it was lunchtime

by the time she had everything to her satisfaction. As good as could be in the circumstances, considering the rotten fabric of the place. At least the air smelt more of pine-scented polish than of smoke . . . Pleased with herself, she found an aged piece of cheddar in the fridge, some stale sponge fingers and a withered apple which, had she been less hungry, she would have thrown out. As she sat eating in the caged silence, she thought of all the thousands of meals George must have had here, alone, in all these years. Did he ever cook himself something good? What had he been thinking all those silent weekends and evenings on his own?

Revived by the food, Peggy then went upstairs. She crept, almost guilty, into George's bedroom. What should have been the marital bedroom, she couldn't help thinking. The sight was much as she imagined it would be: unmade bed, familiar striped pyjamas and a single battered paper-back detective novel on the floor, not a picture on the fog-grey walls. She went at once to the windows: they, too, were secured with the same kind of locks as downstairs. The sour, smoky air indicated they had probably not been opened for years. How could he bear summer nights in such an atmosphere?

It was horrible, his room, Jen. Bleak . . .

The least she could do was tidy it up a bit, have a go at the dust.

By the time she had finished the cleaning of George's bedroom, and the vile bathroom – curtains of cracked plas-tic, plugs of old hair in bath and basin – most of the afternoon had gone. Tired, Peggy decided to return to the spare room for a rest. She would have to set off the moment George came home. If he did come home. For a nasty moment she was stricken with the thought that he might have some wicked plan behind her imprisonment. He might intend to leave her to sweat it out for a while: punishment for the past.

She shivered in the dead air of the spare room. Windows locked there, too. Last night she had not liked to call George in to open them. Now – tea-time it must be – the afternoon sun hot outside, it was unbearable. Better go back downstairs: cup of tea, watch television, hope the hours would not drag too much till George . . . Peggy had no energy to tackle the sitting-room, riled though she was by its dismal state. She sat on the sofa with her cup of tea, switched on a children's programme, must have dozed off.

I was mad by the time he came back, Jen. I screamed at him, I can tell you . . .

She didn't know when it was, but he was standing over her. He carried a bulging plastic carrier from a supermarket, and he was smiling.

'You dropped off, then?'

'Must have.'

'Didn't expect I'd find you here.'

Peggy rallied, sleepiness quite gone. 'You locked me in, you old sod. What did you do that for?'

'I what?'

'Made me your prisoner.'

'Never. You must be daft.' He gave a small, guilty laugh.

'Every window and door in the place locked. I checked.'

'Locked, yes. That I don't deny. You know what I am

about security. But I left the key. Course I left the key.'

'Where?'

'Come with me.'

Peggy followed him into the kitchen, suddenly uncertain. George dumped the bag on the table, went to the brush mat by the door. 'Course I locked the door from the outside – necessary precaution – but I left you this.' With some triumph he lifted up a corner of the mat and picked up the key that lay on the cement floor. He waggled it in her face. 'There, Peg o' my life. What did I tell you? Where, for all those years, did we always put the key at home? Under the kitchen doormat. Thought you wouldn't have forgotten that.'

Peggy sniffed. Foolishness engulfed her. 'Well, I did. I looked everywhere.'

'Silly old you, what? Still—' He looked round in some awe. 'I see you've been doing a bit more than just looking. Tidied up a bit, haven't you? It needed a woman's hand. I'm not much good at that sort of thing, you may remember. Here.' He put his hand in his jacket pocket and pulled out a couple of packets of seeds. 'You take these. A bushy new cornflower we're trying out. You've always liked cornflowers.'

Peggy examined the packets with their optimistic illustrations.

'I haven't much of a garden,' she said.

'Mine's quite sizeable, considering,' said George.

There was silence, then Peggy thanked him and said she'd like to take them.

He tried to calm me down with a packet of his blinking free seeds, Jen: imagine. I said I don't want your seeds, George Jarrett, you can't buy me that cheaply . . .

'I'll be on my way,' she said.

'Better eat something first.' George pulled things from the bag. 'My shopping night, Wednesdays. Afraid you caught me when stocks were low, last night. We could make up for it tonight.'

Any fears Peggy had had earlier about George not taking care of himself now scattered. He had bought a selection of meats and chicken breasts and fruits and vegetables: an expensive rough pâté, French bread, and several bottles of good red wine. His tastes had changed. What was more, oddly, he seemed to have bought enough for two.

'Tell you what,' he went on, 'if you'd like to put something in the oven, I'll nip up to the greenhouse for half an hour, then I'll come back and join you in a nice glass of claret.'

. . . and then he had the cheek to ask me to cook the dinner! I said you cook your own blinking dinner. I said you haven't changed a mite, George: you and your chauvinistic ways that were the breaking of our marriage . . .

An hour later they were enjoying the pâté while the pre-made casserole warmed in the oven. George, against his better judgement, allowed Peggy to persuade him to leave the back door open so that sweet evening air pushed into the smoke and pine of the kitchen, dissipating the obnoxious smells. They drank the first bottle of wine and opened the second. By the time they were into the beautiful ripe Camembert, Peggy found herself weak with nostalgia.

'We did have some good times, George,' she allowed herself to say.

'Some, if you say so,' agreed George, and steered the conversation back to the possibility of a goldfish pond he had in mind for the bottom of the garden.

By the end of the second bottle of wine it was clear there was no possibility of Peggy driving home that night. Departure would have to be postponed once again. Still, there was no pressing reason to hurry home. So when George urged her to stay another night, she did not bother to resist. Once more he wished her a safe journey next day, and said what a nice surprise it had been, her dropping in, and he would leave the light on outside her room. Once more, despite the discomfort of the bed, Peggy fell asleep very quickly.

It was only next morning, going downstairs with my case again, Jen, I realised I'd forgotten to mention the matter of the key. I must admit fear gripped me. He'd had such a funny look in his eye the night before – nothing to do with the wine. And when I looked under the doormat, and there was no key, I knew it. I knew clearly what he was trying to do. He was trying in his horrible devious way to get me back . . . If you've ever had a man after you like that . . .

Quite calmly, Peggy boiled herself an egg for breakfast and made real coffee instead of tea. The kitchen smelt much better now: she sat looking at the lovely show of gladioli in the bed outside, hands round her mug, a comfortable summer warmth within and without. But she would not be caught out so foolishly again. When she had washed up she searched everywhere she could think of for the key to the back door. Unable to find it, she then checked the front door, and every window in the house: as yesterday, all locked. A prisoner again. She contemplated ringing George's office, but decided there would be no point: he was out on his rounds most days. And besides, she would do her best to escape this time, before he came back. This silly nonsense couldn't go on. Or could it?

The morning, Peggy thought, must at least be put to some good use. Back in the kitchen, she went through the groceries George had bought the day before and found ingredients for bread, a cake, veal stew, a gooseberry crumble. She set to work. The thought of the surprise George would have when he returned, reminding him of the good cook she had always been . . . A bee was trapped in the room. Peggy found herself sympathising with its pathetic buzzing.

'We're both prisoners, bee,' she said. 'But it's not too bad, is it?'

It was terrible, Jen, shut in, not a breath of air, dreading him with his frightening eyes coming back. What would he do tonight? Fill me with drink again? I wondered, should I ring the police? I was trembling all over by now, hardly able to think. The monster. Men who want a woman – they'll do anything.

Peggy was kneading dough with a firm hand, a slight smile on her lips. No questions as to why George had shut her in a second time came to perplex her. Rather, she found herself remembering some of the pleasures in their marriage. They had taken long walks, sometimes, in the Lake District, staying at farmhouses on the way. They both liked a bet on the horses, an occasional drink at the pub, quiet evenings in front of the television. It was hard to remember, in fact, quite what had gone so wrong. George had always been a terrible old chauvinist, never renowned for his open mind, but Peggy had become used to all that – couldn't remember the exact nature, come to think of it, of all the irritations and frustrations. Perhaps they had simply been too young, too wrapped up in their own preoccupations, no children to deflect them, to give them a mutual interest. Had they stuck it out . . . by now, they might have reached that state of coasting along in mutual tolerance that a good many people seemed to settle for. They would have had companionship, the comfort of security. Had they stuck it out . . .

I spent that afternoon Jen, going back in my mind over all the awful things about George, thinking how well rid of him I was.

She spent the afternoon impatiently waiting for the delicious things to come out of the oven (the smell of baking bread finally overcame the last traces of smoke), an idea forming in her mind. It made her restless, her idea. Too restless to weigh it up very accurately. She laid the table for tea, chivvied about, willing the hours to hurry until the evening.

'I saw your car. What happened this time?' George began, soon as he was through the door.

'It was no joke, today, George. Locked in again.'

Peggy tried to sound angry. She knew she didn't succeed.

'Don't be silly.' He stomped over to the small alarm clock on the dresser. Picked it up. Produced the key.

'I thought you said under the mat?'

'Under the mat didn't work yesterday, did it? Thought I'd

try our other place today. Remember: the key'll be under the mat or under the clock, we always said. Thought you couldn't be so . . . another day.'

'Well, I was. Stupid, I know.' George, she thought, gave her a funny look. 'There's tea in the pot.'

They both sat down at the table. George cut into the bulging loaf. The crust crackled and chipped under his eager knife.

'I say, jolly nice, this. Haven't had a bit of bread the like of this since . . .' He sniffed. 'Smells as if you've been cooking other things, too.'

'I made supper. Had to fill the hours somehow.'

'Sorry about the misunderstanding, Peg o' my life.'

'That's all right.'

There was a friendly pause. They both spread honey thickly on to the buoyant slices of bread. This is auspicious, Peggy thought. Now is my moment.

Greedy sod, got through my loaf in a flash. I could see he meant business . . .

'George,' she said, 'I could stay a few days if you like. Finish tidying the place up, put some things in the freezer for you. I mean, there's nothing pressing I have to be home for.'

'What about your little cat? I expect you've still got a cat, haven't you?'

'My neighbour Jen sees to her. I could ring Jen, tell her I was delayed for a few days.'

George sniffed again, put down his bread. His hand, his face, were suddenly, visibly, rigid. Peggy was awkward under his new look.

'Funny,' she said, 'I was thinking. You know, if we hadn't been so bloody silly we'd still be together today. None of that divorce business need have happened. We'd be quite happy, used to each other. We'd have security, company, for our old age. Not that I'm grumbling about things as they are, and you don't seem too badly off, could be a nice place here—'

'Vicious neighbourhood,' interrupted George.

'Vicious or not, we would probably have been better off together once we'd got over our ups and downs.'

In the silence that followed her little speech – not quite as she had rehearsed it to herself – George spotted the bee. Too exhausted to buzz, it now tumbled back and forth along the window ledge.

'That poor bee,' said George, at last. 'Must find the window key, let it out.'

'George, did you hear what I said?'

'I heard what you said, Peggy.'

'And what do you think?'

'I think, not on your life, Peg o' my heart. Not for anything. Too much damage caused, no one changed that much, probably. I'm used to it here, as I am. Happy, like.'

There was a silence. Peggy longed for the bee to resume its buzzing. But it had given up.

'Very well. It was just a suggestion.'

'You were always superior to me, see. I didn't like that.'

'Nothing's ever perfect.'

George looked round his newly cleaned kitchen.

'Thank you for tidying up, though. I'll try to keep it . . . You finish your tea. I must get down to the watering.'

George stood up, impatient to be off. Peggy had no appetite for the rest of her bread and honey.

'Keep in touch,' she said.

'Why not? Card at Christmas. That sort of thing. Drive carefully.' He pecked her on the cheek.

'I will.'

Peggy turned her head so that he should not see her face. Ten minutes later she was on her way, suitcase and bunch of hastily picked farewell marigolds on the seat beside her.

She was eager to be home now, could not wait to tell Jen. She arrived before midnight, so rang at once. Jen was a night bird, would be longing to hear from her. She had probably been worrying about why she had not returned on the promised day.

'Jen, it's me, Peggy. Just back. *What* a time, I can tell you. I've been with George. Yes, George, ex-husband George. Trapped! Almost raped! Begged me to stay, wanted me back, *locked me in* for two days till I managed to escape. *I was his prisoner*, Jen! Honestly!'

Peggy kept her friend up for a long time with her story.

Squirrels

Vera Brindle lived alone in a state of dishevelled solitude which the social workers who called upon her could not believe was desirable. They had begun their interfering ways some years ago now and their visits to her cottage were becoming more frequent. One or other of them – sometimes two together like policemen on the beat in a dangerous area – would knock on the door and, when there was no answer, press their faces to the downstairs windows, sheltering their eyes with both hands. Vera Brindle would watch the intruders from upstairs, hidden behind a curtain. On the rare occasions she gave in and opened the door, they would put to her the suggestion of a 'little chat over a cup of tea'. Vera, who disliked both tea and chats, would wave them into the kitchen and enjoy watching their incredulous faces as they looked around the room, making their assessments. She would make no move to put on the kettle. As for the 'chat' they were hoping for – that, too, they quickly discovered, was to be denied them.

Only last week a new young girl had been sent to try out her persuasive powers to make Vera Brindle 'see sense', as they put it. This particular representative of those who know best wore an anxious-about-deprived-people expression which, the old lady knew very well, would be switched off when she went home at five-thirty. She could just imagine the girl hurrying to the kind of party where the boasts of the caring professions meant instant admiration. The girl's narrow little face was contorted with the sort of professional sympathy that made Vera Brindle determine to be unhelpful.

'You must be Ms Vera Brindle,' said this unwelcome creature, when the door was opened a few inches. She was dressed in ugly clothes that signalled there was no frivolity in her do-gooding soul, and hideous, earnest shoes of yellowish leather.

'No, I'm Miss Brindle. I've been Miss Brindle all my life, so there's no supposing, my young girl, I'm going to change to some fashionable title now. And who may you be?'

'I'm Lee Barker. Social Services. But do call me Lee.'

'Certainly shan't do any such thing. I don't know you.' Vera Brindle edged the door open a little wider. She noted the intruder's bony nostrils rear up as various smells began their assault. 'I shall call you Miss Barker, unless you tell me you are a Mrs.' She sniffed. 'Which I very much doubt. Come in, Miss Barker.'

'I don't want us to get off on the wrong foot,' Lee Barker said, once they were in the kitchen. 'I wouldn't want that at all.' Her eyes carried on scouring every crevice of the kitchen. Perhaps she had been warned there was no use asking for a cup of tea, for they did not pause on the kettle. Vera Brindle, enjoying the young woman's unease, kept her silence. She listened to the scrabblings of the squirrels in the roof. Drat the squirrels, she thought. They were usually quiet at this time of day. If this cheeky young do-gooder heard them she'd start writing all sorts of exaggerated reports in her notebook, threaten to send along the pest control man.

'I have news for you, Vera,' Lee Barker said at last. 'There's a nice council flat come up, just a mile or so from Exeter. One of those sheltered housing arrangements. A lovely warden, should you need anything. All mod cons.'

Vera Brindle snorted, furious at the persistent attempt at intimacy, and enraged by the suggestion. But it was useless, she knew, trying to explain that mod cons held no allure. While she could scornfully understand they were part of contemporary utopia, they did not feature on her own list of essentials to a happy life.

'I'm not Vera to you,' she said.

'Sorry. *Miss* Brindle.' Lee Barker gave a patronising smile, which exposed a flash of brown teeth edging a long expanse of gum. Her breath smelt vile. 'Now, have you taken in what I'm saying?'

'I have and I'm not interested. I don't know why you bother yourselves, waste your time, keep coming here. Give the flat to someone who needs it. I'm all right. I'm not moving.'

Vera Brindle put a hand on the table to steady herself. She was not used to speaking at such length. So many words dizzied her. She felt exhausted, but knew she must gather her strength to tell this young woman to go.

'So you can be off now,' she said. The squirrels were scrabbling harder.

'*Miss* Brindle,' Lee Barker sneered, 'there's no use pussy-footing around any more. My colleagues and I have done our best to make you see sense. The time has come for plain speaking. This—' she looked up at the dark ceiling— 'your home, is generally considered unfit for human habitation. We fear for your own safety, Miss Brindle, if you choose to stay. Why, you're not even on the telephone. What if—?'

Miss Brindle licked her lips with the point of a small green tongue. They tasted of salt. Beneath the tight caul of their skin she could feel a prickling, a singing, in their blood. She knew that if she uttered another word her mouth would explode. Teeth, lips, tongue still attached to the messy glob of its roots, would blast off from her face and splatter across the room. So she said nothing, nodded towards the door.

Lee Barker, whose anger prowled up and down her face in mauve coils, responded to the utter negativeness of the stubborn old cow, as this Brindle witch was known in the office, by pushing her nose into a handkerchief. The offensive implications of this gesture Vera Brindle chose to ignore.

'Very well, I shall go for now. But be warned.' Lee Barker's eyes, even in the poor light, were bright with indignation.

'You'd better be warned, too.' Vera Brindle was determined to have the last word, though unsure of her exact meaning.

Lee Barker swung out, tossed her nasty little trousered hips from side to side as she hurried down the path, trailing her hand along the top of the dead lavender bushes. Vera Brindle waited until she was out of sight, then sat down at the kitchen table. She pulled towards her the white plastic weighing-machine that stood like a single symbol of modernity among the debris all around it. A little weighing, she thought, would calm her down. She reached for a slab of very old cake, broke off the hard end, placed it on the plastic dish. One and a half ounces, the clock said. Vera Brindle loved that moment, when the thin red hand raced so confidently to the exact weight. She added a few crumbs. The hand wavered. Miss Brindle smiled. The weighing-machine was the best toy she had ever had. It kept her occupied for much of the day. The interest of guessing what things might weigh, only to discover how right or wrong she was, almost obsessed her. The fluctuating of weight, as bits were added or taken away to the tray, gave her a strange thrill – the same kind of thrill as sudden icicles on a winter morning, or the drone of bees busy among the apple-blossom. Finished with the cake, Miss Brindle took a handful of nuts from the bag of squirrel food. Two ounces, she reckoned. Perhaps just over. She was happy again. Lee Barker and her threats had vanished from her mind.

Vera Brindle had lived in her cottage, a mile from a small village on Exmoor, all her life. Her father had been head gamekeeper on the Bancrofts' estate. Her mother, a house-maid in the big house, had died when Vera was twelve. All she had left was a very large and cumbersome old bicycle, which Vera still rode into the village once a week to collect her provisions. (She could get an astonishing amount into the copious wicker basket that rested, squeaking, on the front mudguard.) Not long after Mrs Brindle's death, her husband's employer had sold the estate and moved abroad. The sale did not include the cottage. With his usual generosity to those who worked for him, Lord Bancroft gave the cottage – only worth a few hundred pounds – to Sam Brindle, in recognition of many years of service. This noble gesture gave a new life to Miss Brindle's father, who for some time had been cast in the immovable gloom of a widower. Now a proud house-owner himself, he set about repairs and with a friend rethatched the roof. This was the happiest time Miss Brindle could remember. Once she had left the village school, she stayed at home, with no urge to explore a wider world, looking after her father and the cottage. In those days, there was fresh paint, new carpet, uncracked windows and an up-to-date calendar on the wall each year.

But this idyllic period did not last for long. Her father, too rigorously stoking the boiler, suffered a heart attack and died two days before his daughter's twenty-first birthday. She broke up the iced cake she and her father were to have shared, and put it out for the birds. It was then she first began to take note of the squirrels, whose grabbing of the food was so much more sly than the birds'. It was then she took up a pencil and paper for the first time since she had left school, and began to make quick sketches. The results, she was in no doubt, were quite pleasing, if not perfect. She began to pin these drawings on the walls. She became aware of a faint sense of achievement.

Once her father was buried, Miss Brindle made some effort to take part in village life. There were those who feared for her loneliness, lack of company – her safety, even. She tried hard to convince them she enjoyed her solitary life and politely turned down most invitations. After a harvest supper, in her twenty-fifth year, a local farmer proposed marriage behind the barn. But Miss Brindle saw this was inspired by nothing more than quantities of beer and the hope of a more instant accomplishment than marriage itself. She took the precaution of not only turning him down, but of giving him so little hope that he thought it not worth the journey to her cottage when he sobered up.

For some years – her squirrel drawings acting as a qualification – Miss Brindle taught painting in the village school. She gave this up during the War to help out in the local hospital. Surrounded by so much death, she became alarmed by the shortness of life. Except for her weekly shopping expedition and an occasional bus journey to the dentist, she spent the best part of the next fifty years in the cottage or its small garden, feeding and drawing the squirrels, birdsong her only music when the old wireless finally broke down in 1951. Always a good needlewoman, she earned just enough money by taking in alterations and mending. To the amazement of those left in the almost deserted village, Vera Brindle seemed happy to lead this uneventful existence. She was never ill, never wanted for anything. A weird old bird, she became; a witchy threat to children. 'Vera Brindle will get you,' mothers would say. 'Vera Brindle lives with the squirrels and casts her spells.'

On the evening of Lee Barker's visit, such an agreeable plan came to Vera Brindle's mind that the social worker's unpleasant behaviour was almost forgotten. She would order a bigger weighing-machine. Fond though she was of the present one, Miss Brindle knew there was a limit to what it could accommodate. And by now she was well acquainted with the weight of most things around her: a slice of cheese, a single slipper, a bag of nuts, two pencils and a rubber. It would be exciting to try out some larger objects, things that would not cause the red hand to dash right out of sight where it hid, alarmed by so much weight, in the bowels of the machine. It would be exciting to weigh the kettle – with and without water – her boots, her big wooden paint-box. With such plans in mind, Miss Brindle began to look forward to the postman's next visit, when he would bring the new mail order catalogue in which weighing-machines of all shapes and sizes were advertised. She would send off for one at once. Fill in the form with capital letters; by then she would surely have found her old biro. She would pay by postal order. Then wait impatiently for the parcel – new things to be weighed all lined up and waiting. Already she could see herself unpacking the machine, making a space for it on the table. The sweetness of anticipation began to seep through her. She had learnt, in her solitude, that the occasional arranging of treats for yourself is the way to divide up time, cause a ripple in the otherwise smooth surface. She had discovered that anticipation of small pleasures, to those who live alone, is a necessity. A rhythm must be created in which there are times of exceptional happiness to counteract the occasions of amorphous melancholy.

So engrossed was Vera Brindle in the thought of her new machine, that at first she did not hear the thunder. She thought the rumbling was the squirrels again. They always danced more loudly at night.

But when, soon after nine, she went to draw the pitiful curtain across the kitchen window, she felt a stab of cold wind pressing through the space between long-dead putty and old glass. As she grabbed the material in her hand, lightning turned the small panes to the colour of watered milk, and she could see they were splattered with hard rain. Vera Brindle shivered, and longed for bed. On her way upstairs, she realised that more crashing above her was indeed thunder. Feeling the bones of the wooden stairs creak beneath her, she clung to the oak rail until the trumpeting outside had stopped. Storms held no fear for her. She had faith in the protection of the cottage, though in the hurricane of 1987 she remembered the cottage walls trembled as trees in the nearby woods fell to the ground with high-pitched, splintered screams.

Vera Brindle turned on the dim light by her bed. She saw that a piece of ceiling had fallen on to the floor. She kicked at the mound of crumbled plaster, automatically wondering what it might weigh. She decided not to sweep it up till morning and glanced up at the black hole it had left. The ceiling all around it was as cracked as an old cup. If the social workers had seen it, they would have gone potty. But it didn't worry Vera Brindle. She was used to it. For so many years, lying in bed, trying to sleep, her eyes would journey over the familiar pathways of lines, the patches that bulged, the baubles of paintwork that reminded her of withered balloons at the end of a children's Christmas party in the Church Hall . . . Long ago, it had occurred to her to have the room re-plastered. But then the thought of the invasion – builders, ladders, wireless, tea – was too awful to contemplate, and the moment passed. As time went by and the ceiling deteriorated, but never collapsed, Vera Brindle's faith in it continued. It would see her out, she thought. Once she was dead, if the whole place crashed to the ground, so long as the squirrels were not hurt, she did not care.

For a moment, unnerved by the whiteness of the plaster on her bruised and threadbare carpet, Miss Brindle considered moving to her parents' room. But no, that was inconceivable. No one had ever slept in there since they died. Their high brass bed was still tightly made up with clean cotton sheets. The piece of carbolic soap, still in the dish on the wash-stand, had been used by old Mrs Barley when she came to lay out Sam Brindle. His daughter could not bear to disturb the room. Besides, her own was quite safe. What on earth had come over her, such a thought?

Avoiding the spread of white dust, she took off her skirt but kept on the rest of her clothes against the cold night. The thunder seemed to be lumbering off elsewhere; just the odd rumble now. But the squirrels were disturbed. They charged back and forth, scrambled about in the darkness of the roof, a mysterious place which Vera Brindle could never quite imagine. Their scurrying footsteps brought to mind different things: most vigorously, the noise of waves on a grey shale beach she had once visited with her mother. That was the day Mrs Brindle had given up her own long wool scarf to her daughter, as they stood pondering the winter sea, saying 'You take it, child – your weak chest.

Never do to catch a chill.' While all the time, as Miss Brindle later learned, it was her mother who had the weak chest, who was to die of pneumonia. So often, in the sub-terranean part of her soul, she had wondered . . . if only she had not taken the scarf, her mother might not have died. Just as clearly, the squirrels revived another sound: the kidney-shaped beans made of glass. They were kept in a jar on the high shelf above the kitchen range, only brought down as a treat on Sunday. Vera would be allowed to tip them out of the jar on to the scrubbed table. They would tumble out with a rush, fast as a small shoal of sparkling fish they came, crimson and sapphire and emerald, sparkling with lights. She would cup her hands around the mound they made, terrified lest one should escape and fall to the floor. Mrs Brindle would carefully choose a few of the beans to make flower patterns. Such imaginative leaves, she made with the green ones. 'How do you do it, Ma?' the child Vera would cry. Her own attempts at flowers were nothing like as good. 'Easy,' Mrs Brindle would say, and shuffle her bent white fingers through the pile of glass, pouncing on exactly the right one needed for her next petal. Vera, despairing at her own lack of talent in this favourite game, would simply run the beans through her fingers, loving the tinkle they made on her palm that was quite different from the scurrying noise they made as they jostled on to the table . . . That jar of glass beans, where was it now? Vera Brindle had never thrown it out. Perhaps it was still at the back of a cupboard somewhere. Might be worth looking for. She would like to weigh the beans, should she find them, on her new machine . . .

Some time much later in the night – no streak of moonlight or dawn paling the curtainless window – Vera Brindle was woken by a thump on her bed. She switched on the light. Edward, the shyest of all the squirrels, was poised, terrified, on the blankets over her feet, claws dug deep into the wool stuff. He stared ahead, not looking at her, jowls twitching almost too fast to see, tail raised high, ready to bolt.

Miss Brindle did not move, but looked up at the ceiling to see the hole was bigger; there was more powdered plaster on the carpet. Poor Edward, what a trauma, falling through the ceiling, she thought. On the other hand, she could not resist a feeling of great pleasure. For so long she had been trying to tame Edward, but he had always eluded her. His father Ernest, a huge animal with reddish eyebrows, spent more time in the kitchen than he did outdoors, while his wife, the lovely but greedy Rose, was a menace among the shelves. Edward's many brothers and sisters, cousins, uncles and aunts had all established that Vera Brindle's cottage was a perfect refuge, both as a place of hibernation and a source of food. They all had their names: the year each one was born was clear in Miss Brindle's memory. And, despite her failing sight, she could identify which junior members of the clan swung and squealed high in the trees. They were her family. She knew and loved them all. In return for her hospitality, they would keep her company just when she most needed it, perching on her chair, or shoulder, or sometimes on her head.

But Edward, strangely ungregarious, could never be won over. This was one of the great puzzles in Vera Brindle's life.

Sometimes she mentioned it when she went to the Post Office to collect her pension, but the busy woman behind the counter, with her orange lipstick, didn't seem interested. And when she tried to tell Jack the poacher, who occasionally passed by, all he had to say was that she was a stupid old woman who should clear the vermin out of her house or the authorities would be after her. He was sensitive to the authorities, was Jack, skulking about after dark. But Vera Brindle held them in no respect. If she wanted to entertain squirrels in her house, she had every right to do so, and no one could force her to evict them.

Up until this extraordinary moment in the middle of the night, Vera Brindle had never managed to persuade Edward indoors, no matter how many saucers of bread and milk, or nuts, she tempted him with, or what olden-days songs she quietly sang – a device which always intrigued the female squirrels. The unexpectedness of his arrival caused her head to spin for a moment. What should she do to reassure him? Her instinct was to put out a hand, coo a few words, offer him a biscuit from her bedside table. But no, she thought, she must resist. Lie down with as little movement as possible, put out the light, pray to the good Lord young Edward would feel at ease at last.

In the dark, she felt a small movement over her feet. Sleepy, she imagined Edward might be sleepy, too. But in the morning he was gone. When Vera Brindle let his large gang of relations in for breakfast, he was not among them.

Later that day, she stood on a chair in her bedroom and filled the hole in her ceiling with a wadding of old rags and dishcloths. She decided not to secure it further with sticking plaster, in the small hope that Edward might fall on to her bed again. His rejection had caused a smarting in her heart that was hard to dismiss, despite the sunny day. The feeling was mixed with pity for his shocking experience, and her own pleasure at having at last come so close to him.

Vera Brindle ordered her new weighing-machine from the next catalogue and waited for its arrival with a force of impatience that made her restless. She found herself unable to concentrate on anything for very long. No sooner had she sat down in her chair to peel a potato than she darted up to look out of the window. An official-looking brown envelope was delivered one day. She took it to the door, spent a long time trying to light a match with trembling fingers, and at last set light to it. It was with considerable glee that she watched the unread threats devoured by a sudden curl of flame. They were followed by a wisp of black smoke that ventured out into the rain and was instantly extinguished. Pleased though she was by her act of conflagration, a fine wire of anxiety now threaded through the impatience; they would be after her again with their suggestions. Vera Brindle turned back so sharply into the kitchen that she alarmed the squirrels feeding from their breakfast bowl of nuts. They scampered away with unusual speed.

That October, there seemed to be interminable rain. The day the postman Alfred came with the parcel, it poured down so hard that the end of the garden was no more than a smudged outline. The guardian trees beyond were scarcely visible against the grey sky. Alfred's waterproof cape, as he hurried up the path, produced no more than a low-watt shine, a flash of dulled yellow. He stood at the door, holding out the parcel, dripping. Much though Vera Brindle dreaded anyone in her kitchen, she felt obliged to ask him in. The poor man was wet through.

Alfred stepped through the door. Vera Brindle quickly relieved him of the parcel, laid it in the space she had cleared days ago in readiness for its arrival. Once he had gone, this huge, wet, friendly man, she would unwrap it infinitely slowly, rolling up the string, folding the paper . . . Alfred's cape dripped on the floor. Raindrops glinted on his white moustache.

'Sorry,' he said.

'That's no matter. Would you fancy a cup of warm milk?'

Alfred, who had been hoping for the more conventional offer of tea, arranged his face into an appreciative smile of acceptance. He stood awkwardly by the sink, his cap just brushing the drooping ceiling. This was the first time in twenty-four years the Brindle witch had asked him in. He had delivered post to her in far worse weather than this. What, he wondered, did the invitation mean? Would she offer him a nut as well as the milk? There seemed to be bowls of nuts everywhere . . . as if ready for a drinkless party. Something to tell the wife, this.

The postman began to look around. In the rain-dark room, nothing was very clear. But he could make out that the walls were completely covered with old scraps of paper, all browned to some degree with age, they were, and uniformly stuck to the wall with a black drawing pin at the left-hand corner, the rest of the paper left free. Altogether, they gave a shaggy impression, a feeling that the walls were ruffled up to keep out the cold, like a bird's breast. Very peculiar, very rum. But Alfred could see that the positioning of the scraps of paper was something of a work of art in itself. They were methodically placed, just overlapping, like a tiled roof. Very precise, very clever.

Vera Brindle handed Alfred a cup of tepid milk. He moved to peer closer at the strange wallcovering. Each one was a sketch, he could just see, sometimes a painting, of a squirrel – sometimes just part of a squirrel, a faded leg, a tail at many angles. The pictures were faded almost to extinction, only beady eyes, with minute highlights, remained distinct. For all that, Alfred – a man, he liked to think, of some artistic appreciation – could see the drawing was fine, sensitive. The Brindle witch was a talented old bird.

'These are beautiful,' he said. 'Bloody marvellous. You could make a fortune, selling squirrel pictures.'

Vera Brindle, who was anxious for Alfred to drink his milk quickly and go, shrugged. The time for appreciation of her art was long past. She was not interested in anything to do with fortunes.

'I don't do it any more,' she said. 'Paints all dried up.'

'Pity, that.'

They stood without talking while Alfred gulped the sour, tepid milk. Rain clattered more heavily against the windows.

'Mustn't keep you from your rounds,' said Vera Brindle at last.

'No.' Alfred brushed milk and rain from his moustache with the back of his hand. His huge presence in the kitchen had turned it into a strange, unrecognisable place that unnerved Miss Brindle. She wished he would hurry.

Alfred stepped out into the rain. He was glad to regain air that smelt of sodden grass and leaves. The stench in the kitchen – rotten food, mould, wet animals? he could not quite place it – had been almost overpowering. He turned to bid Vera Brindle goodbye. She was beside him, rain darkening her clothes.

'You go back in. You'll get a soaking.'

'I'll come to the end with you.'

'I shouldn't advise that, Miss Brindle. Look, you're soaked already.'

But she was walking up the path to the gate with determined stride.

'As for your roof—' The postman spoke more loudly. She was a yard ahead of him now, astonishingly fast on her slippered feet. He wanted her to hear. 'I was thinking, coming in, you should get that seen to. Looks dangerous to me.'

Vera Brindle reached the gate before turning to face him, face shining as rain squiggled down the furrowed skin, sparse white hair sticking up in small points. Her eyes moved scornfully to the roof of the cottage. There was, indeed, a grave dip in the thatch – she had not looked at it for some years. But quickly she realised Alfred was as foolish as the social workers; the roof had been expertly thatched by her own father not sixty years ago and had never caused a moment's trouble, apart from the odd starling caught up in the wire.

'Look at that moss,' she snapped. 'That's been there for years. That protects the thatch, moss.'

'That moss,' began Alfred. But he could see the pointlessness of arguing in the rain.

'I'm not worried,' said Vera Brindle. She gave him a brief wave and was hurrying up the path before he had time to thank her for the milk.

So engrossed in her new weighing-machine was Vera Brindle that she did not notice the persistence of the rain, or its heaviness. She delighted in the hours as she weighed all manner of new things – writing her guessed weight, followed by their actual weight, with her old biro. By evening, she became aware of a smell of damp that was perhaps stronger than usual, though it was always like that on a rainy day. It meant the squirrels would want to come in earlier. She opened the window for them – a pool of rainwater on the sill flopped on to the floor – long before it was dark.

On her way to bed that night, carrying the weighing-machine under her arm, Vera Brindle felt an almost tangible sense of well-being. It could rain every day till Christmas, for all she cared; she would spend her time weighing so many things on both machines. (It was important, she thought, not to desert the old one, just because of the newcomer. Mustn't hurt its feelings.)

In her room there was a pile of rags and dishcloths on the floor. They were mixed with more crumbled plaster. The hole in the ceiling was much bigger – funny she hadn't heard it fall. And at the end of the bed sat Edward, reddish elbows just twitching, watching her.

Vera Brindle managed to stand quite still, wondering what to do. She put her free hand into the pocket of her cardigan, found a couple of nuts, considered throwing these towards Edward. But she quickly abandoned that idea. Nothing must be done to alarm him. So she placed the nuts in the tray of the weighing-machine and put it gently on the floor. Still Edward did not move. His eye was bright as all squirrels' eyes; Vera Brindle suddenly remembered the tiny sable brush which she used for the white highlights in her paintings. After a while, she pulled back the blankets on her bed, slipped into it, not bothering even to remove her slippers. The most important thing in the world, having come this far, was not to scare away Edward now. In bed, awkwardly perched against the pillows, Vera Brindle studied his small body, tense as a trap, ready to pounce at the slightest sign of danger. Rain beat in angry swarms against the small windows. It was cold.

For some time, Vera Brindle lay unmoving, waiting. Then Edward suddenly jumped off the bed, with lashing tail, to the top of the pile of rags and leapt into the plastic tray of the weighing-machine. The noise of his nails, scratching the plastic, unnerved him. But in a moment he was calm enough to attend to the nuts. He clasped one of them in his paws, his jaws working with frantic speed. Vera Brindle, still very cold but dizzy with excitement, strained to see what the machine clock registered. But without her glasses it was impossible. She made a silent guess.

Then she allowed herself a contented sigh. The extraordinary sight, not a yard from her, was beyond her most unlikely dreams. The weighing of a squirrel . . . her ultimate, most secret desire. No one would ever believe her claim that the squirrel had taken it upon himself to jump on to the machine. But that was of no importance, as there was no one to tell. The shock of it all wearied her more than she could have supposed. Her clothes were still damp from the rain. She shivered. Up in the roof above her, Edward's relations began their nightly dance, their tapping feet almost in time with the rain. Very peculiar, she thought, as she fell asleep.

Vera Brindle dreamed of dozens of squirrels lining up to be weighed and of Edward, quite tame now, visiting her every day. She dreamed of sun on her mother's opal ring and the noise of waves breaking on the grey shale. Their crashing became so loud they briefly woke her. For a moment she saw that moonlight on the windows, shredded by rain, lit a room in turmoil: chunks of rock – was it? – on the floor. Black spaces in the ceiling. She heard more crashing, thudding, the high screams of terrified squirrels. Then she saw them raining down on her, flashes of tooth, eye, frantic tail. How kind they were, coming to comfort her. Behind them, she could see a huge slab of ceiling, shifting, unhurried as a cloud. She shut her eyes and struggled to breathe beneath a sudden new weight. Never in all her years of weighing, she thought, would she have imagined her family of squirrels to be so heavy.

Some days later, Alfred the postman returned to Vera Brindle's cottage with another brown envelope. It still rained, and he saw that the thatched roof had fallen in, breaking up the livid green covering of moss.

The kitchen door was locked, the windows shut. Alfred called loudly, but there was no reply. He peered through the kitchen window and could see that among the chaos of things on the table a squirrel lay on its side. He could not tell if it was alive or dead. An iciness went through him, nothing to do with the weather. He hurried away, reported what he had seen.

The rain had at last begun to ease a little when Lee Barker and her colleague, both in turbid anoraks, drove to the cottage. They had brought with them a small metal ladder on the roof-rack. They carried it between them down the muddy path, elated by their feeling of smugness. This would teach the old girl not to listen to those who knew best.

'Stupid daft witch,' said Lee Barker, in her off-duty voice. 'This'll make her see sense at last. The sooner she's sitting round the telly in an old people's home, the better for all of us. We can't keep putting up with all this aggravation.'

'Quite,' said her colleague.

Like Alfred, they received no response from knocking on the downstairs windows. With a gesture of some triumph, therefore, Lee Barker stuck her ladder into what had once been a flower bed beneath Vera Brindle's window. Clumsily she climbed, her huge trainers hesitant on the metal rungs of the ladder.

'Got the mobile on you, Di? Expect we'll need an ambulance.'

'Operation Witch Evacuation, right.' Di, awkward on the spongy grass, tapped her mobile telephone and laughed. She watched her friend push away lumps of rotten thatch that hung over the casement window and look in, pressing her face to the small panes.

Lee Barker screwed up her professional eyes and saw

that there was life in the bedroom. There were squirrels everywhere. They ran up and down over huge lumps of plaster on the bed, where Vera Brindle lay facing the window. She stared back with dull but open eyes. Sitting on the old woman's hand was a squirrel with reddish elbows, a small tuft of her white hair between its paws.

Mistral

I don't know why, and there is nothing I can do about it, but I have this way of irritating people. It's a sad affliction but, as I am unable to change matters, every day is a minefield. I know that at any moment I am liable to do or say something that causes Mr Arthur or Mr Gerald such annoyance they can barely trust themselves to speak.

My name is Annie Hawker. I am housekeeper to Mr Arthur and Mr Gerald, and have held that position for eleven years. Both gentlemen are in their mid-sixties. Mr Arthur was once briefly married to a certain Lucretia. The very thought of this lady brings out the worst in him, though her name is rarely mentioned. There are two grown-up children: Deirdre and Brian. Both of them are over thirty, unmarried, and still searching their way in life. Their telephone calls to their father don't inspire much sympathy. I hear him snarling down the telephone several times a week, though I have reason to believe he is a generous father, and sends cheques to England with some frequency. When Deirdre and Brian come for a visit – some would call it a prolonged free holiday, as I'm bound to observe to Mr Arthur – tension in the house rises. Mr Arthur gets no pleasure from their company, and the feeling is all too plainly mutual. Well, I have to say it: they aren't very rewarding offspring: lumpen, dull minds, lazy, spoiled, purposeless.

Their visits put Mr Gerald into a bad temper, too. He stomps off most mornings, walks the hills or visits friends all day, and then is barely civil to them over dinner. Jealous, I suppose. Mr Gerald was never married, and the children remind him of Mr Arthur's past. Or it may be that he simply finds their ungrateful presence in the house annoying. Which it is. Secretly, all three of us look forward to their departure.

I took the job two years after my husband Simon died in an industrial accident. Arm torn off in a machine in the mill, and he wasn't even a manual worker, but an inspector. Trouble was, he was always poking his nose – in this case, his arm – too far into things, being a conscientious inspector. I knew in my bones some disaster would happen one day. So I wasn't surprised by the amputation, or the complications that followed. Or indeed his death within the week. Nor did I waste much time grieving his departure. Our marriage had never been of a high calibre: we had just chuntered along for ten years, childless, him travelling round the North inspecting, me working for the Inland Revenue.

I had always had a secret inclination to write. But I knew there was no hope there, for all that I was good at essays at school. Everyone wants to write and thinks they can. But there was no evidence to make me believe I'd be any good, or stand a chance of publication. So I abandoned that dream in order to avoid disappointment, and funnily enough quite enjoyed my time at the Inland Revenue.

Anyhow, two years after Simon's death the thought came to me: now's your chance, Annie, I thought. Make a dash for it before you're too old. Go for a complete change. Try a new life.

I started looking at advertisements for jobs abroad, and as luck would have it came upon Mr Arthur and Mr Gerald's within days. The description of the place appealed to me – hilltop cluster of houses in the Luberon region of France. Beautiful scenery, peace, swimming pool, sun: the stuff of most people's dreams.

They were interviewing applicants for the job in London. I went down the night before, stayed with my sister in Barnet so as not to be in a fuss on the morning. I dressed carefully in a nice navy suit and pink blouse. It occurred to me a younger type of person would probably be applying for the job, of the jeans and tee-shirt school, the kind who care more about being in the sun than what they give in return. I wanted to make a good impression, assure them of my reliability, willingness to work hard, and above all my unfailing sense of humour.

Well, it worked. They were a little stiff, the two gentlemen, sitting side by side on a plumped-up sofa. Very tanned, they were, with almost identical thin grey hair. In a word, we liked each other from the start. 'Do call me Annie,' I said, when the interview was concluded. 'None of this Mrs Hawker stuff, now, if you please.' They smiled a little instead of agreeing to this, and made no reciprocal proposal. I realised at once that they were the sort of gentlemen who, at their age, liked to retain a little of the old-school formality, and hoped I had not blundered in my friendly suggestion. Evidently I had not, for they offered me the job, two days later.

Just a week later I fell in love with Le Beau Banc at first sight. They had bought the place, a deserted hillside hamlet, some twenty years before, built a road (still pretty rocky) and renovated the whole place with great skill and imagination. Today, the small houses are a monument to local craftsmen: beautifully converted with mellow tiled floors and lime-washed walls, their old shutters scrubbed and oiled, their old beams stripped and sealed. One of these – quite the nicest, I think, with its little terrace overlooking a vast valley that is always blue with either lavender or mist, is entirely mine. A very far cry from our house in Sheffield, I can tell you. I put up my few things – my picture of Morecambe Bay and my mother's shell mirror and so on – and it felt like home from the start. I can't imagine living anywhere else.

Mr Gerald, being a keen and skilled gardener, planted the whole place, too. There are peach and olive trees, English roses and mimosa. Every path is lined with lavender, and a huge fig tree shades their terrace. Butterflies flutter all day and the crickets sing every evening, ruffling the silence. Oh, it's paradise, as I tell my sister. I know how lucky I am.

The original idea, Mr Arthur told me, was to make the place a kind of commune or colony for artists and writers. The plan was that each would have their individual house in which they worked in peace, and meet for dinner in the evening. But long before my arrival this plan failed. It seemed many a young so-called artist, plus boy- or girlfriend, checked in for a long free holiday full of delights of a certain kind, but in which little artistically was accomplished. So they decided only to put friends and relations in the guest houses: they themselves live in the large main house, which is my responsibility.

To be honest, in all these years I have never quite discovered what Mr Arthur and Mr Gerald actually do. Obviously they are gentlemen of some means, and have no need of regular employment. But Mr Gerald seems always to be on one of the many telephones in his study, often to auction houses in London and New York, as far as I can gather. Very thick expensive art magazines arrive for him every week, and sometimes foreign gentlemen come for lunch. On those occasions Mr Gerald suggests I cook something French rather than the Yorkshire favourites we have on our own. The guests bring with them such funny-looking old ceramic pots which they handle with great care, and talk about in low voices.

Mr Arthur, in his study, is on the telephone a great deal of the time, too, and I understand he has interests in South Africa. But it doesn't bother me that I don't know the exact nature of their professions. All that concerns me is what I have to do to be satisfactory in my job: and that I know precisely.

My employers are gentlemen of routine. They thrive on the domestic timetables they have devised for themselves, and I do my best to see they are not interrupted. It's not hard to take care of them in the manner which they enjoy, because they are easy to please as long as everything is spick and span and meals are on time. They pay me a very fair wage and give me plenty of money for housekeeping, so I am able to call in a plumber or electrician, if need be, and pay him, without having to bother one of the gentlemen.

My day starts early. I'm in the kitchen by seven, all nice and orderly as I've left it the night before. I step outside, enjoying the early morning before the sun has become too hot, and pick a ripe peach or fig for the bowl. I lay the table, blue and terracotta cups and plates from a local pottery, put croissants in the oven and the coffee in the jug. Mr Arthur and Mr Gerald appear regular as clockwork at eight o'clock, each in his blue-and-white kimono.

'Morning, Mr Gerald Mr Arthur,' I say. 'Had a good night, have we?'

I have to admit they don't answer me any more because, I believe, although they appreciate my question is the height of good manners, they don't want to bother me with the troubles of their nights. (Mr Arthur suffers from asthma, Mr Gerald has problems with his digestion.) But I always like to be polite and show an interest. It used to worry me when they gave up answering, but I don't mind any more. I'm used to their ways and they're used to mine.

To be quite honest, the position of housekeeper is an amorphous one, not easy. The problem of address, for a start. I appreciated they wanted to maintain their little barrier, to denote my position as employee rather than friend. So when they insisted on calling me Mrs Hawker I did not object, and soon got used to it. They did make one big concession: I should not call them *sir*, they said, this being a newly democratic world, and as they both had complicated double-barrelled names Mr Arthur and Mr Gerald was the compromise we settled on. That was how they had been addressed by the staff at home as children, they explained, and thought it a charming custom. I agreed.

To begin with, I found it hard to know what was expected of me. What exactly was my place? I never asked the question specifically and they never made it clear to me. Normally, for instance, I would lunch with them at the kitchen table, or on the terrace, but the invitation was never extended should there be a visitor, no matter how often that person came. For some reason they always liked to dine on their own, so once their food is cooked and on the table I have to hang around waiting to clear away. I mean, I've never got on with watching French television – after all these years I haven't managed to grasp the French language at all, though I'm pretty good at making myself understood in the shops. So the evenings are a little bleak, though I enjoy my knitting, or my latest Catherine Cookson. Then again, it's a little confusing when people come for a drink. 'Fetch the bottle of Chablis out of the fridge, if you will, Mrs Hawker,' says Mr Arthur, and in a moment I'm placing it on the table by the sofa, on a tray with six crystal glasses and a pottery bowl of fresh olives. 'And have one yourself, Mrs Hawker,' he often says, when the guests have all been given their glasses. At that point, what am I supposed to do? Early on, I made the mistake of lingering, supposing that having accepted a glass of wine I was required to join in the conversation. I remember the occasion so well: the local architect was there to discuss renovations to the old barn, along with his wife, not an English-speaker, and her brother. Nobody knew each other very well in those days, so I saw fit to fill the rather awkward silence with some comment upon the pleasantness of the weather. As nobody leapt in to follow up my lead, I took it upon myself to compare the climate of Provence with that of Morecambe where, I explained, I had spent so many of my childhood holidays. Possibly I let my tongue run away with me a little, in striving to be helpful, for I remember describing my fondness for whelks. I went on to recall the time I fell off the pier and was rescued by the famous comedian who was starring in the summer show that year. The very thought of all this made me laugh, of course, and it took me some time to realise I was the only one laughing. The three French guests looked completely bemused, and Mr Gerald and Mr Arthur, behind tight little smiles, seemed to be gritting their teeth. Then Mr Gerald came up to me and in a low, urgent voice suggested it was time I began preparing the dinner. I left the room with all the dignity I could muster, as Mr Arthur began to speak to the guests in French, no doubt explaining my extraordinary behaviour.

I have to say, nothing was said. They did not reprove me. And after that, when wine was being served, one of them would bring a glass to me in the kitchen. Well, I got the message: I did not take offence – I'm not one to take offence, it's so time-consuming. I had learned my humiliating lesson and thereafter strove to be the essence of tact. I also realised at that time that there was no question of Mr Gerald and Mr Arthur *ever* being intimates: while they were rarely anything but friendly, they would never be friends. It was necessary to them to keep their distance.

They liked the protection of formality and it was not my place to try to persuade them to behave in any other way. 'Despite the small grumbles, Annie,' my sister once wrote from Barnet, 'you sound very happy. Mr Gerald and Mr Arthur's formal ways of speaking and so on seem to have had their influence on you, too, if you don't mind my saying so. Do you realise you write in a very grand way now? You use lots of new grand words and complicated sentences these days. It's hardly ever you break into your old way of writing.' I had not realised that, though Mr Arthur and Mr Gerald's way of describing the simplest things had always intrigued me. They were elegant in their use of language. Had this really had some influence on my own writing? It was quite a thought. 'It must mean you admire them,' my sister added.

This, my eleventh summer here, has been unusually hot. Mr Gerald and Mr Arthur have never quite accustomed themselves to the heat, and they react badly. They both become short-tempered, petulant, though they do their best to disguise this state. They change their minds a good deal, and give me conflicting orders, all of which is very taxing as the sweat pours down my face in the kitchen. But I try to keep my calm, and reassure them cooler weather must be on its way. Of course, neither of them is getting any younger. In the unkind light of the midday sun I notice that their hair, identical pure white now, is also similar in its thinness. They puff it over their shining pink temples in an effort to make it look thicker than it really is. Mr Arthur goes a funny colour, sometimes, after lunch, and extends his afternoon siesta by at least an hour. Mr Gerald has become fanatical about his pills – vitamins of every kind – and only takes very short walks these days, always with his stick. Time hasn't been particularly kind to me, either: I've inherited my mother's arthritis in the knee, which keeps me awake many hours of the night. And my childhood migraines come back from time to time. But I keep these things to myself. If Mr Arthur and Mr Gerald thought there was any danger of my cracking up, heaven knows what they would do. I may inadvertently irritate them, but I am their prop, their life-blood, their absolute necessity.

Two days ago the mistral began. I've learned to dread the mistral. It's the only thing that makes me seriously contemplate returning to Morecambe for my retirement. All the stories about its weird and unsettling effects are true. As soon as the wind begins to tug at the trees and beat hotly against my window at night, I feel my blood rise. Anxieties turn my skin to gooseflesh. I try to be reasonable, work out what they are about, but they remain nameless. I find it hard to be myself. Mr Arthur and Mr Gerald are affected, too. Their appetites go, and they snap at one another and spend more time on their telephones. 'We must all brace ourselves, Mr Arthur Mr Gerald,' I say. 'It affects us all the same,' I say, and they slam their doors.

The wind started up with its familiar tugging and snapping, blowing my skirts into warm billows above my knees when I go to hang out the washing. It sneaks through any door left open for a moment, ruffling papers and blowing things to the floor. For a few hours I took a positive attitude: the relief, I thought, of a light breeze to stir the heavy heat we had had for so many weeks. But in truth the mistral is not so much light as malevolent. Its aim is to taunt, to goad, to drive you mad. Well, it's not going to beat me, I told myself, as I slammed shut the kitchen window and scooped up the pile of flour I had arranged on the table for my dough. 'One of God's little tricks sent to try us,' I said to Mr Arthur and Mr Gerald at breakfast. Their temples shone with sweat. They answered with silence.

At lunch I could see that both gentlemen were agitated. I put the pot of chicken casserole on the table, then took up a plate to help Mr Arthur first, as I always did.

'I couldn't eat anything hot on a day like this,' he said, and wiped at his forehead with a silk handkerchief.

'But we always start casseroles in late September, Mr Arthur,' I reminded him.

'I tell you, I can't eat a bloody casserole in this heat. I'll have bread and cheese and fruit.'

He looked quite flushed and Mr Gerald, I noticed, was pulling at his earlobe, a habit he has whenever he is out of sorts.

'Don't you worry yourself, now, Mr Arthur,' I said, cool as anything, determined not to be offended by his rejection of my casserole. 'It won't take me a moment to run you up a nice tomato—'

'Did you hear what I said, Mrs Hawker, woman? I'll have cheese and fruit so you can stuff your infuriating concern . . .' He trailed off, picked up a length of bread.

Of all the offensive elements in his response, it was the word 'woman' that got me most, cut me to the quick. *Woman!* Indicating chattel, inferior, nuisance. *Woman!* Never had I been so insulted in all my years here. But I quickly took a hold on myself. No point in shouting back. It was, after all, the mistral that acted like some devil within him.

'And you, Mr Gerald?' I asked, plunging the ladle into the casserole. 'You'll have some, will you?'

'Just a little, Mrs Hawker. Thank you.'

It was a silent lunch. Mr Arthur left before the coffee, his fine poplin shirt darkened with patches of sweat. Mr Gerald anxiously watched him go.

'It's this heat,' he said, by way of conciliation.

'It gets us all down, Mr Gerald.'

'Quite.'

Once I had poured his coffee he stood up and said he would take it to his room. I suppose he no more wanted to be alone with me than I wanted to be alone with him. In this kind of atmosphere it was safer for all of us to be on our own.

'Mr Arthur will be hungry by tonight, at least,' he said with a very faint smile, which I took to be an apology for his friend's behaviour.

'We'll have cold collations,' I reassured him. 'Don't you worry.'

'Thank you, Mrs Hawker. That would be advisable.'

Once he had gone I continued to sit at the kitchen table, stirring my coffee. I could hear footsteps on stone floors, several doors banging. I could hear shouting, though the words were not clear. Then all was quiet. Just the buzzing of several flies and the snip, snip, snip of the wind against the warm stone of the outside walls.

I don't know how long I sat there listening to the frayed

rhythms of the wind. But eventually, true to habit, I stirred myself to clear the table and wash up. Then I went out into the garden. There, the fig and peach trees were tossing restlessly about, their great heads of silvery leaves trying to dodge the nagging and the teasing of the wind. Their usually calm shade was broken into a thousand moving pieces. Butterflies, driven from their resting places, were tossed in the air like tiny sailing boats on an invisible rough sea, and bees clung tightly to the lavender, silent in their concentration. I walked to the edge of the grounds to where the huge oak tree guarded the precipice. Its branches moved slightly, and its leaves snarled, but it acted with none of the frenzy of the fruit trees. It had learned to resist, I thought. I looked down into the great bowl of a valley where fields of lavender and corn dipped and swayed, confusing the bee-eaters. And overhead clouds scurried like lemmings in a dark blue sky. My skirts whipped about my legs. My hair lashed my face. There was not a moment's stillness. I felt so sad, so profoundly, inexplicably sad. The idea came to me that all I had to do was take a couple of further steps to be consumed for ever by the blue of the valley.

When eventually I returned to the kitchen I found, to my horror, that Mr Arthur and Mr Gerald were seated at the table, thunderous expressions threatening their watches.

'Ah, Mrs Hawker,' said Mr Arthur, all polite sarcasm, 'and what has happened to our tea?'

'It's nearly twenty past four,' said Mr Gerald. 'Very unlike you, Mrs Hawker, to have no tea prepared by now.'

There was a moment's quiet, just the wind still tugging away at the windows. Then I let them have it.

'Fucking hell, *gentlemen*,' I screamed. 'For once, just for once in eleven years I'm ten minutes late with your tea. What a disaster. What a bloody disaster! For you two lazy spoilt selfish slobs, that's a *major* disaster, because you're such hopeless bastards you can't so much as switch on a kettle, fill a pot, fetch the butter from the fridge – do you know which the fridge *is*, Mr Arthur Mr Gerald?'

Perfectly synchronised, their flabby old mouths fell open. But their eyes could not meet, nor could they look at me.

'Aren't you ashamed,' I raved on, 'at your absolute use-lessness, your total inadequacy? You employ me to wait on you hand and foot, do your bidding at every turn: you rely on me completely, useless prats for all your money—'

'Mrs Hawker,' said Mr Arthur.

'Mrs Hawker,' added Mr Gerald.

'Calm yourself.'

'Calm yourself.'

'Calm!'

I fact, I did feel calmer, now. I knew my words would come more tightly, with more menace. 'Who could be calm at the thought of a future waiting on two spoiled old sods? Who could be calm thinking that old age would still be darning your socks, getting your porridge just right while my own life just ebbs away? Course, if you live to bury me, I've no doubt you'll commission a nice marble headstone engraved with the tribute *A good and faithful servant* . . .'

'You've gone too far, Mrs Hawker,' said Mr Arthur, dabbing at the string of sweat on his nose.

'Much too far,' said Mr Gerald, running a finger round his damp collar.

'You're not yourself. The mistral, it affects us all.'

'Not yourself, indeed.'

'Not myself?' I gave a nasty laugh that made them both jump in their seats. 'As a matter of fact, Mr Arthur Mr Gerald, that's just what I am being at this moment – *myself*. For the first time in all these years, *myself*. The bit you've never shown the slightest desire to know about, to see. Well, I've only just begun. Sorry to shock you, but there's much, much more I'd like to say . . .'

I saw a look pass between them, then, and Mr Arthur gave an almost invisible sigh. The words I had ready to shoot at them were exploding in my head in such blinding lights that I could not quite read them – something to do with bitterness at the waste of my life, nothing but the satisfaction of two spoilt old men to show for it: the regret at so meagre an achievement, and the sadness – could they not understand the sadness?

They seemed to be waiting for me to go on. But anger had left me inarticulate. Words, insults, evaporated. So I began to moan, a noise similar to the wind. As I picked up the huge pottery bowl Mr Arthur and Mr Gerald looked scared. I thrust the fruit at them, moaning louder. A brilliant aim: figs caught Mr Arthur on the chest, making smeary pink marks on his clean shirt, and bursting obscenely over his fingers when he put up a hand to shield his face. An over-ripe peach slobbered down Mr Gerald's temple. I laughed again. I picked random crockery from the dresser and began to throw it on to the stone floor. The shotgun explosions of cups and saucers and the large dinner plates were pure music: pottery breaks into noisy crumbs. Glass, next. Half a dozen wine glasses landed in the stainless steel sink. They smashed with a high-pitched scream, drowning the noise of the wind. Then a jar of olives – they rolled about the messed-up floor like jet marbles, smearing it with olive oil. The homemade jams: two large jars, Mr Gerald's favourites, burst on to the floor, sticky plums sploshing among the olives and china. And finally the inspiration of a bag of flour. As I picked up a kitchen knife to slash the bag for speed, Mr Arthur and Mr Gerald turned a matching deathly white. In a moment they were whiter still as I held it high and let it scatter down like a snowstorm. I loved its silent descent into random piles that covered everything.

'This is . . .' Mr Arthur stood up, a floury spectre. Flour fell mistily from him.

'. . . too much, Mrs Hawker.' Mr Gerald, still troubled by peach in his eye, stood up too.

Something told me they were right. Besides, the energy was ebbing, just as the words had done earlier on.

'If I've caused you just a moment's thought, Mr Arthur Mr Gerald,' I said, 'then this has been worth it.'

Head very high, I left the room.

That was all some four hours ago. Since then, back in my room, I've been writing like a lunatic. All this stuff. Giving vent to, as they say. Letting it all out. As I pause for a moment I look out of the window and notice the trees are still. A bee-eater on the telegraph wires, eyes speared on to the lavender bush below, does not sway. The wind has died. Only the scratching of my pen in the silence.

Then the buzzer goes, frightening. I pick up the telephone.

'Mrs Hawker? It's almost eight o'clock.'

'So it is, Mr Arthur,' I say.

'Dinner-time,' he says.

'I'll be along, Mr Arthur.'

I stand, stretch. It's one of those dusky blue evenings I love so much. The crickets will start up again now the wind has gone. Funny how much I've enjoyed the writing. The hours just flew. Perhaps I shall try it again. Perhaps that's how I shall spend my time off in my old age, writing stories at last. I brush a streak of flour from my sleeve. I am very calm.

In the kitchen Mr Gerald is laying the table – three places. Very unusual, for I only dine with them at Christmas and on my birthday. He wears one of my aprons. Candles are lighted. A bottle of good wine is open. Over at the oven Mr Arthur is prodding expertly at the chicken casserole and tossing a salad. There's no sign that anything untoward (a favourite word of Mr Gerald's) has ever taken place. China and glass from the cupboard have replaced the missing things on the dresser. There's a bowl of olives – one of them must have been down to the village to buy more – and the flour jar is filled. What an afternoon they must have had! I try not to smile. I say nothing.

'Sit down, Annie,' says Mr Arthur, back to me.

'It's our turn to wait on you, Annie,' says Mr Gerald, without looking at me.

I do as they ask, and we have the dinner of a lifetime.

Now, it's past midnight. Even as I finish this story I find it hard to believe it all happened. The merging of fact and fiction in memory, however soon after the event, is intriguing. How much of what I have described was exactly like that? I have tried to be accurate, but if someone were to ask Mr Arthur and Mr Gerald to describe the events of today, some years from now, I've no doubt they would tell quite a different story. What I do know is that everyone is entitled to such terrible days now and then, and that, in the end, is what Mr Arthur and Mr Gerald understood, and that's why I love them and will work for them for the rest of my days.

Besides, they called me Annie. Of course – and I must stop now, I'm feeling suddenly tired – I know that was only for tonight. Mrs Hawker is how they like me to be, and why not? So Mrs Hawker I'll be again in the morning. But at least I have been Annie for a night.

I set my alarm.

Men Friends

Conrad Fortescue, on his way into the church, trod on a beetle. In the silence of the Norman porch he heard the tiny crackle as it crushed beneath his foot. Looking down, he saw the smashed shell, each fragment shiny as his own highly polished black shoes, linked by a web of blood. Damn, he thought: how Louisa would have hated this – Louisa who would rescue dying flies from summer window-panes. Conrad felt his throat clench. He coughed. Up until this moment he had been all right, in control. Death of the beetle shattered his calm.

He made his way into the church. He was early. Walking up the path banked with expensive wreaths of flowers at the foot of the yews, he had been pleased to think he was probably the first. He wanted time to himself to think about Louisa. But he was not the first. Half a dozen others were already seated, curious vulture eyes upon him, people behaving as if the gathering was for a party rather than a funeral. Conrad took a service sheet from an usher, chose a seat by a pillar from which he would not quite be able to see the coffin. *Louisa Chumleigh*, he read: *1st Sept 1956 – 2nd April 1992*. Not a long life. The organ began to play a Bach prelude. Conrad closed his eyes.

They first met seven years ago, one of those smudged

summer afternoons when the tremor of heat makes everything illusory. He stood on a thyme-planted terrace, leaning
over the balustrade to admire the descending shelves of
impeccably mowed lawns. Friends had brought him to the
house for tea, drinks – he couldn't remember which. He
had stood transfixed as he watched Louisa, in the shimmer
of heat below him, take the arm of an old man with a stick.
She supported him as he stepped from the lawn on to the
path. Her solicitousness – she had no idea she was being
watched, she later told him – was mirage-clear even from
so great a distance. She kept hold of the old man's arm –
Jacob, it was, her husband. They walked towards Conrad,
joined him on the terrace. As Jacob pointed his stick
towards the arboretum, spoke lovingly of trees, Conrad
regarded his wife. It was a case of instant enchantment.
Something unknown to him before.

They had had five years. Five years of adultery, though
Louisa would never use such a word. She had made it easy
for him – writing, ringing, taking the initiative to get in
touch, so that he was spared taking the risk of contacting
her. She never involved him in her deceits. She even managed to make him feel, sometimes, that the woman in his
arms was *free*. But that was the one thing she was not, nor
ever would be until Jacob died. Until that time, her husband came first. If she did not ring Conrad for a week –
and the agony of silent days never lessened – he knew it
would be because Jacob had made some demand that she
would not dream of refusing, although when she did ring
she gave no explanation for her silence. And Conrad knew
better than to ask.

Once, they had managed three whole days together: Jacob was on business in America. Louisa took the opportunity to visit relations in Paris. Conrad followed her on the next flight. Louisa saw little of her relations. On a warm spring afternoon in the Bois, Conrad declared his intention to wait for her: to wait until Jacob, thirty-six years her senior, died. He saw at once his mistake. Louisa, who had been laughing only moments before, retracted from him, though she kept hold of his hand. Conrad, apologising for his clumsiness, felt a lowering of the afternoon. 'Who knows what will happen – then?' Louisa said. 'It's something I can never think about, Jacob's dying.'

Soon she was laughing again. Back in England nothing seemed to have changed. Conrad accustomed himself to the imperfections of loving another man's wife, and privately determined to wait, however many years it might be.

Then, two years ago, there had been such a long silence that Conrad had been forced at last to write. What had happened? Louisa rang at once, her weak voice apologetic. Some wretched bug, she explained. She hadn't wanted to worry him. She had been forced to stay in bed for two weeks.

The bug needed treatment – radiotherapy. Conrad visited her occasionally when Jacob was away. He observed her thinning, beautiful skin gleaming with an incandescent menace. Noticeably more frail each visit, she lay back against a bank of linen pillows in the huge marital bedroom whose windows looked on to the garden. Conrad would look down on the lawns, misted with rain, and see the brilliance of that first summer day. A nurse filtered in and out, filling water jugs, straightening covers. Conrad brought pansies, in which Louisa silently buried her face, and elderberry jelly. She spread it thinly on toast, but could only eat a mouthful to please him. They held hands, talked about the past. But mostly sat in silence watching the rain on vast window-panes. Sometimes, Louisa felt like being up for a while. Once they walked down to the lake and back, which exhausted her.

Conrad learned of her death in *The Times*. None of their mutual friends knew of their affair so, not surprisingly, offered no condolences. He had written at once to Jacob, who replied by return, a stiff polite letter in an infirm hand, inviting Conrad to the funeral and lunch afterwards at the house.

Now Louisa was dead, Conrad would never marry. She was the only woman in whom he had found all the qualities he had never known he needed until he found them in her. He doubted he would ever love anyone else.

The church was filling up: men in black ties, women in dark hats. A large man with extraordinarily wide shoulders sat in front of Conrad, uncomfortable on the narrow bench of the pew, shifting about. Conrad recognised Johnnie Lutchins, a childhood friend. Louisa had sometimes talked about their times together in Cornwall.

Cornwall, Scotland, the south-west of Ireland – Johnnie and Louisa had spent many holidays together. Johnnie's widowed mother had been the best friend of Louisa's mother. She and her son spent much of their time with Louisa's family. Johnnie remembered his first sight of Louisa, a skinny angel in filthy dungarees. *Feeble*, he remembered thinking, at ten: but within the day he had discovered she was tough and daring as any boy. They climbed trees, sailed in brisk seas – the rougher the better, Louisa used to say. They teased an old donkey, put pretend spiders in the cook's tea – always laughing, always daring the other into greater mischief. At fifteen, Johnnie kissed Louisa in the greenhouse among unripe tomatoes. Then he couldn't stop kissing her. When he went up to Oxford three years later, she would visit him several times a term. He was the envy of all his friends, and showed off the beautiful creature at every opportunity. After he had graduated, and found a decent job in antiquarian books, he finally declared his love and proposed. But he had been beaten to it by Jacob – Jacob, a man older than Louisa's own father. When Johnnie had recovered from the shock, he had tried to dissuade her from such madness. Then he had turned to teasing. 'I can only conclude you're marrying the old boy for his money and his house,' he had laughed, bitterly. Louisa denied this. Neither Johnnie nor anyone could stop her from becoming Jacob's wife.

Still, as Johnnie soon found to his delight, the marital state made little difference to their friendship. Jacob, who had known Johnnie since he was a boy – indeed, he was Johnnie's godfather – issued constant invitations to the house. Johnnie was urged to look after Louisa, keep her amused, when Jacob was away on business. Which meant that with a half-clear conscience they could go out together in London. Opportunity was on their side: Johnnie considered himself the luckiest man in the world. He knew Louisa loved him, even if not in quite the same way as he loved her. It was only a matter of waiting . . . sometimes she had frustrated him by her silences, but he knew they meant she was being dutiful to Jacob, and he had no right to be either impatient or greedy. When she had become ill he had spent hours, days, by her bedside, laughing at the many flowers and cards sent to her by 'admirers' whom, she claimed, she hardly knew. Johnnie believed her.

He saw her on the day before she died – asleep, but holding Jacob's hand. The old man sat with fresh tears replacing dried tears on his cheeks, making no effort to brush them away. But when he rang Johnnie next morning with the news, his voice was firm as usual. He was a dignified old boy. He would have been horrified by Johnnie's uncontrolled weeping.

To deflect his thoughts, Johnnie glanced round the church. Hundreds of pansies were woven into ivy round the pillars, and along ledges where they mixed with the reflections of stained-glass windows, and twined into edifices on the altar. Candles burned as if it were Christmas Eve. The pews were full. People were hunting for seats in the side aisles. Many of them resigned themselves to standing. One of those, Johnnie realised, was Bernard Wylie. Johnnie had met him and Louisa one day in Bond Street, very briefly. He had only just caught the name. Later, he remembered to ask Louisa about him. She said Wylie was a solicitor – something to do with her late father's affairs. They had both laughed about the slickness of his coat, with its too-wide velvet collar. Today, Johnnie recognised the coat before the face.

Bernard Wylie wore his favourite coat accompanied by

expensive black leather gloves, and a black satin tie lightened with the tiniest white spots which he had judged would not be offensive. He stood clutching his service sheet to steady his hands, staring straight ahead, feeling the uncertainty of his knees. And he wondered for the millionth time what it was about Louisa that had so bewitched him that his life, since meeting her, had fallen apart.

She had come into his office one November afternoon – some trivial matter to do with her father's estate – wearing a hat of grey fur sparkling with rain. Completely confused by the legal niceties of the matter, she had suddenly said, 'Oh, I give up, Mr Wylie,' and had laughed her enchanting laugh. 'In that case,' he had said, 'let's go and have tea while I explain it all to you very slowly.'

So slowly that their tea at the Ritz drifted into champagne, and then dinner. He had driven her back to her flat, come in for a drink, stayed the night. There had been dozens of nights since – nights and lunches, little notes and presents from her, calls from all parts of the world when she was travelling with Jacob. Then, a year or so before she fell ill, there was the final note. 'I'm awfully sorry, darling B, but we can't go on. I realise now it was all *infatuation* on my part . . . and know it was not real love for you either, but great fun, and thank you.'

For the rest of his life, Bernard would regret not having made his declaration – Christ, he had loved her from the moment she walked into his office. But he had bided by Byron's principle of never telling your love, merely conveying it. Had his conveying been invisible? Too late he wrote to her, pages of the long-contained passion now set free. But she did not reply. The last time he saw her was at a party, laughing in the distance with some unknown man. She had not seen him. Bernard had left at once.

And now instead of Louisa he had a second-best wife at his side who would never know the loving man he once was . . . She nudged him, this loyal, unexciting wife, her sense of occasion offended by the sight of a young man standing not far from them in a dark jacket, grey trousers and no tie. In the unknown youth's eye, Bernard thought he saw reflected the same despair that lodged in his own heart: but it may have been his imagination.

The young man, Felix Brown, had cried for many nights. Cold, exhausted, drained, he feared he might faint during the long service, but there were no seats left. He it was who late last night, and at dawn this morning, had transported pansies from the greenhouse to the church, and arranged them on his own. Only three years ago, Lady Endlesham – as he still thought of her, as he would always think of her – had come into that very greenhouse and admired them. Said they were her favourite flowers. They had talked of planting and pruning, and made plans for the south bed. Felix had done his best to conceal the mesmeric effect the shape of her breasts beneath a pink cotton shirt had had upon him. He had told her how happy he was to be working in the garden. He could scarcely believe he had been promoted to being in charge only two years after leaving horticultural college, he said. Lady Endlesham had smiled, and said they must make more plans. Then he gave her a pot of pansies for her desk.

Some weeks later she came into the tool-shed, admired

his clean and gleaming tools that hung in order of height on the walls. The warmth of that evening was almost tangible. In the stuffy air that smelt of dry earth Felix was embarrassed by the pungent smell of his own sweat. He could also smell Lady Endlesham's scent, a mixture of fragile flowers. In the shadows it seemed to him she hesitated, planning perhaps to mention some gardening matter. Then she put out her arms, and said, he thought – though he could never be quite sure of the exact words – *Come here, you handsome thing*. Handsome? Gathered to him, Felix could hear the racing heart of his employer's wife. They ran like children through the orchard to a hidden place Felix knew. Lord Endlesham was away, she assured him, but not in a rejoicing way. She sounded almost lonely. Felix was twenty-one at the time.

Since then they'd made love in every corner of the garden, and, in winter, in the hayloft. Felix would marvel how one moment his mistress (as he liked to think of her) was laughing in his arms covered in grass or hay, and the next he would see her in the distance walking beside her aged husband, immaculate, admiring the flowerbeds whose geography she and Felix had discussed between a thousand kisses.

When she was ill, no longer able to come downstairs, he sent up a new bowl of flowers to her room each day. The last time he saw her she was standing at her bedroom window – looking for him, perhaps. He was raking the terrace. He glanced up, saw her wave. Then she disappeared. She disappeared, and with a crescendo in the organ music Felix knew at last she was gone. Never coming back to their garden. He took out his handkerchief, blew his nose, realising he was the only man in the church to resort to such weakness at this stage. Through tear-blurred eyes he watched the shuffling procession of coffin-bearers hesitate up the aisle, and caught the eye of his employer, Sir Jacob, seventy-two at Christmas. He was a good man to work for. Felix respected the old codger, but wondered if he could bear to continue the job now the inspiration of the garden no longer existed.

Sir Jacob, seeing young Felix, the first face to come clearly into focus, gave the briefest nod to acknowledge that his floral work in the church was appreciated. Louisa would have been amazed. She loved decorating the church. She and Felix, before the illness, had done a grand job always at Christmas and Harvest Festival. She had been wonderful with the boy. In her usual generous way she had inspired him, encouraged him, suggested his promotion – typical of her, always seeing the best in people, bringing out their qualities.

Sir Jacob trod very slowly, in time to the gentle music. In front of him on the coffin lay a single gardenia. He had chosen it with Felix – the best in the greenhouse. Inside, placed in the stiff hands, was the equally stiff card with its private message of love which would not fade until long after the body had perished.

Beside Sir Jacob walked Louisa's mother, a bent old lady with a still-beautiful profile that had been inherited by her daughter. It occurred to Sir Jacob, as he put a finger on the knife-edge of his collar that cut into his neck, that they might look more like man and wife than he and Louisa ever did . . . Louisa could have been his granddaughter.

Walking down this same aisle, their wedding day – but he hadn't cared then, or ever, what people thought. All that mattered to him was their mutual, perfect love for each other. Which turned out to be proven. While Sir Jacob recoiled at the thought of his own smugness, he couldn't help reflecting that never once in their sixteen years of marriage had Louisa ever let him down, disappointed him, betrayed him. He knew he came first in her life, just as she did in his. He had trusted her absolutely. The only worry they had ever had was about her life after his death. She often said that no one ever could replace him.

The coffin-bearers reached the altar, placed it on its plinth. Sir Jacob and his mother-in-law took their places in the front pew. A shaft of sun, at that moment, pierced the roseate glass of the window above the altar. Sir Jacob remembered Louisa remarking on the strength of its colour – 'a small pink pool on the altar steps, darling – did you notice?' In truth he had never noticed, in all the Sundays he had been coming to this church, until Louisa had pointed it out to him. She had drawn so much to his attention that gave pleasure. She had opened his eyes to the extraordinary qualities of the ordinary, and made him the happiest of men.

The vicar clasped his hands. In the moment's silence before the first prayer, Sir Jacob looked round at the congregation – so many people who would always remember his wife. It occurred to him there was a large proportion of men. Men of all ages, he saw, all with that sternness of eye that strong men employ to conceal grief. He knew some of them: others were unfamiliar. Darling Louisa: untouchable to all but me, he used to say. And she, kneeling on the library floor beside him, would laugh her thrilling laugh in agreement. How proud of her he was! There was nothing like having a wife who was desired by all, but faithful only to the man she loved, her husband.

May the vanity of such thoughts be forgiven, Sir Jacob found himself praying. Then he joined in the general words of thanks for Louisa's life. He could not close his eyes: in his disbelief they never left the coffin. Like so many of Louisa's men friends in the church for her funeral that day, Sir Jacob could only picture her alive.

Easy Silence

For Diana Baring

With many thanks to Humphrey Burton,
my kind and patient musical adviser.

We look before and after,
We pine for what is not:
Our sincerest laughter
With some pain is fraught;
Our sweetest songs are those that tell of saddest thought.

Percy Bysshe Shelley

1

'Where, tonight?'

'Slough.'

'*Slough?*'

'Slough.'

'I wouldn't have thought—'

'Some industrial estate. Some hall. Rather good acoustics, as far as I remember.'

'Slough! I have to say I can't imagine there'd be a very good turn out in—'

'You're wrong there, my Ace.'

'So you'll be back late, you poor thing.'

'Not very late.'

'Slough . . . Mozart?'

William Handle glanced at his wife to assess the precise measure of interest in this question. He knew so well the waterline in her blue eyes that divided politeness from real interest. Tonight, weary after a long day whose tribulations she had relived for him over tea, he judged mere politeness fired the question. She didn't really want to know the answer, she certainly hadn't the heart to be subjected to details of the programme. William spared her.

'Mozart, yes,' is all he said.

'Sure you've got the right –'

William tapped his music case. 'Checked three times.' Since the occasion, five years ago, he had found he'd taken Bach instead of

Brahms to a big concert in Manchester, he had been almost neurotic in his checking.

'Well, then.' Grace patted his shoulder. She registered that the
stiff stuff of his mackintosh had actually cracked. Tomorrow, at
some appropriate time, she would suggest he invested in a new
one. To say anything now would be foolish. William no longer suffered the acute pre-concert nerves of his youth but he liked to
start thinking about the music when he had finished his second
cup of tea. Any deflection ruffled him, though Grace was the only
one privileged to observe such disturbance. She handed him his
violin case, opened the front door. The small car parked in the driveway was pearled with rain.

'Oh dear, what a bother, I won't be able to hurry.' William was
always nervous about his lack of driving skill, especially in the
dark and rain. 'I'd hoped it might have stopped.'

'It's sure to have cleared by the time you come home,' said Grace,
who believed in encouragement.

'Goodnight, my Ace.' William kissed his wife on the cheek.
When his hands were free he liked to cup her chin and kiss her
lightly on the mouth – something he discovered she enjoyed when
they were courting and had become a habit between them. But
lumbered with both instrument and music case, he was only able
to give her what they jokingly called a pre-concert kiss. The cases
barged into Grace's thighs. She backed away, smiling.

'Drive carefully.'

'I will.'

All the way to Slough William had trouble with the windscreen
wipers. They went either too fast or too slow. In neither mode (a
modern word William sometimes reluctantly found he was obliged
to use) did they perform their function properly. The glass
remained smeary, a screen of moving abstract patterns that flowed
from coloured neon signs and streetlights. William was forced to
drive slowly, trying to decide just how near or far he was from the
exploding headlights coming towards him. He feared he would be
late. He wanted to look at his watch, but Grace had drummed into

him so often that a driver should never take his eyes from the road. In her absence, he felt it more crucial than ever to heed her advice, always sound. So he gave up the thought of checking the time.

But tonight something more serious than the rain troubled William. Through the squiggle of disconcerting lights he tried to remember what it was. At a red light (handbrake diligently on), it came to him: Andrew. Andrew Fulbright. Andrew, his dearest friend, his friend of almost thirty years, best viola in any quartet in the country . . . gone. Gone! The fact was still incredible. William could not bring himself to believe that when he reached the dressing-room tonight Andrew would not be wittering on about the threadbare state of his white tie (a mean man, in small respects, he would never deign to replace it), or the banality of the pro-gramme if it did not include some difficult modern composer, or the warmth of the lager provided for after-concert refreshment, or the inconsideration of British Rail for those requiring to travel home late. Dear Andrew! William and the other two members of the Elmtree Quartet were so familiar with his grumbles that their sympathetic responses had become automatic – sometimes in har-mony, sometimes solo, with as little thought as was necessary in playing the opening bars of Mozart's K458. But they were enough to console Andrew – a man quick to recover from his own imag-ined misfortunes if ever there was one. Within moments he would be laughing, tuning up long before reaching the platform with a keenness, a precision, that would make the others smile. And then, no matter how many times Andrew had played a piece, he never resorted to automatic pilot. He always gave his soul to the music in a way that the others – so often tired, bored, irritated – failed to do with such constancy. Now Andrew was gone for ever. This would be the first concert without him.

The car behind William hooted four times in the manner of the opening bar of Beethoven's Fifth. This was a signal William could read. Rather than feel annoyed by the other driver's impatience, he was soothed. It could mean there was another musician on the road to the concert. William obligingly let in the clutch, observing that by now the green light had changed to amber. But he made a dash for it. Didn't want to annoy the chap behind any further. Grace said the slightest hesitation could inspire road-rage these days. William could not imagine what he would do should some angry driver come banging on the window set for a fight. Grace said he should always lock the car from the inside if there was any suspicion of things turning nasty. But William had never encountered any such suspicion, and in the meantime had forgotten how to lock the doors from the inside. In this first-ever possible nasty moment, aware of his vulnerability, he slammed down the accelerator and leapt forward through a glow of red, causing traffic from each side of him to start up a cacophony of hooting, which put him vaguely in mind of Gershwin's tuned taxi horns in *An American in Paris*.

A short while later, his calm returned, his hands loosened on the steering wheel, his thoughts returned to Andrew. The sad fact was that Andrew had been forced to resign untimely from the Elmtree because of 'wife troubles'. He had confessed to William that after many difficult years things had come to a head. It was either bloody concerts, Zara had said, or her. He could take his choice. Zara, addicted to the plural, had screamed at him; music, music, music – she was fed up to here with twenty years of music. So he could either go, go, go, or give in his notice, pronto, and stay, stay, stay. Andrew, being an honourable man and remembering his wedding vows, had been forced to choose his wife. He had given his viola to his son and swore never to play again, thus doubling Zara's triumph.

Andrew's official reason for leaving the Elmtree was increasing arthritis in his shoulder, exacerbated by playing. William (first violin), Rufus (second violin) and Grant (cello) had never heard him complain of this, but did not press him. They set about auditioning replacements. William remembered desolate weeks of listening to young hopefuls – very eager young hopefuls – scraping through their favourite Brahms sonata. Not one of them would bring to the Elmtree players the very particular quality of Andrew, but a choice had finally to be made. William agreed with the other two that a girl, called Bonnie, would be the best choice – though each in their hearts would have preferred another man. Among so many applicants William could remember little of Bonnie except that she had a powerful fringe and a memorable mouth. She had played part of the Walton viola concerto for her audition, which had cheered Andrew: he said here was a girl who liked a challenge. As the others wanted Andrew to be happy with his replacement and her playing was, indeed, original, if a little erratic, the choice was more or less made for them. Besides, time was running out. Zara was looking at houses in Yorkshire, to ensure Andrew was unable to go back on his word, and they were all fed up with auditions. They disliked their power to stifle a dozen hopes a day.

There had been many rehearsals with Bonnie before the first concert together. William had concentrated on erasing the singular and beautiful sound of Andrew's viola from his mind. Bonnie, of the bobbing fringe, did her best. She was quiet, accommodating, quick to respond to any suggestion for improvement. William tried to convince himself that in time he would become used to the strangeness of her presence. For the moment he could see her only as a replacement rather than a being. Certainly she was a good – an especially good musician, they realised after a week or so of playing with her. But as a young girl of flesh and blood, for William, she did not yet exist.

This evening was to be Bonnie's first concert as a member of the Elmtree String Quartet. That was what was troubling William. That was what was making driving in the dark and rain harder than usual. How on earth would it be? Never the same again, of course. Four old friends, so used to each others' idiosyncrasies, so loyal in their disguising of each others' frailties . . . And now they must accommodate a new player about whose attitude, life, tone, mastery of a score they knew nothing. Besides which, this new member, this *replacement*, was not a man. Ashamed of his secret dread and prejudice, William quickly told himself that it was only fair to give this Bonnie girl – young woman, whatever she was – a chance. Help her. She must be feeling pretty nervous. She would need all the support he, Grant and Rufus knew they must give. The whole prospect was nothing less than a nightmare.

By the time William drew up at the hall on the industrial estate in Slough, the rain was so hard the windscreen wipers collapsed altogether, but Bonnie's surname had come to him. *Morse*. Bonnie Morse. Hardly a name to distinguish a programme. He made a mental note to describe every inch of the new viola's appearance, and performance, next morning to Grace. He would end up by trumpeting her name in the funny voice he used to disguise disapproval, and which always made Grace laugh. Bonnie Morse, indeed! How they would agree.

As William ran through the rain towards the lighted door, violin case and music case banging at his clattery mackintosh, he realised that he had not given a moment's thought to the Mozart he was about to play, but consoled himself with the thought that the pieces were so well known to him this would not, for once, impair his performance. More disturbing was the fact that there was a *girl* arriving ahead of him. Back shiny as a seal in the rain. Viola case tucked professionally under her arm. Bonnie Morse herself.

It was a bad start. He had promised the others he'd be there first. Greet this Bonnie. Welcome her. Assure her. As leader of the players, do his stuff.

William pushed himself into a run. He pictured her blundering along corridors looking for the room that the managers of the cat food firm, sponsoring the concert, liked to call the Green Room. It was clear already the choice of the new viola was a mistake. There was bound to be trouble. William felt the ache of a bereaved man as he thought of the absent Andrew. Fired by guilt and melancholy, he attempted to jump a puddle for further speed. He clambered into the air with the heaviness of an insect drowsed by late summer. He slipped on landing. Fell. Eventually, rose again. Cursed Bonnie Morse. In his final wet sprint to the door he tried to calm himself with thoughts of Mozart, but did not succeed.

*

The next morning at breakfast it was Grace who brought up the subject that had occupied William's mind during a long and sleepless night.

'So: how did it go with the new viola?'

'Fine. All right. She's not bad. She's rather good.'

'She?'

'Didn't I tell you, my Ace?' After so many years he was no longer in the habit of passing on the Elmtree's news, usually of no great interest, to his wife. 'The new viola's a she.'

Grace scraped her toast back and forth, spreading the butter till it was an almost calorie-free veil.

'You didn't, no.'

'Well, it didn't seem of much importance. All those auditions, no one particularly outstanding. The candidates were confused in my mind. I suppose I forgot to tell you the one we chose in the end was this young woman, Bonnie Morse.'

'Bonnie Morse?'

'Quite.' They exchanged a smile at the name, as William had foreseen.

'Young woman?'

'As yet I haven't determined whether she's a young woman or an older girl. It's not the sort of thing you can ask. She's got a girlish fringe but womanly hips, I'd say.'

Grace now turned her concentration to thinning out the marmalade in the same way as the butter.

'How could you tell about her hips if she was sitting down playing all evening?'

'I was behind her when she took a bow at the end.'

'Quite,' said Grace after a while. 'When's your next date?'

William shifted almost imperceptibly in the seat of his chair and picked up *The Times* to signal the end of the exchange.

'Northampton, Thursday.'

'Perhaps I should come with you, judge for myself.'

'Not worth it. Wait till she's settled in and we're playing somewhere nearer.'

'It's only an hour's journey.'

'Britten the whole of the second half. You know how allergic you are to Britten.'

'True,' said Grace. 'All right, I won't come. It was just an idea.'

They fell back into the easy silence that was their habit at breakfast. Tea, before William set off for a concert, was the time they liked to exchange news, confirm plans, swap some of the random thoughts that had come to them during the day. It was also the time, especially when the evenings were drawing in, they sometimes fell into a little routine of reminiscence, which reaffirmed, rather than more obvious declarations, their long-married love, and reassured.

Breakfast finished, William put his plate and mug on top of the dishwasher, his single contribution to domestic necessity, and went upstairs. Grace began to hurry with the rest of the clearing, for timing, in the strict routine of daily life that she and William had thrived on for years, was essential. Working daily under the same roof, they decided years ago, would best be accomplished if each of them was able to believe in the illusion that they were alone in the house. Thus skilful avoiding of the other was put into practice – difficult at first, some slip-ups encountered. By now, a habit no longer thought about. They had taken practical steps to ensure there was no danger of a chance meeting in the morning – a kettle and coffee had been installed in William's room, for instance, so that he would not have to come down to the kitchen for his elevenses. This guaranteed they would not have to pass on the stairs, something they both secretly preferred to avoid. For what, as Grace once asked, do people who've been married for a long time *say* when they meet on the stairs? Their desire to avoid any such meeting was mutual, though unspoken. Neither wished to risk the possibility, knowing well that a preoccupied smile or the absence of a jaunty word are the sort of things that can lead to misunderstandings in the happiest of marriages.

Grace waited till she heard her husband come out of the bathroom and climb the stairs to the third floor of the house, to his sound-proofed room. There, she imagined, he would stand at the window tuning his violin, looking out of the window at the severe patch of garden with its orderly standard roses and dark privet hedges, and lose himself in Brahms, or whoever, for the next couple of hours before getting down to the tasks at his desk. If by chance his thoughts turned to her, Grace imagined, then he would see her equally engrossed in her work in the downstairs study, spectacles slipping down her nose, tiny sable brush hovering over the paper as she depicted every vein in a buttercup petal. Her *A Child's Guide to Flowers* had engrossed her for the last five years and the signs were it would take another five to complete. Grace appreciated that William still showed interest in her progress from time to time, and loyally deflected questions from friends who enquired about his wife's date of publication.

What William did not know was that *had* he imagined his wife safely at her flowers, the picture would have been inaccurate. Until at least mid-morning, these days, she was no longer there. Since Lucien had started visiting, her work routine had been destroyed. And what William also did not know was that some mornings, when William took five minutes longer than usual to read the paper, Grace became rigid with concealed tension. For if Lucien had walked unannounced through the kitchen door, which was his way, and William had still been at breakfast – well, Grace dared not imagine what might happen. So occasionally, anxiously watching the clock, she was obliged to chivvy her husband in the gentlest possible way.

'My goodness, it's almost half past nine,' she would observe, taking his plate to the sink to relieve him of this duty.

'My goodness, so it is.'

'You'd better get on, hadn't you?'

'So I had, my Ace. How right you are. The Mendelssohn.' And humming the first few bars, he would be on his way.

William never seemed to notice the urgency beneath her mild suggestions, and the small element of danger gave an edge to breakfast which Grace rather enjoyed.

The morning after Bonnie Morse's first concert with the Elmtree

String Quartet there was no reason for Grace to urge William to hurry. But he finished more quickly than usual, eager to be alone in the safety of his sound-proofed room.

Once there, instead of taking out his violin and drowning himself in the music he loved, as Grace imagined, he slumped into the low armchair, legs slung apart in a matter he would not have considered adopting downstairs. He picked up a pencil and began to tap his teeth in time to a passage from the Siciliana in the Mozart D minor they had played last night. Sometimes he hummed a little, but the tuneless noise depressed him – so far, it was, from the pure sound in his head.

In all honesty, he reflected, last night had been much better than he had expected. Really rather good. A full house and lively applause. Bonnie Morse, he had to admit, had made no mistakes. She had been a little hesitant, perhaps, and a fraction late with one cue – but damn it, the girl must have been terribly nervous, first time playing with such a well-known quartet. She did very well, as Grant and Rufus acknowledged in a brief meeting in the car park, after she had driven off in a small red car, waving cheerfully. Of course, he'd have to coach her a bit, introduce her to the Elmtree's special ways. But that should be no problem. He sensed she would be quick to learn. A bright girl: no budding genius, but a nice touch, an infectious energy which – and here William was reluctant to admit it even to himself – was something the Elmtree String Quartet, after so many years, could well benefit from if it was to keep its impeccable reputation intact.

A worry William tried hard to ignore was in fact not the Elmtree's reputation but its future. He was well aware a quartet with its original members could not continue for ever. They had had a pretty good innings. William often remembered the day he and Rufus, after a village cricket match, sat in the shade of an elm tree with their pints of bitter, and made their plans. At that time Rufus was a keen cricket player – in the village team, he had something of a reputation as a fast bowler. He liked the whole business of English afternoon cricket – the village green, the whites, the teas, the camaraderie. Most of all he liked the fact that his frail wife Iris, slung low in a deckchair, brim of straw hat cutting across her fine cheekbones, cheered him on so enthusiastically. Often he invited William to matches. It was on a day Iris had not felt up to joining them that the two of them had lingered into the late afternoon, and come up with the idea of their own quartet. Rufus already knew of Andrew, who eagerly joined them. It was only a matter of weeks before, through musical friends, they found Grant. There had been no change of cast, since then, till now. Shortly after they had established themselves, played a few lowly concerts, Rufus strained his shoulder by some overconfident bowling. It hurt to play thereafter, so he gave up cricket, declared he had no regrets. Instead, he took up the gentler occupation of Saving the Skylark. A keen ornithologist as a boy, he was horrified by the decline of so many British birds – particularly the skylark, for he was a Shelley man as well as a musical one.

Rufus, William knew, was a better judge of a musician than himself. He had an acute ear. He also knew instinctively how to match players – how well one would balance another. It was he who had assured William – initially reluctant for the wrong reasons – of Bonnie's potential for fitting in with the tone of the other three. It was Rufus, at the audition, who had urged William not only to cast aside his prejudice, but also to think that a change of direction (i.e. the inclusion of a girl) would give the Elmtree the boost it might one day need. At the end of the Slough concert, as the players left the stage, William had touched Rufus on the arm and whispered that he had been right as usual. Rufus had merely given his old friend a curt nod: he was not one who found appreciation easy to accept.

After the concert the members of the Quartet had lingered in the breeze-block Green Room, sipping at glasses of third-rate wine provided by the cat food sponsors. Although they were eager to be off as soon as possible, in appreciation of Bonnie's commendable first performance they stayed a while. It was during this half-hour gathering that Bonnie Morse took her first tentative – and rather charming – steps in getting to know her fellow players. First she admired Grant's cello. She asked permission to run a finger over its strings, which she was readily granted. Then she and Grant discovered that, despite the ten-year difference in their ages, they had shared a music master whom they both admired. William also heard them conversing about a subject that he himself had no interest in at all – foreign food. Grant was an excellent cook, though how he managed in the chaos of his kitchen was hard to imagine. William saw Bonnie revealing a peculiar interest in Grant's descriptions of variations on chilli con carne, and felt that he, as leader of the Quartet, should have his fair share of her attention before it was time to go. When he gave her a light tap on the elbow she willingly broke away from Grant, and cast all her attention on William. Her conversation with him was one that he had had with more people than he could remember over the years but which, the evening in the Green Room on the Slough Trading Estate, was endowed with a curious freshness.

'And you, Mr Handle: are you by any chance a descendant . . .?'

When confronted with this familiar question, William never liked to disappoint. He would therefore give a small nod that could be taken for acquiescence, though if pressed further he would of course explain the discrepancy in the spelling. For some reason, faced with Bonnie's intrigued eyes, he launched without hesitation into the truth of the matter.

'I'm afraid . . . we're spelt differently. No relation.'

'Still, it must be an asset as a musician to be called any kind of Handle.' Bonnie smiled understandingly, showing no sign of disappointment. That was gratifying. William was used to people's interest flagging as soon as they learned he was an *le* rather than an *el*. 'Like contemporary writers who happen to be called Shakespeare,' Bonnie went on. 'I know there's at least one good modern novelist called Shakespeare. Bet that's not a disadvantage.'

William agreed with a silent nod. He was not acquainted with the writer Bonnie referred to, but found himself making a note that the next time he was in a bookshop. . .

Bonnie was leaving by then, tucking her viola case under her arm in a way none of the other players ever did. She smiled round at all of them, thanking them for being so kind – she'd been pretty terrified, she said, but they'd given her courage. Her smile was engaging, pushing dimples into her cheeks. But William found himself more in awe of her mouth in repose, the top lip tipped up in the kind of delicate arc that would have bewitched Michelangelo. All the way home, struggling once more against the rain, William's thoughts had been divided between the mouth, and the fringe that all but obscured the eyes. He imagined that one day – trying to read an obscure score, perhaps – she would flick it back, and a pair of eyes to match the mouth would be revealed.

It was past ten o'clock. William stirred. He had intended to get down to the business of deciding on the Manchester Christmas programme before he started to practise. Instead, his mind turned to the Northampton recital on Friday. Bonnie had said she was quite happy with the proposed programme, but William felt it would only be fair to check her knowledge of the third Britten quartet. It wasn't the easiest piece. He and the others would be prepared to change it for something else – although the programmes had been printed long ago – if she had any doubts.

Secure in the knowledge that Grace, bent over her buttercups downstairs, would never know of this break in his routine – a morning telephone call – William pulled from his pocket the number Bonnie had given him the night before. Somewhere in the muddle of his desk was her official letter of acceptance of the job with the Quartet, with her CV, address and number. But in his impatience William could not be bothered to go through the papers. Instead, he studied the figures written in red pencil on the scrap of paper, trying to determine some clue to her character from the boldness of the figures.

William let the telephone ring for two minutes. No answer. He returned to his chair, wondering at his faintly restless state. Then he rose again, guilty, and took up his violin. Mercifully, his normal calm returned. He carried on practising till mid-morning, when he made his coffee, with two spoons of sugar, which Grace would never allow downstairs, before trying to ring Bonnie once more.

In the kitchen Grace was taking her usual battering from Lucien.

'She's giving me a lot of grief this week,' he was saying. 'Something's like upset her. Don't ask me what. But is she taking it out on me? Hell she is.'

He was referring to his mother, Lobelia Watson, whom Grace had not met – an apparent monster whose general misdeeds and loathsomeness of character Lucien had exhaustively described to Grace since the beginning of their acquaintance some months ago.

'Like, last night. She comes back from her therapist – she's always worse when she's been moaning on to her – and it's like, Lucien do this, Lucien do that, take your wet clothes out of the machine, hang them on the line, whatever. Then it's Lucien you don't understand me. Lucien you don't give a thought to anyone but yourself – how does the bitch know what goes on in my mind? Then she's on about drugs, of course. Every day she's on about drugs. Cuts out little stories from the paper saying some git's OD'd and died, and puts them by my bed like when I was a child she put little jugs of daisies. Bloody mad.'

He picked up his mug of coffee in both hands, looked at Grace. Then quickly his eyes fidgeted away over things nearby – his fingernails, an ashtray on the table, a pencil. Grace had rarely seen him look out of the window or into any distance. It was as if he could not face horizons. He needed to be near the things he regarded.

'You know what I think. I've said it so many times. You should leave home. Soon as possible.'

'How bloody can I?'

'Get a job.'

'How bloody can I? What can I do? Who'd have me?'

'Don't be daft, Lucien. You could do anything you put your mind to.'

'She'd go off her trolley if I left.'

'You'd have to risk that. Most people are quite relieved when their children go. Not many mothers would be happy still to have a twenty-four-year-old son living at home.'

'You don't know my mother. I'm all she's got. All she's got to fucking live for, she says – well, she doesn't put it quite like that, does she? I can't do a thing right in her eyes, but if I left she'd never forgive me. I said to her once, Mum, I said, what happens when I meet some girl I want for more than a night? Want to set up with her? – What did she do? Bugger off and drink a bottle of vodka. Who had to clear up the mess next morning? I mean.'

Grace had heard all this, with variations, many times before. Lucien's way was to start with a blast of angry complaint shot with questions to which he did not want to hear an honest answer. Usually, his morning fury had dwindled after half an hour. The second half of his visit he switched into the young man Grace had grown strangely fond of – still uneasy and inelegant, but lively, interested, curious, amazed by things that seemed to Grace quite ordinary.

'William and I missed Jack dreadfully when he first left,' she said, which was not entirely true, 'but we also felt quite pleased. Free.'

'Yes, well, your Jack. He's a different matter, daresay.'

Grace could see he was simmering down. They sat in silence for a while – a silence as easy, though different, as it was with William. Across this table from the unspeaking William she was always aware of the mutual charge of love and affection, garnered from so many years of happy marriage, that does not need words, queries, analysis. She and William both recognised, and were able to indulge in, the lazy silence of mutual knowing, the unspoken agreement that no effort had constantly to be made. This was the reward for altruistic years together. With Lucien, the silence bore no such mutual recognition. For his part, thoughts were totally of himself. Preoccupation with this 'limited subject', as William, who found his wife's young friend hard to tolerate, once called it, was very fashionable. Grace could see that, and was both appalled and intrigued by such egotism. In the many hours that she and Lucien had spent at the kitchen table (hours lost to her work on the book) there was no denying that Grace, too, was compelled to think only of her visitor. He knew this. He could see questions struggling in her eyes. Her concern was a bolster, nicely doubling his sense of self-interest.

'I suppose you're wondering about me.' This he observed approximately once a week.

'I am, rather.'

'You keep wondering. Come up with any good solutions and I won't half be pleased.'

He gave her a quick smile. A smile that lighted his grey-skinned face beguilingly. Crinkle of dark eyes and unshaven jowls, a flash of incredibly white teeth, despite a regular boast that he never brushed them because of his mother's nagging. (Jack, who had brushed his teeth regularly since he was a child, was now the owner of a very unpleasant smile: dun-coloured teeth fringing over-long gums, inherited from neither of his parents.)

'So how's the book going?' Lucien asked eventually. 'Buttercup a day?'

'Afraid not. It doesn't work quite like that.'

'No, well. You promised I could see some of your paintings. I'm a Damien Hurst man myself, as you know. But I'm nothing if not adaptable. Dead cows one day, buttercups the next. Cows . . . but-tercups – some link there, surely?'

He grinned. At moments like this Grace scorned herself for ever thinking there was something faintly sinister about Lucien. He had the charm of a rather silly schoolboy. A warmth and friendli-ness that had never been part of Jack's character. And Jack had never shown the slightest interest in his mother's work. Grace smiled.

'I'll show them to you one day,' she said. '*You* promised that I could meet your mother.'

'You can, any time.' This was always his reply, but a meeting was never arranged.

Grace pressed him. 'When?'

'I'll fix it. She's in most afternoons after her therapy session. Comes back glowing. From spending so much money, daresay.'

'I'm always free. Any afternoon.'

'Music to my ears.' Lucien grinned again. 'Most people I know are always busy.'

'There does seem to be a lot of competitive busyness about these days, yes.'

'That's right.' Sometimes agreement spurred Lucien to exotic observations that Grace found so singular she would pass them on to William (who was less able to see their interest). But today he swerved quickly back to his mother. 'If I was my mum I'd be bored stiff wittering on every afternoon about myself, thirty-five quid an hour.'

'Some people feel it does them good, talking to a professional.'

'She's one of them. One of her illusions.'

'Everyone needs their illusions.'

'Anyhow, it's not doing any good.'

'It takes time.'

Lucien poured himself more coffee, frowning. Grace sensed he was uncommonly restless today.

'What does your old man do all morning, shut up in his room?'

'Practises. Arranges concert programmes.'

'Maybe I'd better come to one of his gigs,' he said.

'Wouldn't be very up your street, I don't think.'

'How d'you know? OK, I'm into heavy metal, but I can also dig Beethoven. Honest. Like I told you, I'm adaptable.' There was a long silence while Grace imagined the odd couple of Lucien and herself taking seats at one of the Elmtree concerts.

'You don't seem too keen,' Lucien said at last.

'I was just weighing up how much you'd enjoy it.'

'I'd enjoy it. It'd be spooky, great. But if I didn't, we could always walk out.'

'We couldn't,' said Grace sternly.

Lucien took her hand, grinning again. 'Course we couldn't.

Calm down, Mrs H. I was just winding you up. I'd sit there good as anything. Not cause you any hassle, honest.'

Grace shrugged. She tried to withdraw her hand but Lucien would not let it go.

'Well, I'll see what's coming up. Perhaps the next Beethoven.'

'I can take Brahms, Schubert, Schumann, no problem. Anything but Strauss.' He registered Grace's surprise at the list of composers with whom she had not suspected he was familiar. 'Don't look so shocked. We learnt something called Musical Appreciation for a bit at school. I liked those lessons. I remember once snorting a line of coke during *Fingal's Cave*. Improved it no end.'

'I'm not shocked,' said Grace, tightly. Lucien let go of her hand.

'Of course not. You're never shocked, Mrs H, Gracie. That's what I like about you. I'm your piece of rough and I reckon that's what you like about me. You could teach my mum a thing or two, you could. But I won't put you to the trouble. Probably wouldn't work.' He stood up. 'I'm going to go now before you have to ask. Back tomorrow. Thanks for the coffee.' He put his mug on top of the dishwasher, the single gesture he had in common with William, and left with a speed that suggested he wanted to get away fast, he had urgent business to attend. As always, when he had gone, Grace felt a gust of relief – danger over – but also, at the thought of his return tomorrow, an unnerving sense of elation. Their strange friendship provided a semi-secret. Lucien's visits caused a stir in the plain air of the house for which Grace felt grateful. The excitement of his curious appearances was her one infidelity, as she laughingly admitted to William, who had met Lucien only briefly, so was not able to share the view that the youth was worthy of much consideration. To William, Lucien was merely an uncouth young thug who took up far too much of Grace's time baring his tedious soul. He would have preferred Lucien to be banned from the house. Just as keenly, Grace was determined that he never should be. To begin with, the differences of opinion between husband and wife, concerning Lucien, were obfuscated in a web of the merest suggestion as to how each one felt. But of late even these nervous pretences at argument had petered out. Now, Lucien had become a subject never to be discussed and – for William – a man never to be run into. Hence the need for careful timing, and the *frisson* that provided.

The neighbours in Artisan Road had somehow discovered, many years ago, the emptiness of Grace's afternoons and had 'roped her in' for help of various kinds. She was an active member of Neighbourhood Watch, she accepted invitations to wine and cheese parties whose purpose was to discuss Doing Something about a zebra crossing at the junction of Artisan and Hogarth Roads, and for five years running she had organised a group of local carol singers. As the only pianist among them, every November she arranged rehearsals in the Handle dining room, where the singers could secretly try out a descant. As a result Grace was frequently congratulated on the quality of the singers: their high standard earned them an unusual amount of mince pies, and considerable sums for whichever charity they were raising money.

Raising money for those less fortunate, in fact, was an occupation that Grace found more rewarding than most, provided it was on the simple level of going round with a collecting box. She liked a good excuse to wander up neighbouring drives, pass an eye over the disparate tastes of privet, marigolds, or aubretia surfing over a clump of stones. She found it intriguing to glance through front windows, guess at the lives from the small clue of curtain or ornament. She loved the moment of a front door opening (not a very frequent occurrence, afternoons) and the brief exposure to the different smells of halls: the stands of hunched coats, the glimmer of mirror on dark old walls (redecorating the hall was low on the list of priorities in Artisan Road), the flash of patterned stair carpet, the flutter of High Street candelabras. – Grace's eagerness for this particular form of good work was quickly detected among local charitable organisers, and for years she had been amply furnished with opportunities to walk her way round the neighbourhood armed with a tin, or envelopes that must be first delivered and later collected. It was on a November afternoon almost a year ago while on duty on behalf of the sufferers of muscular dystrophy (an annual appeal designed to catch donors before the Christmas shopping season) that she first met Lucien.

The Firs, a few houses down the street from the Handles, was so frequently unoccupied during the afternoons that Grace had almost given up ringing the bell. She knew nothing of its owners except that they were called Watson and had moved in some three years ago. Mrs Watson, rumoured to be a widow, was not a member of Neighbourhood Watch or any other local organisation. Grace had never seen her, but others claimed to have caught sight of her occasionally driving off early in the morning. A high privet hedge guarded the front of the house from the inquisitive glances of neighbours. After a while the more gregarious folk of Artisan Road assumed Mrs Watson wished to keep to herself, and interest in her apparently low-key life soon waned.

The house itself was one of the more eccentric in the road: the ground floor was built of bright red brick, the upper floors were snow-cemmed pebble-dash. High gables were inlaid with dark beams that pointed in random directions, a reference to the Tudor period probably not designed to be humorous, but which always made Grace smile. The house was an exact replica of a doll's house, made in the forties, she had been given as a child. She had spent many happy hours in that house, easily able to reduce herself to the size of the miniature family that lived there, and joined the life she provided for them through her imagination. Though she had never been inside The Firs, each time she passed it she sensed an inner gust of recognition. She felt warm towards it, and curious.

That particular afternoon there was a light on in an upstairs window. Even on dark winter afternoons Grace had never seen a light before. Encouraged, swinging the collecting tin in hope, she hurried into the gloomy area of tarmacked drive behind the privet hedge, and rang the front doorbell.

After a long time – so long, Grace was about to give up – the door was opened by a young man in pyjama bottoms and a T-shirt. He was unshaven, apparently sleepy. Grace felt immediate awkward guilt. Perhaps she had woken him. He held a Walkman in one hand. The wires of his earplugs flopped over his chest. He looked hard at Grace – a mystified, unseeing look as if he could not quite focus – and was puzzled by her presence.

'What?' he said.

'Sorry if I've disturbed you,' said Grace. 'I've come—'

'Do I know you?'

'No. But I'm a neighbour. I'm collecting for . . .' Suddenly confused, Grace could not remember for whom she was collecting. Was it the blind, the deaf, birds, animals, Bosnia? She looked down at the label on the pretext of rattling the tin. 'Muscular dystrophy.'

'I don't know anyone with muscular dystrophy.'

'Nor do I.'

'I'm Lucien.' He suddenly grinned, unplugged himself from the Walkman. 'Let's see what we can do.' He turned away from Grace to a cluttered hall table. The hall was panelled in dark wood, and narrow. Two shut doors. Very few clues, except for a dying pot plant.

Lucien picked up a woman's crocodile handbag – real, Grace realised. He pulled out a twenty-pound note and handed it to her. Grace hesitated.

'That's an awful lot,' she said.

'She can afford it.'

'Sure?'

'Sure. She's ordered a Mercedes. She's got three diamond rings, champagne stuffing the fridge, everything she bloody wants. She can afford it.'

As Grace still made no move, Lucien stepped towards her and pushed the note clumsily into the tin. So near, he smelt powerfully: a sour-sleep smell, smoke, sweat, garlic.

'Well, if you're sure,' said Grace. 'Thanks very much.'

Lucien moved back into the house.

'Where'd you live, then?'

'Reddish House, just down the road.'

'One with all the leaves?'

'That's right.'

'Think I know it. I don't go out much. What's your name?'

'Grace. Grace Handle.'

Lucien thought about that for a long time. Grace wondered if he would ask the usual question, but reckoned he did not look like the sort of young man whose musical tastes encompassed Handel. She shifted, ready to go.

'Want to come in?'

Grace hesitated again. Curiosity nearly overcame her.

'I'd love to. But I have to get round a lot of houses before it's dark.'

'Yeah, well.' He put back the earplugs. 'Tell you what, I'll drop round to your house one day. We could carry on talking. All right?'

'That would be fine.' Unsure that he could hear her reply, Grace nodded. Lucien shut the door. Grace hurried back to the road swinging the collecting box again, this time almost in triumph. What a very curious encounter, she thought. It would make a good story to tell William at supper that night. The sort of thing he would enjoy.

Later, encouraged by William's laughter, she embellished her description as far as she could without breaking the frail fabric of reality. And next morning at breakfast, when the wild-looking Lucien stuck his head through the kitchen window and said he was coming to join them, William recognised the truth of his wife's story. But reluctant to become involved in neighbourly chat so early, he hurried upstairs without finishing his coffee. Uninvited, Lucien quickly took his chair and would have drunk from William's cup had not Grace thrust a clean one at him.

He looked at her furiously. 'Lobelia's bought a leather coat!' he shouted.

'Who's Lobelia?'

'My bloody mother. The one who gave you twenty pounds. I'm going to cut it up, burn it.'

Several replies flashed through Grace's mind, but she made none of them. Instead she offered sugar, milk, toast and marmalade before Lucien returned to his angry diatribe.

That first morning of ranting was eleven months ago.

2

William Handle was a man constantly amazed by his possessions. It seemed to him unreasonable that he should be the owner of a house and its furniture, a car, a violin of some value, and a cupboard full of clothes. He knew his amazement bordered on the irrational, but having come from a family for whom making ends meet was a daily struggle, he felt it was no wonder that appreciation of security and worldly goods should churn so powerfully within him.

Had it been through his own earnings he had acquired these worldly goods, he sometimes thought, then perhaps he would have felt differently. Pride, perhaps. Or at least some sense of achievement, having been able to provide comfort for his wife. But players in a string quartet, no matter how excellent, do not rank among British high earners. They are not the sort of people who have no need of mortgages. When William and Grace were first married they lived in a rented flat in Finsbury Park, a modest place that became intolerable once Jack was born. The combination of a screaming baby and William practising the violin (four hours a day, then) was more than any of them could bear. But there was no money to move somewhere larger.

When Jack was two Grace's mother died, leaving her daughter the handsome estate she had inherited from her husband, a banker. The Handles immediately sold it, enabling them to buy Reddish House, where they had lived ever since, and intended to remain for the rest of their lives. There was enough income left comfortably to provide for necessities, so William regarded his salary as a bonus, not really needed, but useful for luxuries (a new lawnmower, the occasional bottle of good port, a generous pension fund). There being quite enough money for their modest needs, the Handles had little interest in it. Unlike most of their friends, it was not a subject that concerned them.

Buying Reddish House was their only major investment, and one they never regretted. Artisan Road ran through an agreeable part of a suburb of a large town west of London. The artisans after whom it was named may have built modest cottages in what was once a country lane. No sign of them now. The road was a collection of very disparate houses, only a few of which were true to their own period. The Handles' house was one of these: a solid Edwardian building upon which no one had experimented with a Tudor addition or a Georgian front door. Windows were deeply set in the blocks of pale grey stone, though the charm of the stone itself was mostly invisible beneath a thick growth of Virginia creeper, from which the house had taken its name.

William's father was dead by the time they bought the house – a mercy, really, he sometimes thought, for Archibald Handle would not have approved. A frustrated architect himself, he would have preferred his son and daughter-in-law to spend the money on something a little more experimental, something of their age. Ideally, he would have liked them to commission him to design and build something for them. William often imagined what they might have been spared: a glass box with no chimneys, roof of curved steel wings to give the impression the whole structure could become airborne at any moment.

William's father was an architect with ideas so far ahead of his time that he found it impossible to find an employer to share his vision. The only time he worked as part of a team in an office was a disaster. Within weeks he was sacked for urging others to let their imaginations soar, making them restless. He was an unwanted influence. It was unlikely any solid firm of architects would wish to employ him, he was warned. And the warning proved right. Archibald was forced to work freelance for the Council, who kept him under a tight rein. Bus shelters, they kept requesting. Archibald did he best. He sent in designs of the most imaginative bus shelters any council had ever been quick to reject: and in the end produced what the great unenlightened, as he called them, wanted, for pitiful remuneration. The great sadness of his life was that he was never commissioned to design a single private house. The hundreds of ideas and detailed drawings, all filed, went to waste. 'I was never discovered,' were his dying words to William.

On the morning of the concert in Northampton William's departure was delayed by thoughts of his father, combined with appreciative thoughts of Reddish House. He stood just outside the front door fingering leaves of the Virginia creeper, feeling the cold stone beneath them. He felt oddly reluctant to be on his way. What should have been a completely routine day – morning rehearsal at Grant's house, on to Northampton for an early supper before the concert – held none of the comforts that anticipated routine normally provided. Why? He didn't know.

Grace hurried out of the house carrying his violin case. She pretended she had not seen him fingering the Virginia creeper – he was always touching inanimate things, William: making sure they were real; testing their solidity; ascertaining they were not going to dissolve – at least, that's what she imagined.

'You've forgotten . . .?'

'No I hadn't, my Ace. Would I forget my violin? Have I ever?' He slung it on the back seat of the car. In truth he had forgotten it. First time ever.

'So.' Grace crossed her arms under her breasts to make a comfortable shelf for her rapidly beating heart. When Lucien arrived this morning she had had to tell him he must go – William was prowling about, preparing to leave at ten thirty. She had told Lucien he could come back later, but he had left so grumpily she doubted he would, and the equilibrium of her morning had vanished. 'Your plans? I've forgotten.'

'Rehearsal, concert Northampton, home.'

'Late?'

The infinitesimal pause, as William got into the car, served to accommodate a thought so alien it frightened him. It was also too vague to see any clear meaning.

'Hope not,' he said. 'No reason why I should be. Any hold-ups and I'll ring.' This was the comforting thing he always said as he left. Grace pushed her head through the open window. They kissed. William, Grace saw, had his determined-to-concentrate-on-the-road face, which pleased her, for he was not a driver attuned to the possibility of others' foolishness, or indeed to his own. She watched him back into the bush of spotted laurel, which had suffered badly over the years – he had never mastered the art of reversing. He gave her an affectionate nod, obeying her instructions never to take one hand off the steering wheel unless strictly necessary. God bless him, Grace said to herself.

Once William had left behind the perils of the town, and was safely on a dual carriageway where he could meander along at forty mph without annoying anyone, he switched on the radio. He found the station that played the 'popular' classics that usually he avoided. This morning, as always, it was playing gymkhana music: marches, the stuff of pageants and jubilees, tum-te-tee-tum. This morning William needed that sort of crude rhythm to jerk him back to normality. For even now, three miles along the familiar road to Grant's house near Aylesbury, blessed ordinariness eluded him. His nervous apprehension was increased by the fact he could not tell from whence it came. (People laughed at him when he used the word *whence*: but he liked it and had no intention of dropping it because it had become archaic.)

It was nothing to do with Bonnie Morse, he had decided while shaving – having spent some troubled hours of the night wondering if she might be the cause. His new viola player, once he had got hold of her on the telephone, had sounded so ordinary, so practical, down to earth, efficient, shouting against dogs barking in the

background, he was convinced her incredible mouth was a figment
of his imagination, and the ideas that had lapped at him through
the rain the other night were no more than a trick of the mind
brought on by the process of ageing. All the same, the conversation, concerning her familiarity with the fourth movement of
Schubert's Quartet in A minor coming up in a week's time, hadn't
quite stilled him. He rang her again not an hour later. Almost at
Aylesbury, he reran the conversation in his head.

'Bonnie, William Handle here again – so sorry, but blow me if I
forgot to give you instructions how to get to Grant. Bit complicated . . .' At previous rehearsals she had come by taxi. For some
reason she had decided to drive today, which gave rise to William's
anxiety about her finding the way. So often he assumed his own
worries were shared by others.

A fractional brush of a sigh came down the receiver, he thought.

'Mr Handle—'

'Oh I say, do call me William—'

'Well, William, thanks a lot but Grant did me a little map.
Doesn't look too difficult. Think I'll be fine.'

'Right, good.' Grant was an unmarried man, some fifteen years
younger than William. 'See you, then.'

'See you.'

No, it was almost definitely nothing to do with Bonnie Morse.

When William reached the driveway of Grant's house – a converted barn – he saw he was the first to arrive. No sign of Bonnie's
little red car, or Rufus's very old Morgan. He switched off the radio
and contemplated the legs of his new corduroy trousers. They
were the colour of ripe young wheat, and soft to the touch. Grace
had given them to him two Christmases ago. As with every new
garment, he had put them to mature in his cupboard for a while, to
get used to the idea of them before wearing them for the first time.
This morning, unpremeditated, he had chosen to put them on for
no apparent reason, and already he liked them. Good trousers:
Grace had impeccable taste.

Grant had lit the Norwegian stove – which he did only on

rehearsal days, alone he liked the cold – and was making coffee. He had lived in the barn, inherited from his parents years before the converting of barns became fashionable, for as long as William could remember. Both Grant's parents had been musicians. He had spent many evenings of his boyhood listening to them playing, with a group of friends, far into the night round a paraffin stove. It had never occurred to him to be anything other than a musician, though for some time he could not decide which string instrument to make his own. Then by chance, at thirteen, he found an old seventy-eight record of Dvořák's Cello Concerto, which he played on the ancient radiogram (his parents lived in an unwitting time warp into which most modern technology was given no chance), and the decision was made for him.

The cello happened to be an appropriate instrument for Grant, for he was a large man, six foot two with the shoulders of a rugger player. He carried his instrument around as easily as the others carried their violins. His only problem was chairs: the kind provided on concert platforms were uncomfortable, perilous to his massive size. Several had not been able to withstand his weight, and had collapsed beneath him mid-concert. Grant's seating problems had become one of Elmtree's running jokes: something they would have to either explain to Bonnie Morse or – perhaps a better alternative – let her see for herself.

The barn itself was also appropriate to Grant's proportions. Moving across its considerable width, beneath its high vaulted ceiling, he gave the impression of being a man of normal height. William and Rufus and Andrew (no, no longer Andrew, alas) were all dwarfed by the building, as are men in a cathedral. Behind Grant's back the others kept up a barrage of mild complaint about his poor housekeeping – the cold, the chipped paint, the discomfort, the cracked china and barren fridge. They derided his general lack of appreciation of the barn's potential, which needed – as they often told him – a woman's touch. But they also greatly appreciated the space the barn afforded them to rehearse. Without it, their lives would have been far more complicated and its deficiencies, which by now they had grown used to, were of less importance than its advantages.

William let himself in. Grant had cleared a space at the chaotic table to mark a score.

'See I'm the first,' said William.

'Surprise, surprise.' (William was always the first.) 'Rufus has just rung from some garage.'

'What is it this time?'

'The fan belt. Says it'll be OK but he'll be fifteen minutes late.'

'Ah.'

Rufus's Morgan was responsible for several late arrivals a week. But such was his devotion to his ailing car that consideration for his fellow players came second to his determination not to swap it for something more reliable. He and his violin (his wife refused ever to travel in the car) set out on every journey knowing there was a high chance of trouble before reaching their destination, but were never deterred. The Morgan was the excitement in Rufus's life which he could not deny himself. The others, he was glad to say, had come to understand this, and had learnt to accommodate his erratic timing. They had persuaded Rufus always to allow himself an hour in hand when travelling to a concert, and on icy days to go by train or get a lift from one of the others. This alleviated, minimally, the sense of general anxiety on his behalf. As for rehearsals – if ten o'clock was decided upon it was understood that, depending on the Morgan's troubles, ten thirty, or even eleven, would be the actual starting time.

William wandered to the far end of the barn where four music stands were placed in a semi-circle round the stove. (The other players guessed that Grant never approached that end of the barn except at rehearsal time. His entire kingdom seemed to centre round the large cluttered table.) An autumn sun through the barn's tall windows lit up their silvery aluminium frames: they glittered like a small gathering of ghostly trees, thought William. He sat in his usual chair – the chairs, too, were never moved – and took his music from its case. This he arranged lovingly on the stand, bending back the bottom corners, which had been bent a thousand times before, for easy turning. Again, glancing at his knees, he thought how fine were his new trousers.

'The girl,' said Grant. 'Thought she was pretty good, first time out.'

'Not bad at all.'

'She'll shape up quickly.'

'Poor old Andrew. Yorkshire.'

'She said she knows the Schubert pretty well, but I daresay we ought to run through it before we get on to the rest.'

'Daresay we better.'

From time to time William reflected on the nature of his cellist – the puzzle being why he was still adamantly a bachelor. William considered Grant eligible in the conventional sense. He was the owner of a barn and a large (if elderly) car. He was talented, hard working, genial, apparently good looking. Why had he never found, in all the girls who pursued him, one with whom the idea of permanency appealed? Sometimes William would worry about his friend's old age. Grant was in his mid-thirties – surely ripe for settling down, having children? He professed a love of children. 'One day' he sometimes said.

Once William had questioned one of Grant's girlfriends about his ubiquitous appeal. She had been puzzled that William could not see it. 'He makes me laugh – wonderful mimic, does a brilliant William Handle – and he listens. I mean *really* listens. Never pretends. He's rather wise, too.' William had always been aware of Grant's talent as a raconteur – he had entertained the other players on many an evening in a hotel bar far from home – although his 'brilliant Handle' imitation was news, and William had less evidence than the girl of Grant's impressive listening. He so often had his head in a thriller when he was not studying a score, or doing *The Times* crossword (at which he was so good the others had given up competing). But certainly when Bonnie had been enthusing about some exotic Mexican stew, Grant had been listening very hard. Perhaps when it came to his fellow players his sympathetic bending of an ear was not much in evidence simply because, after so many years of habitual short-hand speaking, William, Rufus and Andrew did not furnish him with anything very compelling to listen to.

Rufus came through the door then, smiling. Small triumphs concerning his car always put him in a good mood.

'Sorry, gentlemen, sorry,' he said, 'but what a piece of luck. Fan belt gave up the ghost right beside a repair garage where they actually managed to deal with it straight away. Anyhow, coffee on, Grant? I'm cold.'

'Help yourself. Kettle's not long boiled.'

Rufus, on his way to the stove, put half a packet of digestive biscuits on Grant's table.

'Contribution,' he said.

'Thanks.' Grant did not look up from the score to see the object of his gratitude. He knew quite well if it was from Rufus it would be half a packet of something – the other half having been eaten in the car to keep out the cold. From William it would be slabs of chocolate. Andrew used sometimes to bring his wife's homemade bread and pâté to raise the standard of the average rehearsal lunch – they would miss that. But whatever the offering, Grant was never shamed into producing anything beyond instant coffee for the all-important elevenses.

'The girl, Bonnie, she was rather good, wasn't she?' said Rufus. 'I've been thinking about her. Potential, I thought.'

William, licking his finger to ease the bending of the fragile pages, cast him a look. Rufus was the oldest – just – of the players. Lately he had had trouble with his bones. His back had begun to curve, his shoulders to hunch.

'She said she'd be here on time. I sent her a map,' said Grant.

William's look now swung in Grant's direction. To have sent her a map meant he must have spoken to her, arranged to fax it to her from some shop – naturally the barn did not run to a fax machine. (A telephone had only been installed, at the others' insistence, ten years ago.) A picture came to William's mind: Grant, fax in hand, hurrying down Aylesbury High Street. Normally, Grant never hurried – and indeed perhaps he hadn't hurried with the fax. Perhaps that was an inaccurate figment of William's imagination, this unusual morning. All the same, it was a faintly troubling thought.

Ten minutes later the three men were seated in their usual places, mugs of instant coffee on the floor beside them, tuning up. Notes adjusted to perfection, they put their instruments down again. Looked about them.

'Wonder what we should do,' said Grant, dully.

'Plainly your map wasn't up to scratch.'

Grant ignored this. Over the years it had become an accepted practice to pay no attention to pointless remarks that each one of them made from time to time.

'Expect she'll turn up,' said William. His heels were quietly drumming on the floor. 'Last thing she said to me was she'd be here on time, punctual by nature, not to worry.' William imparted this information with another stern look at Grant. The cellist should know that he was not the only one to have been talking to Bonnie. They sat in silence, then. Waiting.

Bonnie arrived at five past eleven. She knocked on the door but ran in before Grant had time to open it – trailing a backwash of cold air, cheeks the colour of cranberries, carrying a transparent bag of fudge. William observed that Grant stopped by the table, put a hand on its surface as if to steady himself. William and Rufus rose to their feet, bows and violins dithering in the air. William, confused, looked down at his music. The slight lowering of his head, he realised, Bonnie might take for a kind of minor bow, the sort of thing that would be expected of him in the unlikely event of his being knighted for his contribution to the musical world. The thought further confused him. But Bonnie was too caught up in her apologies to misinterpret William's almost invisible gesture, or the sudden rush of russet blood to Rufus's normally pale cheek.

'So, so sorry,' she was saying. 'Everything went wrong. Battery flat, had to get to the station, would have missed the train if I'd stopped to ring you' – here she looked definitely at Grant – 'then the taxi got lost getting here . . . I'm so, so sorry.'

Unaccustomed to such a profusion of apologies, each of the players found himself uneasy. As they struggled for words to assure her she had in no way inconvenienced their morning, they found their eyes following the airborne arcs of her hand in which she clutched the bag of fudge tied with blue ribbon.

'Peace offering,' said Bonnie. 'Please accept. Home-made.'

William saw the sudden jut of Rufus's jaw – a defensive movement he sometimes made if he felt himself to be outdone. Bonnie's fudge had put his own contribution in the shade.

'Thanks very much,' said Grant. 'That'll be nice with our lunch break. So sorry about your car – Rufus often has the same sort of trouble with his. Now, if you don't mind, I think perhaps we should make a start . . .'

Grant, as host in his own barn, sometimes acted as if he was leader of the players, too. William understood this, and had never minded. (Once they arrived at a concert hall Grant made up for his homeground bossiness by remaining absolutely silent on all matters except for the worry of his chair.) But today William cursed himself. He should have been quicker, come up with a command as soon as the girl had stopped twirling her wretched fudge in the air. She ought to be in no doubt, right from the start, who was in charge. Should her loyalties become divided, that could be fatal.

'Here, here.' William's agreement with Grant was so quiet he doubted Bonnie heard. She came bounding across, light on her feet for one of so rounded a figure. Reaching William, she gave a light tap to his knee, touching the soft pile of the new corduroy. She smiled at him alone.

'You remind me of my dad,' she said. 'The trousers.'

Moments later William managed to give the signal to start playing. They were off: the Schubert, for Bonnie's sake. He closed his eyes against motes of dust that dithered on a sunbeam. Also, he felt it safer not to be able to see the faint crease of flesh round Bonnie's wrist, the bounce of her fringe as her head moved and the cushion of her thigh beneath her long wool skirt. Soon, he was lost in the music.

Looking back to that autumn day of the rehearsal in the barn with Bonnie Morse, William remembered only a few things, but they were sharp-edged. He could not recollect, after the Schubert, what they played, only that they had played with more vigour than usual. Then, at the lunch break, the tension that Bonnie had caused earlier seemed to have dissolved. Her willingness to do whatever was suggested to improve a bar, or a passage, had impressed them all. She was plainly a stickler for detail, and her touch had a quality they all recognised. None of them went so far as to give her a word of praise (each one planned to do this privately, later). But if she had not been so impressive the atmosphere, when finally they put down their instruments, would have been very different.

While they ate their packed lunches, Grant turned on the portable radio so that they could indulge in their customary scoffing of the programme that played lunchtime classical choices. They had all sent in dozens of requests, none of which were ever granted, being too esoteric, presumably, for the average lunchtime listener. William remembered Bonnie laughing as the three men sneered at the Strauss waltz that thumped about them.

'Did you know,' said William, turning to Bonnie, 'that the *Viennese waltzes* release a peculiar chemical in the stomach? We're all made queasy.'

'William has his theories,' explained Grant.

Bonnie confessed that she had once sent in a request and it had been played.

'Something so horribly popular they would never have turned it down,' she said. 'Something that I love, as a matter of fact. But I shan't ever tell you what it was.'

'*Liebestraum*,' said Grant.

'*The Gold and Silver Waltz*,' said Rufus.

Bonnie shook her head at both of them. William, not wanting to be wrong too, said nothing. Bonnie swung her ankle as she ate an untidy tomato sandwich, enjoying their curiosity. Lunch breaks were never that merry in Andrew's day, William reflected. Then, the four male players read their papers and did not bother to speak more than necessary.

Most unusual of all, that day, was Grant's producing a bottle of chilled wine (he normally only ran to this extravagance at Christmas). After a couple of glasses, the wide light of the barn suddenly dimmed – it must have been mid-afternoon. William remembered that very clearly, the way the light gave a seriousness to Bonnie's tilted chin resting on her viola. Then, there was the confusion of setting off for Northampton. William offered Bonnie a lift in his car. But she had already agreed to go with Grant.

'Thanks very much all the same, William. Have another piece of fudge, why don't you?'

When had Grant had the chance to ask her? They had all been together all the time. Except for the moment when Grant had taken the wine from the fridge and Bonnie, joining him at the kitchen end of the barn to be helpful, had reached for glasses from the shelf. Grant must have acted with a speed that William would never have guessed was within his capability. Lust the spur, he thought, angrily shutting his violin case. His own journey to Northampton was more than usually hazardous as he raged against Grant's perfectly reasonable invitation to Bonnie – after all, he was much closer to her age than either William or Rufus – and her friendly refusal, offered with a careless shrug as if it was not the slightest matter who drove her to Northampton. What was it that had so tilted the day to an angle he did not recognise, and left him in a perturbed state? William could not answer his own questions. When he arrived at the hall he sat in his parked car for a while, trying to calm himself before he faced the others.

Sometimes, when William was out and she was quite sure he would not be back for a long time, Grace would go to the upright piano in the dining room and play. The day of the Northampton concert she was able to get down to her book earlier than usual, because Lucien, having been turned away due to William's presence downstairs in the morning, did not return. Grace was relieved. He put a kind of pressure on the days that so often made her uneasy. Though when it came to the weighing up she knew she would miss the perverse *frisson* if he never came again.

So often, since he had first come round to breakfast, Grace pondered on why it was Lucien had become such an important part of her life. Sometimes it occurred to her he represented qualities she would have appreciated in a son – a man with the vigour and charm that Jack had always lacked. Sometimes she thought he was the lover she had never had in her youth: wild, unpredictable, not to be relied on, but the kind of love-object who keeps the adrenalin of hope aflame. Dear William had never been like that: solid, reliable, kindly, he belonged to the school of understated romance in which silent appreciation replaces surprise roses – indeed, surprises of any kind. Then, Lucien was both alarming and fascinating in equal measure – the first man in Grace's life ever either to fascinate by rough ways, or alarm. He flirted with her in that safe way which those of different generations sometimes adopt – just enough to make her think what might have been in another time, another place. He flattered her, too, which Grace would have scorned had she not detected beneath the flattery a real admiration. And in her restricted, quiet, conventional life, in which her own artistic efforts brought little satisfaction, and earned scant interest from William, Lucien represented a sympathetic soul to whom, Grace liked to think, she was the sort of mother he would have loved, but never had. The unease he caused her was mostly far outweighed by the pleasure. For in his presence (and this was perhaps the most crucial reason for her attachment) Grace experienced the curious feeling that life had speeded up. 'It's all happening,' Lucien would sometimes say, in the stillness of the kitchen. Although absolutely nothing was taking place, Grace believed Lucien was the centre of unimaginable events beyond her experience, which gave her a vicarious thrill. So for all their actual lack of action, his visits were a kind of magic carpet upon which Grace, for an hour or so, could take leave of her own mundane life.

She began to play a Liszt *Consolation*. Liszt was a composer of whom William – like Brahms and Schumann, he was glad to note – did not approve. 'All right for lightweight fireworks,' he would say, 'a popstar of his age, nothing very serious.' But Grace loved his music, and played it secretly. Lulled by the *Consolation*, she moved her stiff fingers into the first watery bars of *Un Sospiro*. As she played, the smells of the room came powerfully to her: pepper, damp carpet, the leaden smell of old gravy which had infiltrated walls and curtains. Often she wished that, like William, she had a music room of her own.

A sudden awareness of a presence in the room made her break off. She swivelled round on the music stool, whose split leather seat crackled beneath her. It was Lucien. He sat on the polished table swinging his legs. Grinning. Very unusual. Their meetings nearly always began with some burst of rage on his part.

'How long have you been here?'

'Few minutes.'

'You've never come before in the afternoon.'

'Like I told you, I can surprise. Do you mind?'

Grace thought for a moment. Her afternoon at the piano was now blasted.

'No,' she said.

'I didn't know you could play.'

'I can't, really. Any more. I just stumble through a few old-remembered pieces.'

'Sounded pretty good to me.'

'I'm afraid it's not.' She almost smiled. Lucien was fiddling with the sea salt in its crystal bowl. He dug into it with the miniature spoon, making small hills which he then flattened and began all over again. 'As a child I was mad keen. I'd practise up to three hours a day, getting up early so as to get in the time before lessons started. What I really enjoyed was tackling pieces way too difficult for me. It took me six months to get through *The Hungarian Rhapsody.*' She turned her back on Lucien, played the first few notes with one finger. 'I did it in the end, though never really well.'

'Sorry about this,' said Lucien, when Grace turned back to him again. He had spilt a good deal of salt, was pinching it up between thumb and finger to put it back in the bowl. 'Did you have a good teacher, or something?'

'Terrifying. A Miss Spark. My hands would tremble so much I could scarcely play, so she'd yell and scream and beat the piano with my notebook full of furious instructions she'd made in the last lesson – which made it worse, of course. But somehow she pushed me to get things right in the end, inspire me to go on, be better. I suppose she was a sad old thing really. Not much in her life besides teaching dull pupils, or feeding the birds in her cottage in the Malvern hills. When she got angry, which was several times a day, she went purple as a damson – the colour took hours to drain away, so you hardly ever saw her normal skin.'

Lucien smiled. 'Wow,' he said. 'I wouldn't have put up with all that shit.'

'It was all worth it because when she sat down to play – various pieces for me to choose from – I knew why I wanted to go on. When she played, all the pent-up indignation vanished. Her crimpy little fingers whirled along with such joy I was left speechless, time after time. Also, the piano I learnt on was marvellous, the best I've ever played. Steinway grand. It had a little silver plaque nailed to the lid saying *George Bernard Shaw and Edward Elgar played duets on this piano.* They'd been friends of the headmistress in her youth.'

'Wow,' said Lucien again. 'The company you keep. Play something else.'

'What would you like? I've a very limited repertoire these days.'

'Couldn't give a toss.'

Grace spun quickly round and began a Chopin nocturne. Lucien stopped playing with the salt. When the piece came to an end he said: 'Pretty good. You shouldn't have given it up. You could have been a concert pianist, couldn't you?'

Grace closed the lid of the piano.

'No. Never. My last ever lesson with Miss Spark, just before I left school, she asked me what the future had in store. I said I'd like to be a professional pianist. She kept quiet for a very long time, all this plum colour rushing to her face again – her arms, her chest, her hands, everywhere. I thought she was going to burst. Then she said: "If you want my honest opinion, Grace, I don't think you should raise your hopes too high in that direction. You work very hard, you're very able and you feel the music strongly. But you haven't got that extra whatever it is that makes one pianist tower above others so powerfully that the whole world wants to hear him or her play." Then she said: "I hope you don't mind my saying this, but I had the same ambition as you when I was your age. But I knew quite positively there was no hope. I was an accomplished pianist, but I never had that extra God-given talent that you need to make it as a concert pianist . . . So I decided to teach. And, well, it's been a pleasure most of the time, though you might not think so the way I've raged against you to push you as far as I knew you could go . . ." I thanked her for her advice, and took it. She was right. After college I began to teach. I was a teacher when I met William.'

Lucien slipped off the table. He patted Grace's shoulder. She had rarely known him so mild.

'I'd never have guessed. – Are you going to make me a cup of tea?'

'Sorry: I've been going on.' In the kitchen,114 she began to make the tea. 'Once we were married, I gave it up. William tried to dissuade me, but he didn't try very hard. Besides, I was keen to get on with something that would make use of my love of botany. Quite by chance I found I was a reasonably accomplished flower painter, too.'

Lucien looked at her, struck by the shadow of bitterness in her voice.

'You're great, Grace,' he said.

Grace laughed. She brought tea things to the table.

'How's the new girl doing with the Quartet?'

'I don't remember telling you about her.'

'Well you did.'

Grace settled herself opposite Lucien.

'I believe she's doing well. They seem to think they chose the right one. This is only her second concert tonight. What about you? Why aren't you raging on as usual?'

'I'm never angry when Lobelia's away.'

'Where is she?'

'Don't know. Didn't ask. She's back tomorrow or the next day. Wouldn't be surprised if she's off with this new bloke she's seeing.'

'Who's he?'

'How do I know? Only saw him once. She didn't exactly introduce us, did she? Didn't go that far. Tall, fat, baldish. Revolting, I thought. Still I'd be grateful to anyone who'd take her off my hands. In pharmaceuticals, he is, she said. High up in pharmaceuticals. Whatever that means.' He ate a chocolate biscuit. 'Anyhow, I'm starting work tomorrow.'

'Oh? That's good.'

'Walking dogs round the park every afternoon. Some old biddy's prepared to pay me a tenner a time. What d'you think?'

'Well: why not?'

'Only till something comes up. I mean, better to walk earning than to walk not earning.'

'Quite.'

'You're a good woman, Grace. You don't judge me.'

'I've no reason to judge you.'

'I don't want to be judged. Not till I've got it together. In my own time.' He suddenly stood up, the charm fleeing from his face. His eyes had shrunk. His hands shook – he stuffed them into his pocket when he saw Grace noticed. Defensively he looked round the room as if suspicious its contents were about to attack him. Grace wondered if he was going to pick up a plate and throw it. He had done that once before, no explanation.

'I'm off, things to see to,' he said. 'Thanks for the music.'

He left behind half-drunk tea, tranquillity scattered. His sudden switch from calm to inflamed had unnerved Grace. She had no heart to return to the piano, or the book, or even the ironing. She counted the hours till William's return, and tried to put Lucien from her mind.

The Elmtree Quartet arrived in the hall in Northampton – originally a Methodist chapel, a place they had often played – more or less together. Long ago they had abandoned the idea of driving in convoy, an arrangement which would have exacerbated William's neurosis about driving. At one time there had been discussion about buying an estate car large enough to accommodate players and instruments, so that they could all travel together. But what with the financial outlay that would involve, and the arguments it would cause about who should drive, and which was the best route, nobody's heart was in the idea. They were used to the eccentric arrangement of each one being responsible for himself. Though it often caused anxiety and frustration, it was doubtful now that it would ever change.

William always dreaded the seating rehearsal part of a concert day, the assessing of platform, space and general comfort. It was when Grant (silently) and Rufus (muttering) became their most disgruntled. Andrew used never to complain, though his tight face sometimes conveyed the pain that a minor imperfection of the location caused him. William himself, too, kept his silence for as long as he could. When his patience ran out, and he could be bothered, he would berate them. But William was not a man for confrontation, and his scolding was so mild it was scarcely noticeable. By the time he had mustered energy to chide the grumblers, they had taken up their instruments, were ready to go despite the many impediments to their performance. It was all part of the Elmtree ritual with which they were familiar, and acted out from habit several times a week.

In the Northampton hall Grant observed the utter uselessness of the seats the moment he clumped on to the stage. He picked up the chair in his place, shook it violently as if it was a disobedient dog.

'Remember? Same trouble last time, last March. How do they expect a man to play a cello from a thing like this? Bloody ridiculous.' He banged it down on the floor. It made an awkward squawk. The noise alerted Rufus to possible problems. He was the one with the keenest ear for sound quality, and with a small tilt of his head, raising his best ear towards the ceiling, would hold himself responsible for judging the depth of trouble that faced them. Today, curiously, eyes pinched, mouth a short line of disapproval, he said nothing.

Bonnie picked up her own chair, turned to Grant.

'Would you like to swap with mine? It looks a mite heavier.'

Grant glared at her.

'They're all the same. Don't worry. I'll sort something out. Always the same effing problem. Total lack of vision among the chair-providing classes.'

Bonnie laughed and took her place.

'Calm down, Grant,' said William, who had no wish to appear unhelpful. 'I'll get Bob to find you something better.'

Grant looked at William in amazement.

'What's all this? Coming to my rescue so soon?' He turned to Bonnie. 'He usually lets me sweat it out a bit.'

Bonnie smiled: polite rather than amused.

'Well,' said William, mildness concealing his fury. Such disloyalty from Grant was surprising. And now Rufus, he could see, was about to erupt, too.

'Problem here,' pointed out Rufus.

'Oh God,' said William.

Rufus ran a finger along the lip of his music stand.

'Edge seems to have been a bit damaged in transit. Know anything about it, Grant?'

Grant, being the only one with a car big enough to accommodate them, was the one who transported all four mahogany stands. At the end of every concert each player took his stand apart and put it in its cover with infinite care. Grant loaded the bundle into his boot with equal attention, and unloaded them at each destination. He felt keenly the responsibility of this job, and carried it out in a manner that meant scant possibility of damage. All the same, Rufus could not quell his suspicions. Never a concert day passed when he did not examine his precious stand with the eye of one who suspected it might have suffered mysterious harm.

'Have to admit I did take a corner at thirty-five mph,' said Grant, seriously. 'I suppose that could have been the cause.'

William saw him wink at Bonnie. Rufus snorted, unamused.

'Come here,' he said. 'Feel.'

Grant moved over to Rufus. He enjoyed indulging the old boy. Rufus ran a finger along the edge of the stand's lip.

'Pretty rough,' said Rufus, 'or am I imagining it?'

Grant, enjoying his own solemnity, also ran a finger along the wooden lip.

'Very rough, I'd say. Bound to be a distraction.'

'Bit of sandpaper might do it.' Rufus was now worried. 'Anyone got a piece of sandpaper?'

'No one,' said William, 'has a piece of sandpaper. Come along, now.'

'Bob's bound to—'

'When I ask Bob to find a better chair for Grant, I'll also ask him if he can find a piece of sandpaper for you.' William marvelled at his own patience.

Grant had turned back to Bonnie.

'Normally,' he was saying, 'Rufus's problem is the width of his ledge. Seems to be OK for the rest of us, but not for Rufus. Won't hold his pencil—'

'My mute's the problem,' said Rufus, 'not to mention my resin.'

Grant looked at Bonnie. 'You may have noticed that while mutes and resin traumatise Rufus on concert days, at rehearsals it's not only pencils, but also the size of the erasers.' He spoke with mock seriousness. 'We do what we can. We give him the narrowest little erasers we can find by the dozen – birthdays, Christmas, Elmtree anniversaries –'

'They're no good,' said Rufus.

'He still has trouble,' said Grant.

'Come along, gentlemen,' said William again. Out of the corner of his eye he observed Bonnie was looking bemused.

Grant took his seat. He leant back, slung his huge legs apart, squirmed in a way designed to test the strength of the chair. There was an instant crack, a splaying of four spindly legs. Grant flung himself to the ground like a ham actor in a minor tragedy. From the floor, he looked up at Bonnie.

'What did I tell you? Bloody stupid chair.'

'Now come *along*, gentlemen, time's getting on,' said William. He was exasperated by the amusement Grant was causing Bonnie. He called for Bob, the deputy manager of the hall, who was unstacking chairs for the audience. While a new chair was being found, and a piece of sandpaper for Rufus, Grant continued to lie beached on the floor, propped up on one arm, looking up at Bonnie confident of the attractive figure he made – a sort of playboy pose, he imagined. Ridiculous. Undignified. Very unlike Grant. And indeed William, who felt his own sensitivities were more acute than those of his sudden show-off cellist, saw that Bonnie, behind her polite look of interest, was more embarrassed than amused.

'Get up, Grant,' he brought himself to say at last.

Grant lumbered up on to his new, firmer chair, and finding it adequate made no further comment. His sense of humour, usually forthcoming in difficult circumstances, did not ever extend to the matter of chairs that failed him in concert halls all over Europe. Perhaps it was to cover his grumpiness before Bonnie that he had gone through all the foolish acting up on the floor.

As Rufus continued to dab at the offending lip of his stand with a small piece of sandpaper, which in his unskilled hands had no effect, William allowed himself an intense look at Bonnie. She was wearing jeans. He must have seen earlier in the day, just didn't notice. Jeans and a T-shirt. Well, fine for rehearsing. But the thing that struck him was her footwear: red peeptoe sandals through which twinkled toenails painted a metallic green. The sort of shoes in old wartime photographs of forties film stars. But the nail polish . . . Would Bonnie be changing her footwear for the performance?

William felt faintly sick. It occurred to him that he had never had a talk about sartorial matters to Bonnie. At the audition none of them had thought to ask what sort of dress she had in mind that would be in keeping with their own white ties. Grace had berated him for that. You must insist on a dress code, she had said. The girl could turn up in anything. But at the rehearsals with Bonnie before their first concert together, William had not found an opportunity to bring up the subject. Had Bonnie, then, sported her saucy peeptoes, he might have been jolted to enquire what sort of evening dress she was planning. But at those rehearsals she had appeared in black trousers and black suede boots (he remembered thinking they looked rather expensive) and the matter of dress had gone from his mind. At the concert in Slough she appeared in so ordinary a long black dress he could remember nothing about it, and the whole problem of possible sartorial awkwardness dissolved.

Now, he saw a message in the outrageous shoes. The new viola player seemed to be saying that she had no intention of conforming to convention, and every intention of wearing what she liked. William swallowed. He hated the idea of having to curb her, perhaps argue with her, or even cause offence by criticising something that was not strictly within the bounds of his responsibility. But the Elmtree, with its reputation, could not afford to be made to look foolish by the choice of its new member's shoes . . . No, he would have to take her aside. Put it to her gently. God forbid.

His eyes rose from her feet. Her chin rested eagerly on her instrument with a certain tilt that was becoming familiar. She reminded him of a winter robin, beady-eyed, waiting for a worm.

'I think we should begin, gentlemen,' he said, then cursed himself for his mistake. He could no longer refer to his fellow players as gentlemen, with the addition of Bonnie, for fear of being accused of some sort of *ism*. He hoped he hadn't offended Bonnie. Oh dear – perhaps he better not have the shoe talk after all . . . 'Let's begin with the Britten,' he floundered.

'Wretched sandpaper hasn't helped at all,' said Rufus, ruffling through his music. Several erasers fell to the floor.

'I'll give this chair just one chance,' muttered Grant.

'Ready, everyone?' William glanced round. Bonnie tossed back her fringe so that for a second William saw that her large eyes were almost colourless: ice eyes, he thought. But not ice hard. They crinkled as she returned his look with the smallest indication of a smile. She did not seem at all offended by the reference to gentlemen. Perhaps she hadn't noticed. Perhaps there would be no need to apologise. Perhaps . . .

He gave the nod. They began to play.

At seven o'clock Grace was about to draw the curtains when the telephone rang. It was Jack. He usually rang once a week, duty call.

'Oh, Jack.' Grace wondered if he could detect the lack of excitement in her voice. She had never outgrown her youthful sense of anticipation when the telephone rang unexpectedly. When the caller was not some vaguely imagined surprise, she was guilty of a flatness in her voice.

'I see in my diary it's Dad's birthday tomorrow.'

'That's right.' Her own present to William was wrapped and hidden, waiting to be placed on the breakfast table before he came down in the morning.

'I was thinking: celebration. How about we come to one of his concerts with you, then all go on for something to eat?'

Grace paused.

'Mother?' Since he was a small child Jack had always addressed Grace as Mother, though behind her back he referred to her as Mum. Recently his girlfriend Laurel had discovered from her therapist that this was some form of protest. 'Mother, are you there?'

'I was thinking. I mean, why not? Except you suggested the same thing last year, you remember, and somehow it never came off.'

'I had to go to Amsterdam.'

'So you did.'

'Well, how about it? I'd be willing. Over to you.'

'I believe there's something next week in Ealing. That'd be quite convenient for you.'

'Fine: any night.' Considering the exciting life as a chartered accountant that Jack sometimes described, Grace was always puzzled by his lack of engagements in the evenings. 'Check it with Dad and get back to me.'

Grace paused again. She had a sudden impression that there was someone at the window. She turned. It was almost dark. No one.

'I will,' she said. 'But don't be surprised if he's reluctant. You know how nervous he gets if you're in the audience. He knows you've no patience with the Quartet's music.'

Jack laughed. 'Nor he with my sort of music,' he said. 'Well, whatever.'

'I'll let you know. It's a kind offer, anyway. Laurel all right?'

'Busy.' Laurel, second-in-command in a travel agent in Shepherd's Bush, was never not busy. Variety in the answer was supplied by the seasons. 'Heavy early bookings for skiing.'

'Ah.' It was completely dark outside now, but in the extra density of darkness made by the laurel bush across the drive Grace thought she saw a pale, smeary movement. The wave of a white handkerchief, perhaps. A needle scraped down her spine. 'I must get off the line, now,' she said. In these weekly perfunctory conversations between mother and son, they had reached the point where neither found it necessary to give an excuse for ending them.

'Righty-ho. Look forward to hearing.'

Grace went to the window, looked out. Pure darkness, no sign of anyone. She drew the curtains, heart beating fast. This was a relatively safe neighbourhood: the odd burglary, occasional vandalism to cars parked in the road, a spate of bricks thrown through conservatories a few years ago – someone with a grudge against symbols of affluence, it was thought. But Artisan Road, with its good streetlights towering over the trees planted every few yards, was a place the inhabitants were not afraid to walk with their dogs by night. Grace had always felt safe in the house alone, although William insisted she lock the doors when he was out late. Curtains drawn, she put down her possible sighting of something or some-one to imagination. All the same she decided not to wait till she went to bed to lock the front door.

She switched on the hall light. The brightness made her bolder. She decided to take a quick look outside.

There was a man in the porch. A long grey scarf was wound round his neck, hiding his mouth. He was tall, thin, scruffy. He pulled down the scarf and she saw it was Lucien.

'Sorry if I gave you a fright.' The porch light – a lantern of stained glass from Portugal, Christmas present from Jack last year – swung a little in a cold breeze. Its sickly reds and blues and greens cut across Lucien's pale face. His eyes – now red, now blue, now green of the ugly glass – had shrunk back into his head, as they did when he was in one of his states. 'Didn't ring. Saw you were on the phone.'

'Jack.'

'Your son Jack, right.'

'Want to come in?' Grace shivered.

'I won't come in, no thanks.'

'On your way somewhere?'

'Not really, no. Just wandering about.'

'Well, if you really don't want . . .' Grace put her hand on the door, longing to shut it.

'I'll be on my way. Guess what? She's back. She and the phar-maceutical bugger. They come back loaded with all these fat-cat bags of food, start spreading gin and paté and a lot of crap all over the kitchen table, bawling me out because there was a single fag end in the ashtray. Enough to do your head in, she is, they are.'

'Didn't they ask you to join them for supper?' Even as she asked the question, Grace was aware of its presumptuous middle-class overtone, and at once regretted it. Although there was no doubting

Lucien's own origins, he liked to think he had left the middle-classes long ago. In his adoption of 'classless' speech and unattractive clothes, he could be taken for a youth from an under-privileged background. To note any more refined signs through this disguise caused him great offence. Usually, for peace, Grace remembered to ignore the fact that his living just down the road meant they had something in common. She was careful to avoid any reference to middle-class behaviour with which he might be acquainted. So her thoughtless question was a mistake, she realised at once, she would have to pay for. Lucien looked at her with utter scorn.

'Didn't they ask me to join them for supper?' He mimicked her voice perfectly. Then, pulling the scarf back up over his mouth, turned away. Grace waited till she saw he was through the gate, and shut the door.

There was the rest of last night's cottage-pie in the oven, but she had no appetite. She was unnerved. The thought of Lucien prowl-ing round the house at night was disturbing. When he came in the morning Grace felt tense, but safe. William was usually upstairs. If Lucien, spurred by the thought of his mother, had become worry-ingly aggressive, William would have come to the rescue, turned him out. In fact, for all his anger, Grace had only been really alarmed on one occasion. She had innocently enquired after Lobelia, not realising then that *he* was the one who liked to bring up the subject. No one else was permitted to do so. He yelled abuse at Grace for mentioning her very name, and picked up a saucepan drying by the sink. He raised it, swung round poised to hit her. Grace covered her face with her hands, cowered in a corner, terrified by the look on his face. But her fear made him laugh. He scoffed at her for even thinking he was going to attack her. She'd just got on his wick, he said. He was sorry. He put down the saucepan and hugged her, kissed the top of her head. Grace was only partially soothed: the look in his eye had been that of a man temporarily deranged, and her heart had battered for a long time after he left. It was hard to be sure Lucien would never resort to violence, though his good manners (which must have been instilled, somewhere, in his childhood, dreadful though he claimed it was) nearly always came to the rescue of one of his rages. Tonight, though, there had been something sinister about him she had not seen previously. But then, of course – she tried to be rational – he had never come visiting at night before.

Grace did not want to think about the scene up the road when Lucien returned to find his mother and her lover enjoying their innocent dinner. She did not want to think about Lucien at all. It was one of those moments she wished she had never met him. She sat in the armchair by the unlit fire, glanced at the clock. At least four hours before William would be home. What could she best reflect upon to calm herself?

Jack and Laurel – that was the answer. The very thought of them was always soporific. As she imagined her son's earnest, bespectacled face (which bore no resemblance to either her or William, everyone said) her limbs felt heavy, mossy. It was very hard to take a maternal interest in his life – though she did try – for there was little in it to interest. This lack of enthusiasm between parents and son was mutual. Jack had always been a good, dull boy – clever, hard working, cautious. He had decided to be a chartered accountant in his teens, and worked consistently towards that end. Now, for some years, he had been the youngest partner in an apparently 'thriving' firm in Shepherd's Bush. It was buying tickets one lunch hour for an Easter break (alone, all his holidays were alone) to Portugal that he had met Laurel. She was a girl as ambitious in the travel agency world as Jack was in his profession. Recognition of their mutual desire for success drew them quickly together, and four years ago Laurel joined Jack in his depressing flat in Hammersmith. It took six months for him to introduce Laurel to Grace and William. When he did so he called her his 'partner', a description neither of the Handles could bring themselves to say. To them, a partner was a business partner, and Laurel was his girlfriend. Grace could see this lack of co-operation irritated Jack by the way he jerked his head and pulled at his right ear.

(He had done this, when put out or worried, for so long that his right lobe was now considerably longer than his left, but in Laurel's eyes this was no impediment. Or perhaps she did not notice. Grace had judged at once that Laurel was not a keen observer, or surely she would have been demented by Jack's personal habits.)

Laurel described herself at that first meeting as a career girl, and Jack had supported her. 'I should say she is! My partner's a great career girl. She'll go far.'

William and Grace saw there was some truth in that. Laurel was so consumed by her love of the travel agency business that it had inspired even her language. Words such as 'exotic' and 'snow-capped' littered her talk. Early on in their relationship, when she and Jack decided to go away for a weekend in the country, she telephoned Grace to tell her they had chosen 'a very exclusive hotel, river frontage'. Oddly, its exclusivity did not inspire them to many other weekends away: these days their Saturdays were spent in the office, while their Sundays were spent 'catching up on paperwork' at home.

'It's like this, Grace,' Laurel once explained. 'If you want to be top dog, you've got to give it your all. Work must come first.'

'Surely,' Grace had said, 'you very nearly *are* top dog. You could give yourself a break sometimes.'

'No way. There's Danielle above me. When she goes – and I heard her husband's to be posted to Bahrain quite soon – I want to see myself in her chair. The boss.'

'Well, I'm sure you will.' Grace had suppressed a sigh.

During the course of their son's arrangement with Laurel, Grace and William had learnt a great deal about the travel agency business, and were aware they often disappointed Laurel in their refusals to accept her discount offers to almost any exclusive, exotic, sun-bathed, palm-fringed place they liked to think of. Although Laurel herself had only been as far as Spain, on a late-season special bargain tour, her need to acquaint herself with the brochures from all over the world gave her the feeling she knew the places she read about as well as if she had been there. So at the infrequent meetings of Grace and William, Jack and Laurel, there was much talk of places foreign to all of them and of little interest to two of them. (Jack, on these occasions, took a back seat. His only contribution was to agree with all Laurel's rhetorical questions.)

'I'd say Jamaica, with its golden sands, would be nice for you one February.' She was trying yet again to persuade the reluctant Handles to contemplate a 'relaxing break'. 'Wouldn't you, Jack?'

'I'd say yes to that,' nodded Jack.

Grace remembered thinking that surely Jamaica's beaches were white. But it was the sort of reflection best kept to herself. Perhaps they looked golden in Laurel's brochures. William, later, said to Grace that if Laurel tried to sell them one more of her ruddy 'leisure breaks', anywhere, Economy class upgraded to Club class by her ruddy string-pulling, whatever, he'd strangle her.

At every meeting between the two generations Laurel's progress towards being top dog was the main topic of conversation. Jack rarely said much about his office life except that 'it keeps on doing very nicely, thank you'. Once he mentioned that he intended to take up jogging – so refreshing, it was, on the tow-path, fortunately only yards from their flat – in the early mornings. But there was not much to add to this information. And what the two of them never revealed were any domestic plans – marriage, for instance. Grace and William had long since accepted that actual marriage did not seem to be a priority these days among the young, and perhaps that was of no great importance so long as the commitment was there. 'In fact,' William had once ventured, 'if they've not actually tied the knot, and another girl should come along with, shall I say, *wider horizons* than Laurel, then it wouldn't be too difficult for Jack . . . to swap.'

The unsubtle intimations of this suggestion made Grace laugh, but she thought it unlikely. Jack was not the sort of man to whom lively girls were drawn. Her own sadness was total lack of plans for children. Never a mention of a baby, and Grace rather fancied the idea of being a grandmother. Perhaps they intended to marry first.

Should they have a baby in their present state of live-in lovership, or whatever it was called, well, Grace did not know what she would feel about that. Her reflections were interrupted by the telephone again. Unusual, two calls in one evening.

'Hello, Grace? It's me, Laurel.'

'Oh, hello, Laurel.' The voice flat again.

'I was just ringing to say I think Jack's plan about William's birthday treat is a lovely one.'

'Yes, well as I said, I'll . . .'

'So I hope you'll persuade him. We could make a night of it. – You all right?'

'Fine, fine.'

'Mega busy at the agency – as you can imagine. Whole world wants to go skiing. Well, we'll look forward to hearing. I'll say bye for now.'

Grace turned on the television to watch the news. She didn't want to think any more about Jack and Laurel, and the scarfed Lucien still troubled her. By now William and the others would be halfway through the Britten. She rather wished she was in the audience. Perhaps she should start going to more concerts again, as she used to before Jack was born. William would be so pleased. Well, tomorrow morning, his birthday breakfast, she would put to him the idea. Cheered by this plan, she turned her attention to the latest sleaze scandal among politicians. Sometimes, she felt very remote from the real world.

'Good audience,' said Grant in the interval. 'Northampton's woken up or something.'

William nodded. He, too, had sensed a particularly lively attention from the audience. Returning to the platform, he felt more eager than usual to achieve a near-perfect rendering of the second half of the programme.

And then, when the last note had finally evaporated into an intense silence, the audience broke into applause so rapturous that William, Grant and Rufus exchanged looks of astonishment. They were not used to this sort of thing. Quartet audiences were enthusiastic, knowledgeable, appreciative. But they did not usually respond with such eager applause. One or two of them were even standing. There were shouts of *hear, hear!* There were shouts of *more*.

Bonnie, William observed, was smiling a delighted smile, swinging it from one side of the hall to the other. William frowned. Smiling, grinning, was not something the Elmtree players did. In gratitude for the appreciation they were shown, they would stand, give a curt, tight-lipped nod. They would let the clapping continue for a moment or two, then, when William judged it had reached its peak, leave the stage. Nothing worse than to be stranded in the dying fall of applause: undignified. To get off quickly was the Elmtree's way – always had been.

Shocked by the vigour of tonight's applause, after the encore, William remained seated for longer than usual. Rufus nudged his arm. All four players then stood. The men gave a couple of nods. Bonnie's gesture was a deeper bow, a well-trained courtier sort of bow. Then, when she rose again, she stretched out her arms, viola in one hand, bow in the other. She was laughing. Grant, William observed in a quick sideways glance, was grinning. *Grinning*. By God, he'd have to speak to Grant. To Bonnie, too . . . there should be no more of this larking about.

His plans were cut off by further, more hectic applause. Several people were shouting for a second encore. A second encore? They almost never gave two except at Christmas. What was all this? In his confusion, William felt his mouth, very dry, fall open. Warm air from the hall fell like a pad of velvet on his tongue. Rufus was whispering something. Hard to hear, all this confounded clapping.

'Hadn't we better . . . play something?'

'For Christ's sake, we never . . .' But this was no time for an argument, exposed on the platform in front of three hundred people demanding more. 'What could we do?'

'Scherzo of the Schumann A minor?'

Good old Rufus, quick-thinking as always. That was nice and

short and they all knew it well. But Bonnie . . . what about Bonnie? They'd never rehearsed . . . could she manage it? The applause rattled on.

'Fine. Ask Bonnie.' William himself did not want to risk not being able to hear Bonnie's answer. Rufus whispered to Bonnie, she nodded. William mouthed to the elated-looking Grant. Rufus returned to William.

'Better say something.'

William took his point. There was no time to be nervous. He stepped forward. The applause stopped abruptly.

'Ladies and gentlemen,' he said, 'this is un-prec-e-dented.' His voice was oddly high. There was a ruffle of sympathetic laughter. 'As some of you may know, the Elmtree players are not accustomed to giving second encores. But if I'm reading your message correctly, and I think I probably am, what you are demanding is that the arrival of our new poor relation should be celebrated with an especial evening . . .' The words were tumbling out quite easily now, no thought: William listened to himself, fascinated, as if it was someone else speaking. The reference to the musical in-joke about the viola player (always referred to as the poor relation) was appreciated by many in the audience: there was yet more laughter. It was all rather enjoyable. 'Bonnie, here,' he went on when the laughter had died down, 'has gallantly replaced dear Andrew Fulbright, who was sadly forced to take early retirement. But after just one concert we knew we'd found the perfect replacement in Bonnie. And you, tonight, seem to be in agreement.' Bonnie was smiling uproariously, all over the place. 'So just for once, in celebration of her joining our little band of players, we'll give you one more . . . But please bear with us. We haven't rehearsed the Schumann A minor with her. But we'll do our best.'

It was during the Schumann that William noticed Bonnie's sleeves. Previously he had taken in that she was wearing a long black velvet dress, very demure and appropriate, just as she wore at the first concert. Indeed her choice of clothes had been so good – no sign of the alarming shoes – that William had felt there was no need now to have the sartorial discussion he had been dreading. In the Green Room before the concert he had heard Grant complimenting her on the medieval design of the sleeves. William had no idea what he meant by this. To him they were just long, flowing sleeves, a little wider than usual at the bottom.

During the Schumann he glanced constantly at Bonnie to see how she was doing – this was a nerve-racking experience, playing something they had never practised together in front of an audience. As far as William was concerned, it would never happen again. He did not believe in quartets playing two encores. In the event, it seemed to be going better than he could ever have expected. Bonnie was swaying back and forth, afloat on the music, wholly at ease, as if she had been playing the piece with the others all her life. As she moved her arms William saw that the wide velvet sleeves tipped and swung, and as they did so there were strange flashes of shining green: a deep, jade green, it was, that caught the light and was flared for moments with emerald. William realised this green flashing stuff was some kind of lining, designed to intrigue subtly as jewels on a wrist. He was moved to think of the trouble Bonnie must have taken to achieve such beautiful sleeves. How clever she was to have designed of them. He then thought that if *he* was captivated by them in his few glances over his violin, what effect must they have on the audience? Enrapture, perhaps. And audiences should not be deflected by external factors. He would have to speak to Bonnie, after all.

At the end of the piece there was further overwhelming applause, but this time the players scarcely stopped to nod before hurrying after William.

He found Bonnie beside him in a long passage, anxious.

'Have to hurry if I'm going to catch my train,' she said. She folded back one of the sleeves, looked at her watch. A wide band of the green, dimmer in the passage light, was exposed.

'Wonderful sleeves,' said William.

'Aren't they? Antique satin I found somewhere. Feel.'

She took one of William's hands, lay it for an infinitesimal moment on the stuff, soft and downy as feathers. He thought of kingfishers, linnets, greenfinches, moss.

'I'll give you a lift to the station,' he said.

'Are you sure?'

'Quite. It's on my route.'

The station was directly opposite his route home, but Bonnie had no inkling of the lie. Grant came out of the men's dressing-room, already changed. William drew himself upright, as if to look less guilty. Guilty of what, for heaven's sake? Stopping two seconds in the passage to compliment Bonnie on her sleeves?

Grant came right up to Bonnie, patted her on the shoulder.

'Well done,' he said. 'That was a bloody miracle. You played like an angel.'

Bonnie was far more pleased with this compliment than she had been with William's trivial comment on her sleeves. She thanked Grant with a heavenly smile. William cursed himself. He should have been the first one to congratulate her on her remarkable performance.

'Want a lift to the station?' Grant asked. 'I pass it.'

'Thanks very much, Grant. But I've just said yes to William. It's on his way, too.'

Grant gave William a long look in which his surprise, out of loyalty to his old colleague, was indicated only in the almost invisible raising of one eyebrow.

In the car Bonnie said: 'I think if we hurry a bit we might just make it.'

'Very well.' With Bonnie beside him, William's concentration was slipping. She smelt strongly of some flower. 'Is that scent you're wearing bluebell?' he asked.

'Daisy, actually.'

'I knew it was something wild.'

'William: the lights have changed.'

'My goodness, so they have.' Some idiot behind them was hooting.

'That means we ought to go.'

Firm of purpose, William attacked the gear. The engine stalled. Sweat poured down behind his ears.

'I don't think you like driving very much.'

'No.' They shuddered off at last.

'Still, we're nearly there. You're doing well.'

Her kindness burst like a sunflower within him, warming, giving him strength. Out of the corner of his eye he saw her pick up a plastic shopping bag into which she had stuffed the velvet dress. He had not the heart to tell her there was at least another mile to go, complicated by traffic lights, one-way systems and every kind of impediment to speed.

They reached the platform just as the train was leaving. William was too distraught to think clearly. He had let Bonnie down and must be seen to do something. Still in his white tie and tails (knowing he was not a speedy dresser, he had decided not to change for fear of delaying Bonnie), he plucked his handkerchief from his pocket and ran some yards after the train, waving, to no avail. He was stopped in his tracks by the guard.

'Bad luck,' said the man.

'Can't you do something?' panted William.

'Like what?'

'Stop it?' He saw that the train was toy-sized in the distance by now, and Bonnie was laughing.

'I can't, no,' said the guard, who was enjoying himself. 'Whoever you are,' he added.

'Have we a hope of catching it up at the next station?'

'Don't suppose you have. Unless you drive a Porsche.'

'I don't, no, thankfully.' William's knees were trembling. The command he knew he could summon on a concert platform seemed to have evaporated completely, here, on the empty station platform. Bonnie beside him looking as if she was convinced he could solve the problem. 'Well, I don't know . . .'

'The last train's in an hour's time,' offered the guard. He wandered away, the novelty of the scene having worn off.

'That's cool,' said Bonnie. She was beside William, hand on his trembling arm. 'Don't worry. I'll get a coffee. I'll wait. You must go. I'll be fine.'

'Not on your life.' William backed away from her. 'It's all my fault, I'm so sorry. The least I can do is stay with you, get you a drink.'

Bonnie, seeing his determination, did not argue. They sat at a small plastic table in the café, the objects of the place bared in all their ugliness under strip-lighting. William waited for the man behind the counter to finish shuffling an arrangement of rolls bandaged in clingfilm, and show some interest in his order. Eventually the man looked up.

'What, you a ringmaster, or something?' He sniggered.

'One tea, one Diet Coke,' said William, with great dignity. For a few moments, in the pleasure of realising he was to spend an hour alone with Bonnie, he had forgotten about his clothes. The man reminded him of his own absurdity, but he did not mind. In his present heightened mood he was protected from all slings and arrows. He looked over to Bonnie, chin resting on her hands, eyes on the empty platform. What a girl, what a girl . . . What should he say to her? How should he begin? It would be foolish to waste the single hour with small talk.

He fetched the drinks when the man behind the counter showed no signs of performing that part of his duty. Then he moved towards Bonnie, carrying the tray with the same rigid pessimism as he held a steering wheel. But encouraged by her enchanting smile, he felt he might have been crossing the floor of the Café de Paris bearing champagne. He took the nasty little chair opposite her, arranged the tea and Coke on the nasty little table, scarcely bigger than a plate, between them. Bonnie's delight seemed out of all proportion to the gesture.

'Thanks. Great. I say, that was really good, the concert, wasn't it?'

'It was good, yes.'

'What d'you think happened? I mean, I felt the sympathy of the audience was almost tangible. It's not often as powerful as that.'

'It's certainly not, no.' William sipped the disgusting tea to give himself time. He decided to go for lightness of explanation. He moved one side of his mouth, prelude to a smile. 'I think it must have been something to do with your sleeves. The audience was captivated by them.'

Bonnie laughed.

'I thought you were going to say it was something to do with my playing.'

'It was probably that, too. You did so well, though as you know we're all equal in a quartet.'

'That's not quite true, though.' Bonnie looked at William shyly. 'You're an outstanding violinist. Don't know why you're not world famous.'

'No! Really.' William, not often called upon to be modest, was uncertain how to handle compliments of this kind. 'I'm just a regular player. Love my violin.'

'One day, I'd like to hear you play by yourself . . .'

'I'm sure that can be arranged . . .' Dear God, it could. William's eyes left Bonnie's, fearful she might see in them the turmoil in his heart. He envisaged the scene they made as if from the platform on the other side of the rails . . . man of middling years in white tie and tails, beautiful young girl who some might take for his daughter, heads haloed by strip-lighting, horrible little café their pathetic backdrop, all another world from the station scene in *Brief Encounter* . . .

'When did you know you wanted to be a violinist?' Bonnie was asking. 'I always like to know the precise moment when a decision strikes someone like lightning. When there's no doubt any more.'

Well, he could answer that.

'My father was an architect, worked at home. Passion for Wagner. Said Wagner was his inspiration. So we had *The Ring* blasting through the house all day. Did nothing much for me. But he drove my father to design more and more bus shelters with winged roofs – nobody ever wanted them. I think the music was some sort of consolation. Anyway, one day he took his portfolio up to Manchester, where he was going on one of his wild-goose chases. Knowing he'd be away for a whole day I asked my mother if she'd put on something *she* liked. She hunted through a small pile of old seventy-eight records that she took from a cupboard – a hidden store, I think. I'd never seen them before. She put one of them on the old gramophone – one of those radiogram things in an elaborate case of polished walnut – you're too young to know what I mean. Anyhow . . . "You may not like this, son," she said, "but it's the nearest I know to sublime." It was one of the Beethoven late quartets.' William paused, let his eyes meet Bonnie's again. 'That was it, really. I was six. Said I wanted a violin. The music frightened me so much I knew I had to . . .' He paused. 'Perhaps I didn't know what I had to do. A few weeks later, my seventh birthday, they gave me my first violin. Some benevolent old man in the neighbourhood commissioned my father to design a crazy summerhouse, so I was able to have lessons . . .'

'Goodness,' said Bonnie, quietly.

'I do remember very well that feeling of absolute certainty. It was as frightening as the music.'

'Know what you mean. Certainty can be frightening.'

'And you – how did it happen to you?'

Bonnie shrugged. 'I was always fiddling around on the piano, from a very young age. My mum used to play, Blues and stuff. Then when I was about ten I was walking down our road, a hot summer, and heard this music coming out of an open window – radio on very loud. Wow, it was something, I thought. I just stood by the privet hedge, waiting till the end, feeling daft just standing, listening. Then to my horror a fierce-looking man came out of the house, asked me what I was doing, hanging about. Don't think he believed me when I said I was waiting till the end of the piece – think he thought I was a young burglar or something. Anyhow, he said, "Dvořák's Cello Concerto, now you run along." So I ran home, saying the word Dvořák to myself over and over again so as not to forget it. When I got there I told my mum what had happened and said I now knew absolutely *definitely* what I wanted to do: I wanted to play the cello. She said don't be so daft, the cello's much too big. So I said, being perverse, well a violin's much too small – course, I hadn't a clue what size a violin was. So she said why not try something in between? About six months later I played a solo viola piece, can't remember what it was, in a Christmas concert. Got a write-up in the local paper . . . And that was it. Certainty. Just carried on.'

'Well,' said William.

'Boring story, really.'

'Not at all. Another Coke?'

'No thanks. D'you know what I've been thinking?'

'I don't know what you've been thinking, no.'

'That it would be much easier, now I'm with the Elmtree, if I got out of London. I hate the place anyway. If I found somewhere much nearer to the rest of you there'd be no more of these sort of problems.' She nodded towards the empty platform. 'Grant says he knows a neighbour with a top flat to let. Might go and look at it.'

At the thought of her already having discussed her plans with Grant (when? when?) something shifted painfully within William.

'That's a good idea,' he said, aiming for brightness.

They talked about the advantages of her moving, the convenience of Grant's barn, the forthcoming concerts. The hour was gone. William accompanied Bonnie to the train door, patted her shoulder.

'You're a star, William,' she said. 'See you tomorrow, three o'clock. Drive carefully.'

William seemed to remember he had once heard Laurel calling Jack a star: perhaps it was a compliment often used by the young to the old. All the same, he felt himself spinning about the station, dazed, inebriated, hopelessly looking for a telephone. He had to ring home. Grace would be so worried. He found one at last.

'My Ace, oh my Ace. Sorry not to have rung before. Got dreadfully held up – an amazing concert. Two encores.'

'Two encores?' She sounded calm, unworried.

'I'll tell you all about it. I'm on my way now. Don't wait up.'

'I'm in bed already.' Grace laughed, her long rippling laugh that was part of William's being.

'Back in an hour.'

All the way home, a slow and peaceful journey aided by a full moon, William thought not of Bonnie, who had done such peculiar things to his heart this evening, but of Grace. How good their life was. How inestimably he loved her. What a remarkable woman she was – a woman in a million. How he sometimes took her for granted, perhaps. And why, suddenly, this evening, was he accosted by so many loving thoughts?

Grace was asleep when he crept into the bedroom. He kissed her lightly on the forehead. She did not stir.

He got into bed as quickly as he could manage, turned out the light. He always loved those moments of total darkness before sleep came. They produced so many surprises, possibilities. Tonight the last bars of the Schumann sang through his head, bars of twinkling lights: and there was Bonnie, dipping and swaying, flashing her funny green sleeves. She was the last thing he remembered.

3

William passed a troubled night. Weird dreams, restless limbs. Lack of sleep affected him badly. He had to make some effort to go downstairs wearing his usual morning face – an expression, Grace once said, that indicated his inner harmony with life.

On the breakfast table there was a small present, and several envelopes that did not look like bills, one in Grace's handwriting. For a moment, in confusion caused by fatigue, William thought he had been caught out by some trick of time, and somehow Christmas had leapt upon them. Then he remembered.

'Happy birthday,' said Grace.

'Oh my Ace, oh my darling girl. You never forget.'

Grace, as she put a pot of tea beside him on the table, kissed him lightly on the temples. Every year Grace gave William cufflinks for his birthday, and every year William lost at least one of them, if not the pair. This was hardly surprising: he had to wear them at least three evenings a week. Hurrying to change after a concert, eager to be home, it was all too easy to mislay socks, a white tie, cufflinks, studs, pens and other bits of the paraphernalia that haunt the life of a travelling musician. So although an element of surprise had been missing in Grace's present for many years, it was always received with gratitude.

William drank his tea. He needed strength, calm before tackling the envelopes. Grace sat opposite watching the gathering of his forces. She longed to ask him about the encores, and what time he had got home. But even on his birthday it would have been untoward to break their unspoken rule of silence at breakfast. The questions would have to wait till lunch.

The first card was from Laurel: distant view of the Matterhorn with glittery stuff representing snow. The second from Jack: the millionth reproduction of *The Skater*. William had once told his son that he had seen the picture in the National Gallery of Scotland as a child, and given it ten out of ten. Jack must have stored this fact in the back of his efficient chartered accountant's brain, and thought he couldn't go wrong. He had sent it on at least three birthdays in the last ten years. Last, Grace's card. As he slit the envelope William glanced up at her dear, eager face. For as long as he could remember she had been looking at him like that, a look of undimmed expectancy, humour, love. How can I be so lucky? he asked himself, as he did many times a week.

Grace had painted a single flower for him, a thistle. William put on his glasses. He hadn't seen one of her thistles before. She'd done it awfully well, of course. She had real talent. The downy stuff . . . you could almost feel it. When at last she finished her book, it was bound to be a bestseller.

'Must have taken you hours, my Ace,' he said. 'It's lovely, thank you so much.' He opened the card to read the message written in gold ink. His throat constricted. Grace's simple declarations of love always affected him physically – a sign, he knew, that his own love was equally profound, though he was less able to give it expression. He ate a piece of toast.

This unusually drawn-out breakfast was causing Grace some agitation. For the last few days Lucien had been arriving earlier than usual. She dreaded his poking his head through the kitchen window this birthday morning.

'The present,' she said, pushing a small parcel wrapped in floral paper across the table. She looked at her watch. 'Stephen rang last night, wants you to call before nine.' Stephen was William's very fierce agent.

'He does chivvy, that man, doesn't he?' William picked up the small box, began ineptly to unwrap it. Grace cursed herself for having been so lavish with the Sellotape.

At last it was free of paper. William lifted it close to his face, feigning excitement. Get on with it, please, thought Grace . . . Lucien.

William opened the box with the caution of a man half expecting something to spring out at him. There, very close to his eyes, lay a pair of small cufflinks of deep jade set in gold. The green of the stones was the green that had had such power last night. Though in the dullness of the kitchen it was a lightless green – the stones resembled very old eyes in which light no longer reflects.

'I don't know what to say,' William said.

'How about trying very hard not to lose them this year?' Grace smiled.

'I'll try my hardest. They're wickedly extravagant, beautiful. Thank you, my Ace.' He closed the box and put it in the pocket of his corduroy trousers.

Grace began to clear the table. William hurried upstairs to his room, rang his agent.

When discussions of future concerts were over – it was a very long call, Stephen was a ponderous man who liked to embellish the most trivial decision with clusters of unnecessary doubts – William dialled Bonnie's number, giving himself no time to cogitate on the wisdom of this move. She answered at once.

'Happy birthday,' she said. How did she know? 'Grant told me.'

'Thanks very much.' William gave a small laugh. 'As a matter of fact I was ringing you . . .' Why was he ringing? 'Just to make sure you got back all right. Not that safe, these days, unfortunately, young women travelling alone at night.'

Bonnie's turn to laugh.

'If anyone attacked me,' she said, 'they'd get a surprise. I'm trained in martial arts, self-defence. I could throw you over in a flash.' William closed his eyes, saw the enchanting picture of himself plucked up by Bonnie's strong arms. He pictured himself thrown like an unresisting scarf into the air (more Isadora Duncan

than martial arts) and then caught against her bosom. 'I could
even manage Grant.'

'Bet you could.'

The sound of her perky voice enthralled him no less this morning than it had on the station last night – though he didn't much
fancy the idea of her grappling Grant. What could he say now, to
keep her going?

'The other thing . . . I forgot to say last night.' Long pause. Wise
or unwise, this subject?

'Yes?'

'The matter of your sleeves.'

'You loved my sleeves, you said.'

'Yes: yes I did. There's no doubt concerning my personal appreciation.'

'You do put things a funny way sometimes.'

'I'm sorry. I suffer from formality, I know.' Bonnie's laughter at
his admission made him suddenly feel at ease. Heavens, how he
loved talking to her. 'But the thing is, the three of us men in our
severe black and white uniform . . . I was wondering how appropriate even the merest hint of colour is for our lovely new viola?'
Oh dear, had he been too dashing there? The answer was a long
silence. William strained to imagine Bonnie's expression. Perhaps
he should explain himself better. 'I think what I'm trying to say is
this: there should be nothing to detract the audience's attention
from the music. I mean, a single girl among men is going to be the
centre of attention anyway. My feeling is she should probably play
herself down, sartorially, as much as possible . . .'

'William? If you don't mind my saying so, I think that's the pot-
tiest theory I've ever heard.' William swallowed. At least she
sounded more buoyant than offended. 'And I can't possibly go along
with it. I've five dresses for concerts, all black, all long, all with my
special sleeves. In one dress they're lined with black silk – I wore
that at Slough so as not to alarm you my first time with you. Then
there's the green you saw last night, then there's a sapphire blue, a
ruby and a white – that one you'll approve, I daresay. They cost

more than I can afford, those dresses. They've done me well and there's lots of life in them yet. Not for anything in the world am I going to give them up. If you haven't got beautiful arms you might as well have beautiful sleeves. They're my trademark. If we play well enough people aren't going to be distracted by a flash of satin. So I'm sorry if you disapprove, but not for anything would I change my wardrobe for the Elmtree players or any other stuffy old quartet.'

William thought he heard a sigh, the thump of a banged fist.

'Very well,' he said at last. 'I take your point.' He despised his own feebleness – though was it feeble to come round to another's view, well put? 'But I trust they won't be the cause of any more demands for a second encore.'

'They won't. Last night was nothing to do with my sleeves, honestly.' She was gentle again. 'The enthusiasm last night was something to do with your playing, in my opinion. You played like someone . . . well, inspired.'

'Nonsense. We all played the same.'

'All inspired, then. Look, I've got to go now. Grant's going to take me to see this flat, before the rehearsal. See you later.'

'And how do you suppose I wait patiently till three o'clock?' William asked himself out loud, as he put down the receiver.

Downstairs Grace waited nervously for Lucien. She never liked to start work until he had been and gone. In her heart she knew this was ridiculous, and the cause of her being so behind with her flowers. But to take her place at her work table, adjust lights, fetch clean water, lick sable-haired brushes to a fine arrow point, dip into a small jewel square of colour, while decisions about where to begin shifted like small clouds through her mind . . . required tranquil concentration. This was not possible if she knew that at any moment she would be interrupted by Lucien in one of his morning rages.

To fill in time as she waited on the morning of William's birthday, Grace made a rhubarb crumble for supper. There was no concert tonight. They would have Irish stew and his favourite

pudding, and watch an episode of *Great Expectations* on television – the sort of evening that they both most enjoyed, and was all
too rare.

Lucien poked his head through the kitchen window at ten thirty,
so unusually late that Grace had given up expecting him. He
looked exhausted but oddly calm.

'Not stopping,' he said. 'Things to do.'

'Quick cup of coffee?'

'No thanks. I'm off home for a kip. I was up all night.'

'Why was that?'

'Rattled. All this stuff going on.' He straightened himself up,
rubbed a thin hand over his unshaven cheek. 'Mind if I ask you a
favour? Are you free this afternoon?'

'There's nothing much on, I don't think.'

'I've got to take these two bloody great chows out. Round the
park, like. Can't face it on my own. Just wondered if you'd like to
come too?'

Grace smiled. 'I could do with the exercise. I'll meet you at the
park gates at two thirty, all right?'

'Great. Thanks. What's that pie?'

'Rhubarb crumble. William's favourite. It's his birthday.'

'Lucky old William.'

When Lucien had gone Grace realised that too much of the
morning had been consumed, now, to get down to work. She
would hardly have had time to paint a single bluebell leaf (so hard
to achieve the gloss of those leaves, she was finding – she had
thrown away many an effort that had come out lifeless) before she
would have to heat up the carrot soup for lunch. So she arranged
the three birthday cards on the dresser, and began to chop up the
neck of lamb for tonight's stew. That job she had planned for the
afternoon, when her biorhythms were at such a low ebb creative
work was impossible. By agreeing to go with Lucien and his dogs,
which she had no desire whatever to do, her small domestic plans
were upset. She frowned, annoyed with herself.

On the days William was home for lunch a modicum of

communication had become the habit. It was over home-made soup and bread and cheese William informed Grace of forthcoming events in his diary, and she made a note of them on the calendar that hung on the wall. Opinions, or the reporting of events, had no place at lunchtime. These were kept for the few evenings a week they managed dinner together – scraps of talk that shuffled with no very clear pattern, half-sentences that were the understood language of a long marriage.

When William had finished dictating the Quartet's engagements for the following month, November – always a busy time of year, pre-Christmas – Grace braced herself to mention the only invitation that had come to her.

'Jack,' she said. 'Jack and Laurel. They want to come to a concert then take us out somewhere to eat. Birthday treat.'

'Good God,' said William.

'What about Ealing, next week?'

'Perfect.' William laughed. 'Bartok the whole of the second half. They'll hate it.'

'So shall I say yes?'

'You better say yes, my Ace.'

'It might never happen. It didn't last year, you remember.'

'Nor did it. Great relief, too.' He looked at his watch, stood up.

'It's only one thirty,' said Grace. 'You'll be much too early.'

'You know what the boys are like, birthdays. Cake and so on before we start.' Could she see his impatience to be off? If he arrived early enough he might come upon Grant and Bonnie having lunch after looking at the flat. Break up their little twosome. 'Besides,' he added, 'I've got to change my trousers.'

William was again wearing the new corduroy trousers that had received so damning a reception yesterday. He had no intention of risking further painful comment.

'Why on earth? I thought yesterday, thank goodness, you'd decided to christen them at last.'

'Something about them – they're fine for home, not so comfortable for playing.'

'I see.'

William took in his wife's face.

'So I'll put them back in the cupboard, let them mature a little longer, my Ace . . .' She would be warmed by the way he was able to smile at his own foibles. She would like his mentioning the shared joke of his inability immediately to like new clothes . . .

It worked. She was smiling.

'Any plans, this afternoon?' Usually, he remembered to ask.

'Nothing much.'

'I'll be home about seven, then.'

'Rhubarb crumble.'

'Look forward to that. You spoil me. Rhubarb crumble . . . my goodness.'

William arrived at the barn to find that Rufus was already there with Grant and Bonnie. They were all clustered round the table engaged in preparations to celebrate his birthday. A space had been cleared for a large chocolate cake, imaginatively iced and decorated by Grant, who would have been a chef had he not been a cellist. He had not cooked anything for the players since his turn to give the Christmas party. Then, it had been an enormous buffet of over-decorated suckling pig, spiced vegetables and *bombe glacé* that must have taken him days of preparation. William's private opinion was that Grant's real culinary talent was as a pastry chef, judging from the exquisite cakes he made for each of the player's birthdays every year. This one was perhaps his best: an elaborate concoction of chocolate, with crystallised sugar violets glowing through a mist of icing sugar.

William made a quick calculation: if Grant had taken so much trouble making the cake this morning, then he couldn't have had much time to look at the flat with Bonnie. Faintly comforting, that. Rufus was pouring Sambuca into tall thin glasses: this was his contribution to the festivities every year. He took from his pocket a miniature paper bag and tipped four coffee beans into his hand. He was meticulous in his ways, Rufus. It was only lately he had become a little forgetful – times, dates, arrangements (though never a piece of music). This William put down to a recent distraction. Lately, Rufus had become upset to find that the nightingales, that used to sing so regularly in his garden, had left. His anxiety for the decline of nightingales in general greatly increased when he learnt how few were left in England. Between the early seventies and late eighties almost thirty per cent of them had vanished – not quite as alarming as the fifty-two per cent decrease in skylarks over twenty-five years, as he explained to the other sympathetic players, but very worrying to those concerned for the thriving of wildlife. The profits of his charitable fund-raising he decided in future to share between nightingale and skylark, and found himself touched by Bonnie's suggestion for a Sunday concert, which would include appropriate poetry readings, to raise money. Rufus told them that on free summer evenings he would walk in the woods near his house in the hopes of tracking down just a single nightingale. But he was rarely in luck. He missed their music, he said, more deeply than he could ever have supposed a man might miss the music of a bird.

Bonnie, who had volunteered to read several poems at the bird concert, was presently occupied with the decoration of William's cake. She was tipping small white candles from a box. It was clear the shortage of candles would have to be counteracted in some ingenious way.

Bonnie gave William one of her most enchanting smiles.

'I think,' she said, 'we'll have to have one candle for each decade. How many shall I . . .?'

William shook his head. Rufus pursed his lips, carefully placed a coffee bean on each drink. Bonnie stuck four candles into the icing.

'Go on,' said Grant.

Bonnie raised her eyebrows at William.

'I'll leave you to guess,' he said.

Bonnie stuck a fifth candle into the cake. Grant smiled, but restrained himself. Bonnie pushed the candle far down into the chocolate sponge – the half-inch that was left could be taken for any amount of time, long or short, she said. Everyone laughed.

Through the huge window they could see that the sky had darkened. A wind snagged at the few remaining yellow leaves on the two apple trees. It began to rain. Grant lighted the candles and Rufus put a match to the four glasses of Sambuca. The players sat round holding their flaming drinks in the premature dusk, and eating the almost liquid chocolate cake. William remembered that Andrew had always been the one to make some silly sort of toast on his birthday, and a funny speech in praise of William's general exemplary character. But he didn't miss Andrew today. Bonnie was here, next to him, face covered in chocolate like a child. Every now and then she licked a finger, and grimaced with each sip of the burning drink.

William could have sat for a long time round the table, listening to the fragments of quiet talk, feeling the spread of warmth in his stomach from the drink, and the shared safety of the semi-dark. But there was work to be done. He put down his glass.

'Thanks very much, everyone,' he said.

'One more glass.' Rufus held up the bottle.

William put up a hand. 'No, no. We're starting with the E minor Razumovsky. How d'you suppose I'd ever get through the *thème Russe*?'

The others laughed again. They were keen to see how William would do after the Sambuca. He stood, made his way to the stands at the other end of the barn. The others followed. No one put on a light. They shuffled through their scores, tuned their instruments, waited for William's signal to begin. Then the music swooped into the barn and drowned out the sound of the rain.

It was both windy and cold in the park, though here the rain fell only in spasmodic drops. Grace and Lucien walked side by side along a tarmacked path. Each one held a chow on a lead. They were cumbersome, graceless dogs, waddling their fat-furred behinds, pulling, nosing, snorting, generally distracting from any pleasure the walk might hold.

Which was not much. Lucien was in one of his sullen, taciturn moods. He had not shaved for several days and looked terribly thin, thought Grace. Ill. He was plainly bored stiff by the idea of walking dogs round the cheerless park every afternoon, even at five pounds an hour. Grace could not imagine the job would last long. Certainly she would be reluctant to come again. He was no kind of a companion. The wind puffed out his grubby T-shirt, then it fell back on to his hollow chest.

'You must be cold,' said Grace.

'No.' He did up a button of his thin denim jacket. They had been round twice and there were still three-quarters of an hour to go. 'I'll not be standing much more of this,' he said after a while. 'Have you ever seen such horrible dogs? They're like tugs, aren't they? Isn't that right? They're the tugs, we're the liners being pulled out of a harbour.' The very act of speaking seemed to cheer him a little. 'When I was a kid, Portsmouth, I used to watch those tugs doing their stuff. They'd get those liners out to sea then leave them and come snouting back to help the next one. I'd watch the bloody great ship till I couldn't see it any more. What always did my head in was not being able to imagine what it was like, on board, I mean. I kind of imagined it was a sort of palace. Chandeliers and chefs and that – I swore I'd get on to one, one day. Staircases – someone told me they had staircases on liners, all carpeted. Is that right?'

'I imagine so,' said Grace. 'I've never been on one.'

'You've had a quiet life.' Lucien stopped to let his chow sniff round a rubbish bin.

'I have, yes.' Grace shrugged. 'Marrying so young. There was no time to do much before. Since then, with William's commitments, there hasn't been much opportunity to travel. Anyhow,' she smiled, 'the one thing I'm quite sure he would never want is to go on a liner, a cruise.'

Lucien looked at her with haunted eyes. The pupils were unusually large. Grace wished, as she had many times lately, that she had never met him. She wished that he'd never insinuated himself into her life, come to depend upon her in the way he did. Perhaps today, in the park, would be the time to suggest his mornings visits should be cut down . . .

'Wish Lobelia had had a quiet life like you,' he said, 'instead of racing round with her men and parties and drink and that.' He gave a nasty laugh. They began their third turn round the dull path. 'Still, she's going away again today. So she says, that is. She and the pharmaceutical fucker.'

He hunched his shoulders, returned to his silence. Grace knew it was not the right moment. Her suggestion, however carefully put, could well spark one of his rages. She did not relish the idea of confronting his anger alone here in the park.

It was the longest, bleakest hour, that dog-walk, Grace could remember. Whatever Lucien's future plans with the dogs, she would not be accompanying him again.

At the end of the rehearsal the Elmtree players rewarded themselves with the rest of William's birthday cake and mugs of Earl Grey tea. It had been an afternoon out of the ordinary: for William, the combination of Sambuca and the Beethoven had induced a sense of rare deliquescence. But this happy state was impeded by Bonnie's news that the flat recommended by Grant, just the other side of Aylesbury, was perfect. She would even be allowed to share the small garden. As soon as possible she intended to sell her London flat and move. By the end of the month she should be installed.

William, looking at her across the table, felt the only things he knew about her were her smile, her warmth (which was extended indiscriminately) and a little of her music. She was without doubt an unusually talented viola player – by now they all realised this – and the Elmtree would have to be careful not to lose her to a solo career. But he knew nothing of her life: her pleasures beyond music, her taste in food, the books she read, her family, her lover, lovers . . . These thoughts terrified him. He stood up, suddenly unable to go on looking at her twisting the long ends of her red scarf. The not-knowing was an agony he had never experienced before. He felt weak, shaky. But managed a smile as he thanked them all again.

To his amazement Bonnie got up too, and followed him through the dark rain to his car, asked if she might get in for a moment. William unlocked the doors with an unsteady hand. What on earth was this all about?

Once on the seat beside him she was very matter of fact – brusque, almost. Perhaps she wanted William to know straight away that she had nothing more than a business matter in mind. She handed him a small transparent envelope.

'I couldn't be the only one not to give you anything,' she said.

William let the present lie in his open hand. It was too dark to see what it was. He weighed it, his hand moving up and down. Time, he wanted. Time. The rain battered against the windscreen. He could smell her: daisies again.

'Happy birthday.' Bonnie switched on the overhead light. William poured out the contents of the bag – pity about the light. He had liked the dark. Two small silver objects fell into his palm. Cufflinks. They were an abstract, irregular shape. Hideous modern things, as far as William could see. Much like small bits of frozen gristle.

'My sister designs jewellery,' Bonnie explained.

'They're very fine. Thanks most awfully.' The beastly little lumps swirled about in his hand. He could never like them, but because Bonnie had given them to him he would keep them for ever. Make sure he never lost them. 'You really shouldn't have, you know. I mean, we scarcely know each other. Only a few weeks . . .'

Bonnie laughed.

'Last night *you* disapproved of my sleeves, and *I* saw you had horrible cufflinks. I thought the least I could do . . . seeing you'd had faith enough to take me on . . .'

'They were just cheap things. I'd lost my good ones.'

'Well don't you lose these.'

'I won't. I won't.' William could see the complications ahead. Two pairs of cufflinks, now: the official and the irregular. He'd have to think about how to deal with that one. 'Thank you so much.'

'Think I'd better be getting back.' Bonnie switched off the light again.

'Back to London?'

'There's still a bit of Sambuca to be finished. It's good stuff, isn't it? – Yes, then London.' She gave a luxurious sigh. They saw Rufus come out of the barn, lighted for a moment at the doorway, then hurrying towards his car bent against the rain. He was always anxious to get back to his wife Iris, a semi-invalid, as soon as possible. He waved. William imagined Bonnie and Grant alone in the barn, drinking. Grant might go so far as to light the fire. What would they talk about? William contained his own sigh.

'So.' Bonnie turned, leant towards William, kissed him on the cheek so lightly and fast it was as if a feather speeding by in a breeze had touched him and was gone. She was out of the car and running back to the barn: the seat beside him was more empty than it had ever been. This was a tangible emptiness, a most dreadful emptiness he had never imagined could exist. He put his hand on the seat, still faintly warm from Bonnie. This was madness, this was illness – or perhaps just punishment for alcohol in the afternoon. Whatever the cause of the tumult within him, William knew he must take a grip.

He started the engine. Thought of the rhubarb crumble. Thought of his wife's pleasure on his return. His beloved Grace, his dear, dear Ace, whom he'd loved for so long. The weekend, till Monday's rehearsal, stretched like an endless black desert before him. There was an intolerable sense of loss, or losing. Confusion. He did not want to lose. He must take a hold on himself *now*, stop imagining Bonnie and Grant in the barn . . . hurry home, be with Grace, hum the whole way through the first Razumovsky, be with Grace as soon as possible . . . He accelerated, suddenly taken by the idea of driving at speed. The concentration would help deflect the tricks of his imagination. He prayed that God would be on his side, and there would be few other drivers on the road.

*

In fact, once embalmed in the warmth and comfort of the house, Grace all attention with her special birthday smile, the moments of madness receded. He took the (right) decision to tell her about Bonnie's cufflinks, and they both laughed when he showed her the nasty little things.

'I shall have to wear them occasionally, so as not to offend her,' he explained.

'Of course you will.'

On the Saturday afternoon he and Grace made a bonfire of swept leaves in the garden, and it seemed to be a perfectly normal off-duty weekend. Battering heart and tingling limbs had all calmed down and a partial clouding of Bonnie's face came as a relief.

Then, on the Sunday evening, a surprising and unexpected thing happened. She rang. Not his private number upstairs, which he had given her at the first rehearsal, explaining it was his business number, but the main house telephone. Grace answered it in the kitchen, came to tell William the news in the sitting room, where he was reading the paper by the fire.

'Bonnie Morse on the telephone. She says she's going to be very near here tomorrow, visiting someone. She says could she ask herself over before you have to go off to rehearse? Seems there's nowhere to go once her appointment is over. What do you think?'

William scratched his head. He wanted to convey a hint of doubt. Mustn't appear too eager.

'Well, why not? All right with you?'

'Of course. Fine. I'd like to meet her.'

'Suggest she stays for a bite of lunch with us, then we can drive off in convoy.'

'I will.' Grace left the room. William threw the papers on the floor, pulled at his nose, sniffing: a habit when he found himself in several minds. The extraordinary idea of Bonnie coming here of her own volition was both exciting and reassuring. Exciting for reasons he had no intention of articulating to himself: pleasing because he was sure once he could see her with Grace, the two women here under his own roof, that would resolve everything. Extinguish his pathetic little fantasies, put the pieces back together. Finally stop the rocking of the boat.

'She's coming about twelve,' said Grace, on her return. 'I must say, she sounded like a thoroughly nice young woman.'

During a wakeful night William determined not to answer the door to Bonnie, but to be hard at work in his room. She and Grace would thus have a chance for a short exchange without him, and Grace would then bring her upstairs. He had hoped that it would be a bright morning – his studio was at its best with morning sun flung over the shabby old furniture, books and piles of scores – but the weather was disappointing. Solid dark bruise of a sky, flat heavy light. The weather forecast predicted the possibility of snow.

Alone in his room after breakfast, William went through his daily ritual: its precise moves were always the same. They formed a reassuring beginning to the structure of the day. First, he shifted a pile of scores on to his desk, picked out the score he had decided upon on his way upstairs, then returned the pile of music to the floor, but not to the same place it had come from. Thus he provided for himself a small game of hide-and-seek for each morning: his own private way of enlivening his brain first thing. Next, he moved his music stand from wherever he had left it the day before, near to the window. That was the place he always played, looking out over the garden and his neighbours' variously designed roofs. But the stand only kept its place for the duration of his practice. When he left the room it had to be given a change of scene – in a corner, by the sofa, whatever. He sometimes reflected how odd were his solitary ways, but imagined he was not alone in such peculiarities. We design patterns of behaviour for our own security, our own comfort, he thought – patterns that could be derided by those who have no need for the comfort of routine, but are imperative to those who rely on them.

Music stand settled happily by the window, William began Massenet's *Meditation*. This was not a piece in their repertoire that he needed to practise, but wanted to play in the hope of calming himself. He lifted his bow, began the lilting melody that always brought to his mind the scattering of incense, thinning as it rose. Eyes shut most of the time, alone but temporarily safe in the cavern of the music, he did not notice at exactly what time during the morning it began to snow.

Once again there was a reason for Grace to postpone her work. With Bonnie coming to lunch she wanted to make a little more effort than usual. By nine thirty Lucien still had not appeared so she began a haddock quiche. Just as she put it in the oven, and was about to go to the desk, Lucien put his head through the window. His hair and shoulders were covered with snowflakes so fragile that only their outer rims were visible

'Freak day,' he said.

'You're late.' Grace tried not to sound annoyed.

'Does that bug you? I'm bloody frozen.'

'Come on in. But you can't stay long. Bonnie Morse is coming to lunch, and I must do an hour or so before then.'

The wet soles of his feet made marks on the kitchen floor. He sat at his usual place, accepted a mug of tea, then asked for toast. He was in a taciturn mood again this morning, but ate hungrily. Grace wondered when he had last eaten, and what it had been. The food and drink eventually spurred him to speak.

'I gave in my notice. The dogs,' he said. 'Two days of that was more than anyone could take. Went round to the old bat this morning, told her what I thought about her dogs. She didn't seem to like my opinion, screamed bloody murder at me, said how could she be expected to have a mind at peace in her *taxing executive job* – those were her very words – when her chows were shut up all day? I said not my problem, lady, and got out quick. So that wasn't a good start.'

'No.'

'Then the snow. – You look in a jitter. Don't worry, I'm off in a moment. I know when I'm not wanted.'

'Don't be silly, Lucien. I'll make more toast. Are you going to try the job centre?'

'Am I ever? Completely and utterly useless. You know how many times I've been there? Nothing. Nothing suitable. Ever.'

'What, then?'

Lucien lifted his head, closed his eyes, ran his dirty hands all over the stubble skin of his face, fingers moving like a pianist. Grace had seen him do this before. It signified concentrated thought.

'This time, no more mucking about. This time I'm going to have an idea that solves the whole thing. Do something that gets me excited right up to here.' He opened his eyes, slashed a hand across his neck.

'Well that's . . . good. But what sort of thing?'

'Don't ask me that. I don't know yet but I will know soon. But I'm talking the big time.' He shut his eyes again, envisaging something beyond Grace's comprehension. She looked steadily at the pathetic figure he made: thin, unwashed, jumpy, defensive, bleak. How could he possibly imagine that anyone in any area of 'the big time' would be prepared to give him a chance? He suddenly thumped the table with his fist. 'That is, if *Lobelia* doesn't bugger it all up for me again, like she did last time.'

'What did she do?'

'I don't want to talk about it. I'm not one of those who think it's a good thing talking about stuff all the time. The social services people – at one time they kept sending round people to talk to me. Why don't we talk it through? they kept saying. I said I don't want to talk it through, thanks very much, you stupid old cow, so you might as well go. It'd bore me rigid going on about my pathetic childhood, and it wouldn't do any bloody good. So you might as well bugger off and don't send anyone else round. Course, they did. But none of them got anywhere.' Lucien finished his tea, stood up. 'I like talking about other stuff.' He was silent for a moment. Still. 'I like talking to you.' He gave Grace one of his disarming smiles. 'Smells good, whatever you've got in the oven.'

'I'll keep a piece for you.'

'Maybe I should find a girl. One who likes cooking.'

'That's a good idea.'

'Once I've got myself sorted, I'll start looking. – See you.'

Lucien let himself out into the snow. It was coming down thickly now, and covered his thin clothes and bent head within a few yards.

William heard Grace and Bonnie coming up the stairs at five past twelve – he checked his watch. They came upon him so suddenly he had no time to compose himself into an aspect of nonchalance. They opened the door to see him dithering by the window, like a man at loss, violin in one hand, bow in the other. Bonnie, in her instinctive way, made it easy for him.

'William! I say, it's wonderful up here. Your ivory tower.'

Grace, smiling, muttered something about lunch being ready at one, and left the room, shutting the door behind her. So they had exactly fifty-four minutes.

'I rather like it,' said William, feebly, 'I must say.'

Bonnie moved to the window.

'Nice being able to look down on your garden.' She touched the music stand, glanced at the Massenet score, smiled. Could she guess why he had chosen to play it? 'This is where you play?'

William nodded. 'Good view on a clear day. – You've brought your viola.'

Bonnie put the music case on the floor.

'I never leave it in the car. Take it with me everywhere.'

'Won't you . . . sit down?' William felt the constriction of his unease. 'Shall I make you coffee? I've got all the paraphernalia up here, look, it's easy –'

'No thanks. Grace gave me some. – She's lovely, your wife.'

Bonnie's eyes were moving round the room, over hill and dale of all his private things that could be of no interest to anyone, that no one had probably ever looked at with such curiosity – interest? – before. None of the other players had ever been in this room – their occasional meetings at the house were conducted downstairs. Grace only ever put her head round the door and smiled at the general chaos. Molly the cleaning lady swiped at things unfeelingly with a duster once a week. But no one had ever *looked*, in the way Bonnie so pertinently looked. William felt himself moved by her apparent understanding of why things were like they were.

She bounced over to the ailing sofa, pushed up a pile of papers to make room for herself, sat.

'D'you mind? – You know what? I learnt something extraordinary from Grant yesterday after you'd gone. You know I told you it was Dvořák's Cello Concerto that had got me hooked on being a musician? Well, turns out it was the same piece that inspired him originally, too. Isn't that an odd coincidence?'

'Very odd,' agreed William. It was also bad news. The fact that they had this in common was a worrying link. They might, God forbid, see it as some kind of sign, attribute to it an importance that did not really exist. William's spirits dipped. There was a long silence. 'You've been visiting a friend nearby?' he said at last, dully.

'Yes. In Reading. A very old friend.'

Now was not the time to enquire further. One day, in jocular fashion, William would gird himself to ask her questions about her private life. When he knew her very much better. He sighed. Bonnie instantly looked up, pale eyes half-moons beneath her fringe, and gave him a sympathetic smile.

'I rather hoped,' she said, 'this could be the time for you to keep your promise, play to me.'

William was taken aback. He had forgotten his promise. Did he actually make a promise? He certainly had had no plan to play anything today. What could he . . .? Besides, this didn't seem like the right time.

'Oh, I'm not sure about that, Bonnie. I wouldn't like you to hear me at far from my best, and I haven't practised a solo piece for ages.' Her smile waned. 'Tell you what, though: why don't we play something together?'

Even as he asked the question William was aware he had gone

too far: proposed something from which he could not retract. And yet he knew if she accepted his invitation – and it was clear she was about to do so – he would be entering dangerous territory, a forbidden place full of consequences too dreadful to contemplate, should he be so foolish . . .

'That's a lovely idea,' she said. 'How about one of the Mozart duos? There's one I used to play with my teacher at college . . .'

William rummaged through one of his Mozart piles, Bonnie took out her viola. Some immeasurable time later they were both standing by the window, instruments poised. Outside, roofs, hedges, bare trees were now crusted with white. Snow was falling thickly, but straight, so the glass of the window remained clear, sheltered by the eaves. It was all so strange, so unnerving, William feared he would not be able to read the music. Switching his eyes from the moving white outside the walls to his own room, he saw that they, too, were shockingly unfamiliar. He had always believed in the magic of change caused by the presence of a disturbing figure, and here was proof. Bonnie's presence in this, his room, had caused havoc.

He forced himself to meet her eye. She gave a half-smile. He nodded. They began to play together, and the forces William had predicted would be his undoing began their potent work.

They had come to the end of a duo when Grace knocked on the door. The fifty-four minutes had also played their trick, and had disappeared so fast William could not be sure they had ever happened. During their playing a pale sun – which William took to be symbolic – had broken the dark sky. The snow had slowed and was melting even as it fell. They were packing up their instruments. Bonnie glanced at William's stricken face. He would not catch her eye.

He knew she was aware of his ungrounding . . . She put down her viola, came over to him, hugged him with the impetuosity of a child.

'What's the matter? Have I done something?'

William was rigid in her arms, fighting to keep an unreadable demeanour.

'Done something? – Oh, Bonnie. Just: the pleasure of playing with you.'

Bonnie stood back from him now, puzzled.

'You know something, William? Playing with you – with all the Quartet, but especially alone with you – is the greatest privilege I've ever . . . I mean, I can't describe what it means to me. That *you*, William Handle, should play with me! Beyond my wildest—'

'Dear Bonnie,' William interrupted, fearful of being completely thrown by further compliments. 'We must do it again.'

'*Please*. Promise? I *loved* it. What will my mum think? – Come on. Grace is waiting for us.' She gave him a wonderful smile and left the room.

Bonnie's declarations were indeed unexpected. Here was proof, surely, that his feelings were in some ways reciprocated. Bonnie had poured her soul into the music, sending messages too strong to be ignored. She had hugged him, told him she wanted them to play *alone together* again. So many glorious signs unsteadied him. He leant his forehead against the cold window, shut his eyes. It would be a very dull life, he thought, if ordinary days were not sometimes scattered by momentous and unexpected events. Awash with both gladness and horror (what would this lead to?), he followed Bonnie downstairs carrying his violin – for comfort, for safety – wondering how he would get through the rest of the day.

At lunch in the kitchen he was grateful to the two women. Aware of it or not, they made it easier for him than he had supposed. They chattered about music, flowers, cooking. They liked each other. William was not necessary to their conversation.

They left him free to play a strange and frightening visual game. He would look at his wife Grace, and wipe her out of his mind. She simply did not exist in her place across the table any more. It was like playing on an internal computer. One click, and the vision was gone. He was left alone with Bonnie. Bonnie and he, in this alarming game, were alone at the marital table. But it had become another table which he did not recognise.

Grace kept returning, of course. Her powerful presence could not be clicked out for long. This, in fact, was a relief. It proved to William he was not going mad. Had he clicked her out of his mind and she had not returned, that would have been cause for real alarm.

'William? Another slice? You look miles away.'

'Not hungry, my Ace, thank you so much.'

He clicked her away again.

On the journey to the barn for the rehearsal, alone in his cold little car slushing carelessly through wet snow, Bonnie in the wing mirror a few yards behind him, it all became clear to William. Simply: Grace had to go. He could see no alternative, despite the absurdity of the idea. Once she was no longer there, Bonnie could move in to fill the space, the house, his life. They could play, play, play together, making music more divine than he had ever heard. How he would negotiate the matter of Bonnie moving in with him, persuade her of the wisdom of the idea, was not relevant to his present plan to do away with his wife. Later he would think about how to overcome any objections Bonnie might put in his way. But for the moment he must concentrate wholly on how to extinguish Grace, his beloved Ace. It would be nice to think that some outside force would make this possible – struck by lightning while out shopping, a call from her sister in Australia to go there at once . . . But such things were unlikely, and he could not wait too long.

The truth of the matter was that there was no alternative. Suddenly William was able to contemplate the fact quite calmly: he would have to murder his wife.

4

'I don't think monkfish would be too alarming,' said Laurel.

William pulled his gold-rimmed spectacles down his nose and gave her a look he hoped she would interpret correctly: no need to patronise me, thanks very much.

'In that case,' he said, 'perhaps you should choose it.' With the intention of further study, he raised the menu again. It was as big as a pillowcase, and bent awkwardly. After a while he turned back to Laurel, who was biting her lip. 'Think I'll have the *Zuppa di Mammole e Tompinambur* and then the *Calamari ai Ferri con Peperoncini*,' he said, very fast, his Italian accent near-perfect. That'll teach her, he thought.

'The what?' said Laurel.

'The *zuppa* whatever,' said Jack, who pronounced *zuppa* like upper.

So far, as each of the four diners privately recognised, the evening had been ghastly. Jack and Laurel were not lovers of classical music, but had suggested coming to the concert for William's pleasure. If they had thought harder they might have concluded their presence was the last thing William desired: he abhorred the idea of anyone sitting through a concert out of perverse duty, least of all his philistine son. On the rare occasions Jack had suggested coming to hear his father play, he had been careful to choose a programme of composers unlikely to tax his ears. Tonight, Bartok, Haydn and Purcell were about as dreary as a string quartet could produce, Jack

thought, but the overriding consideration had been location –
Ealing. Very convenient for Hammersmith. Grace had suggested the
alternative of a Schubert evening in Leicester the following week.
But with a workload like Jack's and Laurel's, flouncing off to the
Midlands, midweek, was of course out of the question. With the
lack of inhibition that martyrs feel free to indulge, they had several
discussions about the displeasure the Ealing concert would cause
them, but nobly recognised there was no alternative, within the
time limit, that could be considered a birthday treat.

They both devised a way of getting through the musical bit, as
they called it. For some time Laurel had been wanting to work out
a marketing strategy for a hotel in Portugal. As a mere seller of
tickets and information, she was not strictly required to meddle in
the business of promotion. But she had learnt that it could be
advantageous to pick on some foreign hotel and sell it hard with
her 'personal recommendation', which she could give quite easily
without the bother of a personal visit. (One of her ingenious little
plans on her way to becoming top dog.) Such was the busyness of
her working life that the Portuguese hotel had had to be put on 'the
back burner'. The hour of the concert of tedious music, therefore,
presented this opportunity, this 'space' she had been looking for.
Not daring actually to use her calculator while the Quartet played,
during the applause she executed a few sums, and by the end of the
piece of music – which left her cold, as she whispered to Jack – a
complete plan for the Portuguese hotel was dazzling in her mind.

Jack, too, had decided to avail himself of the chance to reflect
upon a business plan concerning the higher, more complicated
realms of chartered accountancy that he so enjoyed. However,
without the relevant papers to hand, this was impossible. He gave
up, concentrated on trying not to fidget. Occasionally he glanced
at his mother, hands folded at rest on her knee, head tipped a little
to one side, benign eyes following every movement of her husband's bow. Jack followed her look to the stage. There was his
father, grim-jawed, eyes half-closed, sawing away at the violin to
make music that, amazingly, the majority of people in the hall had

actually paid good money to come and listen to. Extraordinary, thought Jack. Other people's pleasures never ceased to surprise him. Nor, for that matter, did his parents – a rum couple if ever there was one, completely sheltered from modern life by their adherence to bygone standards, language, behaviour. They were the sort of people who wrote thank-you letters for a minor Sunday lunch, indulged in an excess of precautions – an umbrella if there was a single cloud in the sky, vests in October, the scrupulous studying of ingredients in supermarket food. For years as a child Jack had been embarrassed by his mother's insistence, when they went to visit friends, of carrying a bag of 'indoor shoes' as a precaution against any mud they might encounter on the way. He had given up trying to explain to her that the whole concept of indoor and outdoor shoes had gone out with the ice age, and this was the happy era of the ubiquitous trainer which served all purposes. Why, he and Laurel even wore trainers to the office. But there was no point in trying to persuade Grace. Her prejudice against the trainer was deeply embedded: to her, the ugliness of such footwear (as if that mattered! Jack and Laurel agreed) was so acute that she had learnt to avert her eyes from people's feet in order to avoid the unpleasant spectacle. – Grace and William, Jack had always known, were so bound together in their wayward opinions that they made a formidable force, as parents, to confront. Both so consumed in their artistic pursuits (though Jack found Grace's meticulous rendering of the wild flower hard to think of as art), they had seemed, for all their kindness, impervious to the requirements of a small boy, a teenager or even a young man. All he had ever wanted was their interest, and he had never found it.

Jack glanced back at his mother: the devoted wife, astonishment at her husband's talent undiminished, love for him seemingly unabated. It would be hard for anyone (except Laurel) to agree that Grace was a mother lacking in many respects.

Jack shifted his eyes to the delectable sight of the new member of the Elmtree players, Bonnie Morse. He observed the charm of a pudgy elbow, blanched as mozzarella, that flashed against the red satin lining of her sleeve. He observed the angelic mouth, the bobbing fringe that tantalisingly hid the eyes. He was fascinated by the occasional sight – when she pursed her mouth in concentration – of the shallowest dimple he had ever seen, no more than a small shadow, really, playing about her cheek. As for the large velvet bosom . . . Jack could not help supposing that should Bonnie ever take the risk, say, of a lace *décolletage*, a cleavage as enticing as the dimple would be revealed. (The disloyal thought occurred to him that Laurel's breasts, small and lustreless promontories, were in a sadly different league from Bonnie's. Funny how Laurel was proud of them. She often persuaded Jack to join in their praises.) So intent was his concentration on Bonnie's physical assets that he ceased to care about the boring music: he scarcely heard it. The interval came with surprising suddenness, interrupting thoughts which had wandered some way down a nefarious path . . . Bonnie jogging along the river bank beside him, so he could watch those bloody great knockers jumping about . . . Bonnie – well, he'd have a chance to conjure other pictures later.

It was Grace who realised, as she studied the menu, the extent of trouble Jack and Laurel must have taken to choose the right restaurant. Their concern had obviously been not to plump for somewhere alarming in its inventiveness, and yet not so pedestrian that she and William might suspect, as a very ordinary couple, they were being suitably catered for. As it was, she felt, they had got it just right. This was an agreeable place: starched cloths, comfortable chairs, attentive waiters, lively hush. Among the rather highfalutin Italian specialities that William had gone for with a certain arrogant relish, there were some simple dishes, too. Grace herself fancied the grilled chicken with herbs, some polenta on the side – she had never understood the secret of polenta, so might learn, and even copy. She caught William's eye, smiled. Laurel's well-meaning suggestion about the monkfish had plainly annoyed him. He did not smile back.

Nothing is but what is not, William said to himself. He was inclined to quote Shakespeare at moments of great happiness or despair. Grace's concerned little smile had made his heart bounce and lurch. He needed a drink. Jack was taking the devil of a long time choosing a suitable wine – but then he fancied himself as a wine buff. His praise of William's own choice was always underlined with a trace of a sneer, not that William cared a toss what Jack thought about his choice. While Jack frowned over the long list, made a few comments to the wine waiter designed to illustrate his knowledge, and William fretted, a very junior waiter was permitted the task of putting a plate of nuts and olives on to the table. Laurel, who had been wondering how to dissolve the awkwardness caused by her innocent suggestion to the touchy William, pounced upon them, snatched up a green olive (not forgetting to curl her little finger in her hurry) and hoped the others would follow suit. She believed that the event of the olives and nuts would break the ice, and then there would only be three courses, and some two more hours, of the painful evening to go.

The dish was white, of fine bone china, divided into four. Two sections held black and green olives; the other two, nuts – peanuts and cashew nuts. Laurel pushed the dish towards Grace.

'Have a peanut,' she said, taking a black olive herself. She did not presume that Grace would be fond of olives.

'No thank you,' said Grace. 'I'm allergic to peanuts.'

William raised an eyebrow.

'I'd almost forgotten that,' he said.

'How interesting.' Laurel turned to Grace. She was always fascinated by others' illnesses and allergies, having experienced nothing but excellent health herself. 'How did you discover the allergy?'

Grace gave a small laugh. Aware that everyone at the table was listening, she found herself confused. She never liked to be the centre of attention.

'I was about five or six,' she said. 'Someone gave me a peanut-butter sandwich. I began to wheeze, then choke. I was taken to hospital. To be quite honest I don't remember much about it except that it was very frightening. They didn't know much about allergy in those days, but realised I must have at least a mild one. So I've avoided peanuts ever since.'

Peanuts, thought William.

'Must be rather scaring,' said Laurel. 'I mean, always having to be on the alert. Suppose you ate something you didn't know had ground-up peanuts in it?'

Exactly, thought William, whose hands had turned cold.

'Oh, I'm used to taking care,' said Grace, choosing an olive. 'It's become a habit. But I hope I don't make much fuss, do I, William?'

'You don't, my Ace. Indeed you don't.' The cold shrouded his whole body, now, as a picture of Grace, this time next year, came to him. Grace in her coffin, Grace dead. Luckily the excellent wine was poured: William gulped at it like a desperate man, earning a look of disapproval from Jack.

'Before we go any further,' said Laurel, 'there's something I want to put to you both, Grace and William. Something I think might excite you.'

William sighed. Laurel no longer had peanuts on her mind. Grace managed a look of polite interest. She, like William, could guess the sort of temptation Laurel was about to reveal.

'It's this. It so happens *ear-to-the-ground Laurel* – that's me – has wind of a very special Spring Break to Greece. Of course, as soon as it's announced it'll be booked up. But if you were interested, I could pull strings, probably get you something even more advantageous than the advertised rate . . .'

'How about that, Mother?' said Jack.

'Greece,' said William, with some semblance of a man pondering.

'The islands. Imagine! Place of the wine-dark sea.' Laurel had gleaned this snippet of Homer from more brochures than she could remember. It was *the* quote used in all copy advertising the Aegean Sea. 'A lovely new Swedish cruising ship, air-conditioned, a lecturer, some professor from Oxford . . . or is it Cambridge? Anyhow, all pretty irresistible, don't you think?' Her own excitement at the prospect had caused pink spots on her beige cheeks. They were also splattered on the V of chest exposed by the neck of her Lurex jersey.

'I fear we shall have to resist,' said William. 'The Elmtree's very heavily booked next spring.'

'Oh dear, there's always something.' Laurel gave an irritable sigh. The spots began to fade. 'But if you ask me, William, you do need a holiday.'

'I don't, you know,' said William.

'Nonsense! You push yourself too hard. You need a break sometimes. Think about it.'

'I don't know how you can keep turning down all Laurel's exclusive offers,' said Jack. 'She goes to such trouble.'

'We're not very keen travellers, really,' said Grace. 'You've always known that.'

William caught her eye and gave her a small smile of support. She had saved him the necessity of a much less polite reply. Then, luckily, the *zuppa* whatever arrived, and he was obliged to spell out the Italian pronunciation, which diverted more talk of Laurel's blinking special breaks.

At some time during the main course Jack felt it was his turn to make a show of interest in his father's life. (Duty to his mother always failed him. He could never think of a single botanical question to ask.)

'So: how's the new viola doing?'

Both innocent of the other's vision, father and son saw a white elbow dancing against scarlet satin.

'Bonnie? She's good. She's doing fine. We were lucky to get her.'

'Something of a looker, too,' said Jack.

'Bit overweight, if you ask me,' said Laurel.

'Much better than being too skinny, like a lot of girls these days,' said Grace.

Bonnie was not a subject William had any intention of discussing. The very mention of her name made him feel light-headed. This time next year he and Bonnie could be anywhere. He would be free to ravish her, sleep with her, wake up with her, make music with her – all those Mozart duos to be explored. Bonnie! William filled his glass again. The exquisite wine was

enhancing the familiar sensation that *nothing is but what is not*.
Dully he listened while Jack and Laurel discussed her. They made
no mention of her talent, only her looks. Laurel's mean observations – 'surely a girl with a bust like that shouldn't wear velvet' –
indicated jealous hostility. William could see that a girl like Bonnie
could pose a threat to the dreadful Laurel, but only if there was an
opportunity for Jack to meet Bonnie – which, William would make
absolutely sure, would never happen. Not that any such meeting
would worry *him* – there was no likelihood whatsoever of Bonnie
finding Jack attractive. If William had drunk less he might have
found his son's comments about Bonnie – 'gorgeous knockers' –
outrageous, and he would have challenged Jack to show more
respect. As it was, in his now befuddled state, although the observations were distasteful, William was also aware of a faint sense of
proprietorial pride: here was his son plainly fancying a girl way out
of his reach, the girl William felt closest to in the world. He loathed
the idea of Jack's lustful thoughts of Bonnie, although Laurel's
annoyance was amusing. Perhaps Jack was simply being provocative, entertaining himself by goading her. Well, William could see
the fun of that. She was so very humourless, so very earnest. Surely
Jack would realise, before it was too late, that somewhere beyond
Shepherd's Bush there must be a more life-enhancing girl with
whom to spend his life.

At this very moment Laurel was about to exert her natural lead-
ership (as she saw it). She'd had quite enough of Bonnie talk,
thank you very much (and would make quite sure they never
attended another Elmtree boring concert, thus avoiding the danger
of running into the fat cow with her fancy sleeves). The subject
had to be changed: only pudding and coffee to go.

'I've just discovered *tiramisu*,' she said, 'and my goodness do I
recommend it. Yummy.'

No one took up her suggestion. She sulked through the long
business of disparate puddings, which were eaten in weary silence.
But with the coffee William sensed a faint return of energy, though
his head was spinning: diners, white tables, carnations in fluted

vases, aproned waiters – all were dancing towards the ceiling. Feeling it incumbent upon himself to make an effort – well, Jack would certainly be paying a lot for the terrible evening – William gripped the edge of the table and turned to his son.

'Where are you going?' he asked.

Jack frowned, not understanding.

'Back to Hammersmith, natch,' said Laurel. She was proud of being a resident in the borough of Hammersmith.

William kept his eyes on his son. 'No, I mean in life,' he said.

Jack, who had drunk almost as much as his father, was phased by the apparent seriousness of this question. He looked at his watch.

'Good heavens, Dad. I'm not sure this is the perfect moment to answer that. I was about to get the bill.'

William was delighted Jack was unable to answer. He was not in the least interested where Jack and, God forbid, Laurel, were going in life: he hadn't planned the question, merely released odd drunken words to break a long silence. All he wanted was to get home, go to bed. To his relief he saw that Grace, his darling Ace, was of the same mind: she was gathering up her bag, patting her lips with the napkin. The wonderful thing about their rare excursions out together in the evening was that Grace took care of the driving. There would be no bother about that. He could put back the passenger seat, sleep his way down the motorway, confident of their safe return. Grace's competence in so may areas fuelled William's love for her. He knew his good fortune in such a wife.

'I'll do the tip,' said Laurel, peering at the bill. She took a twenty-pound note from her bag, the gesture a mixture of the discreet and the ostentatious. 'Well, it's been a lovely evening, hasn't it? We should get together more often.'

William could feel Grace's firm hand under his arm, helping him up. In many ways it was a pity she had to die, he thought. As he took his first step on the swaying carpet, the chandelier, which he noticed had become more lively in its movements as dinner progressed, was now intent on actually targeting William. It swung viciously towards him, horrible little candle-lights blinding him. If it hadn't been for Grace's quick reaction – she leapt ahead of him to protect him from its blow – he could have been cut to pieces.

'Steady, now,' Grace was saying, 'you almost fell.'

'Only falling for you, my Ace.'

Behind him William heard Laurel's sneering laugh, and the crude word, typical of her, *tipsy*. Still, so long as he could make it through the jostling tables – which, with Grace supporting him of course he could – the evening would be over. An hour from now he'd be in bed to sleep beside his wife, perchance to dream of Bonnie and the peanut plan.

On the occasions the Handles were confronted by people who wanted to know the secret of their happy marriage, Grace and William were unable to be of much help. Forced (reluctantly) to think about it, they supposed there was some art in simply observing the other one, and reacting accordingly. For the most part there was a mutual desire to avoid any sort of row or confrontation. There was an even stronger desire to avoid analysis of their lives, the eternal thrashing out and 'talking through' their problems, their thoughts, their feelings – the popular contemporary pastime they so abhorred. To Grace and William it would be distasteful, exhausting: there were better ways in which to pass precious time. In this, they were aware, they were branded as the very old, very British school of stiff upper lips. If pressed, they did not mind adding that tolerance of each other's singular ways was a help to marital harmony. But they would never admit, in the name of loyalty, exactly what these ways were. – The ritual of the battle with the bed, for instance. Over the years this had become a smooth operation in which Grace happily accepted her dormant part. William expected, and received, and was grateful for her nightly co-operation.

Grace's contribution to the whole process was vital, but not taxing. Her only duty, on nights that William came home late from a concert, was to listen to the weather forecast. Thus when he returned she could report whether it was to be warm, cool or bitter: and he could judge whether it was a two, three or four-blanket night, or a night of maximum precaution against freezing conditions, when an eiderdown would be added to the appropriate amount of blankets. If Grace for some reason failed to hear the forecast, though William would never go so far as to chide her, his dithering about as he tried to guess at the nature of the night – blankets whipped off and on accompanied by much sighing – was manifestation of his distress. He was also made unhappy by the rare occasions when he had had to leave early in the morning and there was no time to perfect the bed before his departure. Then, he would come home to find Grace reading among crumpled sheets, knowing it was not worth making any attempt to straighten them herself. At such times, not liking to ask his settled-looking wife to get out of bed, William did his best to put everything to rights around her. This was not easy. Grace gave up trying to read, lay passively while the top sheet was slung over her head, blankets were twitched in pursuit of symmetry, and her feet and knees were pushed almost flat as William tucked everything in to the desired tautness. Grace was used to all this and made no complaint. Her happiness lay in William's pleasure when, as master of the bed, he had once again managed to orchestrate pillows, sheets and blankets to his satisfaction.

On the drive home, the night of the dinner with Jack and Laurel, Grace wished very much that William's early departure to London that morning for a meeting with his agent had not meant that the bed was left unmade. In his inebriated state, the customary process would be certain to go less smoothly than usual. Grace, tired herself by the strain of the evening, dreaded it. All she wanted to do was to go to sleep as quickly as possible. She would have been quite happy to throw herself straight down, careless of the bed's turmoil. But that would have distressed William beyond measure.

To Grace's surprise, when they arrived home, William's equilibrium seemed completely restored. His nap in the car – with whimpery little snores that registered his rare consumption of so much red wine – appeared to have sobered him completely. In contrast to his hesitant steps across the restaurant, he bounded up the stairs with an eagerness that Grace failed to understand. At the sight of the rumpled bed he smiled in peculiar glee, as if its restoration was something he could hardly wait to start upon, despite the lateness of the hour.

'Did you listen to the forecast in the car, my Ace?'

'I'm afraid I didn't, no. Didn't want to wake you.'

'Ah, well. Never mind.'

William went to the window, opened it. A shrill blast of cold air stabbed into the warmth of the room. Grace shivered, cursing herself for not having listened to the radio. William licked a finger, stuck it out of the window. Then he turned, convinced.

'More or less freezing, I'd say. Four blankets.'

'Eiderdown?' Just occasionally, Grace liked to humour him. He took her suggestion seriously.

'I'm of the opinion that won't be immediately necessary. But if it gets cold later on, I'll deal with it.'

Grace knew from experience that any judgement of William's in which the word 'opinion' was expressed meant he was unsure, and doubts meant restless nights of leaping up and down to experiment with more or fewer blankets, battling to achieve a perfect temperature between the sheets. Wearily, she began to undress. William shut the window and took up a contemplative position his side of the bed. He surveyed it with a concerned look of one studying a much larger object – a building, or a ship – whose reconstruction required inordinate skill. But after some moments of silent cogitation, seeing Grace struggle to undo her necklace, he broke off his reflections to help. This was uncharacteristic. Normally, nothing could deflect William once he was embarked on his plan for the bed. In her surprise, Grace found herself discouraging him. She could not bear the thought of procrastination, for no matter what charitable reasons. She longed only for bed.

'I can manage.'

'No, no. I'll just . . .' William put on his glasses, turned Grace towards the bedside light, shuffled inefficient fingers among the strands of paste pearls that he had given her long ago. He could feel the warmth of the skin of her neck, soft as kid gloves. He fumbled unnecessarily with the pretty clasp, a paste aquamarine set in a frame of smaller pearls. He wanted to keep his fingers there, ascertaining the vulnerability of the neck he knew and loved. An impatient jerk of Grace's head urged him to undo the clasp. He handed her the small fountain of pearls that trickled from his hand, still warm, their foggy shine quietly luminous in the poor light.

'Thanks,' said Grace.

Then, before she could move away, she felt William's hand return to her neck. Oh Lord, she thought: a sign. Surely, tonight, both tired, so late, the whole palaver of bed-making still to come, it would be better to sleep as soon as possible. William had an early rehearsal in the morning. But she stood quite still, said nothing.

Beneath his fingers William could feel the top joint of her spine, the small dips each side of it. Then he stretched his hand to encompass the indeterminate place between the bottom of her skull and the top of her neck. The muscles, sinews, whatever they were, felt tough beneath the skin. He wondered how difficult it would be . . . He put his other hand under her chin. Her neck was now in a collar of fingers that tightened very slightly. Grace moved her head, puzzled.

'What are you doing?'

'Your pretty neck, my Ace. You always had such a pretty neck.' He laughed, releasing his fingers. He needed words to cover his confusion, some way to disguise the slight unsteadiness of his hands. 'It's funny about necks, isn't it? There's the onset of the dewlap, isn't there? The droopiness that betrays . . . but they don't get thicker, do they? Have you ever thought of that? There's no thickening of the neck, as such, is there?' His voice was rising, shrill. 'No middle-aged spread when it comes to the neck?' He turned away from her, began to pick up pillows, shake each one hard, then smooth its linen case. He was aware of Grace's patient little smile, a slight sigh: no doubt she was under the impression the effects of the good red wine had not yet worn off. 'And you see what I was thinking, undoing your necklace,' he blundered on, 'was that your neck hadn't changed one jot, in circumference that is, since we first met . . . has it? Still the same delicate little . . . stem that I saw arranged in that crimson velvet collar when you were eighteen –'

'– Twenty. William, are you all right?'

'I'm in very good shape.' He could have squeezed that little neck till the life went out of her, bruised the creamy skin that in all honesty showed only the slightest puckerings of middle-age. He tweaked at a sheet.

'Shall I help you with the bed?' Grace asked.

'Good heavens, no. Whatever for?' Strangling was obviously out of the question, though. Grace, the same size as William and possibly as strong, would fight for her life, fling him to the floor, send for a doctor and have him sectioned.

'I just thought . . .' Grace was off to the bathroom, undoing buttons.

Besides, William thought, he would not want to employ physical violence on the woman he loved. He replaced a pillow. Suffocation! That was a thought. But it was said doctors could always tell if someone had been suffocated. Tomorrow, on the train journey to Manchester, he would think more calmly. The matter of murder, which in some curious way did not strike William as at all peculiar to be contemplating, would require an intense passage of concentrated strategy . . . though the train might not be the ideal place. The others would be there, and there would be the distracting thought of spending the night under the same hotel roof as Bonnie. Good Lord, though, thought William: this time tomorrow night – well, anything could be happening.

A few moments later Grace was in bed reaching for her book. (However late, she liked to read a few pages each night.) William took stock: it was one of those awkward occasions when he would have to do his best to make the bed round her – always a frustrating process for them both. As usual William could not quite bring himself to ask her to get out, and his slight hints as to the convenience of such a measure seemed to go unheard. Tonight the pillows were luckily fine – his shaking and smoothing had distracted Grace's attention from his disturbed state most conveniently – but the rest was a shambles.

As Grace concentrated on the silent turning of her pages (she had learnt that almost any movement put William off his stride), her husband anxiously paced the perimeters of the bed, tucking, smoothing, checking, intent on important calculations in his head. The nightly challenge – so very much harder when Grace was in the bed – was to leave the blankets on his side slightly untucked but orderly, and the blankets on Grace's side tucked trimly and tightly, without losing a general sense of balance. Grace shifted very slightly: put down her book, switched off her bedside light.

'Look what you've gone and done! Pulled it all over. Now I'll have to realign . . .'

'William! I'm tired. Why not just leave it? We'll survive one night of not-quite perfection.'

William, on his knees on the floor, arms lost between base of bed and mattress – a position that always put Grace in mind of a farmer helping a troubled ewe give birth to her lamb – suddenly stood up. When the occasion called for it, no one could accuse him of a lack of magnanimity, and the guilt of his neck thoughts was still heavy upon him.

'You're right, my Ace,' he said, 'we'll probably manage.'

His acquiescence was so mild, so unusual, that had Grace not been falling asleep it might have troubled her.

'Grace,' said Lucien, 'I want to ask you a favour. I'm in desperate need of cash. Just a small loan.'

It was ten o'clock next morning. William had left soon after eight, having risen at six thirty in order to give himself unhurried time to deal with the bed. He liked to feel that when he was away Grace would enjoy its perfect state as much as when he was there. Unfortunately, time had outwitted him, and for all his careful planning he had had to rush his packing and breakfast. In his confusion he had left behind his birthday cufflinks from Grace. For some reason they were on a plate on the kitchen table. Lucien was fiddling with them, rubbing them between finger and thumb as a man exercises worrybeads. His restlessness made Grace uneasy.

'I'd never ask unless it was urgent,' he added. 'You know that.'

'For something particular, then?' Arguments shifted within Grace's weary mind. Lack of sleep had made her light-headed, unable to make a decision with her usual fast conviction.

Lucien shrugged, gave her one of his most endearing smiles.

'You could say that.'

'How much do you want? Without going to the bank I've only a bit from the housekeeping in cash.'

'Whatever.' Lucien put the cufflinks back on the plate. Grace picked them up, opened a drawer in the dresser.

'Don't want to leave these lying about,' she said, vaguely. 'I'll never learn to lock the back door.' She shuffled about in the drawer, returned to the table with four ten-pound notes. A look of disappointment dulled the expectation that had enlivened Lucien's expression, but he stuffed them quickly into his pocket. 'I'm afraid that's all I have.'

'That'll help.' This was said so heavily Grace was made fully aware her forty pounds would not be much help in the exigency of the situation. 'Thanks,' he added, after a while.

Grace, mildly curious as to the reason for Lucien's request, did not want to discuss the transaction any further. She knew that any news concerning William was of little interest to Lucien, but in her haste to change the subject she could find no other choice.

'William had to leave very early for Manchester,' she said. 'A concert. Overnight stay.'

'You mean . . . he'll not be back tonight?'

'No.'

Grace saw Lucien registering this information. He pressed his lips together, gave a slight frown.

'Don't you mind being in this great house on your own?'

'Not at all. I'm used to it.'

'I might look in,' said Lucien. 'Check you're OK.'

'That's very kind of you, but not necessary. Really. I'll be going to bed straight after the news.'

'Hint taken. I know when I'm not wanted.' He smiled agreeably. 'But don't you mind your old man going off for a night to Manchester with this new bird, this viola?'

'Of course not. They're all going, all the players.' Grace heard herself sounding more prim than stern. Sometimes Lucien was too cheeky, overstepped the demarcation line between the generations. She was inept at dealing with him on such occasions. 'When they've a concert somewhere too far to get back afterwards, they stay the night. I think they rather enjoy it.'

'I bet they do. – Don't their nights away worry you?'

'Not in the slightest.' Grace frowned. 'Why should they?'

'I mean, I daresay it didn't used to be a problem – they're not the age group to go in search of a bit of skirt after a concert. But since they've been joined by this new young girl – well, you know what men are, given the opportunity.' He gave a nasty laugh. Grace ignored his tone, smiled.

'Don't be silly. Bonnie's a lovely young girl. Young enough to be daughter to all of them – well, perhaps not Grant. No: luckily I've no worries there. William's usually so exhausted after a concert he doesn't even join the others for a drink in the hotel bar. Straight to bed, that's William. Always rings me last thing.'

'Ye of great faith.' Lucien smiled again.

'I trust my husband totally, yes,' said Grace. She did not like the direction of the conversation. It was almost as if Lucien was taking pleasure in trying to alarm her. 'Always have, always will.'

'Quite right, too.' He was teasing now. Perhaps he had been teasing all along. 'My bet is you're a wife in a million. If I could have a wish, it would be to meet a younger version of you.' He stood up. Grace laughed with relief this time.

'You say the daftest things,' she said.

Lucien patted the pocket of his jacket.

'I'll get this back to you as soon as I can. Just got to get a few things sorted.'

'There's no hurry.'

'Thanks again. See you tomorrow.'

When he had gone Grace realised it was past eleven: too late to get down to her painting before lunch. She decided to take the opportunity to walk to the bank, replace the borrowed cash. Lucien's silly teasing had ruffled her. She needed air, exercise, deflection from foolish thoughts.

By the time she arrived at the bank, calm returned. She knew that there was no need to worry about William: it was Lucien who was the cause of anxiety in her life. Why had he suddenly needed money so urgently? The question was too disturbing to contemplate for long. She told herself to give up thinking about the matter, nothing to do with her. All the same, in case Lucien was in need of another loan, she cashed a large cheque. It was one of the moments she felt willing to help him in whatever way she could. Other times her most passionate wish was for him to disappear for ever. These conflicting desires caused her irritating confusion. The time was approaching when, to re-establish equilibrium, she must make a decision about the future of relations with the strange, unnerving, though also endearing Lucien. She could not call on William's help – his opinion of Lucien was obdurately low, would never change. This was something she would have to deal with entirely on her own, and the thought of having to weigh it all up caused her great heaviness of heart.

Alone in his hotel room in Manchester, William felt powerless in the disagreeable silence common to such rooms – silence compounded of nylon carpet, central heating that makes you choke for air, the deadening impact of mass-produced furniture with its easy-to-wipe greasy shine. He sat on a pink armchair, hands sprawled at rest on its arms. It was covered in a bristly fabric more appropriate to toothbrushes than chair covers, which pricked his fingers. The headache that had been troubling him all day had not abated, despite a quantity of aspirin. – To William, headaches were visible things: fungi. The least bad were small, scarcely visible plants in the undergrowth of his head, their own heads pushing against a temple or eye. The worst were the kind he suffered today – obscene, many-headed things whose curly edges thrust against his skull until he thought the very skin would break. Sometimes they shifted, pushing their malleable humps upwards as if to crack the top of his head. Or they would move sideways, leaning so heavily against the socket of his eye he would be forced to groan out loud. Then, for no apparent reason, the mushroom would give up its attack. William would watch it wither down in his head till it was no larger than the dot that used to appear on a television screen before close-down. Once he had tried to describe the agony of the larger fungi in his head to the doctor, fearing they might be portents of a brain tumour. The doctor had chuckled, and praised William for his lucid description of the common headache. They then fell into an interesting discussion on the difficulty of describing the exact nature of pain, and the impossibility of conveying the abstract.

William shut his eyes, neck now irritated by the back of the scratchy chair, and sensed the fungi in his head swell, move, press, pinch. He felt uncommonly depressed. With a headache such as this surely it would be difficult to give of his best in the concert due to start in under two hours. On top of that dispiriting thought, the disappointment of the whole day returned to him. He had been looking forward to it – the proximity, for twenty-four hours, of Bonnie. The faintly nefarious excitement of being away from home for the night – although at this moment he would have done anything to be in his own armchair by the fire, Grace fussing round him with camomile tea. (She was the only person who understood about the fungi, perhaps because of her talent as a botanist.) On the train journey, where he had entertained imprecise thoughts of shuffling along carriages with Bonnie to the buffet car to buy her a cup of tea, she had hidden her face behind newspapers the whole way, and declined several offers of refreshment. Grant, listening to his Walkman, had been lost to them all. Rufus had slept, while

William had stared in acute depression at the rain-blasted land-scape through the windows.

At the rehearsal Grant and Rufus had been at their most irrita-ble while Bonnie, unusually silent, had twice requested to make an urgent telephone call. A friend of her mother's was ill, she explained. But she did not look very worried. William's disbelief added to his general discomfort. What was going on in Bonnie's life? Was some undesirable young man pressing her in some way? – As she hurried back to the platform the second time, full of charming apologies, a sense of urgency stabbed William. He would have to hurry with his plan, put it into practice as soon as possible, or it might be too late. It was unlikely a girl of Bonnie's exceptional attractions would remain alone for long.

The sense of urgency was still with him here in the chair, chaf-ing him inwardly as the fabric chafed his skin. On a tray beside him an indeterminate sandwich shrouded in clingfilm, and a pot of tea, remained untouched. He had no appetite. The others had gone to a trattoria for a pre-concert supper, another thing he had been looking forward to, but in the event could not face. William raised his hands to his temples, and pressed. As he did so, the fungi faded, the pain released him. A picture re-entered his mind, horri-bly bright: *peanuts*.

With a new surge of energy William leapt up, pulled on his mackintosh and hurried out of the hotel. Rain was pouring down, thick as ash. It cut into his tired face and quickly drenched his hair. He ran a few yards down the road, hopeless mackintosh cracking about his knees, to a newsagent he had earlier observed. It was still open: warm, untidy, a smell of faintly rotting fruit, the ugly gauze of neon light falling over its small world. William was convinced there would be packets of peanuts for sale. He picked up a local evening newspaper which he did not want, to swell the bulk of the real purchase he had in mind – or perhaps to dim his guilt – then asked for peanuts.

'We are out of peanuts, very sorry.' The thin, sad Asian shop-keeper shrugged apologetic shoulders.

'Out of peanuts?' Incredulous, William searched his pocket for coins for the newspaper.

'We've had a run on peanuts.'

'Out of peanuts . . .' Thwarted, William's exhaustion returned. He had no energy left to look further for peanuts on this vile night.

'You can never tell what people will be wanting.' The shop-keeper's face, bluish in the savage light, conveyed a disappointment, in letting down a customer, that looked close to his own, thought William.

'Don't worry. It doesn't matter at all. It's of no consequence.' As he handed over the coins he felt a tap on his shoulder. He looked round: Bonnie.

'Just dashed in for a packet of fags,' she said.

She was wetter than William. Her hair was clamped to her head, divided into crab-claw curls that gripped her sparkling face. In the threadbare shop she was the rarest of customers, an illumina-tion: William could see such facts register in the Asian's face. His own heart began to dance.

'What a night, isn't it? Packet of Marlboro, please.' She turned to William. 'What are you doing here? I thought you wanted to rest. – Why don't you come and join us for coffee? It's just round the corner, the café. Very good lasagne we've just had.'

'I'd come to get some peanuts but they're out of them,' William heard himself saying. He knew he was unable to accept her invita-tion, but was at a loss, in his confusion, as how to refuse her.

'You'll not get through the evening on peanuts,' Bonnie laughed.

'I'll be—'

'I really can't persuade you?' She was impatient. William shook his head. 'Well then, see you at the hall.' She was gone, shaking her head, scattering raindrops from her hair. The shopkeeper smiled.

Defeated in his desire for peanuts, William also sensed a certain relief. If there were no peanuts currently available, he would have to postpone his plan for a while. In the end he would have to be constructive, but he was not looking forward to working out the fine details of Grace's demise. In the meantime, the prospect of procrastination for a while longer restored his strength. He was not ashamed of his performance at the concert.

When it was over the members of the Quartet walked back through Manchester's wet streets to the hotel, a cheerless establishment chosen by Rufus in the interests of economy. They gathered in the bar, furnished with more bristling chairs that grazed the thighs, and lit with crude pink lights. Ropes of gold tinsel swung randomly from ceiling to pillar to windows, reminding that Christmas was not far off, though their tired sparkle caused William to think they might well have been in place since this time last year. He could imagine, mid-July, what a tedious task fetching a ladder and dismantling them would be. Better to leave them up all through the year . . .

Bonnie was taking orders for a round of drinks. She snapped off his aimless thoughts with a pressing question about exactly which kind of whisky he wanted. Then he went to telephone Grace. Some indistinct thought occurred to him that it would be better to ring now than later.

'Oh, William: how did it go?'

'Fine, fine. Goodish audience.'

'Good. How's—?'

'Raining up here. Pouring.' Changes in the weather made the only changes in their ritual conversations. 'Any news your end?' William thought he detected a pause fractionally longer than usual.

'No. Nothing's happened. I was just on my way to bed. – You usually ring later.'

'Just thought I'd ring before we had a nightcap.'

'Oh, I see.'

Dear, darling Grace. Deception is so easy.

'So anyway, we're taking the eight o'clock train back. See you late morning.'

'Lovely.' Now there was a definite pause. 'Have you been thinking of me?'

William slammed his free hand on to the small shelf by the

telephone to steady himself. He felt a drift of sweat crossing his face: his shirt stuck patchily to his chest. The question, so surprising as to be alarming, threw him completely. Grace had never asked such a thing in her life. It was not the sort of question they would ever ask of the other one, knowing full well the answer. It was the kind of superfluous enquiry they would laugh at, had they ever discussed it. The reason for it William could not imagine – unless, with her acute instinct, Grace had been reading his mind. He managed a little laugh.

'Of course I'm thinking of you. I always do, don't I, my Ace? What a funny question.'

Grace laughed too.

'It's just been a very long evening. I don't know why. Put me in a sentimental mood or something.'

'My goodness. Very unlike you. But you've put on the alarm?'

'I have.'

'Then sleep well, my Ace.'

William replaced the receiver before she had a chance to say more. He saw he left on it a clammy imprint of his hand. God, he needed that drink.

Back in the bar, Grant and Rufus were sunk deep in their armchairs, eyes heavy-lidded. Bonnie was on the edge of her seat, black velvet skirt rippling over the nasty carpet. She looked anxiously at William.

'Whatever –? You look awful. Here.' She handed him a glass of double malt. William dreaded to think what it must have cost her. 'Also – I've got something for you.' Smiling, from behind her back she produced two small packets of peanuts. 'There! Though I can't think why you'd want them –'

'– No, you couldn't.' Shaken again, William sat heavily beside her.

'All that salt. Terribly bad for you.'

'I know, I know. Thanks all the same.' William slipped the peanuts into his pocket. He took a large sip of the exquisite whisky. 'Thanks for this, too.' He vaguely lifted his glass in her direction, a man whose frailty of indecision was in combat with the strength of his anticipation. Forcing his eyes from Bonnie's lively face, he turned to Rufus, whose eyes were now tightly shut. It occurred to William that his friend looked unusually tired, and suddenly old – though perhaps it was just the dreadful lighting that enhanced his years. In his perturbed state William wondered once again how many years of good playing were left to the Quartet . . . Surely Bonnie would not want to stay for long with this group of men so much older, less vigorous than herself? And then what? William could not bear to think of the whole wretched process of auditioning again, and probably having to settle for someone in a different sphere from Bonnie.

Rufus opened his eyes.

'Think I'll turn in,' he said. 'I'm knackered.'

With an attempt at brightness, William smiled at Bonnie. The last thing he wanted was that any of them should indicate to her signs of weariness.

'Never seems to affect his playing,' he said.

'Think I'll follow Rufus,' said Grant, quickly swallowing the rest of his beer. 'Chance to finish my Dick Francis.'

The two men got up to go, thanked Bonnie for the drinks. For a moment William thought he saw a look pass between Bonnie and Grant – some message? Was this a plot – humour the old boy with a drink or two, then come along to my room? Was this what Grant's eyes were saying? The idea of a third-rate hotel assignation was particularly repugnant: William quickly put it from him, again blaming the lighting for his suspicions, and sank back into his chair. At least he had Bonnie alone to himself for the duration of his whisky. Perhaps after that he could prolong the precious time by offering her another brandy.

As soon as the others were out of sight, Bonnie leant towards William and patted his knee.

'What's the matter?' she asked.

Her touch had lit a fuse in his thigh. It ran riotously upward causing weird, weakening sparks of outrageous desire, love, confusion all through his body. He found it hard to speak calmly.

'Something of a rough night last night. After the concert our son Jack and his girlfriend took us to some fancy restaurant, plied us with very good wine We got home much too late.'

'Then you mustn't be late tonight.' She stroked his hand with one finger, in the mindless way that she might have stroked a kitten, and pushed up his cuff to look at his watch. Her finger whirled briefly on the skin of his wrist. It was almost unbearable. Was this some kind of message? What was Bonnie doing – teasing? William squirmed very slightly in his chair, hoping she would not notice the discomfort she was causing. He tried to concentrate on calming himself down. He thought of pigs' trotters, the sinking of the *Titanic*, the repeal of the Corn Laws.

'No, you're right, I mustn't,' he said faintly.

Bonnie removed her hand. The brisk way she did this – no hint of wanting to linger now she had seen the time – pointed to the disappointing truth: she was absolutely innocent of any delicious intention. Simply being kind to her fellow player, her boss, was all she had in mind.

'You're wearing my cufflinks,' she said, pleased.

'Of course. I'm very fond of them.' Had William been quicker off the mark he would have attempted to tell her, in a dignified and understated way, just what the cufflinks meant to him, how he . . . But her thoughts had flown elsewhere.

'D'you know what? Some fan left me a note tonight.' Bonnie was very pleased with herself. 'Does that often happen?'

'Grant sometimes gets notes from classical groupies. Well, handsome fellow in a largish way. Seems to have something for the girls. A few years back, I have to admit, Rufus and I sometimes had the odd invitation.' Now his own honesty betrayed him. In such a confession, he himself was indicating his powers of attraction were over. But Bonnie, intrigued by the thought of her own fan, did not seem to register the admission.

'Someone called Euan,' she said. 'Depressing handwriting, but wanted to know what I thought about when I was playing? What went through my mind? Could I enlighten him? – Could I, indeed?' She laughed. 'Then he was into all the rubbishy stuff about my looks. How could anyone so sexy – he wrote the word in red ink – be a serious musician?' She blushed. William laughed.

'All very old lines,' he said. He was feeling calmer now. But just for safety he called forth another trio of passion-quelling images: turnips, pug dogs, Grace's aged slippers. 'Whatever you do, don't respond.'

'Of course not.'

'I don't want my new viola ravished so soon.'

Bonnie did not seem to notice the lie. Her innocence made his own longing the harder to bear. But he saw that here, by chance, was the opening he'd been awaiting. Now was the time to ask her something of herself. Did she have anyone –?

'But it's an interesting question,' she was saying. 'What goes through our minds when we are playing? Can you answer that?'

'No,' said William quickly. He loved her serious face.

'I enjoyed the comic bits of Disney's *Fantasia* as a child. But even then I found the serious parts too crude, too neat somehow. – I don't exactly think of anything, but pictures come to mind. When I was a child of seven or eight I heard the *Pastoral* for the first time.' Bonnie hesitated. William put on his best listening face. Damnit, Grant wasn't the only one who knew the power of *really* listening. And this would be no pretence on William's part, of course. He *wanted* to hear all Bonnie had to say. He would be happy to listen through the night. He nodded. She continued. 'My mum said whenever she heard it she saw cows galloping across summer fields, their tails in the air. I've always thought of that ever since. The idea seemed to breed further pictures – but it would sound too foolish, describing them. Haydn's the only one who produces nothing for me so far. I love him intellectually, but find there's no vision there. Still, I'm struggling. I realise it's my fault, not his.'

William bowed his head, avoiding her eye. He was moved by Bonnie's confession, surely not the sort of thing she would mention casually to anyone. Musicians rarely spoke of the effects of their music. It was an impossible subject, prone to pretentiousness. But then maybe he was out of date in this respect, as in so may others. Maybe the young generation all liked to discuss the internal experiences inspired by their playing. He himself would find that difficult, embarrassing. But tonight, in his state of joy brought about by Bonnie's proximity, Bonnie's confidences, he felt he should make some sort of effort to return the honour, try to explain his own feelings.

'I don't see pictures,' he said, kneading his fingers, 'though I shall enjoy thinking of those cows in the future. A very merry image.' He paused struggling. 'What happens to me is that I know whether a certain piece of music is . . . upstairs or downstairs. I can't begin to describe this well, but if it's an upstairs piece then I'm lifted to . . . some sort of life-enhancing place that restores the spirit, gives strength, joy, whatever. If it's a downstairs piece, then I'm consumed in a sort of darkness: a serious place full of mysterious resonances, sounds echoing in some sort of invisible ocean, as in Beethoven's late quartets. I can sometimes feel myself gasping for breath, but always know I'll be saved by the last bar.' He paused. 'Do you know at all what I mean?' His eyes met Bonnie's as he cursed himself. He'd gone way beyond the bounds of propriety. He must have sounded like the pretentious old bore he had always hoped to avoid. But as she nodded, still angelically serious, he found himself adding one last thing. 'The strange thing is, a piece doesn't have to be melancholy to be downstairs. *The Moonlight Sonata*, for instance, is full of light for me. I was very puzzled when I first realised it was an upstairs piece . . .' He trailed off, stricken with the remorse of one who has confessed a long-held secret.

Bonnie nodded. 'I understand,' she said.

William was desperate to break the spell, now: dismiss all he had said as if it was of no importance. Get her to join in scoffing at his fantasies, thus diminishing them.

'Understanding can be the quickest way to an old man's heart,' he said, and allowed himself briefly to pat her knee. It worked. Bonnie giggled.

'You're not that old,' she said.

'No,' agreed William. With any luck she had forgotten the details of everything else he said. But with luck she would also remember they had shared a moment of soul-baring that would bind them, on one level, for ever. William watched the barman pulling the grill across the counter. 'Shall I quickly get you another brandy?'

'No thanks. It's time for bed.' She pushed her empty glass towards the middle of the low table between them, but made no movement to get up. William finished his own drink. There was no more to say. Three lights were switched out, leaving them in the murky pink of a bad sunset. William closed his eyes, wanting to stay with Bonnie in the hideous bar for ever.

'How are you liking it, the Quartet, to date?'

'I'm loving it. You must have guessed that. Playing with you three is something beyond my wildest dreams.' William opened his eyes, saw she was smiling. 'It's like those people who say that playing tennis with people who are better than them makes them play better. I don't know if it's true, but I sort of feel that.'

'You play beautifully.'

'Thanks. I've a long way to go.'

'Of course. We all have. – You don't mind that in a quartet there's no star? The fact that abnegation of sole glory is essential? The excellence of the whole is what a quartet is all about . . .'

'I've always known that, of course. I've never wanted to be a solo star. I've always thought that team effort, when it succeeds, must be much more satisfying than success on your own, with no one to share the highs or lows.'

'Rather an unusual way of thinking, that, in these star-obsessed days.'

Bonnie smiled.

'Well I just want to play for years and years with the three of you, learning from you.'

Touched by these sentiments, William spoke in a voice scarcely above a whisper.

'Well, dear Bonnie, I don't know if we'll manage to do anything for you, but you've certainly inspired us with a new vigour.'

'Really?'

'Really.'

'Golly . . .'

They got up from their chairs. In the lift, a cube of salmon-pink light, William gazed on Bonnie's reflection in the dirty mirror. He saw the absolute impossibility, after their conversation, of suggesting anything so crude as a nightcap in his room. She had signalled her closeness, but by doing so they had gone too far down some other track for him now to switch to lecherous old man. Any untoward gesture was unthinkable. The time to ravish her would be at the moment of offering her his life – a time he must now work towards with all speed, for some small hope had definitely been indicated. In the passage leading to their rooms they hesitated for one moment on the stormy carpet of maroons and blues, then Bonnie reached up and kissed William on the cheek.

'Sleep well,' she said. 'You look tired.'

Then she hurried down the passage, jangling the key of her room. William knew all the players were on the same floor, but in which rooms? In all the hurry of arrival he had not noticed. Where was Grant?

The question did not bother William unduly that night. He was convinced that some step in the right direction had been taken. If he could exert patience, tact, sympathy, then his feelings for the exquisite Bonnie would surely not go unrequited.

A man elated by his anticipation, he got quickly into the narrow bed, pulled up the economy sheets, bounced his head on the rubber pillow. He thought of Bonnie's *Pastoral* cows, of the depths of the invisible oceans she had understood, and her kind peanuts, which could be powdered and added to curry.

Then he slept.

5

'How was your night?' asked William.

'Not at all bad.'

'Good.'

'And yours?'

'So so. Woke up at three, but probably for only half an hour.'

'Oh dear.'

The Handles' questioning of each other's nights was a daily ritual that took place while Grace boiled the kettle and William sat waiting for his tea. There was a competitive edge to these enquiries. Over the years each had learnt that there was sometimes an element of exaggeration in both their own and each other's answers. But each one took care never to describe a night so miserable that it would stretch the other's credulity. In some rhythmic way they were almost equally winners and losers – the winner, curiously, being the one who had missed most sleep. He or she was the one most to be pitied, and yet admired. Due to these morning exchanges they were as well acquainted with the other's nights as they were with the other's days, and to have started the day without an exchange of nocturnal news would have been inconceivable.

Once it was over, they fell into their normal silent breakfast. This morning, two days after William had returned from Manchester (his previous lack of sleep having been compensated for by two rather shamingly good nights), the scarcely enjoyed silence was interrupted by a tap on the kitchen window. Grace and William looked up: Lucien.

Grace moved quickly to the sink, leant across it to open the window. The moment she had been dreading for so long had arrived.

Lucien stuck his head through the window.

'Got a job,' he said, grinning. His shoulders were shirred with a dust of snow. Grace had only seen grey sky outside: she hadn't realised it was snowing again. William, she thought: driving. The double anxiety rattled her heart. 'You here, then?' Lucien looked at William who, feeling accused of being in his own house, halted a piece of toast mid-flight to his mouth. 'I'm early. Sorry. But it's good news.'

'You'd better come in.'

Grace unlocked the back door. She could not bear to witness what Lucien would choose to do next. She moved back to shut the window, snapping off the blast of cold air that had intruded so quickly. When she turned round again Lucien was sitting, apparently at ease, opposite William.

'Coffee?' asked Grace, carefully. She had to convey much in a single word. In the tone of her voice she must indicate to William her disapprobation of this visit, and to Lucien her apologies for not being alone.

'Bit early for coffee. I'll share your pot of tea if that's all right.' He nodded at William, who refrained from any reaction. 'So, William: how's things? How's the new girl, Bonnie?'

In William's indignation, the flight of his toast was again delayed. His shoulders tightened. What was he up to, this repulsive oaf, reading his mind?

'Fine, thanks.'

William had no intention of benefiting the unattractive lout who his wife, in her misguided charity, had befriended, with a more expansive answer. He also had no intention, for Grace's sake, of showing his horror at the situation.

'Good, good. I heard she was doing well.'

William snatched at his toast, and this time caught it. He doubted Lucien had heard any such thing. Grace was unlikely ever to have discussed Bonnie, or anything concerning William, with this brutish young man.

'She's doing fine,' he repeated, hoping, by understatement, to goad a little. Grace returned to the table, pot of tea refilled, and a mug for Lucien.

'I don't usually have this one, do I?' With a fist made clumsy by grumpiness he picked up the mug. It had come from a petrol station, a free gift William had acquired through months of careful hoarding of tokens. Grace remembered the day he had brought it home in some triumph. Lucien's turn to goad, thought William. But if it was Lucien's intention to let the husband know he had a *regular* mug in this kitchen, and all that that implied, he was not going to be drawn.

'Nor you do,' said Grace mildly. Nonetheless, she filled it with tea. This was another necessary double message: she was bound to convey a show of strength to William, pouring tea into a mug Lucien disapproved of; to Lucien, the acknowledgement that he *was* the regular user of another mug, but things had shifted this morning. She sat down, face tight, corners of her mouth twitching. Darling Ace, she's put on her mouse face, thought William.

There was a triple-edged silence that none but Lucien enjoyed. William, hurrying through the last of his toast, was determined to avoid any show of interest in Lucien's news. Grace inwardly prayed that news could be kept until William left.

When at last he got up to go, Grace rose too.

'Back in a minute,' she said to Lucien, and followed William into the hall.

'I need a hammer,' William said.

'A hammer? What, to bash –?'

William smiled very slightly, but friendly.

'Something upstairs.'

Grace took a hammer from a drawer in the hall table. Had it not been so tense a beginning to the day, she might have reflected how strange it was that after so many years William still did not know where certain contents of the house were kept. When she turned to hand it to him she found him standing on the bottom stair. Thus, he was several inches taller than her, looked down on her. This was all very peculiar.

'My Ace,' he said, 'I've been thinking: surely it's my turn to cook dinner?'

'*Cook dinner*?' For a moment Grace thought her husband had taken leave of his senses. He had not offered to cook anything for years. The oddness of the morning was increasing.

'Thought you might enjoy it for once . . . Have a night off.'

'Whatever's brought this about?'

'Who can say?' William wondered how a man can carry on so normally when there is murder in his heart. 'Things just occur to one out of the blue, sometimes, don't they? Good ideas. I suddenly rather fancied the challenge of a curry.'

'A *curry*? Would you know what to do?'

'I've some idea. I'll pick up a few things on the way to the rehearsal. We're having a long session today, so as to have a day off tomorrow.' (A clear day before the funeral was imperative. There were amorphous thoughts in the back of William's mind concerning a flurry of funeral directors, ambulances, doctors.) 'Rufus has to go to his dentist in Birmingham. – I'll be back soon after tea.'

'Very well. I'll look forward to it, my evening off. I may take a drink to the bath while you struggle: what a thought.' Grace gave William a grateful smile as he moved further upstairs.

The smile vanished on her return to the kitchen. Lucien had made himself toast, finished the marmalade, and was banging at *The Times*, crumpling it in a manner which would infuriate William, neatest of readers. His look, as Grace entered, was almost as if *he* was the host, she a guest in her own kitchen. Irritation rose in Grace, as earlier it had in William.

'You shouldn't have come so early,' she said.

'Sorry, couldn't help it. The news got me out of bed early. – We are in a dither this morning, aren't we? Shall I go?'

'William doesn't like guests for breakfast.'

'So he made quite clear. Anyway, I won't be around so much, now I'm working, you'll be relieved to hear –'

'Don't be so silly.' Despite herself, Grace sounded apologetic.

'This job's two days a week.'

Grace sat down. As soon as Lucien had finished his news, she would ask him to leave She dreaded the thought of his still being around when William came down, and she had no idea what time William – engaged in some mysterious task with the hammer – intended to leave.

'So what is it?'

'A centre for the homeless. Helping out.'

'That's marvellous.'

'Yuh. I mean, I can identify with them, can't I? Sort of job'll suit me down to the ground.'

'I'm not sure I can see you identifying with them that much,' Grace said cautiously. 'I mean, you're not exactly homeless, living in a large comfortable house.'

Lucien sniffed.

'A roof over your head doesn't mean much when you're *totally excluded*, does it?' He clenched his fist, punched his temples hard enough to hurt. 'You don't know what it's like, you with your comfortable bloody life, husband and money and that. You can't imagine what it's like not to have a single woman in the world who gives a toss for you. Sometimes the *unfairness* turns into such a rage I just want to blow the whole bloody scene up. Destroy. Put an end to it all. – I can see from your face you don't know what I'm on about. Suppose I can't expect someone from the privileged classes to understand someone from the underbelly of this crap world.'

Grace had no wish to enter this conversation now. She wanted to make sandwiches for William's lunch, get on with her own work. She merely shook her head.

'I can see you're wanting me out,' Lucien went on. 'Even you, Grace. I went and chose a bad time, didn't I?'

Grace looked at him, alarmed, not knowing what to say. She could see the building of one of his worst rages. But then, suddenly as it had come, it dissolved. The bones of his face softened. He gave her one of his most beguiling smiles.

'Don't worry, I'm not going to be awkward. I know you don't want me to go really. It's just him upstairs making you jumpy, aren't I right?'

'Don't be ridiculous.'

'Anyways, Tuesdays and Thursdays I'll be catching an early train, so you'll miss me then. You'll find the three mornings I come very precious, you'll see.' He grinned again, joking. Got up. 'Thanks for the breakfast, as per usual.'

Grace went with him to the door, worried that something in her careful demeanour had hurried him this much. She could afford to delay him just a moment longer, assure him there was no need to dash away.

'What about the promise that I can meet your mother?' she asked.

'*Lobelia*?' Lucien, about to open the back door, changed his mind. He leant against it instead. 'Never in your wildest imaginings could you guess what she did last night.'

Grace allowed a pause. When it pressed too long, their eyes locked. She knew she would have to give in.

'What was that?'

'Tell you some other time . . . But, yes, OK – if you still want to, fine by me. You'll meet her. She's curious about you, too, you know. Before Christmas, I promise.'

'I look forward to that,' said Grace.

'Bye, then. You're really pleased about the job?'

'Really pleased, of course. Good luck.'

Whether Grace's pleasure came mostly from the anticipation of relief at the thought of two mornings off, or for Lucien's sake, she could not be sure. She approached the fridge, trying to rid her mind of anything beyond William's sandwiches.

*

Upstairs in his room, William was finding the task of crushing peanuts harder than he imagined. There were no clear spaces on the desk or table, and impatience fired by guilt made him incapable of bothering to move anything. He settled for the floor. Here, he erected a worktop of two telephone directories, which (cunning thought) would absorb the noise of the hammering. He then opened the two small packets of peanuts (enough to kill an elephant if it had an allergy, he reckoned) and began to bash.

Almost at once he realised his mistake. The peanuts flew all over the place, chipped a little, but not the fine fragments he had intended. He should have left them in the bags. These he picked up and decided the splits could easily be mended with Sellotape, and the peanuts returned. He crawled to the desk, ruffled through the chaos of papers to where he thought the Sellotape might be. His hands, he noticed, were trembling. The tallest peak of manuscripts tottered and fell. Others followed. William sat back on his haunches in a mire of a million musical notes, crotchets glaring at him, crescendos warning him. But at least he held the bent, fluff-bound Sellotape. There was difficulty, then, in applying it to the torn bags, such was the unsteadiness of his hands. But at last the extraordinary task was accomplished. William sensed a kind of molten achievement rising within him, and began to scrabble about the carpet picking up far-flung peanuts.

He dared not look at his watch, knowing that he was already late. Besides, he was rather enjoying the close-up scanning of his worn and grubby carpet. He pondered on its life: who was the weaver of these hardy tufts? And when and where? He was beginning to enjoy the procrastination, provided by such ruminations, as he continued in his curious act of peanut hunting. Then the telephone rang.

'William? Could you manage Prague, Thursday week?' His agent.

Prague? What was the man thinking of? William heaved himself to his feet. He felt it was disrespectful to speak to Stephen, a man who had organised his working life efficiently for so many years, from a position on the floor. Peanuts fell from him.

'The Addenbrooks, booked for months, have had to cancel. John's got a suspected tumour. But I don't want to let Prague down. You'd be doing me a hell of a favour.'

William's mind was working slowly through all sorts of possibilities which might, in the end, make a trip to Prague impossible. On the other hand it would be foolish to put total faith into the power of peanuts, the Elmtree hadn't had a foreign engagement for six months, and there was only one – Paris – pencilled in for the New Year. Pity the lilacs wouldn't be out, he would have liked to have shown Bonnie Prague's lilacs –

'Well?'

'You know I'm not keen on foreign dates, especially this time of year. I'd have to ask the others.'

'I'd need to know by lunchtime.'

'I'm just off for a rehearsal. You will.'

'Thanks, William. Knew I could rely on you.'

Before returning to his knees to hunt the last of the peanuts, William put on a tape of Chopin nocturnes. Music of his youth, Chopin: he scarcely listened to such lacy piano music now, but he remembered its soothing powers. As a student William had secretly relied on Chopin as others relied on Andrews liver salts – balm to a hangover, reliever of inner turbulence caused by late essays. Now, the intensely familiar notes gave a rhythm to his plucking of the nuts, and soon they were all returned to the bags.

The second attempt at bashing was more successful. William was convinced that his secret curry ingredient was now being crushed to a powder so fine that it would be indetectable. In his triumph he swung the hammer down for a final blow that was more wild than he intended, and from somewhere a paper box of drawing-pins was spilt too. Small gold daggers raced for his knees, and bit into his fingers as he swept his hands about trying to gather them in one fell swoop. There was a knock at the door. William quickly stuffed the bags of peanuts into his pockets, but the door opened before he was able to stand.

'Whatever are you doing?' asked Grace, sympathetic.

'Stephen wants us to do a date in Prague next week. Can you imagine?' William was rising to his feet, banging at his trouser legs where drawing pins still clustered like determined burrs. Grace's glance at her husband's legs conveyed nothing of her curiosity.

'I just came to remind you the rehearsal's at eleven and at this rate you're going to be dreadfully late.'

'I know, I know. Everything's conspiring against me this morning. I'm never going to have time to stop and get . . . am I?'

'No, but I will. I've got to go shopping anyway.'

I am in blood stepped in so far, should I wade no more, returning would be tedious as go o'er, thought William.

'Whatever would I do without you, my Ace?' he said.

It was not just the morning, but the whole day that conspired against him. He was almost an hour late for the rehearsal, which gave Rufus – the first time for years he had not been the last to arrive – the opportunity for a smug little smile and some sarcastic sympathy. Grant was in one of his silent, grumpy moods, indicated by much banging of the fridge door. Even Bonnie's smile was less exuberant than usual, when she looked up from warming her hands beside the Norwegian stove. William noticed she was pale. Her lips, usually so rosy, were the colour of skimmed milk. He hoped she was not sickening for something. He would not be up to any more anxieties.

'Sorry, everyone. Not really my fault. Long negotiations with Stephen about Prague. They want us to go next week.'

'Bloody hell,' said Rufus, who shared William's distaste for foreign trips.

'I'll have to put off my medical check yet again,' said Grant, whose regular visits to his private doctor gave him assurance that needed constantly to be renewed. 'Otherwise I've no objection.'

'*Wonderful*,' said Bonnie, with a more eager smile. 'Prague! Imagine. I've never been.'

'Prague it is, then. Let's get down to it.'

They were to run through *Death and the Maiden* for a concert the day after tomorrow in a country palace, where concerts in aid of various charities were held. It was not the sort of engagement any of them enjoyed, despite the above-average standard of the refreshments. The audience, who paid vast sums for their tickets, were smarter than they were knowledgeable, and *The Maiden* was the Schubert they always wanted to hear, perhaps one of the few pieces with which they were familiar. Still, it had been agreed long ago that the Elmtree would be willing to do a certain amount of concerts for charity a year, and Grace always enjoyed the annual outing to the illustrious palace. All the same, William was not in the mood for *The Maiden* this morning, and was ashamed that while Bonnie put her soul into it – she had not played it with them before – he switched into a mode that came from years of familiarity, rather than a burst of fresh energy.

The day dragged edgily. William broke the rehearsal half an hour early, but no one complained. Bonnie offered to make sweet peppermint tea, which she had brought with her, but William declined her invitation. He had too much on his mind to make small talk over tea. Rufus, he observed, dithered in his usual way, torn between not wanting to offend Bonnie and wanting to get home to his wife. Grant conveyed a ridiculous enthusiasm for sweet peppermint, quite out of proportion to the invitation. It was one of Grant's weaknesses: he could rarely light on the perfect spot between reticence and over-enthusiasm. William, anxious not to witness Grant's pathetic eagerness over the boiling kettle for Bonnie, hurried out. He did not want to add to his troubles by thoughts of where peppermint tea could lead his cello and viola.

William was little acquainted with the unease that is caused by the planning of nefarious acts. Until this *illness*, as he called it, of Bonnie, he had always considered himself a reasonably straight and honest man, averse to devious ways, a keen adherer to the truth. But now, with the peanuts in his pocket, gunpowder ready to explode his life as well as Grace's, he was aware of the turbulent consequences of evil in one who is not by nature a wicked man.

When he jerked into the drive, pulled up the handbrake with an unkind ferocity, the Virginia creeper blazed angrily at him through the windscreen. He made his indeterminate way through to the kitchen as if unfamiliar with the hallway, the passage. He was afflicted by all the horror of the familiar becoming unrecognisable due to the blackness in his heart. He shook.

Grace was not in the kitchen. This alone was unnerving. She was always there when he arrived home, stirring things. But perhaps she had taken him at his word, and was indulging herself in a night off. With typical thought she had opened a book on the table at a page of easy, medium-hot curry. Beside it she had put the necessary ingredients. She was an angel, Grace. It was so strange that she must die.

To assure her absence, William decided to go upstairs and find her. He could not risk her barging in just as he was sprinkling powdered peanuts into the mixture. He followed the powerful smell of jasmine bath oil, and the thin sound that the portable radio made of the New World Symphony. Grace was lying back in the bath. This was all very, very peculiar. William was aware that she would notice the intense shaking of his hands, so stuffed them into his pockets where the bags of peanuts gave him courage.

'My goodness,' he said. He remembered an advertisement, widely employed some years ago for bubble bath: picture a girl in a bath towel looking out of the window. Copy saying something daft about wonderful things happen after a bath . . . Grace smiled at him.

'I've left everything ready for you,' she said. 'No need to look in such a panic. I can help if you want.'

William snatched one hand away from the comfort of the peanut bag in his pocket, and held it up in the manner of an agitated conductor urging the wind instruments to switch immediately into pianissimo.

'Good heavens, no,' he said. 'I can manage.' He saw that on the shelf at the side of the bath, in a clutter of potions and fancy bottles, was a glass of white wine. There's madness in the air tonight, he thought. Never in our married life has Grace ever taken a drink up to her bath.

She smiled. 'I'm giving myself a treat,' she said. The fingers of one hand twirled through a clutch of bubbles as if she were sifting through precious pearls, indolent, rich. So unlike Grace as to be astounding.

'I'm delighted,' William heard himself say. 'Sort of thing you should do more often, my Ace.'

Both hands back in his pockets, now, clutching the peanuts, William knew he should go and begin his dreadful task, but he wanted to stay a moment longer. It occurred to him he had not seen Grace in the bath for more years than he could remember. In their early married life, William would sit on a small cork stool, in their chilly little bathroom in Finchley, while Grace lay back gently swooshing the water about – she had never been inclined to soap herself thoroughly. William would watch, fascinated, as the movement of the water contorted the lines of her body, stretching then compressing them, shifting the pale and dark parts of her skin fast and curiously as a kaleidoscope. They would talk. Sometimes Grace would shut her eyes against the steam. Her eyelashes, clotted into pointed spikes, would lie on her cheeks. And long strands of her hair, carelessly tied up, escaped to float on the water's surface, casting snake shadows on the milky body in the water beneath. – Looking at Grace on the evening he planned to murder her, all this came back to William. He continued to gaze, shyly, in awe.

Tonight, he observed (meanly, he knew) the picture had changed a little. Bubble bath was no longer an extravagance. Expensive froth, its smell of jasmine strong enough to reach downstairs, cluttered the water. Grace's body was almost entirely hidden. Half a foot emerged, a knee, part of one breast with its pale centre. Between the bundles of bubbles tiny fjords appeared, their water blue and pink. For a moment William was almost overcome with a desire to plunge his hands in the water, clutch at the sweet familiar breast, and beg Grace to hurry out of the bath, wrap herself in the warm towel and lie on the floor. As they used to, before Jack was born and domesticity cast its less carefree patterns. But then he let his eyes climb up to the neck emerging from the ruffle of bubbles, to the face . . . and the bathcap. That was the change that shocked: Grace's hair screwed up into a pink nylon cap, the scalp straining to join it, the eyes slightly popping from the strain of elastic on forehead, the thickness of eyelash quite gone. Oh my God, he thought: how many years ago did Grace switch from a beautiful young Ophelia in the bath to this middle-aged woman with concern for her hair? How did I miss the moment of metamorphosis?

'Hadn't you better get going?' asked Grace.

In the kitchen William set about making the curry with grim concentration. He had no wish to remember the Grace he had just seen: he wanted to replace the image with their old bathing days. He had always been a profound admirer of Bonnard, could quite understand the artist's preoccupation with Wife in the Bath. He had painted Mathilde for forty years in various stages of nakedness, in and out of the water and, like the youth on Keats' Grecian urn, she never aged. Artistic licence. But had Bonnard ignored the intimations of the passing years, the reality? Or had he not seen them? William wondered. He twisted the empty peanut packets and stuffed them into an empty soup can which he then hid under rubbish in the bin . . . Covering his tracks, the detectives would call it. If he himself had been a painter, and used Grace as his most constant model, would he have concealed the truth, out of love, nostalgia? Or would he have depicted her as she had become? Interesting question . . . William tasted the curry. Rather good. Rice fluffed up. Candle lit. Open bottle of wine on the table. Everything ready. Christ . . .

Grace arrived with damp fronds of hair, despite the bathcap, and unusually pink, shining cheeks. She had not done anything so alarming as to dress up: she had simply put on the clean clothes she was planning to wear the next day. Appreciation for this extraordinary evening flew from her like gold dust. For his part, William was grateful to her for not having chosen to put on some unfamiliar evening garment and thereby add a further air of the unusual to the evening. He would not want to see her carried away on a stretcher wearing a smart, unfamiliar dress, pearl earrings on unconscious ears.

They sat at the table, the curry and dish of rice between them. Grace was smiling, admiring. William knew that the normal easy silence of their suppers must be broken with more conversation than usual tonight: to conceal his minute observation of Grace's condition, he must keep talking. Grace helped William to a large amount of the gleaming curry, then, in her gratitude, gave herself an equal amount. That was good.

'I'm not much looking forward to Prague,' he said.

'But you've always liked Prague.'

'Only at lilac time. We'll be too early for the lilacs.'

William had not had time in his difficult day to go to the library and look up the symptoms of peanut allergy. What would happen? And when? Would Grace keel over, slump into an unconscious state, gurgle in incomprehensible agony? William did not know what to expect. The grip of fearful anticipation in his stomach made swallowing the delicious curry very hard. He toyed with the rice.

'I don't suppose young Bonnie has been to Prague before.'

'No.'

'You'll have to take time to show her around. Take her for a walk over the Charles Bridge.'

'Very overrated place. Not a patch on some of the London bridges, Paris, Rome . . .'

'Oh, William: your expectations are always too high. You're cursed with a sense of disappointment. It makes you such a bad traveller.'

'True.'

Grace, always a fast eater, had got through a third of her curry by now and seemed absolutely fine.

'This is incredibly good,' she said. 'Why've you waited all these years? You'll have to do more.'

'Unlikely. I don't enjoy it, you know that.'

William could see that a fine line of sweat, delicate as a snail's trail, had appeared on Grace's upper lip. He swallowed. It was beginning to work.

'You must take Bonnie to the cathedral,' went on Grace, 'and the Jewish Cemetery, obviously.'

'We're not going to Prague for a holiday, we'll be rehearsing most of the day.' William wished Grace would stop mentioning Bonnie. Grace laughed.

'Your forehead,' she said. 'Covered in sweat! Well, it is pretty hot.'

William dabbed at his forehead with a napkin. Could be that was the reason for Grace's sweating lip.

'Do you mind,' he asked, 'it being so hot?'

'The hotter the better.'

'It doesn't make you feel . . .? I don't know. Some people can't take something powerful as this.'

'Well I can.'

William took a long drink of water.

'I'm not sure I can.' He felt short of breath. His arms, curiously, scorched.

'William: are you all right? You're a funny colour.'

'Think I've had enough. What about you?'

'I'm fine. I'm going to have some more.'

'You're a funny colour, too.'

Grace laughed. Then, suddenly, the laugh turned into a choke. A purple flush streaked over her face and neck. She spluttered and gurgled – a deep, terminal gurgle, William judged it, that came from the chest. He had never seen anyone dying before, but surely this was the death rattle. He leapt up, triumphant and terrified. Banged her on the back. Even as his hand lashed the familiar padding of her shoulder blades, he wondered if he could still find his old black tie, bought for the occasion of his father's funeral. – The choking turned to a scream.

'William! Stop it. You're hurting! I'm not choking.'

'You are.' Hope dipped.

'Not much. – There. I'm fine.'

She *was* fine, now. No doubt of that. William returned to his seat. He was the one being punished by his own hand.

'But you're not feeling . . . dizzy?' The words came hesitantly from William's own spinning head.

'No – why should I be?' She was into her second helping now, wolfing it down with great pleasure.

'You look as if you might be.'

Grace looked puzzled.

'You're the one who seems most affected.'

'I'm fine. Afraid I didn't run to a pudding.'

'There are pears left over from last night.'

Over the rest of last night's stewed pears they both cooled down. William kept his silence for a while, but in his state of disappointed relief he was finally compelled to brush over the subject with the lightest of touches.

'I believe the recipe actually called for peanuts,' he said.

'We didn't have any. I can't say the lack of them made any difference.'

'What might have happened – I mean, had I not known about your allergy and put them in?'

'Nothing, I don't suppose. It was never proved I had an allergy. I expect I've often eaten them without knowing it, and I'm still here.'

Her confidence was a comfort. All the same, William knew he would have to observe her closely for the next few hours.

'That's good, then,' he said. 'But it's worth being careful.'

When they had finished eating Grace moved steadily about the kitchen, no sign of any pernicious effects. Perhaps it took several hours, and the night would be torn with her shouts of agony. For the moment, except for the pinkness of cheeks, she was her normal self, keen to see the news.

They sat in front of the television on the sofa, as they always did when William was home in the evenings. From time to time William glanced at his wife: no untoward signs. Eventually he put a hand on her knee. She smiled. Such rare gestures of affection always pleased her. She could have no idea that tonight the gesture held a particular message of love and relief. They stayed up later than usual, and when they went up to bed, just before midnight, there was still no signs of any deterioration in Grace. In bed William lay tense for a while, awaiting any sudden change, a groan in sleep, a twist of pain. But Grace lay quite still, breathing regularly. William let the last of his fearful anticipation dissolve into a trio of soothing images: tulips, crumpets, nightingales. Eventually he slept too, and passed a good and dreamless night.

Next morning, Grace's normal happy presence was evidence of the complete failure of his plan. This realisation was so confusing he felt physically weak: on the one hand he was relieved beyond measure that he was no murderer, and his beloved Grace was still here with him, not some corpse in a morgue. On the other, the horrendous question persisted: how *was* Grace to be disposed of to leave him free for a life with Bonnie?

And it was Bonnie who preoccupied most of his thoughts during the day off at home. It was only his foul plans yesterday that had deflected these reflections a little. Now, he knew he could not survive the morning making tiresome plans for Prague without ringing her. He picked up the telephone as soon as he reached his study.

'Just wondered how the tea ceremony went?'

'Tea ceremony? Oh, William, it's you. It went very well, thanks.' Did she sound just a touch frosty?

'Sorry I wasn't able to stay.'

'We missed you.'

'How about Rufus?'

'What do you mean?'

'I mean, did Rufus manage to stay?' William coughed, furious with himself.

'He didn't, no. Had to hurry home.'

There was a long pause while William fought down further questions.

'I wasn't really ringing you about your tea-time arrangements,' he said at last, lightly as he could.

'Of course not.'

'I just wanted to check your passport's in order for Prague.'

'It is, yes.'

'That's fine, then.' How could he keep her for a few more moments? 'You're in good shape, good spirits?'

'Absolutely.' She sounded merrier. 'Actually, in rather a hurry. I've got to take the chance of the free morning to make plans about moving.'

'Of course.' With Grant's help no doubt. 'I'll not keep you, I'm sorry. See you tomorrow night.'

The conversation did nothing to dispel his fears – fears he could not quite name, but concerning the predatory nature of Grant. Women, for some reason beyond William's comprehension, seemed to find Grant attractive. The Quartet groupies they had had to deal with in their time – not for some years, it had to be admitted – had always gone for Grant. Women appeared to like great hunks with curly hair and rugger thighs. A touch of musical genius spurred them further. William could not deny that Grant, straddling his cello, was a magnificent sight. His distant, rather grumpy look was apparently an added attraction. William liked to suppose that Bonnie was too clever, too sharp for Grant. His slow (though accurate) assessment of life would tax her patience, though of course she would be charmed by his consideration. William wished that long ago there had been a rule insisting that no personal intercourse between members of the Quartet should take place. But as there had never been a woman player before, there had been no necessity for this rule. And now it was too late. William could only hope that Grant would deem it improper to make any untoward approach to a fellow player, thereby disturbing the general equilibrium of the group. In the past his girlfriends – rarely produced – had been of the thinnish, earnest variety: mature students intent on further maturing rather than getting a job. (William could remember several occasions on which Grant had generously subsidised some of these perennial students.) Surely Bonnie, for him, would be too frivolous, too over the top, too buxom . . . despite her talent.

His ruminations were interrupted by the telephone. It was Dick Lancer, fellow student and for some years closest friend at college. They had not met, or communicated, for several years. Enmeshed in his own thoughts, it took William several moments to bring Dick to mind.

'Oh, *Dick*, yes, why, Dick – my dear fellow . . . how are you doing?'

'Not too bad. Concerts here and there. Best time of year.'

It all came back to William. Dear Dick: freckles and red hair, not a bad cellist but not a good enough one to make history. Then he discovered he had a good baritone voice, and switched to singing. Joined and left several choirs, had a good year when he was the dubbed voice behind a film star who had to sing in a popular film. But ever since he had led the precarious life that is the norm for most musicians: many weeks between solo concerts in regional halls, constant financial worry. He used to visit Grace and William frequently in the past. But since the success of the Elmtree coincided with his own demise, he came less often. In the last few years, not at all. An exchange of Christmas cards was now their only form of communication. So a call from Dick out of the blue was naturally confusing on this troubled morning.

'Just thought I'd let you know I've moved,' went on Dick. 'Dorset. Always wanted to be beside the sea. So when I retired last year I found myself a snug little cottage on the coast. Wonderful.'

'Retired?'

'Well, you know how it is. I could be persuaded, I suppose, in the unlikely event of anyone wanting to persuade . . . I'm trying to rustle up a group of singers in the village.'

'Oh, Dick, my dear chap – that sounds like an enterprising thing to do.'

'– So I was just ringing with a suggestion. Thought occurred to me you and Grace might like to come down for a day or two in the

New Year. Bitter cold, but there's a good fire . . . Haven't seen you for far too long.'

William's mind spun through the re-shuffling of plans a visit to Dorset would mean. He had never been a man keen to leave his own home when he didn't have to – there was far too much going away tied in with his job. But Dick was a very old friend, sounded a bit gloomy . . . it was the least they could do.

'Let me have a word with Grace. In principle it sounds a good idea . . .'

'I shall keep my fingers crossed. Be jolly nice if you could both come.'

Five minutes later, half lost in the andante movement of Borodin's A major quartet, William was unable to imagine a wintry weekend on the Dorset coast with Dick Lancer. Instead, scenes of Prague came to him: Bonnie and he dining on the famous dumplings; Bonnie and he (he might even take her arm) wandering round the cathedral, though God knows how they would get rid of Grant and Rufus. Something would suggest itself. Then it occurred to him – as he lifted himself on the wave of a crescendo, that perhaps, as he was a sane violinist, not a murderer by inclination, it might be a good idea to get to know Bonnie better, weigh up his chances of lasting happiness with her, before making a second attempt at expunging his dear wife.

Just as this thought produced a surge of profoundly felt playing, the comfort was snatched away as quickly as it had come. William faced the picture of Dorset: the dour winter coast, the high cliffs, the snarling sea hundreds of feet below. Grace eager for walks. How easy it would be.

William put down his bow, wondering at this new madness.

6

On the morning of William's departure for Prague Grace made the decision not to tell Lucien of his absence, and felt easier. It happened to be a day that Lucien was working (his second day, the first had gone well) so she was relieved of the anxiety of his appearing while William fussed about his luggage. William always showed signs of neurosis when it came to packing. Grace did all she could to make the preparations less fraught for him. She lay on the bed a selection of folded shirts for him to choose from, she put his passport and foreign currency into the inside pocket of his jacket, so all he had to do was to bang his chest in order to ascertain it was there, and she slipped a list of clothes into his suitcase so that, like a schoolboy, he could check them when packing to come home. (Over the years, so many white ties, silk socks, birthday jerseys and even jackets had failed to return.) But Grace's help did nothing to assuage William's nervous state. He chivvied about the kitchen looking for the telephone number of the hotel in Prague that he had given Grace two days ago.

'William! It's hardly likely to be in the fruit bowl. It's on my desk.'

'Sure?'

'Quite sure.'

'But I'm not looking for the telephone number, am I? I'm looking for the cufflinks.'

'Cufflinks?'

'I'm all of a fluster, I'm afraid, my Ace.'

'Which cufflinks are you after?'

'Yours, of course. My birthday present.'

'Isn't that a little rash? I mean, they're worth a bit, and knowing your turnover in cufflinks . . . I would have thought, abroad, it'd be better to take—'

'No. I want yours. So far from home, Prague, I'd feel safer with your cufflinks.' This was the truth, as William had reflected for some hours during the night. He had come to the conclusion that wearing Grace's cufflinks might be a guard against iniquitous acts, though exactly what he might be tempted to get up to was not clear in his mind.

'Very well,' said Grace. 'Luckily they're insured.' She joined in the search, methodically scanning every shelf and drawer, while William hunted in less likely places – the fridge, the jar in which the washing-up brushes and mops resided. Grace pretended to be unaware of his increasing anxiety. She found it contagious, though. After half an hour's search and still no sign of the cufflinks, she sank into a chair to try to unravel her despair.

'I put them in the drawer the morning you went to Manchester,' she said. 'You insisted on taking the other ones. – I know I did.'

William, too, sat. Exhausted. He glanced at his watch. They'd have to be leaving for the airport in precisely five minutes.

'That's right,' he said, 'I remember.' In fact he had no recollection of what Grace had done with them – just the awkwardness he had felt, rejecting them. But he remembered something else quite clearly.

'You were worrying that your friend Lucien was about to arrive,' he said.

Grace gave him the mildest look of enquiry. She had no recollection of mentioning Lucien. Perhaps William was able to read her more keenly than she supposed.

'Was I? I do believe you're right. Anyway, I know I'll have put them in a safe place. I'm always doing that, then can't find things, aren't I?' Ruffled by William's curious detective powers, Grace was flustered.

'Well we can't keep looking now. Time to go.' William stood. He banged his chest to check the wedge of passport and tickets. Their presence brought him no comfort.

'Stop worrying. They're sure to turn up while you're away.'

'I'm not worrying about the cufflinks, my Ace. I'm worrying about getting to Heathrow on time. The traffic . . .'

Grace contained a sigh.

'If we leave now, twenty minutes before you said we should leave, you'll be there an hour before the others.'

'Good. I shall like that.' William was in desperate need of time for cogitation.

'Very well. Let's go.'

It was William's custom, on the rare occasions he disagreed with Grace, to follow any criticism with a small, placatory tribute.

'There's no one like you for understanding a man's worry about time, I'm bound to say. I'll get my stuff from upstairs,' he said, and gave her a grateful look.

'Remembered your shaving cream?'

William, unable to remember if he had remembered, looked stricken. Five minutes later, Grace driving, William squirming in the passenger seat as he burrowed beneath his overcoat yet again to the reassuring package of documents in his jacket, they set off for the airport.

When Grace returned to the empty house she was aware – as she always was when she had deposited William at some airport or station – of a lowering of spirits. It was not that she minded being on her own. Indeed, from time to time she enjoyed absolute alone-ness. It gave her the opportunity to work uninterrupted. In William's absence – never, fortunately, more than a few days – she imposed upon herself a rigorous discipline, and stuck to it. Long mornings at her desk, an hour's walk after lunch, a decent supper during which she would listen to one of the Elmtree's tapes, early bed with a book. She did not mind the emptiness of the house, the silence. She entertained no thoughts of rapists, burglars, or other such unpleasant surprises. She felt no need to telephone Jack, or friends, for a talk: she was truthfully happy to be on her own for a while, as she had so often assured William. By now he had come to believe it. But that sense of contentment had always been tempered with a very slight lowering of spirits – indeed so slight it was not worth reflecting upon, or mentioning. But there. From time to time Grace had tried to analyse its cause, and came to the sensible, obvious conclusion that it was due to the lack of small anticipation that fired most of her days – the fuel that fires most people who are not in the habit of excitements. The anticipation concerned William's descent for breakfast, or return from a rehearsal or concert: the constant joyful thought of his arriving back home, being under the same roof. This, she knew, was ridiculous. After so many years of happy marriage it was extraordinary that her husband's daily, routine appearances should continue to bring such undimmed reward. But it was so. To be in William's presence she found no less exhilarating now than she had in their youth. In some extraordinary way the essence of romance for her had not dulled. 'The dreary hum of daily life' had done nothing to corrode Grace's appreciation of a husband she loved with her whole being. For such a blessing, when she said her prayers, she gave thanks.

But on the occasion of dropping William at Heathrow for his visit to Prague, Grace sensed that her spirits had dipped a fraction lower than usual. Returning to the house she found herself entering with a certain caution, a flicker of dread. She had no idea from where these feelings of trepidation came: the doors had been locked and bolted. Lucien, safe at work in Reading, would not be waiting in her kitchen.

Scoffing at herself for such sentiments, she made a cup of tea, carried it to the table in the dining room where she intended to put in a couple of hours' work in this always lustreless part of the afternoon. For some unknown reason she glanced through the cloakroom door on her way, checked that all was in order. Multiple coats hung bulbous as always from their brass hooks. The comforting sight gave rise to the silly thought that if a sartorially inclined butcher swapped meaty carcasses for old mackintoshes, then this is what his surreal shop would look like. – Her welling-tons, neatly next to William's, were in their usual place. Nothing odd. Everything fine.

On the table, Grace found the jam jar in which she put her water – an old marmalade pot she had used the first time she had tried to paint a bluebell, and without which she would have felt bereft. It was empty. She had no heart to go to the kitchen to fill it. Instead, she fanned through one of her sketchbooks so that the flowers on their pages were broken into a kaleidoscope of delicate colours. Then she spread open two pages, rested a hand upon them to keep them flat. A tangle of old man's beard and rosehips sprawled from under her palms: the orange of the hips was alive as flame, the froth of old man's beard insubstantial as mist. Rather good, she reflected: and then was puzzled. How could she have allowed herself any such thought?

She started to turn the pages again. Mallow, kingcups, Queen Anne's lace all *done*, nicely executed, finished. Lulled by a sense of achievement, it should have been a peaceful afternoon. Painting things were orderly before her. The ochre light of a winter after-noon gave a soft edge to the outlines of hard things: furniture, pictures, books. It was the kind of light that sometimes pressed through the silent rooms and inspired Grace – sensing a strange quickening of her spine – eagerly to take up her brushes. But not this afternoon. She remained sitting, unmoving, ignoring the list of flowers to be completed. Buttocks squarely pressed on squat chair, she floated, buoyant with wonder at her own inability to move.

Grace had never been averse to solitude. Time on her own was as essential to her as it was to William. To be alone without worry, she had learnt, is a privileged state. Puzzling, then, that today William's absence troubled her in a way so clouded that she could not fathom its source, and that apprehension of something unknown ran round her edges.

Don't you mind your old man going off for a night with this new bird, this viola?

Lucien's question came back to her. William had been going to Manchester. Grace knew perfectly well there had been no funny business in Manchester. Lucien was at his most subversive that day. *Ye of great faith*, he had said.

His unpleasant suggestions had not merited a moment's consideration then. Nor did they now. All the same, nights when William was away might never again be devoid of – not worry, exactly: not suspicion, either. But they might no longer be times of bare, clean solitude of the kind that is engendered by absolute trust. Damn Lucien, Grace said to herself. What right had he to unnerve her with his beastly insinuations – she who had done her best to comfort and befriend him? Thank God, at least, the lilacs would not be out. A foreign tree, in full flower, could turn the thoughts of a man missing home . . . In fact, Grace reminded herself, the real danger was that Prague in November could be a gloomy place. And Bonnie, with her dimples and velvet and sunny disposition, could be relied on for comfort.

Even as such odious thoughts glanced through her, Grace berated herself. It was inconceivable that William would look upon Bonnie as anything other than the new young addition to the Quartet, to whom he should be kind and considerate and fatherly. God forgive her for even contemplating anything else.

Still in search of the meaning of her unease, her mind now switched to Lucien. It was also improbable that he, for all his erratic ways, would ever behave in a manner that was threatening. His visits, his demands, his way of inveigling her into his life were annoying rather than alarming. At some moment soon she would have to try to distance herself, maybe banish him from her life altogether. But that would be less than kind . . . Besides, his existence had come to provide her quiet life with a small *frisson* she might otherwise miss.

Grace rolled a small sable brush on her tongue. It emerged as a crisp little point. She stabbed it into a knob of dried blue paint on her palette, longing for water, but still lacking the energy to go to the kitchen. She must pull herself together, she thought: a

strategy she had always believed in. Think of other things. – The
pepper pots, they needed polishing. Grace glanced at the sideboard. The silver pepper pots were horribly tarnished, streaked
with marks the colour of dried blood. She would enjoy cleaning
them. William would still be on the aeroplane. He would ring
tonight, of course. He was good about keeping in touch when he
was away. She had a nasty feeling there was no more silver cleaning stuff. Poor William: three nights in a hotel bedroom. Grace
dabbed the brush on to paper. The dry paint made feathery
scratches. She must put an end to this idleness, fetch water, get
down to work –

There was a loud bang from the kitchen. The door slamming.
Grace jumped, twisted round in her chair. Lucien was there, damp,
frowning, his waterproof jacket smeary with rain.

'Oh, it's you. You gave me—'

'Sorry. Door was open. Thought I'd drop in on my way home.
Tell you about it. Tell you about day two as an employed man.'

Grace stood. She smiled. A smile feathery as the blue paint, she
thought. Her hands were trembling. To disguise this she brushed at
her skirt, as if banishing invisible crumbs.

'I could have sworn I bolted it. Shall we go –? Tea?'

'In a minute. I rather like it in here for a change.'

Lucien sat on the table, folded his arms, proprietorial. Annoyance rose within Grace.

'Please, Lucien. Not on the table.'

Lucien laughed. It was astonishing with what speed he could
turn from charming to disagreeable.

'We are stressed out today, aren't we? Sorry again.' He pulled out
a chair, sat. 'What's the matter? All right if I sit?'

'Nothing's the matter. How did it go today?'

'Thought you'd want to know.' Lucien was pleased by her interest. He ran a hand through his hair. Grace expected it to return
covered in grease. His fingernails were deep rims, black as hooves.
She had never known him have dirty nails before, and wondered at
this significance.

'Started off all right. That is, Tuesday, like, that was fine. Boring, but fine. Today, the pits.'

'Why?'

'Dunno, really. Can't quite put my finger . . . But they seem to have a problem with me.'

'Oh, Lucien –'

'So I'm thinking it over in my mind. I might not stay.'

'Give it a chance. A week or so at least. It takes time to settle in. What do you have to do?'

'Bit of paperwork. Show the people who come into the Centre where things are. Heat up soup. Boring. Gets to my skull.'

'But surely you didn't expect—?'

'I don't know what I expected, but not this crap. I'm an able pair of hands and they give me this fucking boring job.' He glanced at Grace. 'Shocked you, have I?'

'No.' Grace produced a firmer smile. She was so accustomed to William's mellifluous phrasing it was a relief sometimes to be reminded of the existence of gutter speech.

Lucien got up, came over to Grace. They were divided only by her upright chair between them. He put a hand on her shoulder.

'Wouldn't want to shock you, now, would I? Though I reckon you're pretty unshockable. I reckon beneath that calm little face of yours you're as screwed up as the rest of us.' Grace felt her whole body tighten, as if pulled in by invisible straps. Lucien bent over and looked at the painting of a bluebell: one side of the paper was daubed with the dry blue paint. 'That's good,' he said. 'Not my sort of thing, flowers. But I'd say they're good.'

'They're nothing much.' Despite herself, Grace was warmed by his praise.

'No, really. I mean it.' Lucien began to flip over the pages. 'I'd say they're really pretty good. What do you think?'

The light in the room had dimmed to the colour of wet sable. Grace switched on the sideboard lamp. The yellow-pink was flung over sketchbooks, paints. Lucien's hands. Safer, with the light on, Grace felt. Her heart slowed down. She could see Lucien was in a contrary mood, but there was nothing about him that gave her cause for alarm. In fact, to be fair, after all her anti-Lucien thoughts, she found his interest in her work endearing.

'I think they're reasonably competent,' she said, containing a sigh. 'Nothing more.'

'If you really think that, if you really think you're only "reasonably competent", why do you bother?'

Grace frowned.

'What do you mean?'

'I mean I wouldn't think it was worth anyone's while bashing away at something if the result was never going to be anything more than reasonably competent.'

'In that case, there wouldn't be much accomplished in the world, would there? If only people of real talent worked hard, think of the deprivation.' Grace gave a small, huffy laugh. 'Most people aren't blessed with much talent, for heaven's sake. The Williams of this world are rare. But we like to plod on, hoping to get better, enjoying ourselves. Perhaps producing something worthwhile for others. You learn to live with the realisation that you're never going to be very good. You get used to it. You don't mind that much.'

'I'd say that was very depressing.'

'Well I don't find it so.'

There was a long silence between them.

'At least you don't take yourself too seriously,' Lucien said at last. He took his hand from her shoulder. 'Am I going to be offered a cup of tea?'

'I've already offered . . .' William would be landing by now, Grace thought.

In the kitchen – warmer, brighter, a sponge cake between them – Lucien veered towards the apologetic.

'Hope I haven't said anything to offend.'

'You haven't, no.'

'I was only extending the idea you put up, like about only being reasonably competent.'

'I know you were. Don't worry, I'm not remotely offended. I was just trying to explain I'm fully aware of my own limitations.'

'No bad thing. Quite the opposite from me. I always think I can do anything, and there I am stuck doing f-all. You're the one in the better position. – Where's the husband? Off on some gig?'

'A Beethoven concert, yes.'

'I didn't used to mind Beethoven.' Lucien cut himself a large piece of cake, pushed the plate towards Grace. 'He's always away it seems. Don't you mind?'

'Not at all. As you know. We've been through all this before.' Grace attempted to sound stern.

'You can always call on me, you know. Like, were you to feel lonely or anything.'

'I know, thank you.'

'I'm never far away.' He shoved the sponge cake into his mouth. 'Where's he playing this time?'

Beneath the table, Grace kneaded her fingers. Lucien's mouth, full of cake, muffled his question. She could pretend she had not understood.

'He was in a terrible state, going off,' she said at last. 'He always is. But this time it was worse because he'd mislaid his cufflinks, a nice pair I'd given him for his birthday. – I mean, I'd mislaid them.'

Grace watched Lucien's mashing jaws, the uncouth way he rubbed crumbs from his mouth with the back of his hand. He didn't seem much interested in William's trouble.

'They'll turn up,' he said, when at last he had finished his mouthful.

'I expect so. Things always turn up.'

Lucien began to break up the cake that was left on his plate, the black crescents of his nails punching through the yellow sponge, nudging the jam. He licked three fingers at once. Grace hated the way he ate.

'Haven't forgotten I owe you that money,' he said.

'Any time. There's no hurry.'

'Suppose I'd better stay in the job till I've earned enough to pay you back.'

'I think you should stay in the job, but not for that reason. What does your mother think? She must be pleased you're working.'

'Lobelia?' Lucien looked up with the usual sneer that accompanied any thought of his mother. 'Bloody woman. Wouldn't lower herself to give me a passing thought. Last night she went out in these very high heels: pearlescent, she said they were, proud as punch. I said she looked like a trollop. She said I was scum. We had one of our better punch-ups.'

'Punch-up?' Grace cursed herself for having mentioned Lobelia. She sighed.

'She can push me so far, then I go ballistic. Her fault.'

'You don't mean you –?'

'She gets what she deserves.' Lucien punched his own temples, bored by talk of Lobelia.

'You don't seem keen,' he said, 'to tell me when the old man's coming home.'

'Soon,' said Grace. She wondered what he meant by ballistic, but decided it unwise to ask.

'Well anyway, like I said, you can call me any time. I'll look after you all right.'

'Thanks.'

'I'm on my way now.' He stood up. 'But I'll be round as usual. In and out. – Hey, what's bitten you? What's up?' He clenched a fist, pushed it gently into her cheek.

'What do you mean? I'm fine.'

'White as a sheet.'

'Nonsense! I was in such a rush . . . you usually see me with a bit of rouge on my face.'

'Don't give me any of that rubbish. I know you.'

When he had gone, Grace sat down again. It occurred to her that it was the first time anyone had commented on her appearance, noticed her pallor, for many years. William was not one for observing a familiar face. – What would he be doing now, William? He should be ringing soon.

There was a telephone, nothing but a telephone, on the Formica table beside William's bed. He picked up the receiver, intending to ring Grace, then put it down again. Later would do. There was nothing so far to say. He was exhausted by the lack of event.

On the flight he had insisted Grant, Rufus and Bonnie sit together: he had taken the seat across the aisle. Thus he was not obliged to talk to any of them, and he noticed they spoke little among themselves.

In Prague it was raining. Bonnie, of her own volition, chose the front seat of the minibus, which Stephen arranged for their transport on foreign trips. The three men sat together in one of the back seats, William with his violin on his knee – he would never permit it to travel in the boot of any vehicle. Bonnie gave a running commentary on how beautiful it all was. William had not the energy to argue with her. To him the streets, with their tall dirty buildings, were gloomy as his least favourite parts of Paris. He turned his eyes away from them and rested them instead on the back of Bonnie's head. There was a small arrow of white flesh – her neck – where her hair had parted. William gripped his violin case. He wanted so much to touch her he felt he might explode. Her red wool scarf hung down over the back of the seat. What was the history of that scarf? Who had given it to her? What of her secrets did it know? Was he going mad, asking himself such questions in the streets of Prague? – They arrived at the hotel.

The hotel was the kind that always made William most homesick: a modern box of no character, low ceilings, no air, padded silence, people with suitcases gliding about driven by vaguely indignant eyes. This particular place had been flooded with amethyst carpet, which swirled relentlessly through passages, stairs, reception, bar, dining room. The designers had plainly found a job-lot of amethyst carpet, with imitation flowers to match. They were arranged in prim little bunches on every shelf, table, available space. Each one was placed beneath a spotlight in the ceiling that bore down on the cheap mauve leaves and wire stamens, insults to the humblest peony.

'This is great,' said Bonnie's reflection to William's reflection in the mauve glass of the lift.

'It's terrible,' said William. He felt sick.

Now he remained sitting on the edge of his second-class hotel bed looking at the rain (silenced by the thickness of the double glazing), imagining Bonnie, next door, opening her case, in all her delight at being abroad. She would be shaking out her velvet dress, exploring the mean little room with the sort of gladness in her heart that William feared he would never feel again.

He had decided that he would make use of the dead hours in the hotel room in Prague, sort out the confusions in his mind, make firm plans. So far his plans for murder had been pathetic: a small packet of crushed peanuts fed to one who was not even sure she had ever been allergic to them, and the fingering of a much-loved neck which he knew that even in the higher realms of insanity he would be incapable of strangling. But try as he did to marshall his thoughts towards serious murder, they kept skittering away to the girl next door. He could hear the gush of water. He pictured her in the shower, arms up, pushing the wet hair from her eyes. Mascara running down her cheeks, water running down her breasts. William groaned, bent over like a man in pain.

The telephone rang, a shy, foreign sound. He picked it up.

'Just wondered how you were.'

'Grace? My darling. What are you doing, ringing me? I was just about to ring you.' His heart was thumping like a military drum.

'I wanted to make sure you'd arrived. Everything all right.'

William produced a sympathetic laugh.

'Well as you can imagine, it's not all right at all. Bloody raining here. Prague nasty as ever. Perfectly awful hotel. Otherwise no news.'

'Only three nights.'

'Thank God. You all right?'

'I'm fine. I've been working.'

'Good.'

In the silence that followed a ticker tape of things William could have then said clanked through his mind: *wish I was home, I miss you, I love you*.

'Be sure to bolt the kitchen door,' he said.

'Course.'

'Well, then . . . I'll ring tomorrow.'

'I'll be here.' Of course she'd be there. What foolish things people say to one another to affirm what they already know.

'Bye, my Ace.'

What was up with her, ringing? She never rang.

There was a knock on the door. William picked up his violin case and went to open it. Bonnie stood there, damp hair, smelling of bath essence. She wore a T-shirt with a low neck. There were freckles on her chest.

'You said we had to be off at four thirty for the rehearsal. We've been waiting for you downstairs.'

'Sorry. I'm here. I'm ready.'

'You look as if you've seen a ghost.'

'Very unlikely to be a ghost in a place like this.' William managed a smile.

'What's the matter, then?'

'I'm not much good on journeys. Don't like travelling. Just trying to reorient myself. I can never quite believe that one minute I'm home, and a few hours later I'm somewhere that only a hundred years ago it would have taken weeks to get to –'

'Poor old William.' Bonnie was smiling. 'You're not much good at the modern world.' She moved towards him, put her heavy arms round his neck, lay her head beneath his chin. William feared he might collapse.

'No,' he said. Then, breathless, 'You're an angel, Bonnie.'

Probably she didn't hear. She had stepped away from him again, sympathetic gesture snapped off in her impatience to get going. She took his free hand, guided him along the amethyst passage to the lift. In its small, claustrophobic space, privacy almost tangible, William felt Bonnie's curious eyes on the unusual scarlet of his cheeks. Could she have any idea of the effect of her presence?

In his turbulent state, William was happy for Grant to take charge of administrative matters, as he so often did when he saw William confused by the strange ways of Abroad. Grant chivvied them all into the minibus to the church, checked instruments, music stands, and double-checked scores. He paid the driver and thanked the man in Czech. (He'd been studying a phrase book on the journey, as always unable to resist impressing his companions with a rudimentary knowledge of the language in whatever country they visited. A show-off, Rufus called him. William was secretly impressed.)

In the church of St Nicholas in Malá Strana, for a while they stood, keeping their distance from one another, looking up at the huge fresco of the apotheosis of the saint that covered the nave. William, suddenly realising time was against them, dragged each one from his private contemplation by suggesting they should take their seats at the edge of the altar and begin their rehearsal. Grant, for once, perhaps awed by the baroque flamboyance of the surroundings, grumbled but minimally about his chair. William took up his bow, gave the signal to start. He was conscious of the vast presence of the golden statue of St Nicholas, in the altar, looking down on him, as he leant into Purcell's *Fantasy* as a lone sailor bends his sail into the wind, and composure returned at last.

The first twenty-four hours in Prague, for William, were spent in misery. On the Saturday morning he joined the others for breakfast, was enraged by the miniature plastic pots of butter and jam, and declined to go sightseeing with Rufus, Grant and Bonnie. He had no wish to revisit the wonders of Prague, which in his view were vastly over-estimated, nor to eat disgusting, undigestible dumplings for lunch in some gloomy restaurant – a plan for which Bonnie showed irrepressible enthusiasm.

So while the others made their way to the cathedral, William returned to his blank little room. There, he played his violin quietly to himself for an hour. Then sat in the plastic armchair wondering about the best way to kill his wife – who he telephoned twice, as if the sound of her voice might be inspiration – before he made his way back to the church to sort out the matter of more practical chairs.

On his return to the hotel he ran into Rufus and Grant whose stamina for sights had run out before Bonnie's. She, they said, had gone off to see the Charles Bridge on her own. In a moment of folly William contemplated hurrying there to find her: they could have a few moments alone. The tourist-crowded bridge would not be the ideal place, but better than nowhere. But he soon dismissed this ridiculous idea – sure to miss her – and returned to his room. Lay on the bed.

He was rewarded, half an hour later, by a knock on the door. Bonnie. Bonnie pleased with herself, glowing, impatient, cross. She glanced at the bed.

'What've you been doing?'

'Lying down a bit.'

'You're a chump. A disgruntled old thing, spoiling everyone else's fun. What's the matter? What've you been sulking about?'

'Things on my mind. Sorry.'

'The Quartet?'

'Oh no. It was a good rehearsal. Should be a good concert tonight.'

'That church . . . I've never played in a church before.' Bonnie sat on the bed. William hesitated only a moment, then sat beside her. 'Look what you missed,' she said. She handed him a postcard of a painting: cracked gold background, three round trees, each harbouring a finch. 'Best thing in the Národní Galerie. The others hurried on. I just stared and stared.'

'I remember it. When we were here ten years ago.' Then, there had not been murder on his mind. No Bonnie to cause his wretched state. He turned the card over. *Look what you missed*, she had written. *Love, Bonnie*. Childish kisses scrawled at the bottom.

William turned to her. She was only a foot from him. Their

knees were perilously near to touching. None of this would mean anything more to Bonnie than the proximity to her grandfather. William felt the heat of tears behind his eyes.

'Thank you,' he said. 'I'm sorry I wasn't there.'

Bonnie banged his knee with a clenched fist.

'Well, tomorrow morning, wherever we go, you're coming too. Some church full of bones, Grant suggested.'

'Oh Lord.' He remembered that church.

'He's organising the minibus. You'll come?'

William nodded.

'Now cheer up. Please cheer up.'

'I'm improving by the moment.' Dear God, forgive the lie. He wanted so much to take this warm, soft, sweet creature into his arms that he had to clasp his hands in prayer in order that they should not reach out to her.

'You're a funny one, sometimes. I don't understand you one bit, your moods.' Bonnie was all lightness now, crossness gone. She stood. William, buoyed by conflicting feelings that the danger was almost over, stood too.

'Don't bother your head. Just keep playing like you do –'

The last part of William's sentence was suffocated in the mesmerising skin of Bonnie's neck. She had clasped him to her, once again, in the kind of hug that William disapproved of – the public hug that has now become fashionable in times of disaster or mourning. He felt himself go rigid. He was saddened by her kindness: the sympathy of a grandchild to its grandfather. He forced a smile and pushed her away, awkwardly, as if pushing a heavy table.

'Last time I went to my doctor,' he said, 'there was a notice in the waiting room saying *Hug Someone in Need*. Sentimental rubbish.'

Bonnie laughed.

'Sorry,' she said. 'Now, come on down. There's time for more of that square strawberry jam you're so fond of before we have to change.'

William followed Bonnie down the mauve passage. The smell of her, some gauzy flower he could not put a name to, clung to his jersey. He moved like a man entranced.

The church was packed. Those for whom there were no seats sat on the floor of the aisles. Considering they had been expecting a different, and more famous quartet, this was extraordinary. William found himself moved by their hope of a good evening. Though they said nothing, it seemed that the others felt the same. William looked over the mass of expectant faces – something he used to steel himself to do when he was younger, rarely did now. Then his eyes rose for a last look up at the vaulted ceiling of the nave, where the cunning fusion of frescoes and architecture deceived the eye. 'Illusive architectonic elements,' Rufus had explained, not to be outdone by Grant's phrase-book fluency. The magnificence of it all caused William a certain stiffness of limb and straightness of back. What impressed him most was the fact that Mozart himself had played the organ here – so his eyes, too, must have travelled among the huge figures and pillars. Mozart himself must have sensed that something beyond the material world had been netted in this place of timeless stone, wondrously carved, and holy pictures. With a strange feeling of humility William gave the nod to begin. The Quartet's rendering of Beethoven's quartet in C sharp minor rose with a spirit that he hoped the players would always achieve, but in fact, on more ordinary occasions, they rarely did. In between pieces, shuffling his music, he was aware that Bonnie, perhaps in deference to the holy place, had no coloured lining in her velvet sleeves. He was moved by that too.

Later, tired but exhilarated, the Quartet gathered in the hotel bar for a drink before bed – their custom when on tour. It was an unspoken rule that they never discussed their performance until the morning after a concert. They sat round a small table on seats of quilted mauve plastic, only slightly less unpleasant than the pink chairs in Manchester, sipping at their whiskies and brandies. Each one of them was affected by the audience's appreciation. Each one of them sensed the elation that comes, and lives a while, after a memorable performance. But that was not a subject to be discussed either. There was nothing to say that would further enhance the mutual feeling.

'So,' said Bonnie, breaking the silence at last. 'Trip for tomorrow morning all organised?' She looked at Grant. He nodded. Then she looked at William. 'William's coming, aren't you, William?'

'Of course.' He nodded. He had forgotten what was planned and dreaded to think what it might be.

'Good heavens,' said Rufus. Behind the flatness of his tone William guessed that Rufus might have suspected Bonnie had something to do with William's uncharacteristic decision. There was little, in his quiet way, that Rufus did not observe.

'Minibus is arranged for ten,' said Grant.

There was no life in the bar. Only two others, quietly speaking German, drinking in a corner. William let his eyes trail round the hideous room, feeling the warmth of the whisky. They came to rest on a piano, half-hidden behind a large rubber plant. It was the strangest piano he had ever seen – painted, or glazed, like faux marble. Its iridescent shine was of the mauve that blighted the rest of the hotel. The gleam brought to mind far away things – mussel shells, the breasts of wood pigeons, moonstones, and he felt the old, aching swoop of spirits that so often assailed him in foreign parts. But his reflections were broken off by Bonnie's giggle. She, too, had spotted the piano.

'Do you think anyone would mind?' she said.

Without waiting for an answer, she rose and went to the piano, pushing her way through the tangled leaves of the plant. They clung to her black velvet.

'Not a very good piano,' said the young bartender, to no one in particular.

Bonnie arranged herself on the stool. William, Grant and Rufus all moved a little in their chairs. The Germans put down their beer.

'What are we to expect?' asked Rufus, quietly. He looked embarrassed. To take over a piano in a public bar, unasked, was to his mind showing off. He looked at his watch, a sign that whatever Bonnie chose to play he would soon be retiring.

'My Very Good Friend the Milkman' she began with, ruffling through the notes in a way that would have delighted Fats Waller himself. Then she moved into 'Ain't Misbehavin'' and began to sing in a wispy, smoky voice that reminded William of Blossom Dearie.

The Germans sat up very straight. Rufus raised his eyebrows. The barman stopped polishing glasses, leant on his elbows on the bar. Grant had gone very pale.

It was an accepted fact that each of the three Elmtree men had areas of music they positively disliked. William loathed 'light classics' of a military nature, the 'gymkhana' music he so abhorred on the radio. Rufus could not abide the human operatic voice. Grant was unable to tolerate any kind of jazz. So when Bonnie began to play, surprise and dismay twisted his face. William observed his struggle as Bonnie delightfully husked her way through the verses. When she came to an end Grant applauded her, hands held high over his head, and gave a smile in her direction which she did not see. Her head was down over the keys. She had shuffled into a complicated piece, her proficiency astounding. Grant rose, with a nod at William, and left the bar. Rufus, eager as always to ring his wife, followed immediately. The barman reluctantly pulled the grill across the counter. The Germans, looking at their watches, left the room backwards, their eyes locked on to Bonnie. As they passed William one of them clapped his hands.

'You the father, yes? Congratulations.'

Bonnie was left playing to William alone. She switched from 'Honeysuckle Rose' to a Marlene Dietrich number, 'Falling in Love Again'. Had William had more to drink he might have taken this for some blissful message. As it was, he told himself, it was just a song that came to Bonnie's mind. But he felt the need to assure himself he had not been mistaken.

William rose and went to the piano. He struggled through the greenery, rested his arms on the glistening mauve veins of paint, looked down at Bonnie's nimble white fingers smudging the notes in a way that suggested considerable sentiment.

Never meant to, what can I do? Just can't help it . . .

She tipped up her head for a moment. Gave William a teasing smile. Feeling he might fall, he leant more heavily on the piano. This was all absurd, of course, he told himself. But goodness gracious how convincingly she sang. If she carried on like this he could easily be persuaded his own feelings were in some measure reciprocated . . .

Suddenly she stopped playing. Looked round.

'What's happened? Everyone's gone. Did I do the wrong thing?'

'Course not. Your spontaneous performance was hugely appreciated, I'd say. Did you see the Germans' faces? The barman's amazement?'

'No.'

'We were all enchanted.' No point in saying anything about Grant's dislike of jazz. He would have to tell her himself at some point. 'I never knew you could play, sing. You're a dark horse.'

Bonnie shrugged. With the index finger of her right hand she struck a few single notes.

'There was a time when I wanted to be a jazz pianist. But the viola won.'

'You play beautifully.' Oh, the inadequacy of words when it comes to admiration: when it comes to coded messages to a woman you love. 'Just the sort of music I like. Ruth Etting . . .'

'Ruth Etting? *There's* a heroine.' She struck the first few notes of 'Harvest Moon', still with one finger. The beam of a small, fierce downlight in the ceiling pierced the white skin, the pearly nail. William shifted his position, took a risk. With the upright piano between them, he felt safe.

'I don't feel I know you at all, Bonnie,' he said. 'I feel there's so much hidden.'

'Well, I've not been part of the Elmtree for long, have I? It takes time. You all know each other so well. I could never catch up.' She kept her head down, spoke quietly, then laughed a little. 'Anyway, we're pretty even, there. I don't know you at all either.'

William straightened himself, encouraged. There was no time to work out his answer.

'I'm a combination of the very serious and the wholly ridiculous,' he said, surprising himself. The ridiculous, he reflected, as he stood at attention between the leaves of the confounded rubber plant, was pretty obvious.

Bonnie stood up, smiling at him across the piano. Patted his shoulder.

'I've seen both things,' she said. 'You're also an extraordinary violinist . . .'

'No compliments, please.' William struggled to free himself of the larger jade leaves that were attacking him like slow-winged bats. He followed her to the corner the Germans had vacated. She seemed in no hurry to be off to her room. Such bliss was almost unbearable. They sat.

'Afraid there's no more chance of a drink.'

'I don't want a drink.' Bonnie swung her legs on to the empty chair beside her. The copious black velvet of her skirt gathered into liquid ripples. William's eyes glutted themselves from her feet to her head, where another spotlight charged down on to her shining hair, making a flat halo. Finally their eyes met.

'William, is there anything the matter? Is there something on your mind?'

Startled, William blinked rapidly.

'On my mind? There's a lot on my mind, yes. Always is, I'm rarely blessed with a scoured mind. There are always trails of completely preposterous thoughts gathering, tormenting –'

'I mean, anything special. Anything serious –'

'The thought's always serious when I'm playing, or thinking about playing, or remembering about playing –'

'You know what I mean.' Bonnie sounded impatient.

'I don't. I can't guess.'

There was a moment's silence.

'You've been rather odd, of late.' She smiled kindly.

'Odd? I'm always odd.' William smiled back, relieved. At least she had not homed into anything specific. 'Eccentric, perhaps. Have the others said anything?'

'Not to me.'

'Abroad unnerves me,' William said at last, to break another silence.

'Homesick?'

'You could call it that.' Fleetingly Grace came to mind: her cheerful voice as he opened the front door, the wings of grey hair that she had started to hide behind her ears, her brilliance as a driver, her lemon meringue pies. He shrugged.

'I can't picture your life at all when you're not with us,' said Bonnie.

'Very quiet.'

William sensed his chance had come. He must take it carefully.

'And you . . . is there nothing you're homesick for? Don't you have some . . . eager young man in tow?' Hell, he had blown it. In his hurry he had put it just about as badly as he could. But Bonnie responded with such laughter that her dimples bit deeply into her cheeks.

'"Don't I have some eager young man in tow?" Honestly, William, you put things more weirdly than anyone I've ever met.'

For all her friendly scorn, William felt he must persist. There might not be so good a chance again, for a long time.

'You must be getting used to my manner of speech by now. I can't change a lifetime's habit of distancing formality, though I do sometimes try.'

Bonnie looked at him curiously. She leant forward and patted his sleeve. He was getting used to restraining his hopes whenever he saw her hand coming towards him. He knew it only moved with kindly intent, would never turn into the harbinger of desire that he craved on her part. He let it lie unmoving on his arm, trying to convey the gesture meant nothing to him, for all the currents that blazed up his legs and zig-zagged through his stomach.

'I once went out with a certain Toby of Aldershot for almost three years,' she said. 'But we fell apart.'

'Ah.' William envisaged some vague arrangement whereby the said Toby collected Bonnie each evening, sometimes with chocolates or flowers, and took her to the cinema or theatre or out to dinner. Then escorted her home, kissed her in the porch. The sub-reason of his mind knew this was an insane and inaccurate picture, but he could not bring himself to shift to the reality.

'And then I discovered I liked living alone. Loved it. Solitude, the great healer.'

'You're unusual in that view, though I agree with you. Forced to live alone, I can image myself very content.' As the thought of a past boyfriend was not too depressing, William felt it not untoward to enquire a little further. 'And what field was he in, this Toby fellow?'

'Computers.'

'A funny thing, you know. I've never yet met anyone in computers.' (He knew the power of self-deprecation.) 'Our worlds don't cross much, I suppose. But I'm told you can become very rich if you design programmes, or whatever.'

'Toby became so rich he could only talk about money. He didn't know his Bach from his Beethoven and in the end I couldn't take that.'

'I'm not surprised.' His understanding about Toby, William felt, was forcing them towards a closeness he had not liked to imagine would ever come about.

'I mean, I did try to understand his world. He made no effort at all about mine. Hopeless.' Bonnie frowned, contemplating. 'If you really want to know, the solitude once he'd gone wasn't absolutely unbroken.' She gave a mischievous smile, dimples flashing. 'There've been a few visitors in my life since Toby, but nothing serious. Merely visitations.'

'Visitations is my sort of word,' said William.

'Then it's catching, the way you speak.'

'Much better to keep going on your own than join up with someone less than perfect, just for companionship.'

'Of course. I'd never do that. Is Grace perfect?'

'She is.' William suppressed the fraction of a sigh. He was doing so well it was worth plunging in even further, he thought. 'And now: any visitors?'

Bonnie giggled, blushed. She looked about sixteen.

'Not exactly. Suggestions are made from time to time, but I'm very fussy. I'm not one to say yes in haste. Old-fashioned, like that, I am.'

William shifted in his chair to try to ease the general combustion within him, more lively than ever now Bonnie was responding to the mood of the conversation.

'Glad to hear it.' He spoke in his most fatherly voice. 'As for suggestions, it would be a damn odd thing if a girl like you wasn't besieged by offers –'

'William: don't be silly.' She was pleased.

'If you can take a compliment from a man somewhat older than yourself, I'd say you're an exceptionally . . .' Here, words failed him. 'I mean, take this evening, surprising us all with your piano playing. You made a mighty pretty picture. And sometimes I glance at you when we're playing, and I think . . .'

'What do you think?' She was teasing him, eager to hear how William would explain the feelings these glances gave him. William held her eyes, aware that his own almost intolerable desire was, for a second or two, perhaps mutual. There was no question, of course, of telling her the truth.

'I think . . . how can one so young, and with comparatively little experience, know intuitively about the . . . oneness of a quartet, and yet urge her instrument sing out with its own particular voice . . . ?' He trailed off.

'Oh, you mean musical things.' Was there disappointment in her slight shrug? William had known he would go wrong at some point and cursed himself. He should have taken the risk and told her the truth. Bonnie glanced at her watch.

'It's very late,' she said. 'If we're going to be full of energy for tomorrow morning's expedition, we'd better go to bed.'

She was up and fleeing through the mauve haze of the bar before William could struggle from his chair. She waited for him impatiently. The doors of the lift shut behind them. The closed air was hung with vile old cigar smoke. William placed himself two feet from Bonnie, eyes averted from her. He looked instead at the reflections of the two of them in the mirrors on two walls of the lift. Repeated and repeated, their images were: there they were, smaller and smaller. The last reflection of all, no bigger than a couple of small figurines, illustrated, perhaps, the size of their friendship, relationship, in real life. The tug and pull from Bonnie's eyes, that William had felt so acutely for a single moment while they talked, had disappeared completely. Arms crossed under her breasts, stroking the velvet, she was elsewhere now: dull, flat, oblivious of William.

They reached their floor and stepped into the less obnoxious stale air of the passage.

'What is the nature of this expedition to be?' William scratched his head. God, he did not want her to go.

'We're going to a church full of bones. I told you. Thousands of skeletons. Not for the squeamish.' She giggled.

'How awful. I remember it. I might not come.'

'You've got to come.' She kissed him briefly on the cheek, a noncommittal polite kiss which William had no time to return. She put the key into the door of her room. 'Sleep well.' The door closed.

William knew that Bonnie's room was between his own and Grant's. But this did not trouble him, William was relieved to find. Bonnie had said there were currently no visitors in her life, and Grant was not one to upset the applecart by pressing his case, if indeed, he had designs on Bonnie. And judging from his aloof behaviour on this trip, William, whose opinion on this matter was inclined to shift, had begun to think that seemed unlikely to be the case.

By the mauve plastic shutters of his window he stood pulling at his white tie, unbuttoning his stiff piqué shirt like one in a trance. In his state of acute frustration he knew the night ahead would be a long one. The knowledge that through the thin wall Bonnie slept alone was of some comfort, but not enough to induce sleep. He began humming the slow movement of a Bach violin sonata. It took him an unusually long time to undress, and rather than break off his rendering of the gentle Bach, such was his anguish that he broke a rule of a lifetime and did not brush his teeth.

At three in the morning Grace, who had slept restlessly, woke completely. In her dream she had heard a whistling sound, an eerie moaning. An almost full moon, sharp as glass, stared at her through the open window. She imagined frost outside. She sensed the silence of frost, was glad of the heavy warmth of her bed.

She looked round at the darkness of the familiar shapes of the room for a while, then shut her eyes again. The noise that had been part of her dream started up again. But now it was not a whistle, or a moan, but the howling of a large dog. The howling, in truth, of a wolf.

Grace had eaten several slices of cheese for supper. Cheese at night . . . Plainly her imagination was playing tricks. She opened her eyes again and as a louder howl tore through the night silence, the discs of her spine seemed to shunt together and freeze.

She got out of bed, went to the window, pulled part of the curtain against her chest. The air was icy, damp. Grace began to shiver. Suddenly the silence was broken by a distant wail of a fire engine, or ambulance: a small-toy sound. It set off a further howl, longer, deeper, sadder. It came, Grace realised, now locked in terror, from somewhere in their own driveway. There was a wolf at large, escaped from some far-off zoo, or perhaps from a private keeper. Even as Grace wondered how it could have negotiated a motorway, found their road, their house, without being seen . . . she knew her solution was ridiculous. Should she ring the police, the RSPCA, William?

Grace forced herself to lean out of the window a little to see if . . . there was a movement in the rhododendron bush opposite the front door. Then she heard pounding footsteps, saw the brief sight of a hunched-up figure running through the gate. When it had disappeared from view there was a final howl, louder than the others: a cruel, triumphant, terrifying noise.

Grace quickly shut the window, ran back to the bed, put on the light. She grabbed the telephone and the piece of paper with William's Prague number. Her hands trembled so much that she had to make several attempts to dial correctly. She had no idea what she was going to say. She did not like to trouble William, ever, when he was on tour – he did not like his concentration to be disturbed. But here was the kind of emergency he would surely understand. A few words from William, sometimes, so sensible in a crisis, would calm her.

The number began to ring. It rang for a long time. Grace still shook violently, the man-made wolf howl persisting in her ears.

In Prague, first light was beginning to press through the window of William's room. He had not even tried to sleep, but had read through the long hours, humming through several violin sonatas. The unexpected ring of the telephone charged him with hope so fiercely irrational (Bonnie, sleepless too, was she calling him with an invitation?) that there was no room to suspect any more likely solution to someone calling at this hour.

His hand, picking up the receiver, shook as strongly as did his wife's at home.

'Hello?' Naturally, he'd be next door in a trice. Where was his ruddy dressing-gown?

'It's me. Sorry to call you at such an odd time.'

'Grace! – Grace.'

'I suppose I've woken you. So sorry.'

'You haven't actually. I couldn't sleep. What's the matter?'

'Nothing much.' She gave a small uneasy laugh, the laugh Grace used when she was concealing something like the hiding place of his birthday present or a surprise pudding. 'I just woke from rather a bad nightmare. You know what it's like, a nightmare when you're alone in the house. I felt absurdly scared, put on the light . . .'

'You silly old thing. You haven't had one of your nightmares for ages.' William could imagine Bonnie's face sideways on the pillow, thick lashes resting on her cheeks.

'No. It's so stupid.'

'You keep the light on. Definitely don't turn it off.' He made a great effort to sound sympathetic. 'Nightmares can't live for long in electric light. They thrash about for a while, like a trout out of water, gasping for air to continue, but they can't – they quickly die.' He was rather pleased with himself, able to produce such fluent guff while the warmth of Bonnie under the sheets next door pervaded his whole being.

The shadow of a laugh came down the telephone.

'I knew you'd say something silly and make it all right. I'm fine now, really. So sorry to have bothered you. I'll ring later. Don't worry.'

The wicked thing was, he wasn't worrying very much.

'You go back to sleep, my Ace . . .' William put down the telephone. He wondered if, should Bonnie smile in her sleep, it was a smile happy enough to power her dimples. He felt guilt at his lack of concern about Grace's nightmare, but her strange, rather touching anxiety had been very useful in deflecting the strength of his own imaginings. Rather to his surprise, as dawn began to light the room, he felt sleep approach at last.

7

Grace was unable to sleep for the rest of the night. In the long hours till a concrete dawn began to fill the window, she worked out a rational answer to the disturbance of the night: youths. Recently there had been trouble in the neighbourhood, burglaries and vandalism carried out by a gang of teenage boys who came from an estate some miles away. There certainly hadn't been a gang, exactly, in the front drive – just a single boy with some talent at imitating animal noises. Perhaps that had been their fun for the night – each one of them would target a house and make weird noises to alarm the owner. They probably would not return, but think of some further cruel trick with which to excite their pathetic lives.

Despite assuring herself of all this, Grace was shaky when she got up at seven. She bumped into things in the bathroom. She found herself creeping downstairs as if not wanting to disturb someone. She switched on all the lights against the gloom of the winter morning, put on the radio to furnish the silence. Then she found her usual appetite for breakfast was gone. She ate only half a piece of toast, scarcely touched her tea. Why had she not told William? she wondered. He would have provided some comfort, encouraged her to ring the police, which at the time she had thought pointless. She longed for his return tomorrow, dreaded the thought of another night alone. She rested her hands on the table and wiggled her fingers as if it were an invisible keyboard. Quite suddenly, surprising herself, she burst into tears.

Grace covered her face with her hands and sobbed noisily,

swaying back and forth in her chair. She had not cried for many years. It was a strange, disagreeable sensation: tears pouring down her cheeks and making the backs of her hand, with which she tried hopelessly to rub them away, glisten as if they had been crossed by the trails of several snails. She sniffed and coughed and bent low over the table, trying to ease the pain in her chest. People said to cry was a relief. She could feel no relief. Only the urge to sob more loudly. Perhaps the relief came if you knew what you were crying about. And of this Grace had no idea. 'What's the matter with me?' she gasped out loud.

Even as she sniffed and swayed Grace knew this was no way to comport herself. The question she asked out loud marshalled her senses. She could see what a pathetic figure she made, roaring away, red-eyed, for no more reason than she had been frightened by truants in the night. Her training of a lifetime came into play. She pulled herself together quickly, in the manner her mother would have expected and approved. Blowing her nose, she got up and went to the sink. There, she dampened a dishcloth under the tap and bunched it over her sore eyes. When she took it away she saw she was face to face with Lucien. He was at the other side of the window, grinning.

Grace's unease, beginning to drift away, returned at once. She could not imagine what he was doing here so early in the morning. His normal time nowadays was nine o'clock. Profoundly she wanted him to go away. She had not the heart to deal with him, his problems and his aggressive energy this morning. But Lucien was waving at her, signalling to let him in. Cocky he was – behaving as if breakfast in the house was his right. Wearily, Grace unlocked the back door. He barged in, a fretwork of cobwebs on his lank hair, wet mud on his boots.

'William here?'

'No.' Immediately Grace cursed herself. She had not wanted Lucien to know William was away for the night. She had managed to keep the fact from him. Now, in her unnerved state, she had given it away.

'That means there's no rush, then. Where is he?'

'Prague. He's coming back tomorrow morning – or tonight,' she added, thinking that piece of information might grant her some safety.

Lucien sat at the table, long legs spread like bony wings from the seat of the chair. He must have noticed the state of her face, Grace thought, but he made no comment.

'So: William's gone to Prague, has he? Busy schedule there?'

'There's always a full programme on a foreign tour.'

'What: two concerts a day? Morning and evening?'

'I'm not exactly sure.' She was puzzled by this unusual interest in William's work. 'But I know the last performance is tonight, seven o'clock – some church. Can't remember its name.'

'Ah! Evening concert. Hardly likely then, is it, they'd take a late flight after that?'

'What do you mean?'

'You said they might be coming home tonight.' He was enjoying himself. Tapping the table with an egg spoon, smiling with one side of his mouth. 'In other words, Grace, you lied to me.'

There was no time for Grace to calculate an answer. She folded her arms beneath her bosom, tilted up her tear-marked face, mustering all the dignity she could.

'At some point it was planned for them to come home tonight ... Travel plans sometimes change at the last minute. It's not my business to be absolutely sure of their movements at all times.'

'Quite. But don't pretend. You thought if I knew William was coming home tonight you'd be – well, safer.'

'I thought no such thing,' said Grace with all the suppressed anger of one whose thoughts have been accurately read.

'I'll take your word for it. All the same, it's funny you didn't tell me William had gone to Prague in the first place.'

'I don't see what business it is of yours what my husband does.' Her unusual sternness made Lucien smile.

'Look: I'm not here to quarrel with you. Everyone's entitled to lie if they feel like it. Put the kettle on, sit yourself down, tell me why you've been crying.' Outraged by his audacity at telling her what to do in her own house, Grace felt herself being won over by his persuasive voice – the voice he used when he chose to be his most gentle. Silently she did as he bade, then sat down opposite him with a pot of tea.

'Your eyes,' he said. 'You must have cried buckets.' Without warning he leapt up so fast the tablecloth erupted into a mass of ridges, and snatched the drying-up cloth from the sink. He came towards her. It was bunched in his hands, still damp. For a second Grace thought he was going to hit her. He squatted down, patted at her cheeks and eyes for several moments. Then he leant over and kissed her on the forehead. A blade of foul-smelling breath cut across her.

'So what's all this about? Who's done what to you to cause the tears?'

'No one's done anything.' She sniffed, then smiled. She wanted the drama to peter out now, normality to return. 'I just had a rotten night, headache, felt tired, missed William . . . burst into tears. I don't do that very often. About once a decade.'

'Fair enough,' said Lucien. 'Everyone's entitled to cry, too, if they want to.'

Grace, eyes on his sympathetic expression, marvelled at his capacity to endow statements of the utmost banality with a convincing sense of profundity. She began to make toast, prepare the breakfast Lucien liked. He returned to his seat, eyes following her every movement. The dour winter morning had lightened a little: a hint of light behind putty cloud showed Lucien to be paler than usual. Deep shadows under his eyes. He scratched at his unshaven jowls.

'Work, this morning?' Grace asked. She sat down, longing for him to leave as soon as possible. She longed for the house, the kitchen, to herself. She knew it was going to be one of her lost days – impossible to get down to work or domestic administration – and was impatient to start whatever occurred to her she might like to do instead. A walk in the country, perhaps. Reading her book. Even sleeping for an hour in the afternoon. – Lost days struck her rarely and caused her no guilt.

'Nah. Not today.' Lucien shrugged. 'Matter of fact, and this is what I came to tell you, see how it'd grab you, I've given in my notice.'

The slight rise of Grace's eyebrows indicated nothing more than further enquiry.

'Well, you know how it is. I didn't think in the first place it would be my sort of job, did I?' Grace refrained from contradicting him, gave a slight nod as she remembered his initial enthusiasm. 'Didn't I tell you? Well it was rubbish. All these rules, they'd drive a man mad. I couldn't be, like, my own person there, could I?' Grace felt herself stiffen as she always did when Lucien produced his trendy phrases. But she did not move. 'I had to be one of a team, all consistent, they said. Everyone spouting out the same ideas, rules and regulations. That's not what I'm about. Besides, far as I could see, the wretched homeless we were dealing with weren't benefiting much from what the Centre provides. Far as I could see, what they wanted was more money and a regular decent meal. All that psychobabble was just doing in their heads.' He paused, looked for Grace's reaction. She kept her face closed. 'I did try, though, honest. I put up some ideas. In fact' – he gave a small smile – 'I flooded them with ideas I thought'd be helpful. They didn't tell me in so many words, but I could see they thought I was rubbish, interfering. So I thought: no point in wasting my time here, is there? I'm off.'

'I see.' None of this news surprised Grace. 'So you'll be . . . looking for something else?'

'I might. There again I might not. See what turns up.'

'On the whole not much turns up unless you—'

'Don't you go lecturing me just like Lobelia, thanks very much.' Lucien said this with such an endearing grin Grace felt no affront. 'And don't you worry about me. I'll get myself sorted.'

'I do worry about you,' said Grace. 'I don't know why, but I do.'

Lucien poured himself another cup of tea. It then occurred to him that he should fill Grace's cup. But it was too late. The pot was empty. Grace tried to imagine what was going through his mind as he realised his moment of inconsideration.

'Sorry,' he said.

'I didn't want any more.'

'So: what are you going to do when I've gone? Back to the flowers?'

'I don't much feel like painting today.'

'Pity. Because you're very, very good. See? From what you showed me, I'd say you have bags of talent. More than most. You shouldn't waste it. Get on with that book. Finish it. You'll be surprised at the reaction –'

'Oh, go on,' said Grace. 'You exaggerate. As I told you, I've a minor talent, perhaps. Nothing more.'

'Who says talent can't grow?'

'I don't believe it can. Technique can improve and improve. But actual talent, that actual fire of ability which is given to a few people in unequal measures – I don't believe there's any way in which that can be made to expand.'

'Just shows you're not aiming high enough,' said Lucien. 'In my judgement, and I admit I'm no expert but I do have an eye, you're pretty bloody good. You should carry on not just half-heartedly but with all your energy. See?' He gave one of his fist bangs on the table. He looked convincing.

Grace, completely calm now, felt invisible feathers ruffle proudly round her. No one but Lucien had ever encouraged her in her art, or even been interested in what she was trying to do. William was faultless in his politeness, of course; made some play in showing interest. *Jolly good, you carry on with the good work, my Ace*, he would say, on the rare occasions Grace approached him for an opinion. But she could tell there was no depth to his interest, no real belief that his wife's painting was anything more than a useful little hobby, something to occupy her mornings at home. And here was Lucien, the uncouth stranger and new friend in her life, giving her genuine encouragement. At such moments she felt overwhelming affection for him, chided herself for ever thinking she would like to be rid of him for good.

'You're very kind,' Grace said, more primly than she intended, 'to take such an interest, to give such encouragement . . . Nobody else . . .' She trailed off, fearful of disloyalty.

'Course I'm interested. You're a wonderful woman come into my life, heaps of talent, gives me all these mega breakfasts. You're the sort of woman I'd like to find. Bit younger, I suppose . . .'

They both laughed. They both fell silent. Then Lucien spoke quietly.

'So: did you get my message last night?'

'What message?'

Lucien tipped up his head. Grace could see the straining muscles of his neck. He gave a long, low howl in perfect imitation of a wolf. Even here, in the warmth of the post-breakfast kitchen, lights on, windows shut, Grace felt a blade of ice razoring down her spine.

'Lucien . . . I don't believe it. It was you.'

'Me: the said wolf!' He banged his chest, grinning. 'Now there's a talent I've always had: animal noises. Anything from an elephant to a guinea pig, honest.'

Grace, seeing his good humour, realising he obviously thought of the whole thing as some kind of joke, fought her natural indignation. Determined not to sound admonishing, she spoke in a tight, controlled little voice.

'You gave me a terrible fright,' she said. 'I couldn't think what it was.'

'You can't have thought it was a real wolf? Escaped from a zoo?'

'The thought crossed my mind. One doesn't make much sense, woken up in the middle of the night. I didn't know what it was.'

'Well, sorry and all that if I alarmed you. It was meant to be a message.'

'A message?'

'Just a little signal from me to you.'

'I don't understand.'

'I didn't know William was away, did I? You didn't say he wasn't coming back after the concert. I thought I'd give a few howls, hope you'd come to the window. You'd see me. Or at least know it was me. William would be in bed asleep, and I'd have managed to send you a message. I thought that was a nice idea. A secret that would be between us.'

Grace frowned, feeling the return of uneasiness.

'I'm not sure I . . .'

'No, well, the plan didn't quite come off, did it? You alone, the howling scaring the shit out of you . . . didn't work out as planned.'

This was not one of the occasions when Grace found Lucien's coarse language refreshing. This morning, in her disturbed state, it repelled her. She could not begin to comprehend the motive behind Lucien's curious 'message', and wanted nothing more than he should go, now, at once. Leave her alone. He gave her a look possibly intended to be apologetic. Grace saw it as sly.

'What were you doing, anyway, prowling around at three in the morning?'

'Night walk. I walk a lot at night. Good time to think. Can see you don't approve.'

'You can walk all night as far as I'm concerned. But I suggest you don't go making wolf noises under anyone else's window. Could get you into trouble.'

'Would I? Come on, Gracie. Take that look off your face. I'm sorry the whole thing was a mighty cock-up, and it won't happen again. There. Am I forgiven?'

He turned his eyes on Grace so appealingly, like a small boy forced into contrition but still convinced of his innocence, that she smiled despite herself.

'You're forgiven,' she said. It was always easier to forgive. Lucien clasped his hands as if in prayer.

'In that case, you might grant me a favour. Could you spare me a few biscuits for my lunch? Lobelia's in one of her moods at home, so I don't want to go back there till she's calmed down. And I left my wallet . . .'

Grace, eager to encourage his departure, rose and went to the larder. As she stood by the shelves, contemplating which of the packets Lucien would most like, she heard his chair scraping very slightly on the floor. She stood quite still, intent on listening rather than choosing biscuits. Some instinct told her Lucien was up to something, not merely rising from his chair. She thought she heard a movement by the dresser – a rustle of paper – but could not be sure. She snatched a small packet of chocolate digestives and went quickly back into the kitchen. Lucien was in his chair. He had the air of one who had never moved. Imagination getting the better of me, thought Grace. Put it down to my jumpy state.

She handed him the biscuits. Lucien stuffed them into his pocket, thanked her and hurried out, leaving her no time to enquire when he would be coming again. She wanted to warn him that tomorrow, William just home and tired from his trip, would not be a good time. But she was too late. Standing at the sink, she waved through the window at his back view, wondering how any one man could play such havoc with her feelings in under an hour.

Then she turned back to the dresser, picked up the papers she thought she had heard move. Underneath them was the egg basket, full of brown free-range eggs that were delivered especially once a week for William. Lodged between two of them lay the lost jade cufflinks. Grace picked them up very gently, as if they were breakable as the eggs themselves. She looked at them in disbelief.

Murder, William was beginning to realise, in the mind of one who was not basically evil, was a slippery subject. Time was going by and so far nothing had been achieved beyond one pathetic attempt with crushed peanuts in a curry that had given Grace unusual pleasure. The idea of throwing Grace over a Dorset cliff when they went to stay with Dick was a pretty horrible one, and there was no absolute guarantee she would die. But unless he could think of something better, subtler, he reckoned he would have to give it a go.

The trouble was, whenever he tried to put his mind seriously to the matter of how to dispose of his wife, his thoughts scattered hopelessly, frantic as leaves in a wind. It was a subject upon which he found it impossible to concentrate. This very fact, he concluded, might be his conscience at work, urging him to abandon even considering his nefarious act. But some devil within him persisted: driven by his all-consuming love (was it love? a question he must attempt to answer very soon), the flotsam of thought concerning the murder of his dear wife floated day and night through his mind. Only when he was playing did it disappear.

After William's strange encounter in the bar with Bonnie, whose news of no current boyfriend had so raised his spirits, there was little of the night left. He managed a couple of hours' uneasy sleep and woke to find the curtains of the soulless room bleached by a bland and foreign light. Still four hours till another of the ghastly mauve breakfasts, six hours till the dreaded drive into the country to see the church.

William decided it would be a good idea to employ his time by thinking very hard about the Unspeakable. Calmly he would confront himself with difficult questions, and try to answer them. With any luck, he might arrive at some firm, sane decision. He shut his eyes.

Do I love my wife Grace? he began.

Completely. As much as any man can love a wife.

Do I love young Bonnie?

I suppose it's love, though it doesn't feel like the love for Grace. It doesn't even feel like the love I felt for Grace when we were young.

Are you happy with Grace?

I am. I always have been. I always will . . . be.

Then why do you suppose, being so extraordinarily fortunate in your marriage, that you should want to swap your wife – either hurting her or killing her – for a young girl (a very attractive, sweet young girl, yes, yes) about whom you know little?

Can't really answer that.

Try.

It's not an unusual syndrome. Happily married man (or woman) sees something beyond the safe confines of his or her life, and is irresistibly drawn.

Even if it's impractical, foolish and cruel to act upon this feeling?

Yes.

Mid-life crisis, perhaps?

Don't believe in any of that rubbish. Crises come every year of your life.

I know comparisons are odious, but perhaps we should do a little comparing. It might make you see sense.

Very well. I'm prepared to try anything.

What is it that fires your love for and devotion to Grace?

Pretty well everything. She's as near perfection as you could hope for in a woman. Gentle, kind, considerate, imaginative, unselfish, strong, funny – the list would go on for ages.

Exciting?

Well, not as exciting as she used to be, obviously. But then nor am I. The dimming of excitement on both sides, in a marriage, is perfectly reasonable. To be expected.

In all your years of marriage have you ever looked at, or been attracted to another woman?

Never. Hand on heart.

So: harder question. What is it you love – if it is love – about Bonnie?

Everything I've ever seen, though I admit that's not been very much. Most of all, I suppose, her talent. She's an extraordinary musician. When we play together . . . I'm not going to describe what happens to two people joined together in the playing of a profound piece of music, but its power can leave one weak with gratitude, helpless. The nearest thing I know to ecstasy.

When did you first realise the depth – if it's depths we're speaking about – of your passion for Bonnie?

The day she came to my house and we played some Mozart duos together looking out over the garden. There was snow.

Do you think she has any idea of your feelings for her?

I'm pretty sure she knows I like her. And admire her. She probably sees me as a funny old thing, but age doesn't come into the bond of music.

William: let's be sensible. Is there any reason to suppose that the swapping of the tried-and-tested and altogether remarkable Grace, for the untried, talented young Bonnie, is a good idea?

That is a question . . . to which I shall give further thought on the way to the church this morning, and whenever I have a free moment.

Be practical, too. Have you considered if Bonnie would be party to your plan?

I have.

And?

That's another matter for further cogitation. In many ways she's older than her years. She's aware of the . . . music between us. I daresay she could be persuaded. I think she'd know that in me she'd found a man whom she could trust.

Trust? But you're planning to murder your wife.

That's a plan that's been floating, I agree. Pretty mad. Probably won't ever come off. Can't unfortunately see much alternative.

If you're really set on the insane plan of leaving Grace, you could go for something conventional, like divorce. Thus you'd avoid prison – for surely one as inept at murder as you, would be found out within moments of the act – and be able actually to be with Bonnie. Should she want you . . .

True.

Then why –?

I'd find it very hard to leave Grace. To explain to her. Murder might be easier.

Then stay with her. Abandon for ever all the evil thoughts that have been consuming you, and return to thinking of Bonnie merely as your delightful new viola player whom the Elmtree was lucky enough to have found.

That's the trouble: I can't go back to that.

William: two final, difficult questions.

Thank God we're nearly through. This is all a dreadful strain.

Is it desire you feel for Bonnie?

(Long pause.) That comes into it, yes. (Another long pause.) Well, yes, I suppose I can't deny her presence has a deliquescent effect. I long to . . . But I love her company, too. She cheers me up. I love her playing –

Yes, yes. Now, finally – you would agree your plan is that of a man unhinged, temporarily (let us hope) insane?

Of course I agree to that.

You would agree, therefore, that the only possible thing to do is to come to your senses? Abandon the evil thoughts – in such an essentially good man they're no more than bad dreams that have somehow lodged in your waking fantasies. Let logic, kindness, human charity return to their rightful place, dousing these insane fantasies like a blow torch –

No need to get poetic here. What you're saying is, give up all thoughts of Bonnie, stay happily married to Grace.

That's precisely what I'm saying.

Well, this has all been quite useful, I have to admit. Not an easy business.

Then you'll try.

I'll try.

Good luck.

Thanks.

When this dialogue with himself came to an end William leapt out of bed with unusual bounce and went to the window. He drew back the curtains and looked over the roofs of Prague, feeling pleased with himself. It had all gone rather well. A conclusion – the conclusion in his heart he wanted – had more or less been agreed, and now all he had to do was carry it out. At the moment he felt strong in his resolve. After all, no one had any inkling what had been going on in his tortured mind for the last few weeks: there was no explaining to be done to anyone but himself. All he had to do was screw his determination to the sticking place . . .

remember to get Grace her favourite scent at the duty-free, return to normal. Shouldn't be too difficult for one of his inner fortitude. He drew himself up to his full height, re-knotted the cord of his pyjamas. Grace had always believed in his inner fortitude, and she was a woman of no mean judgement.

Two hours later William was putting his good intentions into practice. Had he not had the serious discussion with himself, he would have made sure his place in the minibus was next to Bonnie. In the back seat, with Rufus or Grant, their arms, thighs, bodies might have had occasion to touch. He would have felt sick from – well, whatever it was that bedevilled him when he was close to her.

As it was William made sure he was the first to reach the minibus, and took the seat next to the driver. He gave no reason for this unusual placing – Rufus was accustomed to taking the front seat whenever they drove together. Rufus's look, when this privilege was denied him that Prague morning, was one of astonishment and irritation. But William didn't care. Both men kept their silence.

On the drive through uninteresting Czech countryside – it put William in mind of many of his least favourite places in England – he concentrated wholly on thoughts of Grace. What was she up to now? Her painting, he hoped. Dear head bent over a sprig of hybrid holly or a helleborous rose. He must remember to encourage her to complete this book with all speed. It had been in the making a good many years, and he didn't want it to die on her. He would suggest a little celebration when it was finished: drinks and supper with the Quartet and a few friends. Perhaps he would compose an aria for her – she had, on occasions, remarked that she wished William was a little more like Schumann, writing pieces for his loved one. Well, William would compose a little song for Grace and get Bonnie to sing in her sweet voice . . . No danger there, a public occasion. He hadn't composed anything for so long. The publication of his wife's book would be an opportune moment.

It was more likely, William thought, that Grace was nowhere

near her paints, but making plans for meals for the weekend.
When he had been away, she always made a special effort to
welcome him with his favourite puddings – Guards pudding,
queen of puddings, steamed orange pudding. William's stomach
ached for such comforts. The Czech breakfast, as usual, had been
the inadequate little squares of plastic strawberry jam flattened on
to bread so hard it endangered the teeth. He was hungry. Hunger
and lack of sleep had spurred, too, some other kind of longing. He
kept his eyes firmly on the road ahead. Not for anything in the
world would he allow himself to turn round and let his eyes pry on
Bonnie in her jeans, and the sloppy jersey which slunk round her
breasts. No. What he thought of was Grace in the bath, his
Bonnard Grace, his dearest Ace, toes mushrooming through the
foam, nipples (faded nipples, in truth) no longer upright but pointing at an endearing angle towards the familiar wedge of her
stomach. Faced with this picture, the uncomfortable feeling mercifully faded.

The minibus pulled up in front of the Kutná Hora Church. The
driver hurried to open each of the vehicle's doors, elated by his
own gallantry. He smiled and shrugged, pointed at the church,
tapped his forehead.

'No good,' he warned.

The members of the Quartet stretched, stood about. William
could not remember how the idea of this expedition had taken
root. Grant's idea, he presumed. Abroad, Grant put himself in
charge of culture, arranged that cities should be explored between
rehearsals and concerts. William and Rufus – and in the old days
Andrew – had always gone along with his plans, but feared they
showed less enthusiasm than Grant expected. Perhaps, now, he put
his hopes in Bonnie. There had been talk of 'rushing her through'
the Jewish Cemetery on their return, if there was time before the
rehearsal. (As far as William understood, this would mean missing
lunch, so the idea would not get his vote.) Grant had also suggested various other visits before leaving for the airport tomorrow.
William and Rufus had not been included in these invitations, and

would not have accepted them if they had. All the same, thought William, it was pretty untoward of Grant to suggest excursions alone with Bonnie. He had no idea whether or not she had agreed to go with him, but rather hoped she had. Just to see Bonnie setting off in the minibus alone with Grant might convince William that her feelings for all members of the Quartet were equal. She would be happy to please each one of them in their different ways.

Rufus was the first one to enter the church. William followed a few feet behind him. There was an old woman – long wool clothes and scarf dripped custard-like from her chair – at a table of post-cards in the porch. No one else. As their eyes grew accustomed to the light they could see that the entire interior of the church was encrusted with bones – human skeletons chopped up and fash-ioned into decorations, chandeliers, deathly designs.

'My God, what a place.' Rufus ran a shaky hand across his eyes. 'It's hard to believe. I'm only thankful the wife isn't here.'

'Astonishing' said William. In the November gloom that fell upon the tapestry of bones there was a faint, ironic brightness which gave them a sense of defiant vitality. They bore no resem-blance to skeletons – the only skeletons in William's experience – in school laboratories. In a pyramid of skulls, at first glance all identical, he could see the flesh of individuals – here a laughing young woman with deep eye sockets, there a surly man with high domed brow. They were ghosts stripped of their ethereality, mock-ing reminders of mortality.

William did not share Rufus's shock. Intrigued, he made his way down the stone steps into the lower half of the church, and began to study the ingenious patterns made from arm bones, thigh bones, spines – the chopsticks of human life. Bone, he thought, had a certain beauty, if you could distance your thoughts from how it once moved, swung, rested, lived, protected the jelly of the eyeball, the mess of brain – how it was the scaffold upon which veins and sinew and muscles and organs were all hung. But to appreciate innumerable bones, formed into this bizarre monu-ment, you had to banish thoughts of the life they had once led . . .

There was a scream. William, deep in his reflections, turned to see Bonnie and Grant some five or six steps above him. Grant had a hand under Bonnie's elbow. The look on his face was one of concern edged with annoyance. Bonnie screamed again, covered her face with her hands.

'Get me out of here,' she wailed.

Grant nodded at William.

'You take her. I want a good look round.'

The cad, thought William. In his own heart, reluctance to usher Bonnie out of this place was mixed with delight at the opportunity of consoling her. This was a genuine reason, he told himself, to abandon every promise made to himself not three hours ago, and help a girl in trouble. Shaking his head, he hurried up to stand beside Bonnie. Relieved, Grant left them to inspect a wall of bones woven intricately as tweed.

Bonnie, one hand still over her eyes, stretched out her other to William. He took it.

'Just get me out of here fast,' she said. 'I'm not going to open my eyes till we're outside.' She was petulant as a frightened young child.

William led her back up the steps, his right hand round her waist, his left clasped in her free hand. He could smell the sweethay smell of her sweat, and was aware her left breast was perilously close to his ribcage. He guided her conscientiously as someone helping the blind, without a word, until they were through the door. As they passed the old woman, she gave a knowing smile over her unsold cards.

'Here we are,' he said, 'outside.'

Bonnie opened her eyes warily. She did not let go of William's hand. They looked at each other, dangerously close, for a moment. Then she broke into a gust of uncontrollable tears, making a terrible noise in the silence of the graveyard. She fell upon William, hiding her head on his shoulder, then moving it up to lodge beneath his chin.

William was alarmed. This was more than he could ever have

hoped for, of course. But Bonnie's sudden melodrama, her uncharacteristic loss of control, would unnerve any man. He felt at a loss
as how to console her. Clumsily he patted her head. His heart was
battering so hard (he could feel hers was, too, for different reasons)
that he felt himself totter against her weight. He splayed his legs to
stand more firmly. Further discomfort was caused by the snarling,
rearing blood in his loins, something he prayed to keep from her,
but in their curious embrace this seemed unlikely.

He had no idea how much time they passed locked together,
Bonnie howling, William muttering useless words of comfort. He
was vaguely aware of Rufus, whose interest in the church must
have expired as soon as Bonnie screamed, sitting on a gravestone
nearby, open guidebook in hand, looking curious. William heard
the chirp of a Czech sparrow, which added a gust of nostalgia for
his garden at home to the general chaos of his mixed emotions. He
was aware of pins and needles in the arm that still clutched at
Bonnie's waist, and wondered for how long he could hold his position of support.

At last Bonnie detached herself from him, very slightly. Her
cheeks were bright pink and drenched with tears. Her long eyelashes were bunched together in shining clumps, each one finely
pointed as Grace's sable paintbrushes. William had to exert every
force in his being not to take her more conventionally in his arms,
and kiss her for eternity.

'That's the most horrible, horrible place I've ever been to in my
entire life,' she sobbed – though the sobs were now more diminu-
endo. 'If I'd known it was going to be anything like that I'd never
have agreed to Grant's revolting plan. He said I might enjoy it. He
must be mad! Perverted.'

'My wife would feel the same,' offered Rufus, from his place on
the grave. 'Incidentally, that ruddy Czech Republic sparrow chirps
a semitone lower than his British counterpart. Makes me a lot
uneasier than the bones.'

William sensed Bonnie smile against his shoulder, annoyed with
himself that he hadn't been the first to divert her thoughts. He felt

the need to take the courageous step of disengaging himself completely, now, from Bonnie. Her sobs had died to the merest whimper: she was pulling herself together, searching in her sleeves for a handkerchief. William produced his own – by chance clean and still folded (Grace was a meticulous woman with the iron). She took it without a word, dabbed at her face, never more enchanting, and causing William's resolve and heart to twist and turn so violently he felt a little faint. Mixed with these turbulent feelings was a deeply shaming delight at Bonnie's anger with Grant. William would not forget what she had said about him. Grant had (innocently, perhaps) tricked her, let her down. Bonnie might not forgive him for that. If there was any possibility of a liaison between them in Grant's mind, surely this morning's mistaken visit had scotched the plan. He had really put his foot in it . . . thank God.

'Just think,' Bonnie was saying, 'it's just pure chance that we didn't live and die when those poor wretches did. We could easily be among them. We could be those horrible sticks of bones, those empty grinning heads.'

William gave a small compliant smile, and shrugged. He could think of no suitable reply to her observation. Bonnie handed him back his handkerchief. He softened his eyes in invitation to her to return to the comfort of his neck if she felt like it. But plainly she didn't. She moved away from William and went to sit by Rufus on the gravestone.

To William's amazement, Rufus patted Bonnie on the knee. It was, of course, no more than a grandfatherly gesture, but not one William had ever supposed Rufus capable of making. Perhaps he had been moved by Bonnie's distress. Perhaps she had the power to move them all.

'Beastly experience, you poor old thing,' Rufus was saying to Bonnie. 'Best forget it. And I have to say it's made me so darned hungry I could eat a whole plate of those revolting dumplings without a grumble.'

Bonnie smiled.

'There'll be plenty of time for lunch when we get back to

Prague,' she said, 'because I've not the slightest intention of going off to see *anything* with Grant.'

This information caused spirals of conflicting sensation to twist through William, who was beginning to feel very cold. One was the jealousy that had flared with Bonnie's smile to Rufus – why had she failed to bestow at least a smile of gratitude on to *him*, William, the one in whose arms she had so keenly fallen? The other was the secret pleasure that Grant was to be spurred this afternoon. That could leave him with a chance to suggest at least a cup of tea in a café, after the rehearsal, while Rufus returned to the hotel to keep up the endless communication with his wife, and Grant went alone to reacquaint himself with the disappointment (to William's mind) of the famous Charles Bridge.

When Grant eventually reappeared, carrying a bunch of post-cards and wearing the smug look of a super-sightseer to whom absolutely everything is of acute interest, a small scene took place which gave further boost to William's hopes.

'D'you mind if I sit in the front on the way back?' Bonnie asked William.

'Of course not.'

'We are in a huff,' said Grant.

'All due to your stupid joke. You said we were going somewhere marvellous.'

'I didn't think you'd take it like that. Anyhow, it is marvellous in a way.' He slammed shut the minibus door.

On the silent journey back to Prague William began to have fears for the concert tonight. Bonnie's rendering of the Purcell was pure delight, but how would she tackle the Haydn F major? He was well aware of her resistance to Haydn, and although in rehearsals she had played competently enough, he wondered if the upsets of the morning would affect her.

But how quickly moods change and anger is dissolved, reflected William, especially when peace is in everyone's best interest. By the time they arrived back in the city Bonnie seemed quite recovered, and Grant was over his temper. He made no mention of his plans to rush her round the sights, and the four of them enjoyed lunch together in a gloomy café, many jokes made against the heavy food. At the rehearsal in the empty church Bonnie played so joyously no one would ever have guessed at her dislike for Haydn. When, after a long session, William suggested to Bonnie she might like a cup of tea in the Square, the other two presumed the invitation included them. While they accepted with enthusiasm – William, scrupulous about expenses, rarely offered to pay for everyone – Bonnie declined apologetically. She felt she needed an hour's sleep to be in best form for tonight, she said. So William found himself round a small table with just two members of his Quartet: two men with whom he had spent so much of his life, in awe of their talent and in the warmth of their friendship, that extraneous chit-chat was no longer necessary. In the easy silence in which they drank their lemon tea, upsets of the morning forgotten, William sensed their brief return to old habits brought relief to them all. Without Bonnie's presence there was no excitement, no possibility of the unexpected observation or question. But there was a restfulness, an understanding, that is peculiar to men who have worked and lived together for a long time in harmony. And although William secretly calculated the hours until he was able to behold Bonnie in her velvet, eyes cast down on her viola, he enjoyed the half-hour alone with his old friends more than he could ever have expected, and had no regrets that Bonnie had chosen not to be with them.

8

It was not in Grace's nature to initiate rows, but her anger on discovering what Lucien had done seethed so furiously all day that she determined to confront him when he arrived next morning. His outrageous act signified it was time to put an end to his troublesome visits. The pity – the affection, even – she felt for him was now far outweighed by her fury.

Her intention was to brace herself for the row as soon as he arrived – she might even refuse him his customary tea and toast – and to be rid of him by nine thirty. Then, putting the whole disagreeable matter from her mind, she would spend the rest of the day preparing for William's return. On the telephone he explained there had been a less than successful expedition to some weird church, and he was tired and hungry and looking forward to being home. God, was she looking forward to that too . . .

Her plans were confused by Lucien's non-appearance at the usual time. Nine thirty, nine forty-five, still no sign. Perhaps, too guilty to face her, he wasn't going to appear at all. Perhaps the return of the cufflinks had been a farewell sign. Well, in some ways that would make everything easier. Grace would not have to charge herself up to shout and accuse. She would be spared his intimidating response – something she had witnessed on occasions if ever she had offered some small criticism. She would not have to resist one of his sudden bouts of charm and persuasiveness should he disagree with the plan to bring their peculiar relationship to an end.

At ten o'clock Grace began her preparations for William's supper. Convinced by now she would not be seeing Lucien today, she felt her usual calm override the obnoxious tumult of the last twenty-four hours, and concentrated on the pleasing rolling of her pastry. With so much on her mind, it had not occurred to her to protect herself from surprise by locking the back door. At ten past eleven she heard it open. There was the familiar sound of Lucien's slouchy tread: and there he was, grinning down at her. Lucien with huge dull pupils to his eyes, damp jacket, thickly bristling jowls.

To one who is unaccustomed to entertaining anger in the first place, to reassemble it once it has faded is not an easy matter. Grace, knife in hand (she had been making such a fine job of slicing the edges of the pastry from the pie dish), stood looking at him in incredulous silence, waiting for a pulse of indignation to fire her.

'There: caught you out, didn't I? Tricked you! Bet you thought I wasn't coming. Bet you thought now I'd returned them I wouldn't be coming back to face the music.' He was smiling. The scoffing bore no malice.

'Lucien,' Grace said.

Lucien took a step towards her. He put a hand on her shoulder. She stiffened. He removed it at once.

'Look, I can explain. I'm no thief – well, am I? You know that. I nick a bit from those who won't miss it if I'm desperate. But in *here* –' he banged his chest – 'I'm not a thief. Besides, I wasn't stealing those cufflinks, I was just like borrowing them. Took them to a pawn shop, got the money to deal with a bit of business, had a bit of luck with another bit of business, repaid the loan, got the bloody cufflinks back and first thing I do is bring them back. You can't fault me there. I'd say that was the act of someone pretty honourable, even in your book.'

Grace sighed. The anger she tried to summon, all the things she had thought of to say, would not return. Instead, she felt an acute weariness.

'It was completely unacceptable, what you did,' she said.

'Well: I wouldn't say that. Not considering the emergency. Course I'm sorry the bit of the business to repay the pawnbroker's loan took a bit of time. People let you down. You can't rely on people.' There was no flicker of a smile at his own irony. 'But the main thing is they're back now. I daresay I'm forgiven, you being the sort of forgiving woman you are. How about we celebrate with a cup of tea?'

Their eyes met.

'No,' said Grace, putting down the knife.

'Come on, now. Where's your sense of humour? I'm hungry.'

'Have you any idea the worry you caused? The misery? I'd only just given those cufflinks to William. He was distraught.'

'Sorry about that. I'm not much of a things person myself. Possessions don't hold much interest. So I'd not be the best at understanding that sort of thing.'

'You could have asked me for another loan,' said Grace. 'I was willing enough to give you one in the first place.'

'No: I couldn't, could I? Not a second one. I'm not a man to take advantage of a friend's generosity – speaking of which I'll get the money back to you any day now, honest.' Lucien sat down in his usual chair. 'Are you going to make me breakfast?'

Grace shook her head without much conviction.

'Just a cup of tea, then. I'm busy. William's coming home tonight. I want to get on with the dinner.'

'Lucky old William.'

Grace went to put on the kettle and get Lucien's customary mug. She could not face an argument about that. When she turned back to the table she saw he was playing with the knife, testing the blade between two fingers.

'You work with a mighty sharp blade,' he said, quietly.

'You have to, for pastry.'

Grace was conscious her heart had begun to beat faster. She told herself not to be so stupid.

'Pastry: that's something *Lobelia* never does.'

Lucien pulled the board on which Grace had been rolling her

pastry towards him. He straightened out one of the ribbons that had been cut from the edge of the pie. With the tip of the knife he sliced through its middle, hand absolutely steady.

'Imagine if that was skin,' he said.

'Lucien! That's horrible.'

'I am horrible, remember.' He gave one of his laughs that reminded Grace of a shaken coal scuttle. 'I used to play with knives as a kid. I liked slicing things. One time Lobelia gave me a rabbit. It bit me, stupid bugger. I ripped right up through its belly with a penknife. That was good fun, at fourteen. – She never found out.'

Grace, unsure whether to believe him, was unnerved by the story. She poured him tea.

'Thanks,' he said. 'I had a rough night. You're a good woman.' He put down the knife. Grace knew she must say her piece before her resolve faded. She sat not directly opposite Lucien, but a little to one side. The sour smell of his clothes, his unwashed skin, had begun to override the smells of cooked apple, lemon and various herbs.

'This has got to stop, I'm afraid,' said Grace. She knew she sounded like a schoolmistress, and spoke with a note of unintended apology.

'What has?' Lucien's sluggish eyes faintly widened in an attempt at humour.

'All this coming here. You come more and more often, uninvited. I can't cope any more.'

'I thought I was welcome. You've always made me feel welcome.'

'It's become . . . too much. You don't know the dread I live in, thinking you'll run into William.'

'Ah, it's the *husband* who doesn't approve. I get it, man. I get it.' Fist bang on the table. Tea slopped on to the cloth. 'I could come later, be sure he was out of the way.'

Grace shook her head.

'I'm afraid that's not possible. I work in the mornings.'

'Not always, you don't.' Lucien laughed. 'That's one of your problems. In fact I'd say some people might quite rightly call you something approaching lazy.'

'I'm not interested in your opinion of my working schedule, Lucien: you know nothing about it. I'm just telling you I want these breakfasts . . . these meetings, to come to an end.'

Lucien sighed.

'Pity, that,' he said at last. 'I've enjoyed our conversations. Looked forward to them.' He picked up the knife again. 'But if that's what you want,' he said.

Silence.

'It is. I'm sorry.' Her victory almost won, to apologise was the least Grace could do.

'I suppose you feel you can't trust me around any more. I'd be nicking the silver three times a week.' He gave the merest sneer of a smile.

'I don't suppose you would.' Grace tried for lightness. 'It's not that. It's just the whole . . . thing of your visits. I can't cope with the tension of them any more. I can't put it any clearer than that, though I realise I'm not being very specific.'

Lucien now held the kitchen knife in two hands. Eyes on its blade, he slowly pushed the tip of his tongue (an unhealthy bluish dun colour) out between his rigid lips. He put the point of the blade against it, pressing hard enough to make an indentation.

'Sharp, isn't it?' he said, suddenly bored. 'Anyhow, I get the picture. I get the picture. So if that's how you feel, Grace, who'm I to go against you?'

He suddenly got up, moved to the sink and emptied the mug with great force.

'Sorry about the waste.'

'For heaven's sake, Lucien. You're being over . . . I didn't mean I didn't want to see you ever again.' Grace stood too, awkward, disturbed by the look on his face. She slipped the knife into the table drawer. This made Lucien smile.

'That's the message that came through. I'm not stupid when it comes to messages. Anyways, no half-measures, that's me. If I'm fond of a person I don't believe in half-measures.' He gave a little toss of his head in the direction of the uncooked apple pie. 'Best let you get back to your cooking.'

Several things clamoured in Grace's head, but she said none of them. She watched Lucien slope to the back door, more hunch-shouldered than usual, and slam it behind him.

When the reverberations of him had died away, she retrieved the knife and went back to trimming the pastry. Her sense of relief was clouded by a measure of foreboding, and somewhere in the depths of her there was a shadow of sadness, of loss.

On the flight home William found himself sitting beside Bonnie. This was not a matter of chance. Lugging her copious hand lug-gage up the crowded aisle she had turned and announced to her fellow players she wanted to sit next to William – a request she had never made before.

'She's in a mood,' William heard Grant mutter, and unease seeped through his tired body. In the old days there had sometimes been tensions or disagreements between the players, but they had been spared of moods (women's moods) of the sort Bonnie had inflicted on this trip to Prague.

Bonnie, having efficiently settled her viola into the overhead rack beside William's violin, bundled herself into the free seat next to the window and patted the vacant seat beside her. She sat in a vortex of twisted things: overflowing carrier bags, scarves, maga-zines, jackets . . . William had no idea how to begin to help her make some order of the muddle. Having sat down and placed his one, small, neat, regulation-sized briefcase under his own seat, he stood up again vaguely aware he should make some offer to help her. There was a look of impatience on Bonnie's face, not the grat-itude he was hoping for.

'Sit down, William, till I've sorted myself out.'

He obeyed, confused. Bonnie shifted herself from side to side, crossly punching at bags and pulling at garments. As she twisted herself about her breasts were slung from side to side beneath the pale angora of her jersey. William shut his eyes. He thought of the ugly woman in the church: of tinned artichokes, marigolds, *The Gold and Silver Waltz* – things that made him shudder. It didn't work.

Bonnie was nudging him. He opened his eyes.

'Can you put these up?' She thrust a pile of bags and garments into his arms. They seemed to have a life of their own, squirming about. He stood, moved cautiously into the aisle to assess the next move. How was he to open the door of the rack, arms loaded?

'Having trouble?' Grant, on the inner seat across the aisle, looked up from the *Guardian* with a satisfied smile.

'Open it for me, would you?'

'I'd consider it.' Grant folded his newspaper very slowly. Rufus put down his book (a new biography of Brahms – to be seen reading the latest musical biography was his only form of showing off) and grinned. Whether it was at Grant's enjoyment of William's plight, or encouragement for William himself, it was hard to tell.

In his own unhurried time Grant rose and opened the overhead rack. Then he sat down again, quickly returned to his paper. William, who was not a tall man, rose on tip-toe and heaved the mass of Bonnie's stuff vaguely in the direction of the empty shelf. His aim was clumsy: he missed his goal by a long way. The bags disgorged their clutter – jackets and scarves poured down over his head and fell to the floor. Grant and Rufus, concentrating on their reading once more, did not seem to notice William's distress. Bonnie, back to him, was staring out of the window. William, conscious of the unravelling of his dignity, began to pick up the things that had spilt on to the floor. After an age of inept dithering, an air hostess came to his rescue. In a trice everything was stuffed neatly into the rack – she was a fine, tall girl with dazzling lipstick that made her mouth look like a cut-out made of Cellophane paper – and William was able to return to his seat. He noticed that Grant's eyes had slid from his paper to the air hostess's athletic ankles, and the observation had a calming effect. Here was proof that Grant's general eye for a good-looking woman had not dimmed. Had he been in love with Bonnie, in love in the way that he, William . . .

then glancing at another woman would have been out of the question.

'I hate taking off,' said Bonnie, when the plane's engines started. 'I can never like flying. – You've not done up your seat-belt.'

She leant across William, hands playing innocently over his stomach and loins as she searched for the two metal clasps, locked them together. Dear God . . . William gripped the arms of his seat, clenched his teeth.

'You look as if you're preparing yourself for take off in a rocket. Relax! And don't worry, I'm not going to make a scene like yesterday among the bones. – Sorry about that.'

William turned to her, smiled. He hoped she would read his silent message of complete forgiveness, understanding, devotion . . .

'We're off the ground,' she said, impressively cool for one who was nervous of flying. But as the plane rose more steeply she covered William's hand with hers, and dug her nails fiercely into his splayed fingers. He would have been happy to die at that moment, he thought. But his bliss lasted for mere seconds. Bonnie snatched her hand away and twisted once more to look out of the window. What a fidget she was, thought William, although impervious to any such annoyance.

'When I was a child I used to think what fun it would be to put a ladder up against the clouds, and climb up and bounce on them . . .'

'Did you?'

They both fell silent, then. William tried to quell the chaos in his head, and the pounding of blood through his veins, by breathing very slowly. Bonnie opened the in-flight magazine – that was the last thing he wanted, to lose her to a magazine. He saw he was in danger of missing his chance to carry on in the extraordinary vein they had left off in the hotel bar. How could he retrieve her attention? Perhaps he should use the opportunity to confront her with a matter, a personal matter, that had been worrying him for some time.

'I want to talk to you about Haydn,' he said at last.

'Oh no: not Haydn. Not here, please. We had Haydn last night.'

'And beautifully you played it, too. Whatever you may feel.'

Bonnie sighed, turned another page of her magazine. She studied a whole-page advertisement for some kind of bath essence. Girl in a bath towel standing at a window. Distant man on a charger approaching.

'You know we're doing the G major for one of the Christmas concerts?' asked William, after a long pause in which he weighed up the wisdom of the question.

'I know that's the plan, yuh.'

'Op. 77 No. 1.' William was giving himself time to think.

'I know that, too.'

'Well, I just think . . . I mean I know your . . . dislike of Haydn in general. But it would be hard to imagine anyone not being seduced by this particular quartet.' Bonnie pursed her lips, causing a flash of dimple. Turned over a page. Beefeaters posed like china mugs beside the Tower of London. 'I mean, it's so merry,' said William.

'Each according,' said Bonnie, after a while. 'Haydn's particular brand of merriment does nothing for me.'

William, mid-sigh, decided to take a risk. Perhaps he could persuade her to take a more tolerant view of the great composer by re-involving her with his secret category.

'It's an *upstairs* piece,' he whispered.

'A what?'

'You remember, I told you . . .'

'Oh that. Yes.'

'You should trust me.' The despair he felt about his love (was it love?) for Bonnie was turning to the bleaker, but more familiar despair, that came to him when defending a piece of music he loved. Perhaps he should try a less subtle, more authoritative note. 'Anyhow: whatever you feel, it's in the programme. We're going to have to get through it. My suggestion is that you listen to it as much as possible in the next few days, and you might find yourself coming round to it –'

'I might. Can we stop talking about Haydn, now? I want to get on with my reading.' Her attention was now on a photograph of a soppy-looking young man and woman on the brink of copulating over a tub of ice cream.

William, puzzling at unknown dark corners of Bonnie's mind, turned his eyes to the small window beyond her. The intense white of a hard-edged cloud filled his vision. He allowed himself to imagine Bonnie bouncing on this white mass, but the agreeableness of the thought did not disguise his feeling of failure concerning Haydn. He had handled that badly. The odd thing about Bonnie was that she made him feel clumsy in his negotiations – a feeling that, in all his experience of dealing with musicians, he had never known before. What a strange, entrancing, difficult, irresistible creature she was. In many ways it would have made for a much happier journey had she chosen to sit next to Grant or Rufus: but then of course he would have been denied these few hours when proximity to her gilded his soul, and did something a great deal rougher to his ageing body.

'You're thinner,' said Grace, as William came through the door.

'Ooh, am I, my Ace? Perhaps. That foreign food.'

They kissed each other gently on the cheek.

'Lovely you're back.'

'Lovely . . .' William put down his small suitcase. Grace picked it up

'I'll just get your stuff into the machine. We can have supper in half an hour. I've done you an apple pie.'

'I bet you have.'

He followed her upstairs, noticing that the weight of his case made her bend quite far to one side. A pretty curve to her spine, he thought. If he'd been a painter, if he'd been Bonnard, he'd have liked to paint a woman carrying a suitcase.

In his study, the thick familiar silence brought a kind of peace to his heart. He shoved a few piles of scores up the sofa, made room for himself, sat. Tonight, in order to avoid talking about Prague, he would introduce the idea of spending a few days with Dick after Christmas. Surely it would give Grace something agreeable to look forward to . . . winter walks together along the cliffs.

Along the cliffs . . . With astonishing force William's original Dorset plan came back to him. Even as it rose before him, bright as Macbeth's dagger, he forced himself to remember his conversation with his rational half in Prague. But since his conclusion, things had happened to shift his firmness of purpose. Bonnie had wept on his shoulder. Bonnie had chosen to sit next to him on the plane. Bonnie's fingers, doing up his seatbelt (he had made sure to undo it himself) had ravaged his good intentions – Bonnie, Bonnie, Bonnie – what was she doing now, alone in her little flat in Aylesbury, not two miles from Grant? Why was he not with her, smothering her dimples with all the pent-up kisses that it was agony to hoard? Why could they not just go off and –

'Supper,' he heard Grace calling from downstairs, and he moaned out loud before rising and forcing himself into his usual, straight-backed, regimental position, expression swept clear of guilt, and prepared to face his dear, dear Ace over her loving apple pie.

For a few moments Grace stood contemplating the whirling soapy mass of her husband's dirty shirts, pants and socks in the washing machine. The domestic sight brought her some relief. William was home. There was nothing to fear any longer. Should Lucien threaten her any further, she would get William to deal with him, see him off, take out an injunction if necessary. (Loyalty kept her from envisaging the scene between the milder man and the aggressive brute.) But she knew in her heart there would be no need for such a confrontation. Lucien's exit had been very final. He would not be returning. The realisation had been sinking more profoundly into her since his departure. By now, along with the feeling of perverse loss, was the thought that without his visits her life would be . . . duller. Lucien's peculiar, erratic behaviour had quickened the days . . . though of course when it came to the weighing up, to be dull and safe was better than to be in a state of constant trepidation.

To deflect such reflections Grace firmly turned her mind to her husband and the quiet evening before them. She could see it all: staccato news from Prague, appreciation for her home cooking, apologies for no news from home . . . then the sinking into their usual happy silence, both relieved to have to make no further effort. She turned her back on the washing and arranged a smile with which to greet William as he came eagerly downstairs.

By halfway through the roast chicken they had finished with carefully edited news from Prague, and the equally perfunctory news of Grace's progress on her book at home. Then, *better take the bull*, thought William, although to switch his mind from a vision of Bonnie – head hiding in his neck, outside the bone-church – would require an almighty effort. His vision of that scene, curiously, was not as it had been through his own eyes – scraps of scalp peeping through her head – but that of an observer some distance away in the cemetery, regarding the odd couple they made: beautiful young girl seeking comfort from an older man. Man's head tilted back to accommodate girl's head in his neck. Man's legs solidly apart the better to support her weight. The clarity of the picture was unsettling.

'Dick suggested we might go and spend a few days with him after Christmas,' he said.

'Dick's last cottage was freezing.'

'I expect there's central heating in this one.'

'Jack and Laurel want to come down for a few days over the New Year.'

'Oh, Lord. Do they?' When Bonnie had reached to do up William's seatbelt, he was near to fainting with pleasure. He would like to lie back and let Bonnie do up seatbelts across him for hours on end. The fantasy began to take a grip.

'They always do. But I expect we could manage Dorset for a day or two.' No more than a day or two, please God, thought Grace. By after Christmas Lucien might change his mind, start his visits again. She wouldn't want him to arrive to find no one at home.

'We could go for walks,' William said, so quietly Grace had to strain to hear him. But he had to say something to disguise the moan that was rising within him, the deliquescence that was rendering him useless under Bonnie's hands, metal fastenings irrelevant.

'Are you all right, William?'

'Quite.' He forced himself upright.

'You're pale. You're not eating much.'

'Along the cliffs,' said William. He smiled, made an effort. 'You used to love walking along those Dorset cliffs.'

'So I did.' Though the last walk she remembered with acute feeling was the one in the park. Those horrible dogs. The incongruity of her and Lucien: him dirty and unshaven making coarse, funny observations, her in a pale mac whose lack of style had never occurred to her before, and her stiff little handbag with its gilt clasp. Funny Lucien hadn't seemed to notice these things. Funny how, walking beside him, the park was quite different from normal.

'You're looking a bit pale yourself,' said William. He suddenly noticed that was definitely the case. Grace's cheeks were usually fine and ruddy. Odd how after a whole breast of roast chicken and tip-top bread sauce she could look so grey. 'Did your friend Lucien take advantage of my absence?' William had no idea why he asked the question – except that perhaps the mention of the rotter's name might spark a bit of colour into Grace's cheeks. He couldn't have cared less how often Lucien came round so long as it was not when he was at home.

'He appeared a couple of mornings as usual. But he's not coming any more.' Grace tilted her head to one side. A small Madonna-like smile, faintly brave, or long-suffering, tweaked the corners of her mouth. There was a long silence.

'Why not?'

Grace gathered up the plates. The thought of the pudding to come made her feel sick.

'Oh, you know. I was just fed up with his visits. I couldn't think why he kept coming, what he wanted, what we could give him.'

'Free breakfasts. Bloody scrounger, if you ask me.'

'You never liked him.'

'I'm not as generous in my opinions as you, no. I could never quite see the point of him. And his visits became intrusive.'

'They did.'

'Very glad he's not going to bother us any more.' Bonnie's hands were in the air, poised to dive on him again.

'Quite.' *You've got real talent, Grace. Your paintings are very, very good.* Lucien's voice was so loud he might have been in the room with them. There are moments when absence and presence are the same. Trying to divide them causes hopeless confusion. William's voice came from a long way off.

'So, anyhow, my Ace, you're a wise woman as always. You've done the right thing, telling him to get lost.' William patted his wife's hand. He noted it had recently changed shape. It used not to have this geography of hillock veins and arid patches of brown skin. Dear God, would Bonnie's plump little hands one day look like this? The thought was calming: he needed calming thoughts. 'And I'll say yes to Dick, then. Dorset.' – From whose giant cliffs this angelic wife with the ageing hands would be flung to her death on the shingle below. The image was unclear, but positive.

'Why not? I daresay we need a break.' Every obscenity Lucien had ever uttered in her presence punched through Grace's mind. Relishing the vile words, she rose to fetch the pie.

'I shall look forward to that, my Ace.' And the thereafter: somewhere, anywhere – it didn't matter – playing with Bonnie. The multitude of duos for violin and viola. Playing far into the night, making ready for their ultimate and imperative union.

After a long weekend (moments relived and relived) William set off on Monday morning for a rehearsal. Despite Bonnie's excellent rendering of the Haydn F major in Prague, he wondered with some dread how she would approach the G major this morning. Her prickliness about Haydn he found hard to deal with. Her resistance was extraordinary, irrational. While it was probably the only weakness in her whole being, it was an awkward one considering the

Elmtree was much revered for its rendering of the composer's magnificent quartets. On the journey to Grant's barn he was so preoccupied wondering how best to convince, approach, persuade Bonnie, that his misjudgement of corners caused much hooting from other motorists.

He had left the house very early – 'just in case your friend changes his mind and decides to return,' he had told Grace. The truthful reason was his anxiety to be back with Bonnie. His acute impatience had spurred him to drive at twice his normal speed, and he arrived ten minutes before the appointed time. Bonnie's car was there, but not Grant's. This was strange.

William went in. Curiosity was now added to his generally nervous state. The main room of the barn was empty, the door to the bedroom open. Bonnie came out of it at once, smiling. Faced with the innocence of her entrance, a sense of relief drenched through William's apprehensive limbs.

'Guess what? You know what I found in Grant's bedroom? A piano.'

'A piano?' William sounded, he thought, suitably surprised. 'Did you, now?' He needed time to fight off the question *what were you doing in Grant's bedroom?* Bonnie read his mind. Laughed, teasing.

'Don't worry. Nothing forbidden going on between your players. I was cold. Went to borrow a jersey.' She tightened the knot of sleeves round her neck. The jersey – Grant had worn it for as long as William had known him – was flung round her neck like a scarf.

'I see. Well, quite. Where's Grant?'

'Gone to get some milk.'

The news so strengthened William's initial relief that he found himself speaking in undue, unwise haste.

'So you arrived very early, then.'

'Not very.' She was teasing him again, the little minx. 'Only now I'm so near there's no reason to be late, is there?'

'I suppose not.' William took off his coat, went to sit on the chair by his music stand. Bonnie seemed not to have noticed the significance of his silly question. 'Tried out the piano, did you?'

'Course I did. A few notes. But it's beyond hope. I said to Grant why on earth have you let a once-beautiful piano like this fall into this state? Why don't you get it retuned, overhauled? We could play together, I said.'

'You could *play together*?' William, who had tucked his violin under his chin, now returned it to his lap.

'Well, I don't suppose we ever would. But it was a nice idea.'

William nodded, swallowed, unable to speak.

Bonnie moved to her own chair, sat. Legs, in their tight jeans, swung apart. She pushed the baggy sleeves of Grant's jersey up under her nose, sniffing. She made a face. She was wearing the devastating angora jersey again, breasts mysterious shadowy mounds beneath it. William closed his eyes, wishing that she would burn the wretched garment. Its effects were so uncomfortable.

'Now, William, I've something to say to you.' William opened his eyes, kept them on her face. All the teasing had gone from her voice. 'I just beg you not to try talking me into the Haydn again. It's counterproductive. You know perfectly well, whatever my private feelings, I'm professional and will do my best. In fact, I practised much of the night – I did, really. So just wait and see. If I've got it all wrong you can tell me where. But don't go banging on about Haydn in general any more, please.' She paused. 'I hope you don't mind my saying this.'

'No.' William searched in a pocket for a handkerchief. He could feel dampness on his brow. 'No, of course not. You're perfectly reasonable. I didn't mean you to practise all night. I know you'll –'

Grant came through the door swinging two bottles of milk like dumb-bells. He was followed by Rufus. A few moments later they launched into the merry, snow-swirling first movement of the Haydn in G major. Throughout the piece Bonnie wore a self-satisfied little smile, so her dimples remained firm. She played with all the joy and brilliance she had conjured so frequently playing her beloved Schubert or Brahms, and her performance was not lost on any of them. Rufus raised one eyebrow throughout: Grant nodded and tilted his head with more than usual frequency.

William himself, confounded, only knew that this was the end for him. Up until this morning what he had felt for Bonnie was a mixture of admiration, friendship and lust. But her unexpected performance changed everything. It could only mean one thing: she had listened, made an immense effort, and was plainly beginning to understand the point of Haydn, whom she had found so hard to appreciate. She had done this for him. At the end of the piece there was a perplexed silence. For William it was the moment when he realised that his previous feelings for Bonnie were now replaced with something of a different order – overwhelming, and absolutely clear: he loved her totally.

It was the custom for the Elmtree Quartet to give a concert for charity every year in the week before Christmas. This was always held in a hall in Reading, and was always a sell-out. Wives traditionally attended. Many years ago Grant, the only bachelor among the players, had brought his girlfriend of the moment, a conspicuous redhead, who had fainted during the Borodin – from boredom, she later claimed – and caused an embarrassing commotion. Since then he had taken the precaution of inviting only his mother, a tiny silent widow whose amazement at her son's profession, as well as his size, had kneaded her knotty little face into an expression of constant bewilderment.

This year it was the Handles' turn to entertain the relations to supper after the performance. Grace always produced a delicious cold buffet and hot home-made mince pies, and William matched her efforts with famously good wine. As always on such occasions he could rely on Grace to do the whole thing beautifully, and was proud that Rufus's (frail) Iris and, in the old days, Andrew's (grumpy) Zara could not begin to compete when it came to suppers.

But this year he dreaded the whole occasion. The idea of Bonnie becoming a guest under his own roof, being friendly and helpful to his wife, was unbearable. He would have to make a supreme effort to appear normal, a good and generous host, equally attentive to each of his guests, yet able to conceal his passion for one of them.

To make matters more difficult, this year there was to be an addition to the party. On the evening that Grace quietly made her list of food (and Grace, it occurred to William, had been particularly quiet these last few days) there was a telephone call from London.

'Hello, William. Laurel speaking, Laurel here.'

'Hello, Laurel.'

Long pause. Perhaps he hadn't sounded as welcoming as she had anticipated.

'Everything all right with you? Long time no see.'

'Everything fine.'

'Brilliant. We're rushed off our feet as usual. Everything happening, time of year, you know how it is. The travel business goes mad with parties. Anyhow, Jack wants a word. I'll pass you over.'

William made a disgusted face at Grace, who smiled in return. It was the first time she had smiled all evening. – He could hear hostile whispering at the other end of the receiver. Then his son Jack came on the line.

'Hello, Dad. Long time no see.' God, they even spoke the same revolting language. 'How's things? Doing all right?'

'Fine, Jack, fine.' William wondered what the final point of this call would be. 'Just back from Prague,' he added, making an effort.

'Prague? Good heavens. You do get about. You should have booked the group through Laurel. She's got some great saving opportunities to Prague, she was saying only the other day.'

'Next time, perhaps. I'll bear that in mind.' After all these years Jack should know that bookings were done by Stephen who used his own excellent travel agent. But William could not be bothered to explain that yet again . . .

'Now, Dad, here's the thing: your Christmas concert. Remember we came a few years ago? Well, Laurel and I were wondering if you'd like us to put in an appearance? How about that for an idea?'

'Good God . . .'

'Mum was telling me the other day it was your turn for the supper. We always enjoy your wine, her food. How about it?'

'Well,' said William.

'We could even stay the night if you like.'

'It won't be that late.' Resistance to the appalling idea was running through William's body like lead. He stood more and more upright till he was completely at attention, stiff, cold.

'No, not by our standards, do see. But if we stayed we could have a drink. Of course, if it'd be a bother on top of everything else, if you'd rather we didn't, then –'

'No, no. I mean yes. Of course it would be fine. Your mother and I would be delighted.'

'Can't say you sound that enthusiastic.' Jack gave a twisted laugh. 'But we thought what a lark it might be. I'd like to talk to Grant again – and what's the other one, Rupert – ?'

'Rufus.' Jack had known Rufus for years.

'Rufus, yes.' A distinct pause. Then a controlled lightness of touch. 'And the girl, Bonnie. We haven't met Bonnie yet, have we? She looked a jolly good sort to me.'

So that was it. Jack, for all his so-called love for the dreadful Lauren, wanted to keep his hand in. Try out his attractions on Bonnie. The thought made William feel so sick he found it hard to speak.

'Bonnie will be there, I hope,' he said at last.

'Some boyfriend in tow?'

The *impertinence* of all this. In his fury a plan came so fast to William's mind that there was no time to consider its wisdom. He would lie.

'It seems,' he says, 'that Grant and Bonnie . . . well.'

'An item, you mean?'

'A what? – Look, I would ask you to be discreet about this, Jack. It's not something any of us mention. It's nothing to do with us, their private arrangement. I know no details. It's just something we've observed, we accept, and we wait without questions until we are told.'

'Right. Keep your hair on, Dad. I'm not that interested. Just said it would be nice to meet her.'

'Quite. So we'll see you at the concert, then. I'll leave tickets at the door.'

'Thanks, Dad. Bye for now.'

'They want not only to come to the concert, but to stay the night,' William said to Grace. He moved his arms, trying to shake off the rictus.

'That's all right. What was it you were saying about Bonnie and Grant?'

In a long moment's silence, William considered. Again, in general deviousness he was now stepped in so far . . . Besides, it would be no bad thing if Grace, too, was under the impression that Bonnie and Grant –

'They seem very fond of each other,' he lied.

'Rather suitable, I'd say. Though whether, in a small group –'

'They've admitted nothing yet, so I can't worry about that sort of thing till they have.'

'Of course not.' Grace returned to writing her list. 'As for Jack and Laurel, I've an awful feeling they're going to make use of the occasion to announce their engagement.'

'Bet you anything you're wrong there,' said William. 'They're too busy for that sort of thing. With any luck we'll escape ever having to be Laurel's parents-in-law. – I say, my Ace: that's a very small helping you've given yourself. Anything the matter?'

Lucien kept his word. He did not appear again and Grace increasingly felt the loss of him. She thought she might send him a Christmas card, but then realised that might be tempting fate. Much though she would like to see him from time to time, she had no desire to return to the state of perpetual anxiety his visitations had caused her. So she did not post the carefully chosen card, and concentrated on organising the party after the charity concert. William, as usual, was averse to discussing any of the arrangements. He liked to leave it all to her, and was always pleased with the result.

In the days before the party Grace had noticed he was more

withdrawn than usual. Jumpy, twitchy. He spent longer than ever tweaking sheets and deciding on the number, and exact position-ing, of the blankets each night. And then he slept badly. Awake herself for many hours in the night, listening for the return of the wolf (whose signal, if it came, she would this time appreciate), Grace felt him tossing about, snatching at the bedclothes he had so carefully arranged earlier. Such a pity, Grace reflected, that the very idea of his own son's presence affected him so badly, for surely it was the thought of Jack and Laurel at the party that was causing him such agitation. But there was nothing she could do about that. She had tried often enough to make him understand that disap-pointment in your children is to do with your own aspirations for them, that they themselves have no interest in reaching. William should be glad Jack was doing so well in accountancy. He should stop regretting the fact that his son had not pursued a youthful talent for chemistry and become a doctor: or even his youthful facility for picking out tunes on a guitar, and become a musician. William was irrationally depressed by the dullness of Jack's job, combined with the heavy weight of Jack's ambition to make his for-tune. He could not bear the fact that Jack – never a very lively or endearing character – now communicated in wince-making clichés in the belief that they gave importance to his utterances. William, so pernickety about language, so worried about its corrosion, was increasingly allergic to psychobabble, marketing babble and all the other contortions that the English language suffered these days: it was no wonder he was so reluctant to agree to get-togethers with Jack and Laurel. Their way of speaking reminded him of the new and ghastly trends of 'Cool Britannia', of which he wanted no part. It offended him so deeply that in their presence he found it hard to conceal his disapprobation. Their company was tedious and unmelodious. And it was mostly Laurel's fault. Before her entry into Jack's life father and son had, in a limited way, got on well enough. Laurel had been the cause of Jack's slippage into the dead-liest kind of self-satisfaction. Though Jack himself, as he once told Grace, loved her for the confidence she had given him. Laurel . . .

Grace could see her flaunting some dreary little diamond ring at the party, boasting of special economy fares to the Caribbean for their honeymoon. She shivered, and pulled back her share of the blankets very gently, so as not to provoke William's ire over the unhappy state of the bed.

But Grace was the first to admit her fears were ill-founded. Perhaps to make up for their undisguised boredom last time, Jack and Laurel behaved well at the concert. If they had brought calculators or travel brochures to pass the time, they refrained from using them. They sat in the front row, with Grace, Rufus's wife and Grant's mother, and gave every appearance of enjoying the music. There was no ring on Laurel's finger, Grace noted, as Laurel clapped excessively at the end of each piece. So they were to be spared the announcement of an engagement, thank God, thought Grace, and began to enjoy herself too.

William, from his seat on the platform, briefly took in the row of disparate relations, then cast his eyes towards Bonnie. He wondered if she would repeat her excellent performance of the Haydn that she had produced in the rehearsal, or, bored now she had achieved William's praise, fall back into mechanical playing. – But she did not let him down. She played faultlessly, enjoying herself, flaunting her new liking for Haydn. Her elbow danced so hard the velvet sleeve slipped higher than usual up her arm, and her hair swung and glinted under the stage lights. At the end of the piece she turned with a smile of triumph (as William saw it) to him alone, and he smiled curtly back. Their shared secret, which the audience could not guess at, blasted William's concentration. Shuffling through his music for the Schubert in A minor (Grace's favourite quartet, chosen on purpose) he glanced down at the front row again. Unlikely Laurel would have enjoyed the Haydn. Amazingly, she was clapping hard. So was Jack. His eyes, William could not fail to see, were on Bonnie, penetrating the velvet quite brazenly. William swung round on his seat, glared at his son. The applause stopped. There was a moment's puzzled silence – so menacing was William's look, no one could have failed to notice it. His reward was to observe a deep and ugly flush suffuse Jack's face. Jack then turned to Laurel with a stupid, guilty grin.

Rufus nudged William's elbow.

'Get on with it,' he whispered.

William gave the signal. They began to play the Schubert. Grace, puzzled by Jack's enpurpled face, wondered what had caused William's apparent anger. Her eyes trailed over the players, dipping and swaying, locked in their music. She then looked towards the Exit door at the side of the platform. She watched it open slowly. A head peered round, scanned the audience. Within a second it was gone.

Lucien.

Dear God, Grace thought. He's back . . . Lucien's back. What had he in mind now? In the heat of the hall she felt herself turn very cold. What was he up to? What was his new plan to torment her? Grace kept her eyes on William. She hoped to be lulled (and also invigorated by its occasional intimations of stormy weather) by the andante, which she loved so much.

At the end of the concert Jack and Laurel hurried out with Grace to drive her home, so that everything could be finalised before the others arrived. It was clear their good behaviour at the concert had caused them considerable strain. As soon as they arrived at the house they made straight for an opened bottle of William's claret, and drank two glasses very quickly. Grace was left to manage on her own.

In her scurrying to arrange food and light candles she had no time to ponder further on the extraordinary flash-sighting of Lucien, and half thought it might have been a figment of her imagination. But the effect was in the trembling of her hands, her clumsiness lighting the tree. On her knees searching for the switch she crashed into the lower branches so hard that the coloured balls flashed and swayed dangerously. Laurel, scarlet cheeked, squealed.

'Take a care, Mother,' shouted Jack. He made his single contribution to the evening by heaving his mother to her feet. Once she
was upright he slapped at the pine needles on her shoulders. 'Keep
your hair on,' he added. 'Not exactly a large party. Nothing to
worry about, is there?'

Grace wanted to cry. She wanted to run away, leave them all to
it. She said nothing.

When the others arrived they marvelled at her efforts: the table
full of food, the smell of a stew of long-marinated meat and herbs,
the baskets of Christmas roses propped up against holly, the
candlelight. William poured wine, Bonnie delivered the glasses. An
efficient team they made, he thought. It occurred to him the
evening might not turn out to be as bad as he had anticipated. As
the guests drank quickly and seemed interested in talking to each
other – in the odd way that people who know each other well
suddenly do at parties – this feeling grew. His only concern was for
Rufus's wife, Iris. A narrow woman in a nervous little dress, he
noticed she kept to the less bright parts of the room, not speaking,
but appearing to listen. When someone pushed the door further
open and light increased, Iris stepped quickly back into relocated
shadow. She took care to avoid the Christmas tree – fearful of
reflections of the glass balls on her quiet grey skirt, perhaps,
thought William. 'She never likes to stand out,' Rufus had once
confided. There was no danger of her doing that tonight. William
made his way over to her. Flushed by Bonnie's presence in the
room, he felt the concern for one less fortunate than himself that
came from the certainty of his own secret love.

'My dear Iris,' he began, 'why not come and sit by the fire?'

'Thank you, William. I am a little chilled.'

It was no wonder Rufus was so constantly attentive to his wife.
She looked too frail to last many winters. The idea of her death was
unsettling. What would happen to the Elmtree should Rufus become
a premature widower? Iris's pathetic little hand, fretted with high,
blue veins, shook as she held her glass. William swore to himself that
never again would he scoff at Rufus for ringing home so often.

Perhaps it was a couple of glasses of his own good wine, combined with Bonnie's presence (Bonnie's existence), that heightened William's sympathy for a woman to whom he had paid almost no attention, and showed nothing more than polite interest, for so many years. Whatever the reason, he determined to sit next to her for a while, concentrate on her completely. He ushered her to the sofa by the fire. Slowly, she sat. But before William could take his place beside her, Grant pushed his tiny old mother, turtle head emerging from a shell of shawls, down into the cushions. Grant's tangible impatience caused him to push the old lady too hard. She fell stiffly back, and seemed unable to rock forward.

It was one of those moments when several things happen very fast. In retrospect they become a fluid stream of flashing lights, their order not quite clear, but their significance underlined by the main discovery of the moment.

William glanced round the room. No sign of Laurel. Everyone else happy. Grant hurried out of the door holding two empty bottles. William was left to tilt his mother to a forward position. Having accomplished this small charitable gesture, he exchanged a smile with Iris – in a smaller flash he remembered how beautiful she was when Rufus first met her – and heard Iris enquire after the old lady's health and comfort. His proposed seat now taken, he placed himself of the arm of the sofa next to Iris, and gave every appearance of attending to the valetudinary conversation taking place beside him.

In truth his attention was caught by Bonnie and Jack, who sat in small chairs (brought down from upstairs) turned to face each other in the window. The drawn curtains – a swirl of tulips unnaturally plunging and soaring across stretches of nasty blue, which William had always disliked – were the backdrop to Bonnie's familiar evening shape of black velvet. Set against the mad flowers, was her expression troubled, eager, amused? William could not be sure. Jack was half-hidden from William's view by the Christmas tree. But he could see his son's shoulders were hunched in a show of intense concentration. As a child Jack had always hunched himself over whatever the object of interest – his trains, a comic, a fancy penknife. As a grown-up the position was familiar when he concentrated on a wine list or the *Financial Times*. Now, he was horribly hunched towards Bonnie.

'Once you've had your stomach out – you've nothing to fall back on,' observed Grant's mother, to no one in particular. 'Don't you agree?' She stretched out a hand, still muffled in shawls, to touch William's knee.

'Oh, I do.'

'It's all part of the process,' Iris added.

Her mysterious observation faintly intrigued William, but nothing could detract from his study of Bonnie and Jack. Jack was the speaker. Low voice, but William could detect a few words.

'. . . came, not expecting anything . . . don't suppose . . . ever been so moved . . .'

'Really?' A sweet surprised smile from Bonnie, innocent of the rubbish she was being fed.

'And . . . I don't know . . . mind me saying, Bonnie, the sight of you . . . the most beautiful violinist I've ever seen, and do you know what?' Here Jack leant further towards Bonnie, whispered something in her ear. She pulled back at once, laughing, blushing.

This was intolerable. William stood. Grace caught his eye.

'Isn't it time to eat?' she said. 'Get everyone to help themselves.'

'Where are Grant and Laurel?'

'I don't know about Grant. I asked Laurel to take the brandy butter out of the fridge.'

With a quick glance at the window – Bonnie and Jack were stirring, standing, pulling apart reluctantly as wet wool, William thought – William left the room. With burning face he hurried to the kitchen. There he found Grant and Laurel, eyes locked, by the dresser. Laurel, holding her (third or fourth) glass of wine in one hand, was picking invisible fluff from Grant's collar with the other. Her face was a lustful scarlet, and shining.

'. . . and I could get you at least fifty per cent reduction to Corfu, off-season,' she was saying.

Grant, on William's entrance, turned, startled. He had the dappy look of one who had for a brief moment seriously been attracted to the idea of a cut-rate Greek holiday.

'Great,' he said, to no one.

Laurel touched his hand.

'You've only to give me the signal.'

'Laurel!' William shouted so loud he surprised himself as well as the others. Laurel, still webbed in her dream of a conquest of a client (possibly more, the handsome brute), turned to him with no flicker of guilt. Her eyes were dreamy, stupid.

'William?'

'Grace told you to get the—'

'I did.' She nodded towards the table and a bowl of brandy butter. William clasped his hands, desperate. Things were completely out of control. And he must get back now, see what further outrage his son and colleague were up to – though not for anything would he leave Grant and the appalling, predatory Laurel on their own. Grant, for all his size, wouldn't stand a chance against Laurel.

'It's time to eat,' he said. 'Back in there.'

Something of his perturbance must have penetrated Laurel's insensitive skin, for she hurried out, head high, secret smile to Grant.

'Christ,' he said. 'Your daughter-in-law's a fast mover.'

'She's not my daughter-in-law and I hope she never will be.'

'I sympathise there.'

'I'm sorry if she embarrassed you.'

'Takes more than a tacky little travel agent to embarrass me, worry not.'

They looked at each other with the understanding of old colleagues who have weathered many years of minor incidents that have no lasting effect on the whole.

'Let's eat, then.'

'I'll offer Laurel a sausage on a stick, see if I can send her a little public message.'

'Behave yourself, Grant.'

Back in the sitting room Bonnie was sitting on the floor talking to Iris and Grant's mother. Jack was standing by the tree, plate and fork in hand, eyes on Bonnie's back. Rufus was attempting to engage Laurel in conversation, but she was digging without interest at her Elizabethan stew, puzzled by her lover's moody look. Rufus got little response.

Grace, always a thoughtful hostess, saw to it that everyone's plates were piled. But she herself could conjure no appetite. She found it very hot in the room. Stifling. She had only sipped half a glass of wine, but the candle flames and tree lights were all bending and swaying as if in a wind. She moved uncertainly towards William. He was standing alone by the piano, a bleak, bemused look on his face. But then William had never enjoyed being a host. And this evening, for some reason she could not clarify in her mind, Grace was beginning to agree with him. Parties were no fun for those giving them, particularly when the guests were both disparate and difficult.

'You all right, my Ace?'

'Hot. Isn't it very hot in here? I'm going for a breath of air.'

Grace slipped out of the room. She stood for a few moments in the hall, arms crossed under her breasts, hugging herself. She listened to the thin weave of voices, the occasional laugh. She studied the huddle of alien coats on the hooks. She longed to know if Lucien's appearance was a signal, and meant he would be here in the morning.

Grace moved towards the front door. It was one of those high-waisted Edwardian pieces of design, with stained-glass panes at the top – the bust – that cast multi-coloured patterns on the floor when the sun pushed through. Such doors, in their demureness, reminded Grace of nineteenth-century dresses.

She found herself opening it. She stood by the narrow margin of cold damp air, grateful for its relief. Outside, three parked cars shone with damp, and the laurels, entangled in a dim moving fog, were indistinct shapes, no detail of leaf or branch. Grace shivered. About to shut the door, she looked down. On the step was a milk bottle surrounded by a circle of six tangerines. A feather of folded paper was sticking from the neck of the milk bottle. Grace bent and picked it up. Unfolded it. She read its message by the light in the porch. *Happy Christmas*, it said.

Grace stood there, reading the scrawled words again and again. Eventually she gathered up the carefully arranged tangerines, and took them to the kitchen. In her excitement she dropped them on the floor, watched them roll towards various points and under the table. No sooner had she knelt to retrieve them than Rufus came in carrying empty glasses.

'Can I help?'

Dear Rufus! Just as William had felt unaccountable warmth towards Iris, Grace was conscious of an extraordinary beneficence towards Rufus, simply because he was inadvertently caught in the slip stream of her own delight. – He was much more efficient than her, catching the rolling tangerines, handing them to her to arrange in the fruit bowl.

'Very nice evening,' he said. 'You always do these things so well.'

'Very modest,' said Grace. 'But thank you.' She did not care a damn if he noticed her blush, her dithering, her general sense of ungrounding. From now on she would enjoy the peculiar gathering. Thrilled by the knowledge that somewhere out in the shadows Lucien was, or at least had been lurking, she knew that she would now enter into the spirit of the evening. For her, the party had only just begun.

Perhaps, sifting all these things in her mind, she had the look of one preoccupied: for Rufus made no effort to engage her in further conversation. He went back to the dining room. Grace remained leaning against the sink luxuriating in one of those times when, at your own party, you can snatch a solitary moment, not having to speak or attend to anyone. In the quiet space of an empty room it can almost seem as if it was a normal evening and the guests did not exist. Grace was in a semi-trance of contentment. Then, she heard a shout.

She made her way back to the others, peeped round the door.

She saw what everyone was looking at in a freeze-frame moment. Laurel and Grant stood face to face in front of the Christmas tree. Grant was cramming a large sausage into her mouth, too fast for her to chew. There was absolute silence except for a glugging, a strangled giggle, from Laurel. Her scarlet cheeks bulged from side to side, her eyes flew about. Near to choking, she put her hands against Grant's chest to steady herself rather than to push him away. For all her discomfort Laurel managed to convey she was enjoying the scene: centre of attention, shocking everyone.

'Leave off, Grant! You'll choke the girl.'

Grant turned briefly to his mother, whose squawk of warning broke the spell. He laughed.

Grace's eyes flew to Jack. He put down a plate of half-finished food. The gesture was heavy with menace. He moved solemnly towards Laurel and Grant. On his way, passing close to Bonnie, he briefly touched her shoulder, giving it a squeeze. Grace tasted bile in her throat.

Jack snatched the sausage from Laurel's mouth, flung it carelessly across the room. It knocked over a glass. Then he hit Grant hard on the cheek. A hollow, watery sound. Spectators gasped in its wake. Iris clasped Grant's mother's hand.

'It was a *joke*, you idiot.' Grant held his cheek.

'Some joke.' Jack moved a pace nearer his target. His first punch had been very minor compared with what he had in mind.

'Jack! What are you doing?' Laurel pawed at him, trying to push him away from Grant. She was making a dreadful noise. He brushed her away, clenched his fist, landed another strong thump on Grant's nose.

Grace saw blood stream across Grant's face like a warning flag. There was a ragged chorus of screams, alarmed pleas to stop. People were shifting, moving about, embarrassed, not knowing what to do. William, hands held up like a man surrendering, was pushing past Rufus to reach his son. In the moment of confusion Grace noticed how pale were his palms, the skin grained like rice.

'Stand back, Dad,' shouted Jack, 'I'm not finished.' He held up a fist again. William, relieved by the command, gladly obeyed it. He'd felt he had to make some gesture of defence – though who to defend was a moral problem. There was small likelihood of his being very effective in stopping a fight between two men considerably larger than himself.

But Grant, several inches taller than Jack, had had enough. One feeble jealous hit he could have accepted without reciprocating. A bloodied nose was a different matter. He lunged at Jack – unsteady on his widely placed feet – and managed to spin him round at the same time as clubbing him on the side of the head.

Jack fell heavily against the Christmas tree, knocking it over. He lay among its branches, blood from Grant's fist smeared across his cheek, one eye swelling. Fragments of coloured broken glass were scattered on his dark jacket. Several unbroken balls hovered on the floor, each one with its tiny window of light reflecting a particle of the scene. They were quickly smashed by chaotic feet. Jack groaned, others screamed. Laurel sobbed into the curtains, pulling the tulip material round her like a cloak.

'Do something, someone!' she groaned, but offered no help herself.

Grace saw William and Grant take Jack's hands and pull him into a sitting position on the floor. Grant's blood gushed on to Jack's trousers and the carpet. Bonnie took Grant's hand, led him out of the room. Grace could not decide who to attend to – Grant was hurt worse than Jack, but Jack was making more fuss.

'Thish has all got out of hand,' he muttered. Sitting there in the mess of blood and chips of glass, he looked both pathetic and revolting. Grace hated her son at that moment.

'Let's get him on to a chair,' suggested Rufus, who seemed to be the only unperturbed man in the room.

'What were you *doing*, bashing up Grant like that, you bastard?' screamed Laurel from her curtain cocoon.

Jack turned his blackening eye on her.

'What were *you* doing, you bloody little flirt?'

'Shut up, you two.' Rufus spoke on William's behalf. 'Let's get this mess cleared up.'

Given the command, everyone helped. Grant's mother lowered herself on to the floor. She moved slowly round the room on all fours, picking up minute specks of broken glass. The old lady was still swathed in all her shawls, and William, despite the whole ghastly business, could not help noting that in her likeness to an old sheep she provided an element of humour. Rufus replaced the damaged tree, Iris dabbed at the blood on the carpet with her handkerchief soaked in mineral water, Grace swept around replacing things very quickly, and William poured new glasses of wine for everyone but Jack and Laurel.

Jack sat in his chair, brushing himself down, watching the clearing up all round him. Sullen, he made no effort to help or to speak. The looks of disapproval, launched by the helpers, he defended with a hostile jut of his jaw. He did not look at Laurel, whose sobs had turned to snivels. She still clutched at the protective curtains. The feeble bitch, thought Grace: and loathed Laurel, too.

'Thish has all gone horribly wrong,' observed Jack, at last, to no one in particular.

'You can say that again.' Laurel let the tulips fall from her.

Jack looked at her. 'I don't know what you think you were doing.'

'You've never been able to take a joke. A bit of fun.'

'Not my idea of a joke, oral shoshage.'

Grant's mother looked up from her position on the floor near the grate, bewildered. 'Moral?' she asked. 'Where does moral come into all this? I think you owe my son an apology.'

'He's not getting a bloody apology,' said Jack. 'Not on my life.'

'You always spoil everything.' Laurel moved close to Jack. She touched his only slightly swollen eye with one finger.

'Leave off. Take your ruddy fingers off me. We're going home.'

'You bastard. You're not going to forget this.' Laurel burst into fresh tears.

'You're staying here as planned,' said Grace to Jack. 'You're in no condition to drive.'

'We're going home, Mother, so don't interfere.'

'You do what your mother says, my boy,' said William. He was conscious that he had been no very great help in the general shambles, and here was an opportunity to exert himself without danger of further confrontation. He carried two glasses of wine out to the kitchen for Bonnie and Grant, keen to leave the disagreeable scene in the dining room.

Grant sat at the table, head tipped back. Bonnie dabbed at his nose with a scrunched-up wet dishcloth. She touched him very gently. William stopped. His heart had remained calm during the fight. Now it lurched and stumbled. He put the glasses on the table.

'Anything I can do?'

'Thanks, no. Bonnie here's a very fine nurse.'

'I'm sorry about all that – my son. I don't know what –'

'Don't mention it.' Grant's voice was thick beneath the dishcloth. 'I'm sorry I couldn't resist giving him a dose of his own medicine.'

'He deserved it. Should teach him a thing or two.'

'Daresay the sausage was a poor joke, and Jack had had a lot to drink.'

'No excuse.' William shrugged.

Bonnie stood back to appraise her work on Grant's nose.

'Pretty good,' she said, smiling at both of them. 'Almost as if nothing had happened.'

'Let's carry on as if that was the case.' Grant stood, ruffled Bonnie's hair. 'Thanks. Don't let this stupid business spoil your party, William. Grace has done it all so well. Let's go back and finish up the food.'

He left the room but Bonnie did not follow him.

'Sorry about your dishcloth,' she said, and threw the bloody clump into the sink.

'No matter –'

'– and about events in general.' She gave him a look (didn't she?) – a look that penetrated his turbulent being, a secret acknowledgement of something William did not dare to name. 'I have to say – forgive me if this is rude – but your son Jack doesn't take after his father.'

William smiled. Shrugged.

'He's trodden a dull path since Laurel came into his life.' God Almighty, Bonnie was right up against him, the warm velvet of her pushing against the length of his body, her heavy arms flung round his neck – as she so often flung them.

'But as for *you*, William, you're a wonderful, wonderful host and no shoddy behaviour can spoil your party.' He could smell the claret on her breath. How much had she drunk? Not that William cared . . . *in vino veritas*, he believed. All he asked was to remain where he was, propped up against the dresser (fortunately) for ever, listening to her sweet words. He patted her shoulder with a hand that raged to cup a breast.

'Dear Bonnie.'

'You're a man in a million. We all think so – Grant, Rufus, me of course.' (Here, William rather wished the others had not been included among his admirers, but in the general bliss of things it didn't really matter.) 'And what I'm demanding, here and now, is a Christmas kiss.'

Bonnie placed her glorious mouth on the astringent line of William's own. Her lips did not part, but pushed. William kept his eyes open so that the out-of-focus muddle of thick lashes and the exquisite pores of her nose filled his vision. Faintness shot through his body, emptied his head. Bonnie moved away.

'There. Thanks.' Her cheeks matched the holly berries on the table. There was a deliquescence in her bearing that spoke of the effects of William's superb wine, it had to be admitted. But why not? He would buy her a lifetime of Montrachet '85, given the chance. 'I mustn't leave out Grant and Rufus, must I? Kissing.' She giggled. 'Here. Come on.'

William took her hand. They made their way to the door. The marvellous thing was the he knew that the others surely would not be dealt the same *quality* of kiss. It would be public – theirs had been private. What's more, at the kitchen door Bonnie let go of his hand, quite rightly. She would not want the others to have any idea of the absolute oneness that she and William had just experienced. No: it was their secret, and William had every intention of keeping it too.

In the hall they saw Jack and Laurel dragging their feet upstairs.

'I persuaded them to stay,' said Grace. 'They were both way over the limit to drive.'

They watched the couple turn the corner towards their room – not looking back to bid their audience goodnight.

'At least,' said William, 'they don't look very engaged.'

Bonnie laughed at this. She laughed so hard William half suspected it was her way of cheering them all. (Their almost passionate kiss had of course cheered *him*. His being was now privately burnished beyond measure.) Her laughter, he could see, worked on Grace and Grant. The evening, which had been so thrashed and spoilt by his son, now righted itself in Bonnie's gaiety. He judged there could be some enjoyment to be had in the hour or so before the guests began to go.

In a muted way, there was. The remaining guests ignored the bloodstains on the carpet and the smashed balls on the tree – the inside skins of these delicate, broken balls were visible: they gleamed like mother-of-pearl, flushed with a paler version of their outside colour. The guests ate more than they really wanted for fear of disappointing Grace, and talked of Christmas plans. William refilled glasses, and dreaded their departure. Ten days holiday: ten days without Bonnie. He knew Grant was driving her back to her flat in Aylesbury – of course that made sense, but he could not like the thought, even with Grant's mother as chaperone. He knew Bonnie was travelling north the next day to be with her own family for a week. Here, he and Grace would have their usual quiet Christmas, but beneath the surface there would be both yearning and agitation which he must keep from Grace. And then, the dreaded few days with Dick. The walk on the cliffs.

It was Rufus who, at almost midnight, suggested they should

end the evening with a few carols. He was always keen for a sing-song, secretly a little proud of his resonating voice – in his youth he used to sing a lot of Schubert *lieder*. Grace loved the idea. She clapped her hands, said she'd find her book of carols.

But Grant, apparently unaware of her offer, looked at Bonnie.

'Bonnie'll play for us,' he said.

Bonnie smiled. Grace sat down again.

'I didn't know Bonnie played the piano,' she said.

'One of her hidden talents.' Grant gave Bonnie an encouraging smile. 'As we discovered in Prague.'

William saw the disappointment sweep over his wife's face. He knew how much she would have liked to have been the accompanist.

Bonnie got up, moved over to the piano. Pale flakes of light showered across her velvet skirt like a rush of sunlight through leaves. She moved magnificently, everyone's eyes upon her.

'I haven't played a carol for years,' she said. 'But I'll try.'

Bonnie had no need of Grace's music book. She could play anything by ear. She drifted through a few minor chords, warming up, trying out the piano. Grace felt an irrational tightness within her. She recognised a gift she herself did not have, would never have. The huge waves of the evening, stilled for a while when the fight was over and Jack and Laurel had gone to bed, now returned, almost swamping her. She turned to William. He stood in an awkward position, like a man trapped in volcano lava and made rigid. His eyes were on Bonnie's back, expressionless. He was wonderfully conscious that after all there had been no opportunity – and probably no desire – for her to bestow Christmas kisses on Grant and Rufus. The thought gave him profound satisfaction.

'Silent Night', Bonnie began.

'*Stille Nacht*.' Rufus, also proud of his German, made it impossible for the others to join in. He had no intention of being denied his solo. In the past, his rendering of the carol had moved people to tears. This was not to be the case tonight, but he would give it his best. Glancing round the room he saw that Grant's mother was asleep, Iris was twisting her engagement ring, and Grant was lighting one of his revolting cigars. Only William and Grace, in their unmoving postures of listening, seemed appreciative.

'*Heilige nacht,*' he went on, and moved one hand to his heart.

9

'How much further?' asked William.

He glanced at Grace. She was a fine driver, hands firmly on the wheel, nicely spaced as if guiding a ploughshare – eyes never leaving the slow lane which, she felt, was the appropriate place for their small, uncompetitive car. He always enjoyed being driven by Grace, even if her rigid keeping of the Highway Code meant that, just as when he was at the wheel himself, their journeys took longer than most people's. But he had learnt from experience that to press her to accelerate, even a little, was counter-productive.

'Not much.' Grace had answered the same question twice since they'd been on the motorway. She was used to William's anxiety always to *get there*, and to *get back*. She knew there was no use in guessing at exact miles (which confused him) or approximate hours and minutes (which annoyed him). Vague assurances soothed him best. But this morning he was in a particularly impatient state.

William turned on the radio. Delibes's *Flower Duet* mushed through the car.

'Heaven forbid. Hundreds of requests for that bloody awful piece, and the requests granted three times a week. The People's Music, I suppose.' He snapped it off. As usual William enjoyed raging against such 'classical' programmes. 'There she goes again,' he scoffed, as the presenter produced one of her dumbfoundingly simplistic explanations in the soppy voice of a *Play School* instructor.

'Nothing you can do about it,' murmured Grace, automatically. That was usually a pacifying reminder, too. Though not this morning. William's contempt blew off him like snow in a wind.

'I shall write to object. Been meaning to write for ages.'

'So you have.' Grace smiled as a very long vehicle roared past them, agitating the small car a little in its slip stream.

In the silence that fell between them for the next fifty miles both Grace and William reflected on the Christmas break. Each had felt, for private, unacknowledgeable reasons, the days had dragged unusually slowly. The old sense of blissful privacy, which for years they had enjoyed in the annual break from concerts, eluded them. But both of them were so preoccupied with their own thoughts that they did not notice the other's distraction. Once Jack and Laurel had left – after a disagreeable breakfast the morning following the party, when they tried, through their hangovers, to justify their behaviour – Grace and William fell into their normal Christmas holiday pattern. They exchanged presents beside the tree, went to both midnight mass and matins in a distant church, where there were no enraging hybrid services and extraordinary requests to kiss your neighbour.

William poured glasses of the left-over excellent wine before lunch, and proposed a toast to Jack and Laurel.

'Let us never, ever invite them to another party,' he said. 'I never thought my own son could behave in such a brutish manner.' Still smarting from the vision of Jack's eyes scouring Bonnie, William spoke with feeling. 'Vulgar, provocative. For once in my life I felt quite sorry for Laurel.'

'*She* was no angel!' Grace was loath to be uncharitable at Christmas, but Laurel's blatant flirting with Grant had shocked her deeply. 'Grant must have been revolted.'

'He was.'

'Pity about the tree. I've more work to do on the carpet.'

'Still.' William searched for comforting words. 'I daresay there's a certain gory pleasure to be had reflecting on the most horrendous party, and at least it ended nicely, Rufus enjoying his star turn.'

'It did,' said Grace. Having been passed over as the pianist was a slight she would keep to herself – for her, the most affecting part of the whole ghastly evening.

They agreed the party was an occasion best put swiftly from their minds. Over the guinea fowl and Christmas pudding their silence was easy as ever, only broken to rejoice in not having to share their minor festivities with Jack and Laurel.

Alone by the fire, though, Grace fretted about Lucien. Where was he? What was he doing? Was he putting up with Lobelia for the sake of a roof over his head? Or, unable to bear her company even for a few days at Christmas, when relations by tradition join uneasily together, had he opted for some friend's floor, or a depressing squat? Most of all she wondered about the meaning of his message on the doorstep. Was it a mysterious sign of goodwill, despite the (probable) end of their friendship? Or was it a threat? And then, what if he needed her? If he came round and found the house deserted . . . Grace did not like to think of what Lucien might do if he was in one of his irrational moods. She must remember to make sure William locked every window and double-checked the alarm. Fortunately he was by nature security conscious – much more than her. So he would be pleased to think for once she was paying attention to locking up the house. Her insistence on making sure everything was as impenetrable as possible would raise no suspicions in his mind.

Even as she planned the barricading, Grace felt guilty. By not being here, should he want her, she would be letting Lucien down. And that she had no wish to do. He had disturbed her life in an odd way – most unpleasantly – but he had also been her supporter, her encourager, the one who brought a glitter into her steady life. She had insisted he go because his deviousness had driven her into a nervous frenzy. But she was still fond of him. She always would be. In truth, should she be asked which man meant the most to her, her son Jack or Lucien, the answer would come with no hesitation. It occurred to her she had never worried about Jack as she did about Lucien. Her son had never given her so much pleasure, and he pained her in quite a different way. The fact was that she could not love Jack in a way that she had always imagined a mother should love a child. And now here she was overwhelmed by protective, loving feelings for a strange, alarming young man she did not know well, but was drawn to in a way that unnerved her. The idea of not being there for him, should he turn up, needing her, was almost unbearable.

While Grace tormented herself downstairs, in his room at the top of the house William played the first movement of Schumann's A minor quartet – a movement of spirited wistfulness, he always thought – to himself to reflect his own yearning for Bonnie. Even the sound of her voice on the telephone would have been a consolation – bloody miles away in Northumberland. The small part of his being left over from his agonising about Bonnie was faced with an equal problem: how, precisely, to send his dear wife over the cliff . . . *If the assassination could trammel the consequences*, he thought, all would be well. But it was never as easy as that. Just to shove her over and hope she would end up as an untidy splatter on the shingle was naïve. Someone would be bound to see him. His shock-horror might not convince a coroner. (It should: he *would* be shocked and horrified, mortified, even – but better not chance it.) Then there was the matter of regret. There was no doubt he would suffer regret, not to mention guilt, so vast it would be hard to overcome. But one thought of Bonnie, the scent of her hair as her head rested those few sweet moments on his shoulder, and he was able to put aside imagining how a murderer would be punished, even if not caught. How, how should he execute the foul deed?

On the day after Boxing Day, a grimy morning of extreme cold, William went up to his room and stood looking out of the window. The garden was tense with frost. There was not a glimmer of sun to sparkle the bare branches, or the ivy in their grip of rime. William took up his violin and started to play his part of one of the Mozart duos he'd played with Bonnie. The sweet, dry notes – as so often happened when he played alone – cleared his mind of peripheral matters and an idea began to unfold. As the sound of the instrument bit into the room, at first the idea wafted unclear as an underwater plant groping though a disturbed river bed. But when it reached the surface its shape was sharply defined. There it was. Clear. Obvious. Terrifying.

William stared at his solution, behind shut eyes. As an idea it certainly held great risk. But if he acted with great care . . . it seemed pretty foolproof. In his excitement he speeded up the andante. He ran this new, bright picture over and over again in his mind. He felt the strength of evil intent. He knew what it felt like to be a criminal, feel no conscience, exult in the idea of an unforgivable deed. These were dark places of the soul he had never travelled before, and he felt afraid, but determined.

By the time he reached the end of the andante cold sweat clenched his brow, his 'heat-oppressed brain', and he had not the heart to go on to the scherzo.

William's friend Dick was not a man with any interest in comfort. His cottage, once belonging to generations of coastguards, was so close to the water that storm waves frequently flew up over the walls and sizzled down the chimney. The thickness of its walls ensured that no hurricane could destroy it, but provided no warmth. Inside, there was a greenish smell of damp. A few haphazard rugs were scattered over the stone floors. Their mottled reds and blues had clashed into each other, turned into an inky aubergine. Their edges were worn down to a lace of crossed string ribs, pathetically bared. The slumped sofa and two armchairs, both of which looked as if they had crash landed many years ago and had not the heart to right themselves, were covered in old rugs gloomy as the carpets. Despite a fire in the grate, it was bitterly cold. Grace did up her second cardigan and wondered if they could find an excuse to reduce the length of their stay.

But William was fond of his old friend Dick and was determined to make light of the cottage's shortcomings. He rather enjoyed short spells of acute discomfort so long as they were on British soil. They made him appreciate all the more the comforts of home. He stood in front of the fire warming himself, unaware that its limited warmth extended to only one bottom at a time. Outside the small window the wintry sea, horribly close, bashed at rock and shingle. Dick, he was pleased to see, was pouring sherry from an old bottle that obviously spent most of its time undisturbed, dusty sentinel to a small gathering of minute glasses.

'So, William, old man . . . what news from the larger musical world?'

Dick handed over a glass. The sherry looked solid, like an amber stone. William did his best to smile, felt his mouth slide in a lop-sided manner. He hoped he appeared to Dick nothing more than a little stiff and cold after the long journey.

'We did the Haydn in G major at the Christmas concert. Went down quite well. I remember you liked that . . .' He mentioned Haydn, of course, because it was a secret link to Bonnie. The thought of her warmed him more than the sherry. Dick looked puzzled.

'Did I?'

'You did, Dick. I remember distinctly. I've a special fondness for the Haydn Op.77 No.1, you said. Love all three of the late quartets, you said . . .' William felt completely mad, had no idea what he himself was saying.

'Did I really?'

'You did. As a matter of fact . . .' William now paused, giving himself just time to calculate the danger of his next remark, 'Haydn's been the cause of a spot of bother. Our new member of the Quartet isn't drawn to the music – resists it, almost.'

'Bonnie? Really?' Grace raised her eyebrows. 'You wouldn't have thought so, from the way she played the other night. She was brilliant.'

'Don't tell me your new member's a woman?' In his shock, Dick passed a glass unsteadily to Grace, making the sherry sway.

'I'm afraid she is.' William gave a small chuckle. He wondered what would happen if he suddenly shouted: *And I love her!* 'We didn't look for a girl, of course, as you can imagine. But in the event she turned out to be by far the best candidate.'

'Good heavens. Could cause you a lot of bother.'

Grace laughed. You could only laugh at such prejudice.

'Not so far. But I warned her: any trouble, and you're out, I said.' His head spun so fast between truth and untruth that there was no hope of making sense.

'Very wise,' said Dick.

'I suppose the only trouble she could cause,' said Grace, 'is if she actually set up with Grant. You seemed to think they may be . . . well.'

'Early days yet,' said William tightly. Grace's remark re-chilled the heat on the back of his calves, which had been building up slowly. But it was his own fault, he knew. Shouldn't ever have planted the idea in the first place. Better never to be the first to mention Bonnie.

They lunched in the icy kitchen: cabbage and sausages. William had no appetite. He looked across at Grace, smiling bravely against the cold, and felt the unease of the knowing who look upon the innocent. This could well be her last meal. He wished it could have been of a higher standard. She would have liked a bread-and-butter pudding. William was running through all her favourite puddings in his head when they heard the whiplash of rain against the small window. The grim sea view outside was now obliterated by mist through which thick slanting water stabbed against the cottage.

'Pity,' said Dick. 'There goes your chance of a walk. Better tomorrow.'

'Pity,' agreed William. The reprieve for twenty-four hours was a mixed blessing. The extra time in Grace's company was of course a bonus: on the other hand it would be a relief to get the foul deed over and done with.

'But I can cheer you with good news,' said Dick. 'One Perdita – Perdita Beccles – is to join us for supper tonight. My betrothed.' He looked from one to another of the Handles with a tentative smile. 'That is, we're to be married in the spring. We met in the choir. She's a lovely voice. You'll like her. Wonderful wife material. Just what a man needs. I'm aware of my luck . . .' As he trailed off Dick lifted his glass of flat lager, as if intending to propose a toast to his absent wife-to-be. But then he thought better of it and took a noisy gulp.

'That is good news,' said Grace, with another of her genuine smiles.

'Very, very good news,' added William.

'A man needs a wife. Especially in a place like this.'

William and Grace nodded, joined in complete appreciation of that fact. But only a small part of William's being rejoiced in his friend's good fortune in finding wife material in such a God forsaken place as this: for the rest he worried how the long, cheerless afternoon would be spent in the wind-battered guest room in the eaves. Grace – whose good behaviour was exemplary – would listen to Dick's wedding plans, and with any luck take a hand in preparing the supper.

Perdita Beccles arrived promptly at seven in a rain-darkened mackintosh, carrying a paper bag of apples whose rosy sides protruded through the sodden paper. The bag burst at the moment of entrance. The fact that everyone then scurried about chasing the apples that bobbed along the floor was a God-sent aid to the introduction, William reflected. This was a perfect cover for his dropped jaw, his look of amazement.

William had had no idea quite what to expect of his friend's choice of wife. The mean thought had occurred to him that a woman of some forty years who lived in a small coastal village and sang in the choir would automatically fall into a type: a type that represented safety and security, wonderfully lacking the dangers of an attractive face. But on the other hand the beautiful name Perdita gave rise to thoughts of Bonnie-like nubility, tossed blond hair, incandescent skin. It would be an irony, he thought, if into Dick's brave solitude some kind of minor goddess had walked.

But once the apples had been hunted down and safely trapped in a hideous bowl, William was able to observe that this definitely was not the case. Perdita Beccles came from the first part of his imaginings. She was a large woman: huge, pastry-coloured hands, huge feet in gloomy shoes. Her red hair was cut in a childlike bob. She had one of those nervous smiles that even as the lips begin to spread suffer a change of mind long before the full width has been gained, and flick back to a position of tremulous repose. Well, she was nervous, poor woman, William supposed. Here to make an impression on her fiancé's old friend, the well-known (had Dick thus described him? William wondered) musician and his wife . . . understandable. But she was obviously nice. Niceness flew off her. She dispensed the solid-looking sherry efficiently, her big hands making the glasses look small as thimbles. When she strode across the room her permanently pleated skirt flipped nicely about her knees . . . Nice had so many definitions, William remembered, most of them far from the general lustreless meaning understood today. Recalling one of his snippets of arcane information, it came to him that in the seventeenth century, nice meant slender, thin, unimportant, trivial . . . not at all what he meant about Miss Beccles.

'Pity about the weather.' She was addressing him, handing him a glass of amber.

'Rotten luck, yes.'

'Missing your walk.'

'It'll be fine tomorrow,' said Dick. At the sound of his voice Perdita Beccles blushed. William warmed to her.

'Oh, I don't know. It's often like this.' William appreciated her pessimism. 'Still, you must go up the cliffs. Whatever the weather.'

'We will, we will,' said William with a shudder. He had the ridiculous impression that she could read his thoughts, this huge, nice, red-haired woman: could tell just what William would be getting up to high on the cliffs. Should a murder trial take place she would stride nicely into the witness box and declare that she had known, the night before, exactly what William's plans had been. She had seen into his mind.

The kitchen, at supper time, was slightly warmed by candle power: Perdita had lighted several fat church candles (she was able to acquire them wholesale, she said). Draughts from the curtainless window bent their flames every which way, making shadows fly about the walls, tempering the ugliness of utilitarian pots and pans, crude china. An anorexic chicken was carefully divided, a mush of cauliflower passed back and forth, tepid gravy poured, surprisingly good wine sipped. Grace (who seemed to be enjoying herself more than she could possibly have imagined, which was good, considering this was likely to be her last night on earth) listened to Dick and Perdita's stories of life in the village choir, and they in turn took a wonderful interest in the progress of her book. Behind William's own expression of vivid interest in all that was being said, his mind seethed with speculations upon his old friend and Perdita Beccles. Was there passion, there? he wondered. Apart from Perdita's initial blush, and a small pat on the shoulder Dick gave her in reward for his plate of food, they seemed unmoved by each other. William glanced at Grace, cheeks burnished by the wine, eyes crinkled with interest, still-pretty lips ready to leap into a smile of appreciation. He remembered her when they first met: her translucent skin, her energy, her laugh. He wanted to touch her all the time. Her absence drained him, her presence invigorated him. It had remained thus for the first decade of their marriage, and when the daily excitement began to dim the pleasure of companionship and understanding made a substitute with which William had no quarrel. It wasn't till he met Bonnie he realised that he must have been missing the thrill, magic, spark – whatever it was between man and woman that makes glorious chaos of every day. Unconsciously, he must have been waiting for its return.

And now all his love and desire for Bonnie was so overwhelming that his dear Grace had to make way for her . . . Did Dick and Perdita feel such ungrounding sensations? William doubted it. They were, of course, middle-aged, the time when unmarried people in search of a spouse are driven by considerations of a practical nature – mutual interests, agreement of where to live – more than blood-curdling passion. But William reckoned that Perdita and Dick stood a good chance. He noticed small, bluff looks of contentment that passed between them, a certain light in Dick's eyes that had never been there before. And once supper was over they were at one in their desire for a little musical entertainment. Back in the sitting room the fire was stoked up, and Dick opened the lid of an old, upright piano. It bared its stretch of yellow notes, challenging. Dick shuffled through a pile of music. Perdita, almost gaily, handed William his violin, which he had forgotten to take upstairs.

'Very well, just to oblige,' he said, for this sort of spontaneous music was not something he would ever encourage.

Dick began to play 'Linden Lea'. William joined in, the notes coming back to him from somewhere far in his past – school perhaps. Dick's fine baritone voice filled the room. A few bars later the sound was marred by Perdita's contribution. She had one of those caricature choir women's voices, penetrating, harsh. But she was smiling, happy, her hands clasped as if in prayer.

William glanced at Grace. She sat by the window. Behind her, old curtains – boiled so often their flowers struggled in a colourless fog – moved in the draughts. She was staring at the fire, her body tense in the act of listening. If she had looked up and caught William's eye she would have smiled. He could tell her opinion of the whole quaint evening matched his own, and she was enjoying herself. That was a very good thing indeed, he thought once more. In a pause between verses the wind, freed of the competitive music, whined at the cottage walls like a petulant singer previously ignored. Did the others feel the strangeness of the evening? William wondered. Or did it emanate solely from his own wicked heart?

By the next morning the sea had battered itself into a dour swell, the waves no longer spuming with angry frost, their edges scarcely chipped. A grey, rainless sky, still, but patches of intense light indicated the sun was struggling to emerge. Just the day for a good walk on the cliffs, Dick said at breakfast: he was sorry he and

Perdita would be unable to come because of their duties in church. Unless they should all go together after lunch . . .? When William saw Grace wavering over this idea he was quick to remind her that they did not want to miss the best of the day, have the view obliterated by the early dark of a winter afternoon.

Grace agreed immediately. Her speed in agreeing with him when she (almost always) saw the sense of his point was another of the things he loved about her. They drove the few miles to West Bay, parked the car. When they had last visited the place many years ago when Jack was a boy, it had been high summer, crowds of people, blue sky, ice creams. Now there was no one about. Deprived of their summer tenants the blocks of flats were dolorous, curtains drawn. Kiosks were boarded up, torn posters, four months out of date, waved from the walls of closed shops. The clapboard restaurant in which they had once enjoyed an evening of fine fresh cod had the eyeless, empty look of an upturned boat deserted on the shore.

'I don't know about this,' said Grace. She shivered, looked down at William's feet. 'Were we right to come? You're wearing your slippery shoes.'

'So I am.' William laughed. There would be a bit of hard work, rekindling her enthusiasm for the walk, but if he made it sound like a challenge it shouldn't be too difficult. 'I do believe I've forgotten my boots, too. But never mind. I'll manage.'

'Perhaps we should just go along the beach.'

'No, no. I'd come a cropper on the stones.'

'Very well. But don't blame me if you fall.'

The irony of Grace having hit upon his exact plan was almost too much for William to bear. He took her arm for support. If all went well there would be no time to blame her, because in her struggle to pull him to his feet she herself would slip easily over the edge. It was a simple, excellent, foolproof plan. *Accident at West Bay. Wife of famous violinist falls to her death* . . . The headlines danced across the raw grey sky.

They turned towards the cliffs – vast, shaggy precipices, their rocky sides the dun colour of wet sand. They reminded William of pictures he had seen of Egyptian rockface; there was a foreign imperiousness about them, nothing endearing, like the white cliffs of Dover, or the tufted cliffs that guard Sussex coves. They had doubtless seen many an unhappy soul fly from their heights to death on the hard shore below. There were probably human bones to be found among the skeletons of dead gulls, were someone to start digging through the stones.

'Steep climb,' said Grace.

'Good for you,' said William.

They stood looking at the high cliff ahead of them. In summer it had been covered in thick blue-green grass, the kind that reflects sunlight so brightly that it looks slippery as oily water. Now, under the winter sky, grey light was attached to every blade. It was threadbare grass thinly flung over the earth and rock beneath, and caused William to shiver.

'You're cold,' said Grace

'No, my Ace. Am I ever cold?' A blast of wind from the sea snagged at his trousers, flattened the creases against his calves. He ached to be in his study, violin beneath his chin, shuffling through the piles of music looking for something to play against the inclement weather, Grace safely downstairs hard at one of her puddings.

'Sometimes,' she said. 'Let's get moving.'

As a drowning man is said to see his whole life pass before him, so William, as he puffed up the slope beside his wife on their last walk together, saw fragments of the many walks they had taken over the years. Mostly they had been in Britain: Brancaster beach in December, its loose cover of over-sand, usually swept on erratic journeys by winds of varying strengths, pinned to the heavier stuff beneath it by a netting of frost. Yellow sky – Van Gogh yellow, Grace had pointed out, ever accurate when it came to colour – throwing paler yellow shadows across the tight sea. Not another soul: width of horizon and height of sky all to themselves. Grace's fingers, the ends that protruded from the mittens, were blue with cold but she said she did not feel it. William took each hand in turn and blew on it. He remembered thinking that when there was no music, then to be in a silent place with Grace was all he could ever ask. – There was Mull, a miniature shell-shaped cove of pink sand where small oaks grew among the rocks, and sheep had found something to graze upon. And the beach near Lisadell in Southern Ireland, where primroses overstepped the boundaries of their copse and flared in the sand. There, Grace had put her head on William's shoulder and said that for two whole days she had been able to put the worry of the teenage Jack from her. – Sometimes they had been abroad – walked through fields of lavender near Apt, and the crowds of dancing sunflowers which, through half-shut eyes, seemed to be advancing towards the sun with rush-hour fervour. Grace thought them strangely ugly. And from such brightness to the grey streets of the unsung city of Milan, pausing to rest swollen feet in the crypt of St Ambrogiano, where the skeleton of the saint exuded a whiff of ancient life in his ecclesiastically burnished robes. They were alone with the saint – so often on their walks they were blessed by being alone. It was in Milan on a foggy morning, in an empty gallery, William had come across the small Leonardo painting of *Il Musico*: a young man holding a score. To his delight William realised there were actual notes on the score – no lazy smudge of paint, and had taken out his notebook and copied them down. At home, he played them – they amounted to nothing very much, but it had been an interesting exercise which he had confessed to Grace. She had laughed so hard tears plumped up her eyes. She said it finally proved she was married to an eccentric genius.

'Careful,' she said.

They stopped for a moment, panting, halfway to the cliff's top – turned to look back at the small town in its hibernating garb, the fields beyond it a graph of shut-down mobile homes. By swerving the eyes from land to sea the ugliness was banished. William looked down on the hard grey shore, and across the stroppy glinting of the waves that met the sky at some indeterminate place, and caught his breath, and heard the thumping of his heart. He tried to cast off the past walks cobwebbing his mind to concentrate on this, last, present one, and felt the courage drain from him. He turned to Grace. Her cheeks were crab apples. The edges of her hair, escaping from her woolly hat, danced across her forehead and round her neck, greying tendrils that reminded him of her years of love and devotion. She was fitter than him – no doubt of that: scarcely out of breath, her mouth twitching, ready to smile with its next burst of enthusiasm.

'Come on,' she said. 'We're nearly there.'

Grace, less burdened than her husband, began to climb again with a light step. The visit she had dreaded to William's old friend had turned out to be a great deal more enjoyable than she had expected. She had warmed to the ungainly Perdita with her fierce bossy singing voice, and her conviction that making music round the piano was still a good way to pass an evening. She liked the unpretentious, friendly Dick: his apparent obliviousness to cold and discomfort, his keenness to be a good host, his complete lack of ambition to aim for some recognition in the musical world. Surprisingly, she had enjoyed herself, though she could see William – who'd been the one so keen to come – was less happy. Well, there had been major problems in the night due to a duvet, an article of bedding William abhorred with such intensity that his usual powers of calculation as to balance and weight had simply exploded, withered, died. He had spent the night in his overcoat. Grace put his morose look down to lack of sleep. For her own part the single shadow on her enjoyment was the thought of Lucien trying to get into the house – wanting her, needing her, expecting her. But she reasoned quite successfully with herself: Lucien may have committed an act of theft through necessity, but he was not a regular burglar. She could not imagine him shinnying up drain-pipes, testing window locks. The house should be quite safe. And on their return she would hold out no longer, but get in touch with him. She would not let herself dwell on the fact that self-consolation can be a great deceiver, and was finding as much pleasure in this walk with the panting William as she did in all their walks.

During the last twenty yards of the steep climb to the top of the cliff, William kept his eyes only on the ground: the slippery winter grass and Grace's ankle boots – what she called her walking boots, as if journeys round the suburban streets at home required sturdy footwear. They were made of sherry-coloured leather, soft enough to mould round her bunions. William thought of all her shoes lined up neatly in the cupboard. Each pair bore the faithful imprint of these swollen joints. Their reflections of their owner's imperfections William had always found rather sad. A few bars of Borodin's Quartet in A major, the second movement, came to him. *Better get on with it*, he thought. For they had reached the top.

They stood looking out at the muffled horizon. The cliff top jutted out so far that from where they stood it was not possible to see the shore. Grace took a step backwards, to be a little nearer to the fence that divided the rough grass from the tame undulations of a golf course. She had no liking for the edges of high places. She would never lean over the rails of a boat. She feared driving along narrow mountain lanes. To see William widen the space between them, as he took two paces towards the edge, made her heart beat riotously.

'Come on,' he said, and held out a hand. He smiled – not so much a smile of encouragement as one signifying he was spiritually removed from the present. Grace had often seen that smile when he was playing, particularly andante movements. Bracing herself, she joined him. Did not take his hand.

'Couple more feet and we'll be able to see the shore,' William said.

'I don't want to see the shore. I know perfectly well what it looks like. Don't be *silly*, William. You know I hate—'

'Very well. I'm not forcing you.' He felt the burning of his face. Things were not going exactly to plan. He moved nearer to the edge, stopped at a clump of shiny leaves, similar to spinach but more rubbery. He had never seen such leaves before, wondered if Grace knew what they were. – Two more steps and he would be over. He craned to look down at the beach, its grey stones reduced to a lead pencil line hundreds of feet below.

'William!' Grace's scream was dulled by the damp air, but carbonated by the terror within it. William turned to placate her. In that careless moment, shocked by her face, his foot slipped. He fell.

Even as he crashed to the slippery ground some infinitesimal part of his mind registered that his plan was now working all too well: *he* should fall, and in Grace's struggle to pull him up she would be pushed over the edge . . . What he had not calculated was his own petrified feelings as his legs thrashed into the air. Only the top half of his body was supported by land.

Grace's desperate hands were on his arms and shoulders, pulling. She shouted at him to grab the leaves. He saw that she was crouched on the ground, trying now to hoist his legs back over the cliff edge. Spittle on her lips. Immense strength, from somewhere, for suddenly his legs were supported again: wet grass soaking his trousers. His own death now averted, some clear point in the chaos of his mind and body urged him to take his chance before Grace retreated.

In her panic, for all her fear of edges, Grace had no intention of retreating. She pulled at William, urging him to get up, move away from the edge. He lay strangely recumbent, moaning. Then he began to kick, and struggle, squirming like a man having a fit. Grace's terror was renewed – just as William intended. How would she ever have the strength to prevent his sliding off? She grabbed at his hair. In return he rolled over, releasing his head from her fingers. Grace, weak with relief that they were both now squarely on terra firma – danger over – let down her guard. This William saw at once, realised it was his moment, his final chance. With a terrible shout of 'Over you go', he shunted her towards the edge again. His awkward, half-crouching position denied his arms their full strength. Nonetheless, Grace rolled obediently towards her death. As her body moved within inches of the cliff's edge, William watched fascinated, scarcely able to believe his brilliant strategy had been executed so well. Questions ripped through his mind:

would he hear her screams as she made her flight down to the shore? How would he judge the efficiency of an undertaker advertised in the Yellow Pages?

As Grace found herself bundled to the cliff's edge, her last thoughts were of exasperated love for William. As usual, when disoriented by some kind of crisis, he could never tell his *reverse* from his *forward*. In his panic he had meant to roll her back towards him – 'Over you go' – and had made his usual muddle . . . Which this time was about to be the end. For Grace saw the distant shore, hundreds of feet below, awaiting her. She could not bear to look. She tried to scream, but terror had strangled her voice. She shut her eyes.

In darkness she moved her hands, free from William who was now clutching at her hips. The black behind her lids was torn with frantic prayers. She knew that William was trying his best to save her, pull her from danger. But in case he was not strong enough, there was perhaps still a chance to save herself . . . Blindly Grace flung a hand further. Suddenly her fingers were filled with icy rubber leaves, the strange sprouting foliage she had earlier been unable to name. She pulled at it. It did not give. It was strong. A life-saver of a plant. With one hand locked firmly on a bunch of leaves, she managed to heave herself round to what she imagined was in the direction of William. Only then did she dare open her eyes. She was right. The cliff edge was behind her. She lay like a beached fish facing the golf course, the cluster of distant roofs of the village. William, too, was on his stomach, hands splayed on the earth. His face was very close to her own, eyes enlarged with fear, the poor dear creature. She knew he had been imagining life without her.

'Oh my God, my Ace.'

William's voice came to her like a rudder. He ceased to push or pull her. She kept her eyes on him. To have reconstructed their struggle for life would have been impossible. How they had arrived here, now several feet from the cliff edge, awry on the wet ground, she would never know. William hoisted himself into a sitting

position. He patted her on the shoulder, then rubbed at the marks
on his trouser legs. He had saved her life – though for a moment it
had seemed as if in his distraught state he had definitely misjudged
the rescue. Not for anything would Grace ever admit this to
William, but at one point it had felt as if he was pushing her
towards the edge, rather than dragging her back. But perhaps it had
been a hallucination, caused by the general terror. Grace saw
William's cheeks were a nasty red, his forehead slashed with mud.
He gave her an unabashed look. At least he was taking it all coolly,
as she would expect.

'That was a near thing,' she said at last, and gave a small laugh
that was thickened by encroaching tears.

'It was indeed, my Ace,' agreed William. The thump of
Prokofiev – da di da-di da di da, *Romeo and Juliet* – was now so
loud in his head that he shook it violently, trying to stop it.

'You saved me,' said Grace. William turned the shaking into a
nod.

'I did, my Ace,' he said. 'Just managed it.'

Grace lumbered to her feet. William looked up at her in awe.
She put out a hand, helped him to his feet.

'If it hadn't been for those strange leaves, God knows, we might
both be . . . by now.'

'Or one of us might have been,' William added. 'That would
have been worse. Shall we walk on a bit? Or are we too cold and
shaken?'

'I think we are.' Grace put her arm through William's. 'I think we
should go back.'

Very slowly they began to retrace their steps back down the
cliff, several yards from the edge. In their delicate journey William
realised there are few kinds of happiness more potent than relief,
and for the time being, Grace safely beside him, this warm thought
dispelled all regret at the abortion of his plan. That was something
that in the warmth and safety of his room he would have to think
about further.

Dick and Perdita were still in church by the time they returned

to the cottage. This afforded them a little time to repair themselves – change into dry clothes and stoke up the fire, seek further
calm in an early glass of sherry. But a sense of shock was deeply
embedded within them both and their chief desire was to get home
as soon as possible, distance themselves from the scene of their
cliff-top experience. So when their hosts returned, they confessed
their need to get back this afternoon rather than next morning –
William remembered vital calls that had to be made concerning a
concert in Denmark. Dick understood, was impressed. Can't interfere with the heady life of a world-class musician, he said, meaning
it. Had William not been so full of other sensations, his old friend's
reasonableness would have induced guilt.

To make up for their sudden departure, Grace and William made
a great effort over the Sunday lunch. They made light of their
minor accident, converting the real terror into a funny story.

'I shut my eyes once I'd grabbed William,' Grace explained, 'not
daring to look. At one moment I could have sworn he was pushing
me the wrong way, *over* the cliff. But of course I was completely
disoriented.'

Dick and Perdita laughed so loudly that the strain in William's
own contribution to the hilarity could not be discerned. Beneath
the table he kneaded his cold fingers, longing for his violin, and
wondered what the next move in his grand plan should be. After
the near miss this morning, he was aware that his determination
for success was less firm than it had been. But in order to be available for Bonnie he must, of course, not waver. Some new idea
would come. Meantime, for once in his life, he had no appetite for
the rice pudding that Dick had so kindly prepared long before
breakfast. When he declined a second helping Grace raised her
eyebrows. Luckily, she seemed to think it was the only really odd
thing that had happened during the visit.

10

'How was your night?' asked Grace.

'Not bad: not bad at all, my Ace. And yours?'

'Fine, fine.'

On the morning after their return home, Grace and William fell automatically back into their normal routine, their daily enquiries as to the other's well-being. For once, both lied for their different reasons. Instead of exaggerating their small nocturnal disturbances, here they were both declaring their rotten night was not bad, fine. Very unusual, they both thought, avoiding each other's eyes.

Grace, on getting up, sensed a stiffness in her limbs that had not been there the day before. She noticed bruises on arms and thigh. One ankle was swollen. It was painful to walk (but not too bad). She was determined to disguise her hobbling. It would be better to make no further reference to yesterday's fall. At the time it had all happened so fast that the impact, the potential horror, had escaped her. But in the night *what might have been* had brutally assailed her, been the cause of her wakefulness. Now, she found herself shaky, eager to lose herself in her painting to deflect the trauma.

Further agitation was caused by the thought of Lucien. Some instinct told her he would return, at last, this morning. He could not know it was far from the perfect morning. William seemed to be in a jumpy state equal to Grace's own. She could see the inner quivering, despite his firm mouth and bright countenance, and imagined that he, too, was suffering shock from their near escape. It was not a morning Lucien would receive any welcome from William.

But Lucien did not come. The Handles kept their silence during breakfast, both willing the time to speed towards their various escapes. Grace finished her second cup of coffee. She longed to glance once more at the window, both dreading and longing for the sight of Lucien. But she resisted, for fear William would detect the process of her mind. She placed one hand flat on the table, fingers pointing towards him. Through the veil of his own preoccupations he recognised this was some kind of unusual appeal.

'Hello, my Ace.' He patted the strangely placed hand. 'Busy schedule today, have you?' In reply Grace smiled, nodded. 'Well, I must be on my way, too. There's the Bournemouth concert to grapple with.' He hurried from the room.

Grace knew there was no hope of settling down to paint until later. Much though she wanted to escape into the shell of her work – sable brush, thin colour, delicate stamens to be depicted with infinite care – she knew she could produce nothing of any value until she had walked off the restlessness that nagged at her. She put on her thick coat, boots and scarf and left the house. She did not bother to leave William a message. He was unlikely to come downstairs till lunchtime, would not discover her shirking.

It was a raw grey morning, bitterly cold. Frost tinselled the hedges that divided her neighbours' gardens. Lighted windows threw their reflections on to trim little front lawns, making a strange geometry of gold on the frost-white grass. Grace walked slowly, painfully. With no one to see her she did not try to disguise her limp. She was aware of encroaching self-pity. She wished the visit to Dorset had never taken place. She wished she had never come across Lucien. She longed to see him.

At the end of the road she stopped, wondering whether to turn right or left. She had had some vague plan to go to the bank, but there was no need for this chore. So instead she turned left. Once round the block, she realised, was all she could manage with her ankle. Home, she would have to bandage it.

She hobbled a few yards along Beauchamp Road – houses more exposed than in the Handles' road, a wary look on their mock Tudor façades – and looked up from the pavement to see a familiar figure loping towards her. Lucien: definitely Lucien. He wore a long, shaggy coat she had not seen before, open to reveal a thin, unbuttoned shirt . . . how did he manage never to catch cold? Her mind dithered on these motherly lines while her heart tipped up, unbalancing her. Lucien was almost upon her: brisk, unshaven, smiling as soon as he recognised her. She was glad she had had a few seconds to observe him before he had seen her. They stopped simultaneously, a yard apart.

'Well,' said Lucien. 'Grace. Whatever –?' He looked down at her foot. 'William been throwing you downstairs?'

Grace smiled back. She felt a warm flush of blood roaring across her face. Her fingers, in their angora gloves, burned.

'Slight accident,' she said. He was thinner. Spiky wrists jutting from the short sleeves, more bruised than her own arms. What on earth had he been up to?

'I was thinking of coming to see you,' Lucien said. 'Been a long time.'

'It has.'

'Enjoyed your Christmas?'

'It was quiet.'

'You got my message?'

'Thank you, I did.'

'Seemed you were having a party. Didn't like to intrude.'

'Just the members of the Quartet. We get together every Christmas.'

'Very exclusive, like.' Lucien hunched his shoulders, frowned.

'Not at all.' Grace gave a small laugh. 'What've you been up to? Working?'

Lucien stamped his foot. Nails in the sole of his boot made an ominous clash on the pavement.

'I've been here and there. Thought I'd send you a signal, though. You know me – signals. That's what everything's about, signals, isn't it?'

'I suppose so,' said Grace, after a while.

'Were you to ask me about my Christmas – '

'– I'm so sorry, I –'

'Were you to ask me about my Christmas . . . well. Bloody nightmare.' Lucien searched in the deep pocket of the wolf-like coat, found a loose cigarette, lit it with the last match in a crumpled pack. Inhaling, he tossed the empty pack into someone's garden. The puff of smoke, paler than the sky, which whistled down through his nostrils, had an evil smell that Grace could not quite distinguish. Sour milk, sweat, gutters. 'Lobelia was out of her head. Jewels, lace stockings, silver eyelids, prancing a-bloody about. Fridge door kept bursting open, so much stuff. She gave me a poncy scarf, silk one side, cashmere the other. Can you imagine? I've just been and flogged it. – I couldn't stand the whole scene. I left. Went to London.'

'I'm sorry,' said Grace. Standing still, the weather had begun to bite into her. She put her hands in her pockets, shifted her weight. Her feet were so cold she could not feel them.

'So,' said Lucien, inhaling ostentatiously again, 'are you not going to ask me back for a cup of tea, this bloody freezing morning?' He gave her one of his most endearing smiles. But behind the question Grace saw a hint of mockery. An array of alternative replies flared through her mind. One thing was quite sure: she could not answer truthfully. Lucien would have no patience with William's presence as an excuse.

'I'm not sure it's the perfect time,' she said with a small frown to indicate she wished it were – 'I'm on my way to the surgery. Got to get this ankle looked at . . .'

This time Lucien's smile was nakedly mocking. He nodded several times.

'Aren't you going in the wrong direction?' he asked.

'I was just going round the block, seeing how I got on. I mean, if it didn't hurt too much then I wouldn't have bothered the doctor. As it is, it does . . .' She trailed off, wishing now she had told the truth.

Lucien seemed convinced. His scorn melted fast.

'Sorry I doubted you,' he said. "S'matter of fact, I was thinking of coming round to pass on an invitation. Seems Lobelia is all psyched up to meet you. Really wants to. Tea and cakes and stuff. What d'you think?'

Grace swallowed.

'That would be nice, sometime.'

'This afternoon?'

'This afternoon?'

'Why not?' Lucien's look challenged her. 'Get it over with.'

William never asked where she was going in the afternoons. She had nothing planned. She could, in all truth, get her ankle bandaged at the surgery: Lucien's house was only a few yards down the road. Besides, she was curious, always had been, about the dreadful Lobelia. She had been looking forward to this invitation, had almost given it up. The idea, though unnerving in its spontaneity, was appealing.

'I think I could manage that,' she said. 'About four o'clock, shall we say?'

Lucien nodded. He ground the half-smoked cigarette into the pavement.

'Don't say I didn't warn you, though. She's off her trolley. She's a whore, a self-obsessed trollop only after one thing –'

'Lucien.' Grace put a hand on his arm.

'Well, two things. Money comes into it.'

'I'll be the judge for myself. No need to go on.'

'As for her appearance – you'll be shocked. Don't know how you'll manage to keep a straight face.'

'I expect I'll manage.' Grace wanted to be on her way, now. The cold was dreadful, and there were so many things to reflect upon before the visit this afternoon. 'I must –'

'You be on your way. I'll tell Lobelia to get out the red carpet.

May see you there.' Another thought occurred to him. 'Mind you, if you two get together, where does that leave me?'

He swung round on a heel, hunched his shoulders and strode off down the road. Despite the cold, longing to move to restart her circulation, Grace remained where she was for a few moments, staring at his receding figure. It was hard to know what to make of the meeting. Lucien had done nothing to assure her their friendship had resumed. Rather, he had given the impression that although he was not displeased to see her, and had carried out a duty by asking her to come and meet Lobelia at last, she had become part of the flotsam of his past. Not needed any longer.

After a while she turned back in the direction of home, heart still battering.

It came to William, in the blessed silence of his study, that to ring Bonnie and enquire after her Christmas would not be untoward. There would be no reason for her to suppose that his call was spurred from any motive other than friendliness. There was a rehearsal tomorrow morning, but he did not think he could survive another day without hearing her voice. Besides, in the long sleepless hours of the night, the thought returned to him that before he made another attempt to expunge Grace, he should be quite sure that Bonnie would be willing to take her place. It would indeed be foolish to murder a much loved wife and be left with nothing. But in the early days of his obsession with Bonnie, his own crazed desire had blasted all reason. He had been foolish – he now saw – in his blindness. And even as this new uncertainty about Bonnie's willingness to be part of his plan grew, so did he find that the desire to murder his wife was on the wane. His New Year's resolution, he decided, was to make assurance double sure. If Bonnie gave any further hint that his feelings were reciprocated, and she fancied spending her life with him, then he would make just one more attempt at the foul deed. But if there was any doubt, then he would let the whole matter rest: continue to want her, from afar, but remain with his dear, good Ace.

William made a place for himself on the sofa between the piles of music. He put the telephone on his lap. His hands were unsteady – he was beginning to realise that general shakiness of limb was the price of a troubled conscience. He tried to think of things to calm himself: waterfalls, the shade of willows, cucumber sandwiches. He pictured Grace at work downstairs, earnest little head bent over her daisies. Since the dreadful Lucien had ceased his morning visits, she had retained her old serenity over the toast and marmalade. Much less fidgety, thank goodness. Less flicking her eyes towards the window, thinking her anticipation went unobserved. William appreciated that the repellent lout was Grace's latest good cause, but she'd done more than her bit for him. His sudden disappearance was a merciful relief. If he ever returned . . . William would be bound to express his opinion very firmly.

He picked up the telephone, hand still fretting. Dialled Bonnie's number – engraved more deeply than any other number had ever been in his memory. She sounded breathless: the delicious breathlessness he knew so well when she dashed in, never quite late, for rehearsals, bosom erupting gently under angora of opal grey, or a childish blue or pink –

'William! Sweet of you to ring. How are you? How was your Christmas?'

'Quiet. I was just ringing to enquire after yours. No trouble in Northumberland?'

'Trouble?'

'I mean, you had a good time? Family all well?' Here, he was presuming she had a family. He had no idea what it consisted of, apart from her mother. How pathetically little he knew of her.

'All great, thanks. We had snow. Wonderful. I walked the dogs for miles over the hills. Needed the exercise.'

'Ah.' He could just see her: bunched up in warm jackets and scarves, storming up the stony hillsides, dimples ablaze, sheep scattering, dogs – Great Danes, Labradors, wolfhounds? – the background barking he so often heard meant nothing to him – bounding about beside her. He wasn't a dog man, could only guess she was not a lapdog girl. God what he would have done to march beside her holding her cold little hand – or, more likely, not holding it.

'And you?'

William, entangled in his fantasy, floundered for a moment.

'Dorset,' he said at last. Heavens, he must pull himself together or the girl would think something was amiss.

'Bet you and Grace didn't do much walking. I can't imagine you walking.'

'We did a bit . . . up the cliffs. But, Bonnie . . .' He squeezed shut his eyes, fighting to control his voice. 'I know there's a rehearsal tomorrow. But it happens I have to come into Aylesbury this afternoon to the dentist.' He was so shocked by this unexpected, unpremeditated lie that he had to stop. What on earth was he saying? But yet again having entered in so far, he could only continue.

'Poor you. Something bad?'

'Nothing very much. It was just that when it's over it occurred to me that I should avail myself of the opportunity to be given a tour of your flat . . .'

'William! Honestly!' Bonnie laughed. 'I thought I'd managed to cure you of your verbal flatulence. A few days apart, and back it comes. What you mean is, you want to drop in for a cup of tea?'

'Would that be convenient?'

'Why not?' Her voice had surely lost a little of its bounce. Should he retract the suggestion.

'I mean it was only a silly idea. I wouldn't want to impose.'

'It's a lovely idea. I'll expect you whenever.' She gave him the address, said she had to dash, her voice full of warmth and friendliness again. And in just four hours he would be with her, alone.

The thought left William incapable of any immediate action. He flung himself further back into the sofa, aware that hundreds of sheets of music were falling, slipping over him, scattering on the floor. He shut his eyes, the better to imagine: but not to imagine too far. What would happen? Would there be a chance at last to declare himself? Could he extract from Bonnie some inkling of what she might feel for him? Dear God: it would probably be his only chance. He prayed that the right words would come to him, and that the chance would not be wasted.

William had merely picked at his fishcakes at lunch. Grace's pale face signalled her surprise: she was used to appreciation – daily appreciation, he had learnt, brought its rewards – for her cooking. Perhaps, though, he thought, it was her ankle that hurt more than her feelings. But in his hurry to be off he somehow forgot to ask how it was, now tightly bandaged. And Grace said nothing. Dear Grace.

In his state of nervous excitement his driving suffered. Every few yards he seemed to do something that annoyed other drivers. People hooted and signalled rudely at him – all very puzzling considering his careful keeping to the kerb at a very slow speed. Eventually, partly because he was far too early, and partly to seek a few moments' respite from taunts of the modern motorist, he drew into a garage There, as always, he had trouble filling the car with petrol. He had written several letters, both to *The Times* and the Minister of Transport, suggesting that the return of attendants to fill cars for customers would be a step back towards the decent service motorists had been accustomed to a couple of decades ago – but had received scant gratitude for his idea. Hands still unsteady, he did his best. But the eager pump fulfilled its job long before William had expected, gushing wasted petrol not only over the flanks of the small car, but also over both legs of his trousers. There was nothing he could do, he realised, about smelling of petrol – the sort of thing Bonnie would notice and perhaps notch up as incompetence on his part. He would just have to make a joke of it. Self-mockery, lightly put, usually worked in such circumstances.

To fill more time, William studied flowers in their Cellophane cones, lined up on a bank of green plastic shelves on the forecourt. Daisies, chrysanthemums, and the odd freesia bowed among dull greenery, a couple of bunches of those roses he had never seen growing on any bush – two feet of stalk topped with a hard nipple, no less, of dark, scentless flower that never opened. Where did they come from, such roses? Who on earth found them desirable? Bonnie would know such flowers were garage flowers, but perhaps if he bought her *enough* she would still be quite pleased. He banged round his pockets for his wallet.

Moments later he found himself stuffing half a dozen lustreless bunches on to the back shelf of the car. He realised too late that his view was now impaired, and would cause further hazards. But he had not the heart to stop and rearrange them, and continued on his careful way.

Despite his lingering, William arrived half an hour before the appointed hour. This was a good thing, he thought: he'd have time to calm down. Perhaps to work out his approach – though each time he tried to calculate what that might be, in the last few hours, his mind had turned to an unhelpful blank.

He parked very skilfully alongside the kerb a few yards from the small fifties block of flats about which Bonnie had enthused on a number of occasions. To the untrained eye it looked pretty ordinary. A narrow strip of grass and just one weeping silver birch divided the communal front door from the road. No view to speak of. But Bonnie must have rented it for its convenience to Grant's barn and rehearsals, and no doubt it was a great deal cheaper than whatever she had left in London. However unprepossessing inside, she would have made it agreeable, of course. William had complete faith in Bonnie's taste (based only on her velvet evening dresses and her choice of biscuits when it was her turn to go out for elevenses). He watched the hands of the car clock creep intolerably slowly towards three thirty, and wondered for how long his heart could bash so hard without exploding.

Bonnie's flat was on the first floor. There was no lift. William clattered up the lino-tiled stairs, one hand on the wall for steadiness. Then he was there, outside her front door. A cheap, uniform front door, no embellishments, but painted the grey of so many of her jumpers. Trust Bonnie to choose such a colour to distinguish her territory . . . To while away just one more moment before ringing the bell, William glanced up at the floor above. Its front door was an identical grey . . . With a pang of melancholy William was forced to assume this was a regulation colour for all front doors in the block. Strange how profound love endows the object with all manner of mistaken attributes, he thought, and rang the bell.

Bonnie faced him before he had a moment to compose himself. There was a brief flash of her beaming face, then her arms were round his neck, noisy kisses on his cheeks. She smelt of summer flowers – sweet peas, perhaps, though there was also a hint of onion, of garlic.

'A visit at last,' she said. 'I was beginning to think you'd never come. You and Rufus – you haven't exactly shown much interest in my new flat. You haven't exactly been pressing for invitations, have you?' The dimples flashed, William shook his head, registering the fact that Grant did not come into the category of friends who had shown no interest in her new habitat. But then obviously . . . it was Grant's friend who owned the flat, Grant who found it for her. No doubt she had rewarded him with the occasional drink, or supper. William did not like to think how many times – though innocently – Grant had been round. He did not want to calculate the depth of Grant's acquaintance with Bonnie's dream flat.

William followed her into the sitting room, ungrounded by the warmth of her welcome.

'Well, this is it. Nothing very grand, as you can see. Sit yourself down. I'll make a pot of tea.'

No, it was nothing very grand, William was bound to admit – indeed nothing very memorable or even particularly agreeable. A very standard room, in William's opinion – low ceiling, rather grubby white walls, random bits of furniture, uncomfortable-looking chairs, a dying pot plant at the blank little window. Altogether disappointing, surprising. William had been so sure that however fundamentally plain her apartment, Bonnie would have made it into a sort of magic cave of warmth and colour. He had imagined bright cushions, lively pictures, a mass of plants. As it was the room indicated nothing of Bonnie's life. You could never have guessed she was so good at velvet dresses and delicious biscuits. But then perhaps she just hadn't had the time to start work on it yet: or perhaps she could not be bothered. In any case, it was of no consequence. The fact was he was here at last, and he must take his chance.

Bonnie was pouring boiling water into a teapot in the kitchen end of the room. He saw she had laid a small tin tray with two cups and a plate of ginger biscuits – the especial thin ones that she always managed to find.

'I have to say I'm feeling pretty low,' she said.

William's heart leapt. He was good at ministering to those in a miserable state. There had been many occasions on which his sympathetic listening had apparently been of great help. He knew the best thing was not to enquire why her state of gloom had come about. She would tell him in her own time.

'I had to make the decision to leave the dogs in the north,' she said after a long moment of sad reflection. 'It simply wasn't practical having them here. No time ever to exercise them properly, and there'd been complaints from the neighbours about their barking.'

As high as William's heart had leapt at the thought of her predicament, now he knew its cause it plummeted equally low. There was very little he could do to console someone for the absence of a dog – consolation that came from the heart, that was. He hated dogs. Indeed he had often thought that *should* Bonnie ever agree to his proposal, the problem of the dogs was one he would dread confronting.

'I'm so very sorry,' he said, 'but I daresay they're much happier in Northumberland, all those walks.' He hoped he sounded suitably dolorous.

'I miss them dreadfully.'

'I bet you do.'

'Why don't you sit down?' Bonnie nodded towards the low armchair beside the electric fire. Its wicker bones were covered with a colourless rug made pale with white dogs' hair. Having no wish to add to the mess of his petrol-stained trousers, William chose instead the slightly more buoyant-looking sofa, half occupied by Bonnie's viola. Its springs squawked as he sat, reminding him of the sofa at home. Dog talk now out of the way – with any luck Bonnie would spare him the details of her loss – he felt happier, though uncertain as to how to proceed.

Bonnie settled in the dog chair, put the tray down on a low table of faux wood and spindly legs, much like one he had once seen in Grant's barn. She was lit from the silky grey light that came through the high window. Even in its poor wattage her hair shone like a bird's wing, the fringe so long that as usual it all but hid her eyes. It was all William could do not to leap up and ravish her, clutch her round body to him till she squealed for more. He shifted. Above her, on the shelf above the fire, was a photograph of her and a good-looking man, arms about each other. Bonnie followed his look.

'My brother,' she said.

'Really?' God, the relief. William could see that if this room was all he was going to be shown of the flat – and as it was far from a grand mansion of architectural delights, to ask for a tour would not be appropriate – he would be unable to find many clues. Bonnie handed him a cup of tea, a plate and biscuits. 'You'll enjoy Bournemouth next week,' he said. 'We've a wonderful following there. Always a marvellous audience. The Dvořák . . . They love that.'

'Have you come here to talk about Bournemouth?' Bonnie pushed back her fringe. For a second there was a flash of wide, pale forehead and the ice-coloured eyes. Teasing, William thought.

'No.'

'Funny thing is,' she said after a while, 'outside your music I know nothing of your life, despite a few hints in Prague. – You and Grace. Can't imagine it.'

The idea of her *trying* to imagine it was surprising. It brought a measure of comfort. It meant that during some of the long hours that he had spent thinking of her, she had been thinking of him.

'Grace and I, we've been married a long time. Very happy and all that. She's a woman in a million. All the same . . .' He clasped his hands, raised his shoulders with the effort of an attempt to say what he desperately wanted Bonnie to know. 'All the same, I'm gravely alone.'

There was a moment's silence in which Bonnie looked as if she wanted to laugh, then restrained herself.

'Gravely alone! I know what you mean, though *gravely* probably applies more to you than to me.'

'Quite. I can't imagine you grave.'

'But you can imagine me happily alone?'

'I suppose so. I hope so.'

'Because that's what I am.'

Whither, now? He had dared, she had almost understood. But they seemed to be slithering off the path. He must play for time, return more gently.

'You're set up nicely here,' he said, feeble in his attempt.

Bonnie shrugged.

'Haven't done much yet, as you can see. Not sure I can be bothered. I don't see myself here for ever.'

'You're thinking of moving?'

'Nothing definite. But I think of this as a temporary place. It doesn't feel like anywhere permanent, does it?'

William shook his head, which was spinning. The room was becoming a quicksand into which he felt himself sinking. Did Bonnie mean that her time with the Elmtree was temporary, too? That she was thinking of moving on? But to question her further would be to risk an answer he had no desire to hear.

There was a long silence.

Then William said: 'Do you ever think about Clara Schumann?'

'Not much, why?' Again Bonnie halted a smile. William's switches of thought confounded her, amused her.

'That poor woman. I think about her a lot.'

'What do you think?'

'Well, she wore herself out, didn't she? Wore herself out loving. But it was Brahms I feel really sorry for.'

'He gave her the rough time, didn't he? Wouldn't commit himself, used her, dropped, her, used her —'

'Oh, all that. I don't deny that.' William sighed, braced himself. 'But the *Julia* Schumann part of the story . . .'

'I don't know about that.'

'Clara's daughter. He'd known her as a young child. Watched her grow into a glorious young creature, apparently. Brahms was obsessed by her. Couldn't do anything about it, of course, because of Clara.' There, he'd said it. Some inspiration had produced this introduction to what he wanted to say. Bonnie looked interested.

'Old man's lust?' she asked.

'I suppose you could call it that.'

'Sad.'

'Where's the dividing line – lust, love? Such cases are always sad. Though I don't know why they're always assumed to be nothing *but* lust. Love is often the driving force.' He said this lightly, with a smile. Bonnie responded – unless he imagined it, in the fading light, with a slight deepening of her pink cheeks. His inspiration now seemed to be failing him. Here was another impasse, and he had no idea where to turn next. – 'But you, Bonnie: what's in store for you? How do you see your future? Any plans?'

Bonnie laughed. She probably had no notion of the importance of his questions.

'How can I possibly answer such things? I'm far too young to be sure of concrete plans. All I know is I just want to go on playing and playing, getting better. I take each day as it comes – don't you remember doing the same, when you were young?'

William took two slow sips of tea, stung. He glanced at his watch. Time was running out.

'Daresay I did, though I remember always being rather boringly precise about what I imagined was to happen next. You could say I was old even when I was young . . .' He smiled again, attempting to win her back on his side. Not having planned a strategy had been foolish: things had not gone the way he had hoped. There had been no indication of reciprocated feeling – and now he was lost. Soon he would have to go. Just one more question, jokingly put . . .

'But your heart – not engaged? You must have hundreds of young men queuing up for your favours . . .' God, he sounded so old. Intrusive, too, despite the lightness of tone. But this time Bonnie laughed with a depth of good humour.

'Honestly, William! Do you ask your son all these questions? But, no, right, I'll tell you. You're sitting next to the love object that most engages my heart.' She looked at her viola. 'OK? But I promise you one thing, in case it'll bring any comfort. If ever things change, and I have to leave the Elmtree, I'd give you *masses* of warning, I promise.'

'That would be very kind.' But that was not what he meant at all.

'As it is, that's far from my mind. But you could replace me in a flash, no trouble.'

'Never.'

'Nonsense.'

'You'd be irreplaceable.' William's hand suddenly shook so hard he had to put down the cup.

'That's very sweet of you, but not true.'

'You've probably no idea how high a regard I . . . we all have for you.'

'And you've probably no idea how much I realise how lucky I am to be part of such a quartet. Beyond my wildest dreams, honestly.'

'Your only trouble is that you're so damn beguiling I sometimes want to—'

The telephone rang, cutting him off. Bonnie leapt up. On the way over to answer it she patted William affectionately on the shoulder. As soon as she picked up the receiver she giggled. William put his head in his hands. He could not be sure if she had taken in his last crumbled declaration – and if she had, was she affronted, amused, pitying, what?

'N-o,' Bonnie was saying. 'About five, I should think. Come about five.' She put down the receiver and returned to the fire, but not to sit. William glanced at his watch: twenty to the hour. He must go before she was forced to suggest his leaving. He stood, drooping in his failure. Bonnie did not urge him to stay. In the skidding of her look, the flicking of her skirt, he observed a slight impatience for him to be off. Her next visitor was the one that mattered – of that there was no doubt. His thanks, their farewells, were brief.

'It was lovely that you came, William, really . . . any time.' Kisses on both cheeks again. Then the sad journey down the stairs, the melancholy of knowing he had achieved nothing, messed up his chance. Plainly it would take much more work on his part to persuade Bonnie where her free heart (could that be the truth? he wondered) could come to rest. He must gather his strength, his patience: think more clearly about how to win her, how to do away with Grace . . .

The streetlights were on, their beams shimmying down into an evening mist. William unlocked the car. He saw the back shelf still crowded with the garage flowers he had forgotten to give her – probably a good thing. Might have been over the top, caused her more embarrassment. Waste of money, but still. Grace wouldn't want them . . . He'd have to stop and throw them over a hedge on his way home.

William drove more jerkily than usual, invoking the rage of more than the usual number of motorists. He tried to turn his weary mind to the comfort of the warm, familiar kitchen that awaited him at home. Scones, perhaps. Strawberry jam. Grace. His dear, innocent Ace.

But he found the house in darkness. She was out – where, for heaven's sake? It was unlike her not to be back from shopping by five thirty. As he turned the key in the door it occurred to him that this final nail in his despondency was more than a little peculiar, considering his ultimate plan was for Grace to be gone for ever.

*

At approximately the same time that William was waiting outside Bonnie's door, wondering what to expect, Grace stood outside Lobelia's house in an identical state of nervous anticipation. She rang the bell, waiting to be faced by the vulgar, hedonistic woman she had heard so much about.

Lucien opened the door. Grace was immediately surprised by his scarlet jersey, new and expensive looking: very unlike him. Perhaps, Grace thought, he did not sell *every* present from his mother. Her look rose from his jumper to his face. He stared at her with dead eyes, as if he had just woken and did not recognise her.

'Oh, it's you,' he said at last, and indicated she should come in.

There were no lights on in the narrow hall that Grace had seen on her charitable visit. Mournful wooden panelling and shut doors made it near dark.

'She's in there, or will be,' said Lucien. He pointed to a door at the end of the hall. 'Go on in. I've got to go out.' He moved towards the open front door.

'Aren't you going to introduce us?' Grace knew he would scorn such conventional politeness, but dreaded the awkwardness should he disappear with no word.

'You'll recognise each other.' He gave the faintest smile and was gone, banging the door behind him.

Grace stood at a loss in the hallway. The *rudeness* of him, she thought. For a moment, angry, she contemplated leaving, too. It had been his idea, this meeting: the least he could have done was to have introduced her to his mother, made a little polite small talk before leaving them on their own. But to leave now, the arrangement having been made, would be as badly behaved as Lucien. Grace went to the door he had indicated, knocked, and went in.

The room was empty. No lamps lit in here, either. It took Grace a while to accustom her eyes to the dim geography of the room, lighted only by a darkening sky over a narrow garden outside. It was a cheerless place: too many dark armchairs herded together like animals before a storm, shoals of tasselled cushions clinging to the sofa, a reproduction of Landseer's *Stag at Bay* over the fireplace. Grace unbuttoned her coat, wondered what to do. Lucien had not alerted his mother to her arrival: maybe, in his perverse mood, he had not even told her the time Grace had arranged to be here.

She sat on one of the Dralon-covered chairs. On a small table beside her there was a photograph of an enchanting small boy in a silver frame. Lucien, she supposed, and sighed. How on earth had such a sweet innocence turned to . . . whatever it was he had become now? Ten minutes passed very slowly.

Then there was the sound of footsteps upstairs. Grace stood, doing up the buttons again. She faced the door. It opened. The woman who stood there was backlit by a single light in the hall that she must have switched on. Grace could only see that she was small and thin, in her mid- or late-sixties. Probably the house-keeper, she thought. From what Lucien had said, Lobelia did little in the house herself.

'Who are you?' asked the woman.

'Grace Handle, Lucien's friend. He told me Mrs Watson wanted to meet . . . He arranged that I should come this afternoon –'

'You're Grace Handle?'

'I'm sorry – weren't you expecting me?'

The woman came into the room, shutting the door behind her. She touched a switch. Balloons of cautious light spread from vari-ous lamps.

'I'm sorry to sound so unwelcoming. No, I wasn't expecting you. Lucien is always a little imprecise about *when* things are going to happen. He simply said one day you would come.' Her small mouth twitched. Grace could now see her clothes: all grey, a cro-chet cardigan over a demure silk blouse.

'And you . . . are?' Grace was still fighting to establish the woman's identity. Perhaps she was an elderly relation living here: someone Lucien had failed to mention. The woman clasped her hands, looked puzzled.

'I'm Lobelia, Lucien's mother. – Won't you sit?'

Grace's own amazement was reflected in Lobelia's small, pale face. United in their disbelief, both women stared at each other in astonished silence before finally sitting in two of the armchairs that faced each other. Grace was the first eventually to break the silence.

'I have to say this is very strange. I was expecting . . . someone quite different.'

A frown gathered on Lobelia's forehead. She dabbed at it with one hand, and made an effort to replace it with a weary smile.

'As was I,' she said quietly.

'There can't be any confusion, can there? It's the kind of thing that makes one think one is losing one's senses.'

'A feeling I've lived with for many, many years,' said Lobelia. 'Do take off your coat, or is it not warm enough in here? I'll get some tea in a moment. But I think we should just . . . establish the truth of the matter first.'

'I think we should.'

Lobelia sat very upright, tiny in the huge chair, hands clasped on her grey flannel knee, ankles crossed. She reminded Grace of a nineteenth-century governess.

'The fact is – and forgive the surprise I'm afraid I could not hide – I imagined someone so entirely different . . . that it's difficult to believe you're the Grace Handle I've been hearing about for so many months.' She gave a small sigh. 'The woman Lucien had described a thousand times is a tyrant, no less. A – hussy: could that be the word? Vulgar, loud, demanding . . . He said he met you when you came round collecting for some charity.'

'That's true,' said Grace. Her chest had become so tight it was hard to expel the words.

'And in those few minutes you became totally . . . obsessed by him.' Lobelia looked down at the floor. 'Please forgive the word, and all its connotations. But it's the word he used, over and over again. *She's deranged, Mother*, he used to say. *After me every moment.* Once, he even suggested the police should be called in – protection from the nuisance you were causing him.'

The women's eyes met.

'I don't believe it,' said Grace. 'And yet I must, because it's very close to all he told me about *you*.'

'And that was?'

'It would be painful to tell . . . But in essence I was under the impression you were a fiend of a mother – cruel, uncaring. There was some man he referred to with considerable dislike –'

'Some *man*?'

'Some . . . friend. A certain consumption of drink was mentioned.'

'*Drink*? Oh my God. I don't know whether to laugh or cry. There's been no man friend in this house for thirty years. There's nothing to drink but sherry for the vicar's occasional visits. What was he saying?'

'There must be some explanation,' ventured Grace, kneading so hard at her wedding ring that it hurt her finger.

Lobelia took a small linen handkerchief, thin as a wisp of ectoplasm, from her cuff, and dabbed at her nose. Her eyes were dry, but beaten.

'There is,' she said. 'There's an explanation, but no solution.' The handkerchief was refolded, put away. 'There are many modern names for his trouble. As far as I'm concerned he's just mentally ill. Mad.'

'I'm so sorry,' said Grace, after a long silence. She knew she must concentrate only on Lobelia. This was no moment to think of herself.

'I've lived with the hell of it since he was twelve or thirteen. He's been seen by everyone you can think of: in and out of those curing places. Nothing's done a scrap of good, made a jot of difference. It's rather – well, worn me down.' Lobelia flattened her hands on her knees. 'The trouble is, I've never been able to give up hope, to accept the fact there is no hope. So often, you see, he's almost convinced me he's as sane as the next person – as sweet as they come. Funny, considerate, touching . . . then at the flick of some invisible switch he becomes someone else, an enraged, frustrated, wild creature it's hard to recognise. – He's a congenital liar, always has been. The truth does not exist for him. It's not a concept he's ever been able to understand. In many respects I've learnt to recognise the lies: but even after so many years he can catch me out . . . In the case of you' – she looked straight at Grace – 'I initially thought he was making it up, all these stories about this wild woman who lived down the street. But the stories were so consistent, went on for so long, with such venom, that I thought there must be something in it. Perhaps I could help, I thought, by meeting this raving Grace. That's why I suggested a meeting. Long ago I suggested it.' She paused to give a difficult smile. 'I suppose,' she said, 'the thought of us here, so astonished by each other, is causing him a lot of amusement . . .' She was bitter, dry.

'I imagine it is.'

'Tea – I'm so sorry. Can I get you something?'

'No, thank you. Really.' Swallowing would be impossible.

'When he comes home this evening there will be that hyena laugh all over the house – that dreadful, dreadful laugh. Manic. And his animal noises. Sometimes he howls like a wolf.'

Grace nodded.

'*If* he comes home,' Lobelia went on. 'Often he doesn't. Often he's away for days – weeks sometimes. Comes back with no warning, stinking clothes, thin as a rake, never says where he's been. He's always in need of money. If I refuse him he . . .' She looked round the room. 'So many of my ornaments gone. All the silver. But what can I do? Turn him over to the police? Turn in my own son?'

'Has no one been able to help?'

'No one's been able to help because he's not prepared to co-operate. He's not interested in changing. He seems to get a strange kick out of his weird life. I have a horrible feeling he's – well, as you can imagine, spurred by drugs. I never ask, of course. I never admonish him. I've been trying to keep up my role of the one person who is consistently kind and understanding, no matter what. The only way I've ever succeeded has been to assure him that my love is unconditional. It doesn't get me – or him – any-

where. He just takes advantage.' Her position in the chair had
slumped a little now. She gathered the thin revers of her cardigan
across her chest, looking as chilled as Grace, still in her coat, was
feeling.

'Christmas,' Lobelia went on, 'this Christmas. All had gone
relatively well for twenty-four hours. He gave me a pot of cycla-
men – I hate to think where it came from. We were just in the
middle of our Christmas lunch – I'd cooked non-Christmas
things because he hates that sort of food – when suddenly he got
up, face like thunder, said he couldn't stand any more and walked
out. He only came back this morning, still wearing my present of
a nice jersey. He didn't mention anything about your coming this
afternoon, that's why I was taken aback by finding you here. I'm
sorry.'

'Don't think of it,' said Grace. Pity for this wretched woman had
seized her body, tightening her chest so that it was hard to breathe.
'Compared to you, my experience of Lucien is nothing: but I've
become used to his unpredictable ways. And, like you, I've seen his
other side, so many times. His sympathy, his interest, his encouragement. It has to be said I've grown very fond of him.'

The women's eyes met again.

'I love him,' said Lobelia. 'I love him whatever . . .' She kept her
silence for a moment. 'I try endlessly to work out where it all went
wrong. His father walked out when he was six. They got on so well
together. Perhaps it was something to do with that. It must have
been something to do with that. Desertion. Betrayal. The standard
results. – His father went to live in Australia. No contact with
Lucien ever again. You can understand . . .'

'Of course.'

'I did my best. But a woman on her own can't hope to be both
mother and father. When he began to go off the rails there was no
one strong enough to discipline him. One thing led to another.
And his hate for *me*, the woman who caused his father to leave, as
he sees it, seemed to grow. I've failed him completely. But I can
never give up hope. I can never give up believing that one day

something will finally snap and he'll be magically changed back into a normal, loving son . . .'

'Meantime,' ventured Grace, 'aren't you afraid, living with him? I mean, your safety . . . Do you ever consider that?'

'I'm used to his rages.' Lobelia shrugged. 'He's violent sometimes, but never towards me. Throws things about, bangs doors, abuses me in obscene language – but never causes any harm. I'm used to him. Perhaps what might appal other people has become the norm for me. Of course I live in fearful anticipation, wondering what he'll do next. But no, I'm not afraid of his attacking me. I don't think he'd ever do that. I've no worries about my own safety.' She paused. 'But you: what about you? I hope he hasn't made your life too much of a misery? Threatened? Stolen?'

Grace slowly shook her head. She had no intention of adding to Lobelia's troubles by telling of her own experience of Lucien's misdeeds.

'No,' she said. 'I've been aware of his unpredictability, his short fuse, his confusion and despair, sometimes. I think the constant adding to the stories and descriptions of you have been the only major deception . . . so puzzling. Perhaps it was his way of getting sympathy from both of us. But, as I said, I've grown fond of Lucien. He would come round, listen to me playing the piano, look at my rather minor little paintings . . . be full of encouragement. Often he was such good company. The difference in our ages seemed not to matter to him at all. You could say that he brought quite a . . . sparkle into my rather quiet life.'

Lobelia looked briefly gratified. Perhaps she had not heard a word in her son's favour for many years.

'I'm glad,' she said. 'I'm relieved. And now we've met, now he's negotiated to blow his fantasy, what will happen, I wonder?'

'Perhaps, together, we could be of some real help,' suggested Grace, aware of the feebleness of her remark. Two ordinary, well-meaning women were not the stuff of aid to one as disturbed as Lucien.

'Perhaps we could,' agreed Lobelia. Grace could see she had

little faith in the idea either. 'At least there will be no further point in his spinning ridiculous tales about the two outrageous women, Lobelia and Grace.'

Both managed a small smile.

'We should keep in touch,' said Grace.

'We will. It's wonderful to have met you, to know you're so near if anything . . . But we must be absolutely sure not to let him think we're in collusion behind his back. That would drive him over the edge.'

'Of course,' said Grace. She stood up, suddenly longing to be out of this dark, sad room. Wanting to be at home with William, muttering over his tea about the Bournemouth concert, unaware of Lucien's betrayal raging in her heart. 'I mustn't keep you any longer,' she said.

'Please come again,' said Lobelia, standing too.

'Perhaps you'd come round and visit me one day? Lunch, or whatever would be convenient.' She very much liked the idea of seeing Lobelia again: the possibility of friendship. But a look of confusion, fear, passed over Lobelia's face.

'I haven't had much of a social life for years,' she said, lightly. 'But yes: one day, perhaps. I'd enjoy that. Thank you.'

In the dust of the hall Grace saw that she was several inches taller than Lobelia, who glanced nervously towards the front door.

'I daresay we're both in a state of shock,' she said, quietly, 'having discovered –'

'– what we've discovered. Yes, I daresay we are.'

There was a moment of touching awkwardness (as Grace thought later) when neither of them knew what kind of farewell was appropriate. Kissing the other on the cheek passed through both of their minds. But being women of a certain age and constraint, even the bond of Lucien was not enough to force the gesture of friends (as the young, these day, are wont to employ after only moments of acquaintance) into the meeting of what were, after all, still strangers. They held out tense hands at the same moment, shook briefly, but with a firmness that confirmed Grace's hopes of a future friend was not the stuff of fantasy.

'Goodbye, Mrs Handle. And thank you.'

'Grace. Please call me Grace.'

'Well – goodbye.'

'Goodbye.'

Outside it was dark: mere frames of light round curtained windows. Streetlights shone glossily on to the bare branches of cherry trees, in their iron cages, that were planted randomly along the pavement. The cold cut into Grace's body, ignoring the thickness of her coat. She hurried home – almost ran.

There, she realised the extent of her lateness. She had intended to be back long before William, and had failed. Guiltily, she removed his tea things from the kitchen table. Where was he? She wanted to tell him about her extraordinary afternoon *now*, not wait till supper. But even as the idea struck her, she knew it was foolish. He hated to be disturbed when he was working, and she imagined he was struggling over something to do with Bournemouth.

Automatically, Grace took carrots from the fridge, began to chop them. Her hands were trembling, clumsy. *Lucien*: how could he –? How could the man who had inspired that *sparkle* have been planning all along to rip her to pieces? However could *she* – surely a reasonably good judge of character – have been taken in by him, regarded him in many respects so highly? How could she never have been really afraid of him? The unease she had felt in the past was as nothing to the depths of the trepidation that shook her now. Released from her self-imposed composure in front of the pathetic Lobelia, Grace wanted to bellow her anguish, to beg William to protect her should Lucien ever appear in the house again.

She gave up on the carrots. Dragged herself upstairs, no longer caring about William's annoyance at being disturbed. But when she reached the top floor she heard him playing. This was so unusual, his playing in the evening, she paused to wonder if anything had gone amiss in his own afternoon. A bad time at the dentist, perhaps.

Grace stood on the small landing outside his door, listening. She did not recognise the piece, but it was in a minor key. The sad melody kept disintegrating, like cloud. The notes, muffled through the door, rose and fell and chased each other warily, as if afraid to catch each other and destroy the pattern of despair. No: she could not go in. William must finish his piece innocent of her presence. They had always respected the other's privacy in their various, rare times of suffering.

Grace turned to retrace her steps downstairs. But then, halfway down the top flight, she sank on to a stair and buried her head in her arms to weep unheard against the music. Her misery stretched wider and wider, like ripples in a pond of sluggish water. The discovery of Lucien's insanity was bad enough: the thought of expelling him once again, completely from her life, which surely she now must do to protect herself and William from danger, was very much worse. It might even be impossible, she thought, as William played on and on.

11

An observer looking through the Handles' kitchen window later that night would have been struck by the appearance of normality. Grace had bright – if wary – eyes: no trace of tears left. William, having returned from some amorphous land in which music magically restores, now showed no sign of the disappointment or self-condemnation at his own clumsiness that had racked him that afternoon. One of the great blessings of a marriage in which words are so few is that signals are accepted, unquestioned, respected. So if Grace had any intimation that William was troubled – the very slight shaking of his hand persisted – she had no intention of asking *why*. Equally, if William suspected Grace's own afternoon had been in some mysterious way ruffled (and he did wonder at a certain flickering in her normally steady smile) then the decent thing was to keep his queries to himself. Unlike Jack and Laurel, who were forever 'putting their feelings on the table and thrashing them out', as they called it, Grace and William had learnt the luxury of privacy. Such was their trust in each other that jealousy never imposed. The code of behaviour that had established itself over the years, untroubled by analytical discussion, worked very well for them. They both knew, however, that should something that could not be shouldered alone enter either of their closed lives, then some indication to the other would not come amiss.

Grace considered this as she prodded at her sponge pudding.

She had no appetite. William was helping himself extravagantly to custard. Grace judged the receptivity of his mood: the events of the afternoon pressed so hard upon her she felt compelled to recount, in a vague and general way, what had happened.

'At last,' she said, 'I've met Lobelia, Lucien's mother.'

'Ah! That's where you were,' said William. 'Unusual name.'

'I was curious, as you can imagine.'

'Meeting Lucien's mother would not have been something that lit my own curiosity, but I quite understand yours. I mean, considering your high regard for her son. – Interesting, was it?'

'Not at all as I expected. Lucien had given a very false picture of her.'

'Never imagined he'd be much concerned with the truth.'

'Far from the appalling woman he described, she was rather nice. Cowed, gentle. I liked her.'

'Any possibility of her becoming a friend?'

'Perhaps.'

'That would be good, my Ace.' William was intent on more custard. 'I mean, there's not a rich mine of friends round here, is there? Perhaps this Lobelia woman could fill a gap. Be very convenient, living so near. As for young Lucien, he seems to have stopped using us as a free café. Good thing too.'

'In many ways.' Grace did not bother to conceal a small sigh. She could see that William's concentration on the subject of Lucien and Lobelia was waning fast. She felt she had failed to lay strong enough clues. But some instinct stopped her from admitting her sense of trepidation: her desire for William's assurance that, if Lucien came round again, he would be there to protect her. Equally she felt incapable of confessing the perverse feeling that, despite her horror at Lucien's behaviour, she could not bear the idea of not seeing him again. And if friendship with Lobelia meant that Lucien – by his own hand – deserted her, then that potential friendship might have to be sacrificed.

'Bournemouth: I'm driving down with Grant,' said William, after a long silence in which his thoughts scurried eagerly away from

Grace's favourite topic of Lucien – a topic now unfortunately enlarged to include his mother.

'Oh?' Grace stirred herself. 'That's unusual.'

'Rather a good plan. Grant and I haven't had a moment together for ages.' A further plan was so tentatively etched in his mind that he could not be sure of its outline. But its very existence meant that William looked forward to the drive with Grant.

'What about Bonnie?'

'Making her own plans. Taking a train from London, I think she said.'

'Poor old Rufus. His car in this weather.'

'Rufus'll be all right. He's bringing Iris in her car. She always loves Bournemouth. Wants to retire there.' Bonnie danced before him, confused in the custard – smiling down at him as she stood before her grim little fireplace, mourning the loss of the dogs (for which, surely, he'd shown more than enough proper sympathy). Perhaps he had underestimated her friendliness, her regard for him. Perhaps, though not even conscious of it yet, at the back of her mind the idea that life with a violinist she declared she admired greatly was nudging its way into existence. The thought cheered William immensely. Tomorrow, facing her at rehearsal, he would make yet further sympathetic noises about the dogs, gradually worm himself into her heart. He might even suggest, if the concert went well as usual in Bournemouth, they open a bottle of champagne in the hotel bar afterwards. He had heard Bonnie telling Rufus of her fondness for champagne.

'Anyway . . .' he said. 'My Ace.'

'If Lucien ever appears here again one morning . . . please tell him he must go.' Finally, desperate, Grace quietly exploded. William merely raised an eyebrow.

'Happy to see him off, any time. The rotter. Glad you've come to see what a worthless rotter he is.'

'*William*. He's . . . ill. Don't you see? I just want to make sure.' She glanced round the room at their collection of things, remembering the cufflinks.

'Anything you say, my Ace. I'll do whatever you want. I'm at your service.' He gave a small, distracted smile. *William*, said Bonnie in his mind, *here I am, yours*. For some peculiar reason he was beginning to feel more optimistic. He knew he would be able to face Bonnie at the rehearsal next morning with a look of outward calm, and real progress might surely be made after the Bournemouth concert. 'You're a good woman,' he added, after a while.

Grace was pleased with the compliment, but puzzled, too: they were not words William had ever employed before to cheer her. But then he was in a slightly distracted state – no doubt about that. Worrying about Bournemouth, she presumed. But in the gentle flurry of clearing the supper things, and returning to her own thoughts of the afternoon, Grace soon forgot that William had addressed her so oddly, and smiled at her with a smile that looked as if it was destined for somewhere far beyond her.

William enjoyed travelling in Grant's car. It was large, with soft comfortable seats, almost armchairs, very warm, and quiet. It occurred to him that perhaps he and Grace should turn in their rough little model for something more like Grant's stately chariot, although neither of them would be capable of driving it with suitable aplomb.

The other pleasure was Grant as a travelling companion. He kept his eyes on the road, drove with a mixture of caution and dash that William could only admire. Also, he did not see the necessity of conversation unless something of real pertinence occurred to him. Indeed they listened to the whole of the Prague Symphony before either of them uttered a word. It was Grant who broke the silence, and he happened upon the very subject William was wondering if he could bring up in an innocent manner.

'We'll be at Bournemouth station in plenty of time to meet Bonnie,' he said.

'That's good. You're a nippy driver.' William studied the profile he knew so well: large eyes, Roman nose, amused mouth. He had one of those timeless heads seen both in Greek statues and at contemporary bus stops. Something of a wild Roman about him – he'd be the only member of the Quartet who would look good in a toga – and yet something of the reticent Englishman, too. Grant was *good* – good in the biblical sense, which was something William admired profoundly. You could rely on him in a crisis (he had been a great help at the Christmas party). You could count on him to put others before himself. His foibles were trivial: disorganised (his imperviousness to the mess of the barn William could never understand). He was sulky, sometimes, stubborn; more awkward than was necessary when it came to the chair provided to sit upon at concerts up and down the country. As a cellist he was no Rostropovich. But, unhampered by ambition to be a star, his concern always to do his best as part of the Quartet – there, he could not be faulted. When finally some woman captured his restless heart, thought William, she would be unusually fortunate.

'What was she doing in London?'

Grant shrugged.

'Don't ask me. She doesn't keep me in touch with all her plans.'

Had he said *any* of her plans, William would have felt happier. As it was, he was stung to think *some* of her plans were imparted to Grant. Almost *none* of them did she tell him. But he was being ridiculous.

'Can't imagine her life, really, outside her time with us.' He calculated this innocuous little opener might produce a nugget of information.

'It's good she's moved to Aylesbury. Much easier.'

'Easier for what?' William sniffed.

'Well, easier for her.'

'You've seen her flat?'

'I found it for her, if you remember.'

'So you did. Does she seem to be happy there?'

'Seems to be.'

'That's good.' William liked the fact that Bonnie plainly had not told Grant about yesterday's visit. He turned up the volume on the wonderfully uncomplicated-looking radio. Another musical interlude would give him time to work out his next step. But it was Debussy piano music, not Grant's favourite sort of thing. He switched it off again.

'I sometimes worry,' he said, 'that she'll be off quite soon. I mean, she's so young, so good. Someone will snap her up. Some job far more exciting and lucrative will lure her away.'

'We went through all that when we decided to take her on,' said Grant. 'We all agreed it was a risk worth taking.'

'So we did.' William sighed. He felt a sudden desolation, more from the prospect of Bonnie leaving them than from the future of the Quartet. Perhaps now was the moment to put this to Grant.

'Rufus and I,' he said, 'will have to think about retiring one day.'

'No need to think about that. It's not as if engagements are dropping off. In fact, with Bonnie, we haven't been so in demand for ages, have we? Perhaps she's given us a new life.'

'I think she probably has. But the fact remains. Rufus and I . . . are probably past our prime. We should bow out on a high, shouldn't we? But I like to think the Elmtree might continue in some form. I often wonder if you . . . could keep it on. With Bonnie, maybe. Shouldn't be too hard to find a couple of excellent violinists. There's so much young talent about.'

'That could all be a possibility,' said Grant.

'Of course,' went on William, after a decent interval, 'if Bonnie got married, hitched up, involved with someone – you know the kind of thing I mean – then I suppose there'd be no chance of keeping her.'

'Oh, I don't know.' Grant shrugged again. 'Depends. Women are so independent these days. Keep on with their careers, fit them in with children and so on.'

'True.' Pause. 'As far as you know, does she have any sort of . . . arrangement?'

'You mean a man?'

'I suppose I do.'

'As I told you' – Grant was smiling – 'she keeps her cards pretty close to her beautiful chest.'

'Her beautiful chest: yes indeed.' William smiled too, to disguise his slight alarm. To hear Grant applying adjectives to Bonnie that he, William, only used in the most secret part of his mind was faintly disturbing. But he saw it was the moment to dare to push a little further. 'Damn attractive young girl,' he said.

Grant thought about this.

'Though I don't think she has the faintest awareness of her own attraction. Very unusual. She seems to be utterly without vanity.'

'I'm with you there. A rare specimen of her generation.'

'There are a lot of very good specimens among the young,' said Grant. 'You just don't happen to know them.'

William enjoyed such mild teasing on Grant's part.

'Not among Jack and Laurel's friends, there aren't.'

They both laughed. William's affection for Grant had been deepened by the journey, he thought, as they reached the outskirts of Bournemouth. What's more, he was comforted by the knowledge that Bonnie's private life was a mystery to Grant, too. It was right that it should be so, of course: there would be something distasteful about the single, attractive female member of the Quartet confiding her hopes and fears to her fellow players. And until she made a definite announcement about future commitment to some stranger, there remained hope that William – in a way he was still not able to work out – might win her lasting love and affection, her life.

When William had left for Bournemouth Grace stood at her desk knowing it was yet another morning in which extraneous matters would keep her from work. She flipped through her sketchbook, searching for a Pulsatilla Vulgaris Alba she had intended to finish. The pallid little flowers with their stiff little leaves so horribly *carefully* drawn, as she now saw, filled her with gloom. Her conviction that her talent – if talent you could call it – was very minor indeed pressed upon her. Perhaps the knowing, deep within her,

that the ultimate book – if ever it was finished – was not going to
be very good was the reason she so often found other excuses not
to persevere. Because she did not really love what she was doing,
but had chosen it as an alternative to her own piano playing when
she met William, she did not feel compelled to keep at it in the sort
of disciplined way that William practised his violin, always trying
to reach a few steps closer to perfection. In the case of her flowers,
Grace thought, she had neither the energy nor the desire to strive
for perfection. And this morning, ankle still hurting, the knowledge of Lucien's strange behaviour causing pain that could not be
shifted, and William away enjoying himself for twenty-four hours,
it occurred to her she should give up altogether. Stop pretending
this magnum opus was worth pursuing. Throw it away, perhaps,
and start something quite different. She picked up the folder of finished paintings, devoid of even less liveliness than the sketches.
How could she have believed Lucien when he was so encouraging
about her ability? Surely that was just another of his lies. Her work
was fit only for the fire.

Grace lifted up a picture of a clump of violets, awkwardly placed
on the page, it now seemed. She was about to tear it in half when
the telephone rang. She put it down again.

'Hello? Mrs Handle?' A woman's voice she did not know. 'This is
Lobelia Watson speaking.'

'Oh, Lob –, Mrs Watson.' Grace could not remember exactly
what agreement they had come to about how to address each other.
But it was nice to think her new, possible friend was ringing so
soon. Usually, there were no calls for her in the morning.

'I just thought you'd like to know that soon after you left yesterday Lucien came back in a high good mood. I haven't seen him
so happy for ages. He was laughing, joking, said it had given him
a terrific kick, as he called it, thinking of us being so amazed by
each other.'

'I'm glad he enjoyed his little joke,' said Grace. 'I mean, I suppose it was quite funny.'

'Well,' said Lobelia, 'it was rather protracted. Descriptions of you for months, building up this shocking picture. But Lucien's like that – once he's got an idea in his head he'll stick to it, ever more devious. I suppose it's all part of his . . . trouble. I suppose building up the picture was all part of his enjoyment.'

'I'm glad he's happy again.'

'It's always a relief, though it may not last long. He was so – touching, really, last night. Offered to make me a drink, even made a stab at laying the table. At supper we had a perfectly civilised conversation – history of art. Well, I was once a mature student.' She gave a self-deprecating laugh. 'He said he wanted to find out everything I knew about Van Gogh, God knows why. He did go out later, but kissed me on the cheek on his way out. Nothing like that has happened for years. I couldn't believe it. And this morning I found him down in the kitchen before me, boiling the kettle. All very mysterious. Wonderful.'

'My goodness,' said Grace.

'He was the one who suggested I rang this morning, make some kind of plan for us to meet, perhaps. I was going to leave it for a few days . . . I was wondering whether . . .?' Her eagerness, her uncertainty, quivered in Grace's ear.

'Why don't you come to lunch on Friday?' Grace suggested. 'My husband will be away rehearsing, but it would be a lovely excuse to spend the morning cooking us something.'

'That's really so kind. If it isn't too much trouble, I'd love to.' Lobelia paused. 'Oh, with all these arrangements' – she gave another small laugh, as if awed by unaccustomed plans for lunching out – 'I almost forgot Lucien's message. He said would I tell you he was planning to come round to see you today. He said he'd not been round for ages. He was looking forward to seeing you.'

'Thank you,' said Grace.

But when she had put down the telephone she realised that part of her was not looking forward to seeing Lucien at all. That is – it was so confused in her mind. She *longed* to see him, God knows she had missed him, but also, his madness confirmed by Lobelia, she was now afraid of being alone with him. What exactly made her suddenly nervous of his presence she could not explain. Perhaps she could not be sure she could contain her furious disappointment in him, and if she gave vent to her anger he might well react in some irrational, perhaps violent way. It would have been fine if William was upstairs in his study, ready to come to her rescue in the event of a sudden outburst of temper. But to be in the house alone with him, after several weeks of no real communication, filled her with apprehension. She thought of the wolf howling, the disappearance of the cufflinks, the extraordinary lies about Lobelia. She thought about the unknown part of his life, whose clues came in his dishevelled appearance, his large-pupil eyes . . . and she felt a vulnerability that had never struck her before.

As she remained standing at her desk, looking at the mist-dull laurels outside in the drive, a sense of urgency added to her weighing-up. Suddenly she knew that she could not be here, alone, when Lucien arrived. It would be foolish – dangerous, even. She would be letting him down, of course: her absence might spur him to some future revenge. But she would have to take that risk. The important thing, right now, was to *go*. To check the locks on all the windows, set the alarm and be off.

As she rushed about the house no plan came to her of *where* she should go for twenty-four hours – she merely thanked God that William had gone with Grant and so the car was free. Something, she thought, would come to her. She stuffed her night things into a small bag, took the housekeeping money from the kitchen drawer so that there would be no need to stop at the bank. Ten minutes after Lobelia's call, too amazed by her own unpremeditated actions to summon any coherent plan, she swirled out of the drive only wondering whether to turn right or left into the street.

After so many years of performing in public, William and the others knew that it was only very rarely that a group of performers would achieve 'lift off', as Grant crudely called it. When it happened – sometimes spontaneously and surprisingly, sometimes anticipated due to a sympathetic location or a piece of music loved by them all – its boost would tide them over the less memorable evenings, as they waited for it to recharge them again at some unknown date.

Bournemouth, William was pretty certain, would be a lift-off evening. It was in Bournemouth the Elmtree had first won ecstatic reviews in the national press. They had returned every year, certain of support from their loyal fans – many of whom had been at that first concert. But the cheering thing was that for the last few years there had been many young people in the audience, too. William enjoyed finding a few pieces that would keep this new generation from thinking the Elmtree were strict traditionalists. Dvořák's Quartet in F, the *American*, a regular every year that had come to be known as the 'Bournemouth special'. An early Mozart, and Brahms were usually included in the programme, while the 'spice', the new element, was couched between them. This year William had chosen a piece by Alan Rawsthorne. He looked forward to the reaction.

The concert had been sold out for weeks – it always was. The hall was packed. A crowd of young was standing at the back. William led the players on to the platform – edged, as always, with ranks of poinsettias so popular with producers of musical concerts. He sensed a lightness of being, enjoyment, before a note was played. The applause – again, as always – conveyed the warmth of the audience's welcome. At such times William was able for a few moments to put aside his usual feelings of inadequacy as a musician, and believe that the Elmtree Quartet could make some contribution to the happiness of a few hundred people.

William observed that Bonnie gave one of her extra special little bows, accompanied by a dimpled grin. At this, the applause thickened and William found himself smiling. He had kept meaning to say something to Bonnie: suggest she should join the others only in the one, uniform bow at the beginning. But he had not the heart to do so, and would say nothing this year – after all, it was her début, here. She had to introduce herself to the audience, many of whom might be mourning the loss of Andrew. And certainly, before she played a note, she seemed to have won them over. As her sleeves swung William caught sight of flashes of scarlet satin lining – she only wore the scarlet at especial occasions, he thought, and smiled again at the catcalls that came from the back of the hall. He took in the audience as best as he was able with lights shining into his face, and could just observe that in the front row, her tense, pale face shrouded in a filmy scarf, was Iris. For a second William was struck with guilt: perhaps he, like Rufus, should have brought his wife to this concert. But then Grace never liked staying in hotels, wasn't keen on the Dvořák, was much happier at home in front of the fire . . .

A keen silence fell now as the musicians, sitting, tuned their instruments. William checked each one of them with a look. They were all ready to go. He nodded. They bent their way into the first teasing notes, the pastoral lilt, of Dvořák's Quartet in F. All thoughts of Grace vanished as William disappeared into the music.

As the wife of William Handle, an annual guest at the hotel for many years, Grace was able to check in with no difficulty. She was shown up to his room – the red carpet of the endless corridor seemed to move towards her like those flat moving escalators at airports: an illusion caused by the long and tiring day, she thought.

The room had a high Edwardian ceiling and elaborate cornice. The furniture did not match the grandeur of the architecture, but the bed and chairs looked comfortable, and there was a television and a mini-bar. Grace, who was both hungry and tired, helped herself to a packet of crisps and a gin and tonic – very unusual, for her, but she felt she needed it, deserved it. She had driven at least a hundred miles, unable to decide where to stop, where to stay. It was only when alone in a tea shop in Marlborough that she realised she wasn't that far from Bournemouth, and the sensible thing to do would be to join William, surprise him, and drive him home in the morning.

Grace, in the flush of the hotel room, began to enjoy herself. She took the drink into the bathroom – an extravagance of faux marble and white towels, and had a long bath. It occurred to her that if she hurried she could reach the concert hall in time for the second half of the programme. But she knew there would not be a seat. She did not fancy standing on her ankle, and she did not want to hurry. Her mind soon silvered with the gin, she felt safe in the steamy warmth of the bathroom, hidden in bubbles that smelt of pine forests, hair damp on her forehead. Later, in her dressing-gown, she watched the news on television, bad ankle resting on a Dralon stool. A second gin and tonic nudged the thought that, pleased and surprised though William would be to find her here, he might be less than delighted to find her in her dressing-gown, with its traces of breakfast on the lapels, badly in need of a wash. So she dressed again: the skirt she had been in all day and the spare (crumpled) jersey she had thrown, panicking, into her suitcase. Then she returned to the armchair to watch a cooking programme: only two or so hours and William would be here. She had made the right decision, she thought to herself. He would understand, be so pleased. Grace smiled to herself.

Their time on the platform was immeasurable. William was suddenly aware that the end had come when the audience, frozen in their delighted listening, returned from their private reflections to clap. Applause rolled on and on, an unstoppable surf crashing into his ears. He had broken his usual rule about encores and given in to Elmtree's greatest fans with *two*. Andrew was plainly not mourned: Bonnie had won over this enthusiastic crowd completely. Her bows and smiles – even a small curtsey, which caused a trill of laughter among the clapping – were completely over the top, though William knew that once again he would never scold her. Dimples, shining hair, flashing velvet – no wonder they loved her.

Despite the enjoyment of the audience's appreciation, William would not let himself spoil it all by staying too long. With a final, curt little bow – the applause still echoing like ocean depths – he

led the players off the platform. Bonnie swirled about, drunk on
what she called the 'magic'. Grant muttered 'bloody lift-off', several
times, while even Rufus acknowledged with a smile that it had
been the best evening for a very long time. William himself was
dazed by the knowledge that they had played their best, and their
best had been rapturously acknowledged – perhaps there was still
a year or two left for the Elmtree in its present form. More forcefully in his mind was a picture of the near future – the hotel's
elegant bar where, for once, careless of economy, he *would* order
champagne, see Bonnie's delight. And then, and then . . . who
knows? Were he to engage her in a conversation she felt compelled to continue, perhaps she would accompany him to the large
room overlooking the sea (he had been adamant about that, when
making the bookings), where they could explore the mini-bar and
draw back the curtains to let the moon play tricks on the vast
spaces of carpet patterned with red roses.

'*William!*' Bonnie had taken his arm. 'They're wanting you to
sign.'

They were outside the stage door, a flurry of lights and cold
breath ballooning up like captions from a dozen heads or so.
William disentangled himself from his reveries, pulled a pencil
from his pocket. Bonnie was right. Some old woman had shoved an
autograph book up against his chest – politely, he guessed, for the
real object of their desire was Bonnie. Scraps of paper, programmes
and autograph books were swarming round her. She left William's
side, laughing. This sudden moment of fame, of public recognition,
had ignited her spirits to heights William had never seen before.
She was signing her name again and again, leaning against people's
shoulders and arms. William exchanged a look with Grant, who,
like him, had been caught up in the slip stream of Bonnie's popularity and had signed a few programmes. As no more requests for
their signatures were forthcoming, they were happy vicariously to
enjoy Bonnie's success. Rufus was nowhere to be seen. He didn't
approve of such vulgar post-concert behaviour, as William knew,
and had gone to meet his wife.

At last Bonnie finished signing for her fans, and joined William and Grant. The three of them walked back to the hotel, Bonnie deliquescent, giggling, incredulous.

'I've never known anything like it! What an audience! And then all those mad people wanting my autograph . . . I mean, I never thought the day'd come . . .'

'Pipe down,' said Grant, nicely. 'We don't want your head swollen.' He took her arm.

'Don't be silly, Grant. I know it's a one-night wonder.' She offered her other arm to William, who quickly took it. This, he felt, was the meaning of walking on air. He wondered how far the one-night wonder would go. 'Look at the sea,' Bonnie squealed, suddenly anxious to shift attention from her own success. All three paused for a moment – a rum little trio, as William thought – and obediently looked out at the ebony water, its shallow crests just lit by the moon and the lights on the front. They listened without speaking to the percussion of waves breaking on the shore, then moved on again, more seriously.

For William, the emerging from darkness into light was always of particular significance, both metaphorical and physical. He had never grown accustomed to coming from the gloom of the subterranean passage of a concert hall into the shocking blast of the stage lights. So blatantly illuminated, he felt disagreeably exposed. His eyes were confused by the sudden change. It always took him some moments to dispel these feelings. (The others seemed not to be similarly affected.) But then he was a man who preferred shade to sun, shadow to revealing light. He regarded himself as one whose rightful place was in dark corners: not one who sought the limelight, or any other kind of light. In this respect he felt an affinity with Rufus's wife.

But there were occasions in his life when this diffidence about moving from darkness to light, far from playing its usual unkind tricks, delighted him intensely. He could never tell when this was going to happen. The bonus moments struck him unawares. They had not happened often, but the few occasions were unforgettable. The first he remembered was as a young child. He had hidden beneath a table, blind in the darkness made by a thick cloth. Eventually tired of his game, worried by the anxiety in his parents' calls, he crept out into a room astonishingly bright with lights and candles, and glass balls on the Christmas tree, each one stamped with a tiny reflection of part of the room. He had not remembered the brightness when he had gone to hide. The contrast of five minutes in a black world had conjured the brilliance. The child William had sat there in speechless wonder as he was welcomed back.

Another time, as a young man, he and a friend had swum into a large cave on the coast of a Scottish island. The adventure was less agreeable than they had anticipated. They perched on a wet rock inside the cave, listening to the thud of black water against its walls, then voted to leave sooner than they had intended. Outside, sun had put a blowtorch to a previously dark sky, leaving it shorn of all cloud. Instead, dazzling opal light stretched from the highest point of the heavens and flowed deeply down into the sea. Journeying back to the shore, William felt as if he was swimming through pure light. He secretly harboured the experience for many years – though several times he had been tempted to tell Bonnie – and often he relived the occasion when he was playing Schubert, who was to him a musician wonderfully capable of conveying light. – When he looked back on that swim, William recognised it as one of those times in a life that constitutes inexplicable importance. Something shifted direction within him that day. He was conscious that the vague possibility of making music his life changed, amorphously, as he swam back through the light, to something stronger: determination. The feeling grew from that day forth.

On the evening of the successful Bournemouth concert William was unprepared, as always, for one of his dark-to-light experiences. Elated by the appreciation of the audience, he was also intoxicated by the walk back from the hall with Bonnie. She had kept an arm through his – the fact that her other arm was linked with Grant's William regarded with no great significance. The sea air ruffled their hair and slapped at their cheeks. From the dappled darkness of the street – neither the moon nor illuminated windows nor street lights did more than perforate the real darkness of the night – they walked into the Cinderella world of the grand hotel. There, William found himself delightfully stupefied by the perfectly normal evening lights. It seemed to him that suns and moons and stars shone from every alcove, making watery rock pools of the patterned carpet. There was a sense of movement: liquid light, again, it was. And what tricks it played: burnished mahogany furniture rocked, as if on a gentle sea. Armchairs jigged, and the glass petals of chandeliers were turned to living flames. Nothing was still, nothing was dark. William rubbed his eyes.

'Come *on*,' said Bonnie, interrupting the enchanting illusion. 'What are you just standing there for? The bar! Let's go to the bar.'

She was still there, warm beside him, arm through his. Grant was no longer on her other side. Where was he?

'Grant's gone on to order the promised champagne in case you changed your mind.' – God, how the girl could read his mind: though on a night such as this he would not even toy with the idea of ordering any lesser drink.

They moved together through the hotel lobby – William, stately, dazzled: Bonnie impatient. It was a moment or two, he realised, of pure, present happiness. So often such happiness is easily enough recollected in the past, or anticipated in the future. But rare it is to capture it at the moment of striking: hold it to you for a small measure of time before consigning it to recollections. What an evening, what an evening, thought William.

The bar, when they reached it, was crowded – very different from the gloomy mauve place in the hotel in Prague. Rufus and his wife were seated at a table, guarding three empty chairs. Grant was making his way through the crowd with an opened bottle of champagne in a silver bucket (very good champagne, William noted with alarm). A waiter followed him with a tray of tall glasses. Bonnie, who had detached herself from William's side so quietly it was some moments before he felt the chill of absence, now had her arm round Iris, expressing delight in her presence. (Christ: Bonnie's friendliness was ubiquitous.) William lowered himself into a large armchair next to Rufus, who nodded with the gravity of a man determined to enjoy himself for the sake of the others.

When a group who have participated in some binding activity reach the moment of celebration, there is often a dip in the proceedings, a sense of anticlimax. As they sipped their drinks William wondered, now the headiness of their success was over, what they would talk about – four people who saw and worked with each other most days, who knew each other so well. And Iris: she in her quiet, huddled way meant there would have to be some stricture on in-jokes and anecdotes about events unknown to her. It would be impolite to start explaining things to her – increase her sense of being the outsider. So, once they had drunk to their own good health and the future of the Elmtree (something William had no wish to dwell upon, despite feelings of optimism earlier in the evening), how would the celebration progress? In his still ungrounded state, William raised his glass and looked rather desperately at Grant. Grant did not let him down. He began to tell stories about his time in a youth orchestra – familiar to Rufus and William, new to Bonnie, who found them rather too funny for William's comfort. But as a second, and then, glory be, a third bottle of champagne were drunk he, too, found Grant's power as a raconteur was exceptional.

'You ought to have gone on the halls,' he mumbled to the spinning disc that was now Grant's head. But as no one agreed – or perhaps they hadn't heard this unsteady contribution – William turned his mind to the engaging of Bonnie's attention. He put a half-empty glass of champagne determinedly down on the table. If he didn't stop *now*, it would be too late to intrigue her with some idea so fascinating that she felt compelled to follow him to his room, listen while he philosophised, or confessed about the cave day, or whatever, for the rest of the night. If he didn't pull himself together *now*, it would be too late to make a dignified approach to the curtains, and pull them back to reveal the moon. – Had anything quite so ridiculous been his plan? He suddenly could not be sure . . . But he could hear himself laughing, loudly.

'William's letting his hair down,' said Grant. Bonnie went over to him, smiling her agreement. She punched him gently on the forearm. In return, Grant squeezed her wrist. William stopped laughing, and looked away. When he glanced back again they had moved apart. By now Bonnie was talking to Rufus. Maybe the moment of familiarity with Grant had never happened. William could not be sure. Nothing was clear.

But through the buzz of conversation he could hear the whine of poor-quality music. He turned. In an alcove where the bar met the larger reaches of the lounge, two musicians had taken their stand, a violinist, and a pianist. For some inexplicable reason they were dressed in a way that suggested matadors, or Spanish gypsies – high-waisted pink satin trousers, frilled shirts, and waistcoats of many coloured glass. Perhaps to detract from their playing, William reflected: certainly to add to his confusion. Through the swirling of his head it occurred to him that others thought more highly of these musicians, currently slooping through 'Some Enchanted Evening'. There was applause, private smiles as people remembered their own enchanted evenings. Then, heaven forbid, Bonnie was making her way through the tables of drinkers, viola in hand. What a one she was for snatching opportunities to show off. You couldn't take her to a hotel bar without her leaping up to entertain, bring added life to the place. At the thought, William smiled to himself. While it was not in his nature to approve such behaviour, she performed with such verve and charm it would be hard to condemn her.

Bonnie whispered something to the violinist as he finished his dreadful jiggling of the C string. He smiled, instantly flattered by the heavenly creature in velvet offering to join in. At this point William heard himself groan out loud as he noticed the warm, flirtatious way she made some suggestions to the fourth-rate violinist. *Oh no, please God* . . .

Bonnie had no intention of looking at any member of the Elmtree for approval. She was enjoying herself. It appeared as if this was the kind of spontaneous fun that she believed every serious musician should allow him or herself from time to time. With any luck, she seemed to be saying in the wiggle of her hips, Rufus and Grant would join her. Even, perhaps, William. She glanced at his horrified face, smiled, and launched into 'Let's Do It'. Her fellow players, unused to her speed, dragged behind her.

'Let it swing,' she shouted, to encourage them to speed up. She wiggled her hips even more and shook her sleeves. And suddenly her new fellow players joined in her tempo, inspired. The music thumped. And William, looking round, saw an extraordinary thing: the dozens of people in the bar seemed to be enjoying it. People were standing. Some were clapping to the beat. Some were mumbling the words. Stranger still, Rufus – Rufus the quiet contained man – had joined them. He had got up, was bending his knees, intent on a kind of rhythmic bounce. Then Iris joined him. Pulling her shawl more tightly round her she, too, rose and joined the singing, with the prissy mouth movements of a singer in a Bach choir – but with a look of total enjoyment on her worn-away face. As for Grant: he was behaving like a weightlifter relieved of his weights – clapping his great hands above his head, jacket arms shooting up to reveal a vulgar set of glinting cufflinks William had never seen before, and certainly would have to speak about . . . Grant was bawling his head off, leading this motley choir in a verse of bawdy words. It was unbelievable.

Even as he remained in his chair, middle-aged bottoms jumping about all round him, William felt the isolation of being the odd one out. Scarcely knowing what he was doing, he pushed himself to his feet, clapped his dry hands, found his shoulders heaving in time, saw his feet slither agreeably on the carpet, felt the aching need of Bonnie in his arms, a dancing partner. – Bonnie herself, jigging about like a crazed puppet, was pretty out of focus: but William was able to observe very red cheeks highlighted with a glitter of sweat. Weak with love for her, William forced his gaze beyond her lest he should not be able to control the tears he felt encroaching his eyes. While his feet dithered uncertainly about William made himself keep his eyes from Bonnie: he focused on the horizon beyond the bar, where crowds of jigging spectators jammed the lobby. There he saw something akin to Banquo's ghost – an illusion made manifest from the fabric of his conscience. But it was no spectre in a woolly jumper. It was Grace. The familiar figure of his wife. Grace, it seemed, had come to get him.

With the last remaining rational fragments of his mind, William was still just able to ponder on whether others saw her (if indeed they observed her at all) through his eyes: or if, as he gazed upon her in wonder and alarm, he was seeing her through the eyes of all these singing strangers.

Grace stood completely still, both hands on the handle of her old black bag. She wore the skirt she had put on that morning, and a jersey for which William had never felt any fondness, with its yolk of Fair Isle pattern slung from one shoulder to another. Among all the sequins and satins she made a very plain figure. William aimed a blurry smile in her direction. He could not bring himself to stop his shoulder twists, and small rhythmic claps of his hands. In the confusion of conflicting feelings he realised that his heart raced towards her, loving. His dear Ace – so very unusual – had come to join in the fun.

In her hurry to leave the house Grace had not thought of packing clothes suitable for an evening concert, or a drink in the bar of an expensive hotel afterwards. She regretted this as soon as she was met by the blast of central heating in William's bedroom, but also she did not really care. In her flight from the potential alarm of a visit from Lucien, nothing mattered except the protection William could provide.

After her bath, having given up all ideas of going to the concert, she enjoyed a room-service supper, pushed in on a trolley of silver domes that she lifted slowly, excited. The mixed grill and *pommes dauphinois* were something of a disappointment, as was the chestnut pudding with a name more delicious than the pudding itself. Still, it was all such a novelty, being waited upon, that Grace's enjoyment, combined with her feeling of safety, flourished. She watched television till ten thirty, then decided to go downstairs. In her hurry to surprise William – she could not wait to see his face – she ran down the endless curving staircase, her progress silenced by the dense carpet, rather than take the lift. By the time she reached the first floor she could hear the music from downstairs, and smiled at the thought of how William and the others must hate having to listen to such stuff as they sat over their nightcaps.

Grace pushed her way through the crowd. The heat was worse, here: it made the Shetland wool of her jersey prickle her chest. She continued to move her way slowly forward, observing that some of the drinkers, in their smart clothes, made a passage for her, as if they recognised an especial kind of species in need of its own furrow. The music was thumping some song from a fifties musical – Grace could not name which one. It was the kind of thing that puts silly smiles on people's faces as they recollect past moments of their own romances finely tuned by memory.

Then Grace came upon those she was looking for, and beheld a sight she had never imagined she would witness: there before her were members of the Elmtree String Quartet *drunk*. That is, she told herself, if not rolling drunk, then *seriously inebriated*, and apparently enjoying themselves. Rufus was dancing by himself – if you could call it dancing – shuddering like a bird shaking water from its feathers, eyes rolling behind his glasses. Grant, Tarzan of the crowd, held his arms high as if swinging from an invisible branch, while William seemed intent on small hops accompanied by painful-looking twists of his shoulders. His bow tie had made its way round his neck and was lodged beside one ear. As for Bonnie – in her place next to the third-rate pianist, she was murdering her beautiful viola as she tossed her head to the sloopy beat – fringe flinging every which way, light streaking over the moving velvet of her dress. What on earth . . .?

Grace stood looking from one to another of the musicians. So unusual a sight rendered her helpless. She did not know how to proceed, where to go.

Then she was aware of applause, catcalls, people moving towards the bar again. Rufus's hand was on her arm: dear, kind Rufus, always to be relied on in a crisis, even if he was not entirely himself tonight, due to unforeseen circumstances.

'Grace,' he said, 'how nice you've come. Why don't you join Iris on the sofa? Can I get you a drink?'

'Very good idea.' Now, William was beside Rufus, more animated than sheepish. 'Oh, we're having such fun, my Ace, aren't we? Very surprised to find you here but lovely, lovely . . .'

Grace never received her drink because apparently her appearance signified some midnight chime that said time is up, and the fun seemed to be over. Bonnie moved away from the strangely attired musicians. Deprived of her presence, they lacked inspiration for another number. Grant was clumsily putting her viola in its case, Rufus and Iris had disappeared. Grace felt a sense of disappointment. Having caught the Elmtree in so unlikely a situation, she would have enjoyed witnessing a little more, to make sure her eyes were not deceiving her. But she and William seemed to be gliding towards the stairs. William's arm through hers was purposeful, though his smile skidded about in his dishevelled face.

'Tremendous fun we're having,' he said.

'So I see.'

'So *good* you decided to come, my Ace. Though there was no need.'

They were climbing the massive staircase. The densely carpeted treads could have been a rockface, William had to search for each step with such difficulty. But Grant was just behind them. Grace was grateful for this, knowing she could not cope on her own if William should fall. Grant came with them to their room, took William's arm through the door. William seemed both surprised and amazed by such nannying. He moved towards the window – a mere scrap of his now obsolete plan still left in his mind – bent on drawing back the curtains to greet the moon he was to have faced with Bonnie.

'Where is she?' he asked Grant.

'Signing autographs still at the bar.'

William gave a snort.

'Shouldn't encourage that sort of thing.'

'Come off it – just for one evening. It was fun. You said so your-self – several times.'

'Oh yes, I suppose it was fun.' William was loosely soldered to the floor. He swayed a little. 'Well, thank you, Grant. Goodnight, then.'

'Goodnight.' Grant smiled at both Handles and left the room. Only one so keenly attuned as Grace, to the slightest hint of ine-briation, could have noticed the uncertainty in his own step.

William turned to his wife, tugging at his bow tie. It missed the centrepoint of his collar, and went scuttling towards the other ear.

'There was no need to come,' he repeated, finally fed up with the tussle round his neck. 'Nothing but fun, old dance tunes – you saw for yourself. Nothing but that sort of thing going on. I mean, I wasn't up to anything with Bonnie.'

At this admission of innocence Grace, on her way to help William, came to a halt. She decided to control her laughter.

'What?' she said.

'I said there's nothing between . . . just because we spend a night under the same hotel roof.' There was a buzzing in William's ears, a sensation of drowning. What the hell had come over him, men-tioning Bonnie? Putting thoughts into Grace's head? He gave a twisted smile, accompanied by a sudden leap of his eyebrows, to indicate he was pulling her leg, indulging in a late-night joke. 'I mean, no hanky-panky. Nothing *whatsoever*, my Ace.' By now he spoke so quietly Grace had to strain her ears to hear him.

At that point Grace laughed so suddenly, and with such force, William found himself tottering to the bed, where he sat down heavily.

'The very idea! You and Bonnie! *You and Bonnie!* I can't believe you thought I had any suspicions and had come to spy on you!' She moved about in her laughter. The jersey scratched more uncomfortably at her chest. William was pleased to see he had afforded her so much amusement, but was puzzled as to why she should find the idea of him and Bonnie *quite* so funny. 'I've never heard anything so absurd, William!' she went on. 'Bonnie's a beautiful, talented young girl: you're a wonderful musician too, but near retirement, *old* . . . Can you imagine Bonnie thinking of you as anything but a father figure? Your joke is so far-fetched it's ridiculous.'

'Really?' William was battered by his wife's noisy response to an admission he had not meant to make. But in the whole confusion of the latter part of the evening there had been no time to wonder at her motive for turning up. In a muddy way he had wondered if it had been due to some vague suspicion of his inadmissible love – guilt, the dark twister, at work. His only concern had been quickly to deflect her from the truth – and it seemed he had gone the wrong way about it. He cursed himself for ever having mentioned Bonnie and his innocence. 'I'm glad you find it so funny, the very idea of some young girl regarding me as anything other than a—'

'I do, I do.'

At last there was silence between them. William wanted to get up, shut himself in the white cube of the bathroom, lull himself back to sobriety by the rhythmic brushing of his teeth. But he had no energy to move.

'Why did you come, then?' he asked eventually. A quick glance at her face. Solemn, now. Pale.

'I was afraid Lucien might decide on one of his visits. I didn't want to be alone in the house when he came.'

'Lucien? Oh, that. Him.' Grace could see William struggling to remember old preoccupations, the normal world of minor anxieties light years away from this gilded room. 'You never liked the Dvořák,' he said at last. 'If I'd thought you'd like the programme I would have invited you.'

'No: I never come to Bournemouth.'

'Nor you do.'

Grace went to the mini-bar, helped herself to a miniature bottle of whisky. William looked at her in astonishment.

'Well, you're right. You're safe, here,' he said with a vague wave of his hand. Come to think of it, Bonnie was safe, too, in her room. Elbows in the air, perhaps, sleeves swinging as she struggled to undo her zip.

Grace sat down in the overstuffed chair of olive nylon velvet. As she sipped cautiously at the drink she watched her dear King of the Bed confront the challenge before him. Once he had managed to pull himself upright, he regarded the hotel bed for a long time, hands on hips, assessing. Despite the alcoholic fuddling of his brain, no deficiency in its making escaped him. Imbalance of sheet and blanket, meanness of the corner turns, inadequate weight of eiderdown that would have to be supplemented with blankets hidden in some drawer or cupboard . . . Grace watched as William battled with these things. There followed a strange performance as sheets slipped through his infirm hands, refusing to obey his instructions. Pillows lobbed on to the floor. Mahogany cupboard doors were flung wide as spare bedding was searched for: a pile of blankets toppled from a high shelf on to his head. He floundered, moaning, cursing.

Grace, from her position in the armchair, following his every move, did not smile. The ridiculous figure William made did not bother her, annoy her, amuse her. She was only glad she was not home on her own, and that she had been able to dissuade William of his daft illusion of the very possibility of something going on with Bonnie. Drink, on the rare occasions he overstepped the mark, did not make William a wiser and better man.

Grace did not know what time it was when eventually he sank on top of the bed in a twist of blankets. They had not succumbed to his regimentation so, finally exhausted, he had silently given up. Grace had no intention of trying to undress his recumbent figure, though she did remove the white tie. In the morning . . . well, knowing William's dignity would somehow be reinstated, they would order a lovely room-service breakfast before driving home.

Grace drew back the curtains and saw the moon was so low in the sky it sat on a plate of its own reflection in the sea. Strangely, she did not think of Lucien, only of her need for sleep.

But she did not sleep well. Unused to several drinks, ungrounded by the spontaneous visit to Bournemouth and the strange behaviour of the members of the Elmtree, she relived the evening over and over again – a harder-edged version than the reality bounced off her skull, keeping her awake. When first light appeared, before the noise of traffic began, Grace heard the faint brush of sea on the shore. High tide, she supposed, and was tempted to dress and go for a walk – paddle, even. But then she pictured William waking in his rumpled clothes, cold and confused, wondering where she was – and changed her mind.

Instead she made her way into the claustrophobic bathroom, ran a bath, filled it with sweet oil that turned into a cloud of iridescent bubbles. *This isn't me*, she thought, as she lowered herself into them, scarcely breaking their fragile crust. *This is Katharine Hepburn in a third-rate film.* Luxury. An unusual episode plucked from normal life that will make us laugh when we remember it. William will see how funny it all was. Oh, how we'll laugh . . . She trailed a hand through the hillocks of miniature rainbows, in her drained, dreamy state half expecting Humphrey Bogart to put his head round the door.

The head that did come round the door was a terrible sight: hair standing up like electric wires, eyes strung with red veins, skin pale and shining as a peeled onion. William had discarded his jacket but had given up a struggle with his braces which, slipping from his desolate shoulders, just kept a grasp on his half-mast trousers. He shambled in.

'Thought I heard you.' He put a shaky hand to his temples as if to silence his thoughts. Moved nearer the bath. 'What time is it?'

'About five thirty.'

'Early, then. We were late last night.'

'You were.'

It was this kind of grasp of things, this not giving in to self-pity caused by foolishness, that Grace would always admire.

'You all right?' she asked.

William sat on the three-legged stool, gazed down at his bubble-covered wife. Something vaguely came to mind.

'Fine.' He touched the other temple. 'I'll be even better after breakfast.'

He registered the forgiveness in the reddened face that sat, decapitated, among the bubbles. She was a good woman, Grace. Uncommonly understanding. No doubt of that. Curiously languorous, this morning, too. William had been expecting questions, explanations. There was none. Instead, she said:

'I read somewhere recently that a very easy way to kill someone was simply to lean over a full bath and pick up their legs. They can't struggle like that. They can't keep their head above water.' With one finger she made a small passageway in the bubbles.

For a moment William could see a ribbon of her skin beneath the clear water. The vague idea stirred again. Why was it that so often long-married couples could guess at each other's minds? But there was no time to reflect on what Grace had said. She was offering him a last chance to act, and unless he took it he might never again have either the will or the energy for a further attempt.

'You mean like this?' he said, with something close to a laugh (a back-up laugh, as he saw it, so that if he failed he could say it was all a joke). With no forethought, no coherent plan, he leant over the bath. He plunged both arms into the bubbles, felt for Grace's legs, lifted them (how surprisingly heavy they were) with a supreme effort. The legs came crashing *up*, streaming with bubbles that melted fast as snow in sun. A few stuck in clusters of unshaven hair before they burst . . . Down went her shoulders. Her head disappeared completely. Bubbles raced to fill the gaping wound of water into which it sank.

In the next moment of absolute silence William realised he had succeeded at last. This was it. Grace drowned. Water-logged. Dead. In a moment he would haul the body back up through the bubbles,

further soaking the shirt sleeves that clung to him. He would pull
from behind her shoulders. Having seen a similar incident in a
thriller last week on television, he knew that was the easiest way.
Then he would ring for help. 'Quickly! My wife has had a terrible
accident . . .' Distraught words would come ringing out.

He looked down at the water swaying over the corpse, and felt
a tear in one eye along with a sense of panicky triumph. Then he
found himself ashamed, but smiling nonetheless, at the silly sort of
thought that comes to a man in a crisis – would a bath towel be an
appropriate shroud?

Two, perhaps three seconds passed. Then the steamy quiet in the
murder place was broken by a gurgling noise. Suddenly Grace,
emerging from the bubbles, was struggling like a wild thing. She
kicked. William lost his grip on her legs. They slipped from him.
He felt a blow from a foot on his jaw. He had not calculated her
strength, or his own lack of it. Once again, as on the cliffs, he
realised he was no match for her. He reeled back, tipping up the
stool, landed on the wet floor. Grace's head appeared over the side
of the bath, purple face, hair a black net clamped to it. She was
screaming. William began to scrabble up on to the stool. Oh dear:
nothing for it but to give up. He attempted a laugh, to make sure
she realised it had all been a silly joke. She was appearing like a
volcano in reverse, sliding *up* out of the bubbles, ungainly breasts
resting on a ledge of rainbows that were now thinning like sleet
attacked by rain.

'What are you *doing*?' Grace shouted – William had never heard
her shout so loudly. But then, more quietly, 'Trying to kill me?
William!' His name was uttered with a dying fall. William felt his
heart clench with remorse. He managed another minor laugh.

'Don't be ridiculous. It just occurred to me to disprove a silly
theory.'

'I could have drowned.' She was shaking her head, digging fingers into her ears.

'Of course you couldn't have drowned. I wouldn't have let you
drown, my Ace, would I?'

Grace looked up at him with a wonderful smile.

'I don't suppose so. I don't suppose you'd be much good at living with guilt – or without me. Though sometimes I have the feeling I've no idea what goes on in your mind. Pass the towel, will you?'

Her sudden calm, her benign expression, William found more unnerving than her previous roaring. He had an uneasy feeling that this near-death experience, if that was what it had been, had in some way been a watershed (in all senses of the word) for Grace. Perhaps she was unconscious of this herself. But to one who had observed her (from time to time) for many years, it occurred to William that the experience had provided her with a weird satisfaction, an unusual elation. Perhaps, after such a long and mostly silent married life, the funny little drama, the shouting, the pretence of danger had released something within her. He hoped to goodness that it would not mean, henceforth, a change in their customary reticence. He did not relish the thought of Grace switching from a character who kept her thoughts decently to herself, to one who believed they might be of benefit to her husband.

'Here you are, my Ace.' William passed the towel and retreated. He had no wish to see her lively form emerge from the waves, reminding him of the flesh structure that padded out her dear old clothes, scarcely noticeable in their familiarity: to look upon what went beneath them, this morning, would be more than he could bear.

Alone in the bedroom William took off his damp shirt and trousers, put on his dressing-gown, stood gazing out of the window at sky and sea that looked as if they had been knitted together with dull wool. A gull screeched, hurting his head. Triple images would be no good at calming his battered state this morning: it would have to be sounds. He summoned to mind the cooing of wood pigeons, the trill of a Scottish mountain burn, the second movement of Schubert's Fifth Symphony. But to no avail. The appalling pain of mushrooms swelling against his skull, pushing into the paper of his skin, worsened. He sat on the rumpled bed, in which he had had no more than a few hours' sleep, hands hanging between parted legs, eyes closed.

Grace crept in to dress. She did not want to disturb William, or pain him with the necessity of conversation. She returned to the full support of the armchair, placed her hands on its arms, wondered how to pass the time till seven, when they could ring for breakfast. William, briefly opening an eye to ascertain her position in the room, caught sight of her damp hair and was put in mind of shredded beetroot. He quickly shut his eye again against the disagreeable image – already, he realised, he was suffering his punishment. God's wrath was in the loathsome picture of the wife he loved. But he knew that once his head had recovered she would look herself again.

Each in his and her own way, William and Grace found comfort in the silence that came so naturally between them. They let it engulf them, familiar with its restorative powers, until a chorus of gulls outside jarred their peace, and Grace stirred herself to order porridge, kippers, coffee. She knew that William would be obliged to eat them. It would be part of the pretence that he was not suffering, a further part of the act Grace held in high regard. By the time they arrived home, late morning, their grip on normality would be complete. The episode in Bournemouth would be snuffed out as if it had never existed, the hum of daily life would resume untroubled.

William saw these things passing through his wife's mind as she ordered the gargantuan breakfast with quiet glee, and the pain in his head moved to his heart as he thought of Bonnie. So close – just down the corridor, sleeping deeply, no doubt, against the gulls' cry. But for him, now more than ever, out of reach, out of bounds, a possibility no longer.

12

The following morning, at home, head now light and clear, William took the unusual measure of going to his study before breakfast. He wanted to lean against a wall, make sure of his bearings, steady himself. He was exhausted by the Alpine range of hopes and disappointments over Bonnie: he needed rest, calm. Besides which, a tide of reasoning was beginning to approach: the melancholy thought that even if he made another foolish attempt to get rid of Grace, there was still no reason to hope that Bonnie might want him. Come to think of it – and coming rationally to think of it was not an agreeable prospect – Grace in her great wisdom had probably been right . . . *absurd . . . Bonnie's a beautiful young girl . . . can you imagine her thinking of you as anything but a father . . .?* Grace's voice persisted in his head. He could not shut it out or ignore its sense. Music might solve things, though he had not the energy to take up his violin. (Somehow, before the Beethoven concert the day after tomorrow, he had to pull himself together.) He put on *The Trout* because the CD happened to be in the player. Then, leaning against his favourite wall, opposite the window, he settled to listen to the sun dancing through water, the fish engaged in its mellifluous acrobatics, and the ache of Bonnie's absence, the hopelessness of ever being able to show his love for her, was eased a little by the musical water. When at last he left the room to go downstairs, he was conscious that it was with the gait of an old man. He was bowed, stiff, shuffling. Safe at home, it would nonetheless be a hard day to face.

As he reached the hall the telephone rang, drilling the silence. William picked it up with an irritated swipe. He did not like people to ring before nine.

'Are you all right?' asked Bonnie.

'Of course I'm all right.' William steadied himself with one hand on the banister.

'No need to sound so cross. You looked pretty rough yesterday. I just wanted to make sure –'

'I'm *fine*. There was no need. Good night's sleep put me back on track.'

'Glad to hear it. I mean, it was an unusual sort of night, wasn't it? But really good fun. Think we all enjoyed ourselves.'

'Yes,' said William. He wanted never to hear the word *fun* again.

'See you at the rehearsal this afternoon, then.'

'Oh Christ, I'd forgotten that. I thought it was tomorrow morning.'

'Will*iam!* We'd better have a long go this afternoon, you said. The Beethoven. The cavatina will calm you down.'

'So I did.' His heart was battering uncomfortably. However could he put the girl from his long-term plans when she continued to have this effect upon him? 'See you there.'

It was Bonnie's friendliness that was so confusing, made it all so difficult. She didn't *have* to ring him, enquire after his well-being. Neither Rufus nor Grant had thought to do so. As a matter of fact, they hadn't even thanked him for the three bottles of champagne, put on his bill, which William had had to pay yesterday morning – thus adding shock to his hangover. 'Bloody hell,' he muttered to himself, very out of sorts. How unappreciative is mankind.

He braced himself for his late breakfast and Grace's half-smile, which she employed as her disguise for concern: it never fooled William, but in the game of marriage he had learnt it was easier to appear to accept a spouse's offering as the truth, rather than provoke complications by asking questions.

When Grace opened the kitchen window a gust of mild air, out of character with January, came through the window. Intimations of spring, she thought: and the wicked idea came to her that, rather than getting down to painting this morning, she would go and buy pots of hyacinths and narcissi, cheer up the kitchen. Her ankle was better. She would like the walk.

Grace was not surprised that William had not appeared at his normal time. As far as she could judge, he had a lingering hangover to deal with, though naturally he had made no mention of this – had not even enquired about the whereabouts of the aspirin. Grace had caught him rummaging through unlikely cupboards. She would, of course, go along with his ignoring the whole situation, but in her own subtle way ensure he was in good shape for the next concert. Porridge, she thought. That should help. She would also suggest he open his study window to let in this glorious, downy air. Then a nap before supper, perhaps? As always it was difficult to judge the delicate line between bossiness and kind suggestion. But Grace, who had had a good night's sleep, felt confident she could work her gentle plan subtly enough not to arouse William's sensitive defences.

So busy was she making her calculations that she gave little thought to Lucien. Then, as she ate her own breakfast opposite William's empty place, he came to mind once more. She looked up at the open window, half expecting to see him: hoping he would come, fearful of the consequences if he did. (William, in his present delicate state, would react in a far from polite way to any visitor this morning.) Grace could not help feeling that Lucien *had* been here yesterday. There were no signs, no clues: he had not been able to get in, but she had an irrational sense that he had come to find her, and discovering she was away had left – what? angry? disappointed? Guilt struck. Perhaps her flight had been cowardly. She should have been there for him. If he had been in the endearing mood Lobelia had described, it would have been a pleasure. He would have asked to have seen her latest paintings – chided her for not having done more. Encouraged her. They might have made a little expedition together: gone to lunch in the Post House, or taken a bus to Oxford and visited the

Ashmolean. Grace would have liked an adventure of that sort: its scale would not have alarmed her, though Lucien's presence would always cause her unease. But by leaving, full of silly alarm, she had forgone, perhaps, the joy of a day with Lucien. Also, had she stayed, she would have remained innocent of the foolish antics of the Elmtree – the evening in Bournemouth she wished in many ways she had never witnessed, despite her curiosity at the time.

Still, if Lucien had come round yesterday and found the house empty, it was likely he would try again today. She would find out from Lobelia what he had been up to – Lobelia! At the thought of her, Grace's mind turned to the nurturing of a new friendship – slowly, quietly – visits to each other's houses, consultations about their gardens and books, then a gradual crescendo into wilder things. Grace envisaged trips to England's great cathedrals, perhaps, or even a day in Paris (Eurostar there and back) to look at pictures and lunch by the Seine, the kind of thing that William could never be persuaded was a prospect of delight. Grace pictured herself and Lobelia wandering down the Boulevard St Germain arm in arm, on a fine spring day, blue sky. Then William came into the kitchen. It was ten o'clock.

He took his place at the table, picked up the teapot with a hand that shook very slightly. The considerate silence that had lodged between him and Grace since their return from Bournemouth was broken by a scream – a scream from outside. Then the splattered sound of running footsteps.

A woman's cheese-white face appeared at the window. Fright had infected her eyes with an unnatural, myxomatosis bulge. Grace recognised her. She lived a few houses down the road.

'Let me in!' she shouted. 'The telephone! There's no one else in anywhere – there's been an accident or something – '

Grace ran to the back door. William stayed where he was. It seemed to him a shotgun had been aimed at the kitchen table. Grace, in her hurry to rise, had pulled the tablecloth awry. Toast had fallen from the rack. Cups and saucers were askew. The strange woman kept up her damn howling. The possibility of a quiet, restoring breakfast was over. The drama, whatever it was, did not touch him. He sipped his tea.

But over by the dresser the wild woman, sweat and tears pouring down her cheeks, was screeching into the telephone.

'Number fourteen! Watson, yes. *Quickly*, please. There's blood everywhere. I think someone may be dead. Yes, I said fourteen . . . straight away, please . . .'

She put down the telephone, turned to Grace.

'I couldn't get an answer from Lobelia's door – delivering eggs, I always do every Wednesday morning. So I went to knock on the dining-room window, saw all this –'

Even William noticed a terrible, denser paleness drench her face. She broke into a wailing sob. It bent her double. Grace pushed a chair beneath her. She half collapsed. Her words, in a further attempt to describe the scene, were incomprehensible. William carried on drinking his tea, still detached from the scene a yard from him, still annoyed that the plan for his morning was now upset.

Grace patted the woman's shoulder. She knew at once what had happened – Lucien had tried to kill himself, and had succeeded. A sour black nausea rose in her gullet. She felt the discs of her spine loosen, making her useless, floppy, and yet her hands were on the hysterical woman's shoulders trying to calm. She knew it was her fault: she should have been here when Lucien wanted her, not dashing off in that cowardly way. It was because *she* had been, insanely, on her way to Bournemouth, where she was not wanted, that Lucien was now either dying or dead.

'I'll boil the kettle,' she heard herself saying, 'get you a cup of tea.'

'They can get in through the back door,' sobbed the woman, 'the key's in the shed. Lobelia always left it there so Lucien didn't have to take it with him and lose it –'

'William?' Practicality swung through Grace like a pendulum. Her time to break down would come later. 'You'd better go round, wait for the ambulance. Give them the key. I'll come as soon as I can.' She spoke in the terse snapping tone of one in whom reason surmounts shock.

'Very well.'

William rose reluctantly: the potential seriousness of the situation he could no longer ignore. He looked mournfully at the untouched toast, and left through the back door, avoiding a further glance at the sobbing woman and Grace's stricken face. It was so curiously mild, outside, that he abandoned the idea of returning for his scarf.

William pottered down the road, wondering why he was not gripped by any particular sense of urgency or trepidation. The hysterical bearer of the news had most probably exaggerated, in common with many of her sex, and the drama she described was no more than some minor accident. If by chance Lucien *had* done himself in – well, not good riddance, exactly, but typical of the self-obsessed, no-good rotter that he was. If that was the case, William hoped Grace would not take it upon herself to feel guilt, blame herself in any way. There could be no one less to blame.

Whatever was in store, William enjoyed the exceptional softness of the air, the faint creases of blue teasing their way through the sky. A lilac bush in one of the neighbour's gardens showed the first swellings of buds. The sight took him to Prague, to Bonnie.

He turned into the Watsons' front drive. There were large windows on the left of the front door – similar in all but detail to those at home. The dining room, he supposed. Scene of the . . . whatever.

William was puzzled by two reddish marks, like distorted cobwebs, on one of the windows. He hesitated for just a moment. Then he went on, a faint tremor behind his knees. Two feet from the window the marks were clearly distinguishable: the prints of two hands, cast in blood, held up side by side as if in horror. Or perhaps in triumph. From the thumb of each print a single streak of blood had run further down the window and come to rest in a congealing clot, impairing the almost perfect pattern. William swallowed. He moved very slowly over the last foot of tarmac, edging away from the grotesque red hands. Then he stepped into the soft dark earth of the flowerbed. It sank beneath his feet. For a second he had the impression it was lowering him into the ground, giving him reason not to look. But its beneficence only went a few inches. He could not now avoid looking through the window.

Directly opposite him was a wall-length sideboard of gloomy wood. A long mirror hung above it. Through this he could see a reflection of himself looking through the window at his own reflection, the red hands – alone in space on the invisible glass – just a few inches from his head. There was a breadboard on the top of the sideboard, and half a white loaf. A bottle of sherry, a pepper pot. William let his eyes rest on each object for a long time, dreading moving on to the next for fear of what he should find. He had no wish to look again upon the floating hands so near to his own head.

The bread *knife* – where was that? As the question asked itself, William sensed the schoolboy detective within him: the realisation that none of this was quite real, and at any moment there would be a rational explanation.

His eyes drifted to the white tablecloth, which had been dragged to the far end of the long table and left in a whirlpool of unshining damask, reminding William of the kind of unmade bed that he would find a challenge . . . The rumpled mess of the cloth, he then saw, was scattered with gashes of scarlet blood. His eyes followed the bloodlines downwards. They led to a dense purple pool on the carpet – dark on dark, the viscous substance only distinct from the fabric in its dull gleam. – And there, too, the bread knife, scarlet blade, bloodied handle. Inches from it . . . a foot. No: two reddened feet without shoes. Legs to the knee, in pale torn tights, ladders white as tapeworms crawling up through the blood that drenched them. Whoever had been attacked had been pushed under the table. So, thank God, William could see no more of the victim. Drawing his eyes away from the scene – and yet still conscious he must avoid the floating hands – William turned his stupefied gaze towards the right-hand wall of the room. There, a decorous pattern of small framed etchings was stamped like flags in a sunset of blood: a great scarlet fan of the stuff had splattered almost to the ceiling. The stabbing, or slashing, of the body must have been conducted with an almighty force to produce such a high gush of blood. On the glass of the etchings threads of blood still crept down, only stopped by the frames. William's eyes hovered on down beneath the bloodied wall to a low cupboard. Just one piece of decoration, here: a glass case caging a stuffed owl. This, too, was lashed so thickly with blood that only one dead glass eye and a few deathly breast feathers were visible. The owl appeared to be the second victim in the attack.

William turned his feet in the earth, stepped shakily back on to the tarmac drive. He had no idea whether he had studied the bloody spectacle for a matter of seconds or for hours. Disinterest, cool, calm, had flown. He shook. The warm air had turned every part of him to ice. He felt very close to vomiting, and swallowed back the sick that rose in his throat. But he was no longer alone. Suddenly a different nightmare confronted him: the flashing of blue lights, wailing sirens, shouting. Several men in green, slashed with livid yellow bands, were running towards him.

'Know how to get in?' one of them shouted.

William nodded. That was why Grace had sent him. To let them in. To help. To rescue the owner of the bloody legs. He tried to move, but his feet would not work. The paramedic – the word came to William's mind like a string of lost beads, an agreeable word – took his arm. Somehow they reached the shed by the back door. The man, the *paramedic* (how gentle, how comforting was the word) found the key on a nail. He unlocked the back door. Despite his haste to reach the victim, he had thought for William. He was a marvellous man, this paramedic, a credit to his profession. When all this chaos was over William would write to some high-up figure in the NHS . . . the green arm supported him through the dark hallway, lowered him to sit on a stair.

'You just stay there, mate,' he said. 'And don't look at anything. I'll be back soon as I can.'

Two more green-and-yellow men then rushed past William, into the dining room. He heard one of them swear. Then the door was slammed shut. A moment later it opened. William saw another flash of scarlet-and-white tablecloth before he looked away, so dizzy he reached for the support of the banister. He wondered if he could stop himself from spewing out the bile that had risen in his mouth again. The man who had helped William was back in the hallway, speaking on a mobile telephone. He looked up at William.

'Police need to be here pretty quick,' he said. 'Whoever did this was out of his bloody mind. Nothing we can do till the police arrive – she's dead. You look done in, mate. I should stay where you are a bit longer, if I were you.'

'You look pretty shaken yourself,' said William, quietly. But the man was shouting at the police. He didn't hear.

Moments later police tramped in, scarcely glancing at William on the stairs. The dining-room door was opened and quickly shut again. He heard voices on mobile phones. He heard obscene exclamations. One of the paramedics came out with a deadly white face and hurried towards the cloakroom. William put his head in his hands. He wanted to see and hear no more. This was a real murder, he supposed. The very thing he had been playing at, *contemplating*, made manifest. He crouched over his knees, wizened with self-disgust, horror, fear. Too shaken to stand and leave, he longed only to be with Grace, to hold her hand.

In her own state of crisis Grace dealt with the traumatised neighbour as quickly as she could. She provided tea and brandy, and suggested she should stay until she felt stronger. Then, asking the woman's forgiveness, she said she must now go round to the Watsons' house. However terrible the scene, she wanted to be there.

'Lucien was my friend,' she said.

'Lucien your *friend*?' For a moment incredulity broke through the woman's sobs. 'That psychopath?'

Grace hurried out of the house. How long had William been

gone? she wondered. Ten minutes? Two minutes? Time turns such somersaults in a crisis. Silly, irrelevant questions speared her mind. They were cut short by the sight that confronted her as soon as she turned into the road: twenty yards ahead, outside the Watsons' house, an ambulance and two police cars were parked. Their blue lights turned silently, but sickeningly, throwing ugly streaks of electric colour on to laurel and yew. A crowd had gathered, recognisable neighbours.

Grace ran. She pushed her way through the spectators. A length of fluorescent tape had been strung across the entrance to the driveway. She tried to duck beneath it, but was stopped by a guardian policeman.

'Sorry, love. No one allowed.'

'But he was my friend.'

'He? – Sorry.'

Grace stood her ground. She had never felt more determined. Besides, William . . .

'My husband,' she said, 'went ahead to let everyone in, to get the key. He's in there. I must be with him. Surely . . . please?'

The policeman hesitated. He scanned her eyes bleakly, as if studying an out-of-date driving licence. Evidently he saw something that prompted him to think again.

'Very well,' he said, lifting the tape, 'only don't say I said so.'

Hurrying round to the back door, Grace did not see the red hands at the dining-room window, or the vile scene inside. She made her way through the kitchen – mud all over the floor, poor Lobelia – to the dark narrow hall, where she collided with another policeman.

'Who are you, may I ask?'

Grace considered. Who was she in this unreal morning, Lucien in some kind of crisis, police and ambulance men running amok through the quiet grey privacy of Lobelia's house?

'I'm a neighbour, and William Handle's wife,' she said at last, words all bending as if in a breeze.

'Chap on the stairs?' Grace nodded, though she had no idea

what he meant. 'He's a bit shocked just at the moment, poor bloke. Soon as we've sorted this business someone'll take care of him.'

The policeman moved to one side, letting Grace pass in the narrow passage. She looked up to see William, some half-dozen stairs above the ground, sitting with his head hidden in a cradle of unsteady hands.

Grace moved quickly beside him, leant against him, but did not touch his hands.

'I'm here,' she whispered. William moved his shoulders.

'Good,' he said after a while. 'Christ almighty, my Ace. – What I've just seen.'

Silence.

'Is he . . . by any chance not dead?' Grace knew that if she did not ask quickly she would break into tears, and gathering information would be harder.

'Is who not dead?' Suddenly William raised his head from his hands. Grace was surprised to see that confusion, rather than shock, had gathered in his eyes. It must be the shock, though, that was making him so stupid.

'Lucien, of course.'

William sighed. He turned to Grace. She could see the movement cost him great effort.

'My dearest Ace, I don't know what's going on, but there's no indication your friend Lucien is dead.' He watched a smile begin at the edge of her mouth: could read her thinking: *Lucien's alive, the rest is all bearable.* She was in for a shock. He took one of her cold hands.

'Lelia –'

'Who?'

'What's her name, his mother?'

'Lobelia –?'

'Lobelia, it seems, is the one . . . who hasn't escaped.'

'*Lobelia?*'

'From the way they're carrying on, I assume she's . . . From what I saw through the window.' The Handles' hands tightened. 'Don't ask me about it.'

'No. – But Lucien: where's Lucien?'

'I know nothing, my Ace. No more than you. Nobody's mentioned Lucien. Naturally this lot can't say anything.' He glanced at the policeman by the dining-room door. 'I can only imagine that your poor new friend, Lola –'

'Lobelia –'

'– could be the culprit.'

Grace unlocked her hand from William's. She stared at the curiously ecclesiastical glass of the top half of the front door, an Edwardian entanglement of labourers, sheaves of corn, doves, poppies, and ribbons with no purpose other than ludicrously to entwine the elements of the pastoral fantasy. The reds and blues seared her eyes. The orange ball of formalised sun pressed like a hard ball in her throat. In the chaos, the coloured glass window was the only thing that remained unmoving.

'Lobelia was about to be my friend,' she said.

'I know, my Ace. I know.'

'She's probably all right.'

'Could be.'

'She can't be dead. Lucien would never have done anything like . . . He was a bit unbalanced, yes. But not dangerous. She must have done it herself. Lucien must have driven her over the edge, but not . . . There must be some mistake.'

The doorbell rang. The policeman opened it. For a moment Grace's eyes were relieved of the coloured glass. Two men in white overalls came in. One of them was pulling on a glove of thin, milky stuff that reminded Grace of a cawl. In place, the hand looked ghastly, armed for its task. The men seemed to know by instinct their destination. The policeman merely nodded in the direction of the dining room and they slid discreetly through the door, shutting it firmly behind them.

'Jesus,' said William. 'How many . . .? Now, my Ace . . .' He put an arm round her shoulder.

Another policeman appeared beside the one standing on guard. He whispered something, glanced at William and Grace.

'You two on the stairs,' he said, 'I'm sorry to disturb you but we've got a job to get on with. You are?'

'Mr and Mrs Handle,' said William. 'That's an le, not an el.'

'Mr and Mrs Handle: what, neighbours?'

William nodded.

'Number six. Reddish House.'

The policeman took out a hand computer, tapped something into it.

'We'll be round to ask you a few questions later. But now, if you don't mind, I must ask you to move. We've got to search the house.'

'What for?' asked Grace.

'My wife's feeling sick and faint,' said William, speaking for himself.

'Just a while longer, then. But don't mind us if we get started.'

The two policemen, suddenly athletic for their cumbersome size, lumbered up the stairs. Grace had to lean closely to William to let them pass. Her eyes returned to the sickening glass vista in the door, while her mind ran amok: strange how shock, disbelief, shatter firm images like gunshot. Lucien's face was full of cracks in her mind's eye. She could not recall his smile. Only the strange look, which had so often spurred her fear, in his eyes.

They listened to the two men going from room to room on the first floor – opening and shutting cupboard doors, slapping at curtains as if Lucien might be hiding like a child. Grace hated the idea of Lobelia's house being so violated. Though if she was not actually *dead*, and no one but William – whose opinion in a matter so far from real life was not to be relied on – had suggested she might be, then Grace could of course help restore order. But perhaps, after all this, she might reasonably want to move elsewhere, far away.

They heard the men climb stairs to the third floor. Two doors open and close. Then, a thick laugh, like anthracite being flung from a coal scuttle. Grace had heard that laugh before – Lucien at his nastiest. It was followed by a command, indistinct beneath the shoals of laughter.

Lucien must have been in his room, waiting for them. Grace

glanced at William. William had been sitting here, alone on the stairs. Lucien had never liked him. In his unbalanced mood Lucien could have taken the chance for further revenge.

'I think we should go,' she said, tears on her cheeks.

But William did not move. They heard, now, three pairs of unco-ordinated footsteps coming down the top staircase. Then crossing the landing. Simultaneously Grace and William looked up.

Lucien was between the two policemen, handcuffed. His bloody shirt stuck to his chest. He moved calmly, unperturbed. The laughter had stopped but he was smiling (not the encouraging smile Grace knew, that used to raise her spirits). This was no defiantly brave face. He was enjoying himself enormously.

Grace and William rose quickly, shakily, hand in hand. They hurried to the bottom of the stairs. There they leant against a wall of hanging coats for support. Grace heard the creaking of an old mackintosh behind her. She could not take her eyes from Lucien's cheerful face.

They watched as the awkward threesome negotiated the narrow stairs. At the bottom, Lucien stopped. He wriggled his hands as well as he was able, constricted by the handcuffs. His palms were crimson, the nails black as they had always been of late.

'Left my bloody signature, didn't I?' he said, his look somewhere between Grace and William. 'I signed my best piece of work – *Lobelia.*' His eyes slammed directly into Grace's. 'Can't imagine what the fuck would've happened now you two got together, you and *her.*' The smile whipped away. Grace winced, as if struck. The mackintosh behind her moaned. Lucien's captors urged him to move again. He did not resist. The three of them went through the front door. William and Grace could hear jeers, whistles (peculiar for such a discreet neighbourhood) as he was led to the waiting police van.

The front door was shut again. Grace and William stood helpless in the dark hall. Grace saw that on the table, beside a dying poinsettia, stood a collecting tin for some charity. She remembered that it was because of her own charitable work, collecting from the neighbours, she had first encountered Lucien – a strange, endearing creature with an irresistible smile: nothing to do with the cold grim figure, stiff with self-satisfaction, who had just so bloodily gone through the door in handcuffs. – A criminal, a murderer.

'I don't believe it,' she whispered.

'I think we should go home now, my Ace,' said William. 'Through the back.'

The dining-room door opened again and a paramedic with a kindly face appeared. In the instant that the door was open William was able to see that the blood hands had been wiped from the window.

'I've a moment,' said the man. 'Can I drive you two home? You want to take it easy.'

William tucked Grace's arm into his, met the man's well-meaning eyes.

'Thank you very much,' he said, and drew himself up. 'But we only live a few yards down the road. We'll be all right, see ourselves home.'

'Tea, with plenty of sugar for the shock,' said the man.

'Thank you,' said William again, surprised by the firmness of his own voice, but still confused by what it all meant. 'Plenty of sugar, then the rehearsal this afternoon. Beethoven B flat major, the Op.130 . . .'

The paramedic looked on without understanding as the Handles made their way to Lobelia's back door. He knew that shock takes many forms.

William, with Grace heavy on his arm, began to let the first bars of the Beethoven into his mind. Outside, the sky was a pure but fragile blue, and the earlier warmth of the morning had increased by several degrees.

Grace sat in her chair by the telephone like an angel. Back lit from the light outside, William saw her as he had seen her so many times in her youth: soft, quietly pretty, visible strength beneath the gentleness and patience. She had rung Rufus, Grant and Bonnie: explained there had been an emergency – 'a friend of William's and mine died this morning.' William would be a little late for the rehearsal. (No one had actually told her that Lobelia was dead. From William's silence – he said nothing of what he had seen – she assumed this was so.) Each member of the Quartet suggested the rehearsal was cancelled. But William was insistent it should go on. He wanted as much as possible for life to continue as normal. An hour or two sitting quietly, a couple of aspirin and a bowl of Grace's soup, and he would stop the confounded shaking. Grace looked reasonably calm, but then she had not set her eyes on the carnage.

'Are you quite sure you don't mind being on your own for a while this afternoon?' he asked.

'Quite sure. I daresay I'll collapse a bit, do my weeping.' She patted her chest. 'Then I'll be fine.'

William made an effort. He knew he must ask the sort of question he most disliked – the kind it was his habit to avoid, and to replace with understanding silence.

'Wouldn't you like me to be with you when . . . you do your weeping?'

'What on earth for? Certainly not. What a funny question.'

She *was* an angel, Grace. Letting him off the hook, even in a crisis.

'I just thought . . . Well. It's all so horrible. Lucien: your friend. I didn't much like him, as you know. But he was your friend.'

Grace turned to look out of the window. William regarded her profile keenly, as if for the first time: familiar, it was, and yet there seemed to be a new sharpness. So odd, how unexpected events can change or enhance physical things. He had never understood that.

'You know, if I hadn't followed you to Bournemouth . . .' Grace was saying. 'Some instinct made me leave very fast. I had a feeling he was coming round here . . . Of course, it might have been perfectly all right. It so often was. But I was afraid, I'll never know why. It's horrible to fear someone you're fond of . . . and if I had been here, I might have deflected him in some way. It might never have happened. That's what will haunt me for ever.'

'Thank God for your decision. You, here, alone with a deranged . . . It doesn't bear thinking about. Don't let's think about might-have-beens, my Ace. Too dreadful to contemplate. I mean, it could so easily have been . . .' He quivered. 'Just thank God you were spared.'

Grace saw two level tears appear in his eyes.

'But Lobelia . . . to think he *brought about* the thing that he then couldn't cope with. He urged us to meet so that he could enjoy his sick joke, play the last card in his appalling game. Then regret – or whatever it was – drove him overboard. I don't understand. Especially as Lobelia said he had been so sweet and calm just two days ago.'

'No point in trying to understand an irrational mind. He was a dangerous psychopath, the sort of man who shouldn't be allowed out for his own good. Or for the sake of others' safety.'

'We don't know that.'

'I think we do, my Ace.'

'I don't know why I was so drawn to him.' Grace was speaking almost to herself. 'I felt he needed protecting. I thought I could help a bit.'

'Who's to say why we're drawn to people? When the match is unlikely . . . ' William paused, also thinking aloud. He wasn't much good at this sort of thing, but he felt he ought to keep trying. 'When the match is unlikely, when irrational passion or affection are the only link, rather than anything more cementing, practical, well, it can cause all sorts of trouble. Suffering.'

Grace seemed not to notice the effort in his voice. She could not, of course, ever guess the evidence on which he based his small homily. Of that, William would make sure, she would remain innocent for ever. She went on looking out of the window.

'Oh, William,' she said at last. He could see she was near to breaking.

'It's not often ordinary people like us are neighbours to such atrocity,' he said, feeling himself beginning to flounder, 'but we mustn't let it darken our days. Whatever you feel about having let Lucien down, you must see that you were blameless. I doubt that having been here would have stopped him in his murderous path. In all innocence you befriended an evil, mentally disturbed man. – Probably nothing as dramatic as all this will happen in our lives again, thank God.' He stood up. 'Now, I must be getting on.' He paused, waiting for Grace to move, too, offer to warm his soup. But she still sat looking out of the window, an unbreachable distance from him. So after a while he left the room and began inefficiently fumbling at the stove. It was the first time he had made his own lunch for years, and in the horror of the morning it gave him an unexpected feeling of satisfaction. As he left the house, he heard the telephone ring.

William arrived early – not late as Grace had warned – at Grant's barn, so he drove on some way till he came to a bench on a small common. The feelings that had raged within him on the drive over – detracting dangerously from his concentration on the road – had to be quelled before he confronted the others. He had no intention of embarrassing them by his shaken state.

He sat on the bench, eyes on a block of council offices across the common. Then they shifted to a small boy kicking a football. He watched every innocent move of the boy's foot, listened to the small sound of boot against leather. There was very little time to work out what he must do, and he realised that in his shocked state it was not going to be easy. But plainly the most important thing was to protect Grace, persuade her that guilt was the last thing she should feel. He could see that would be a struggle, but he would not give up. Even harder, because it must remain unspoken, would be the dealing with his own unforgivable past behaviour. How *could* he, a sane, gentle musician, ever have allowed himself to contemplate the murder of a much-loved wife, simply because of some irrational desire for a young girl? Perhaps his intention had never been deadly serious: until this morning he had never understood murder. It was something you read about in the papers, distant from your own life, the stuff of a different world, or fiction. He had thought it could be easy, tidy, painless: peanuts, a fall from a cliff (not that tidy), drowning quickly in the bath. He had never dwelt on the possibility of blood – the obscene gallons of blood that can spurt from a human body, drenching the killer, lacerating yards of wall, carpet, cloth . . . He had never intended anything like that for Grace. His imagining had been of a bloodless end. He had planned it would all be easy – if he really *had* planned – had he? Had he? Looking back, it was now hard to be sure of his intentions, of anything. His strategies, as he always really knew, had been half-hearted – impractical, foolish, bound not to work. What on earth had he been playing at? Perhaps his intent to murder was no more real than his intent to win Bonnie. But nefarious thoughts are scarcely less evil than nefarious deeds: he, too, therefore, was no less a criminal, no less a despicable human being than Lucien. Self-hate, disbelief at his own unbalanced behaviour, *shame*, all thrust through him so powerfully that death itself for a moment seemed compelling.

So William got up from the bench, walked back across the park to the car. The boy with the football smiled at him. Innocence crossing the path of wickedness, William thought. But the boy's cheerful face spurred a little hope: not only would no one ever need to know what had been cankering his being for the last few months, but also there was time for redemption. The asking of forgiveness, the receiving of pardon. From this very moment – he unlocked the car door with his usual difficulty – he would repair his misdoings. *The remembrance of them is grievous unto us, the burden of them is intolerable.* He waved to the boy, who looked surprised.

In the barn the players were tuning their instruments, shuffling through scores. William stood at the door looking at the familiar scene – players at one end, the usual muddle at this, the kitchen end of the place – and the picture acted as a placebo. It occurred to

William that though he could never understand how Grant could thrive in so disorganised a habitat, he could see the comfort of it. Drawers were open: things hung, swung, seemed close to falling: the back of each chair was padded with jackets and scarves. There was a feeling of pleasurable life here. Grant's *joie de vivre* pervaded. (At Reddish House, the sense of order in all but William's own room meant a certain lacking of vitality.) This horrible day, walking into the warm chaos provided by Grant, William felt grateful for his unconscious way of making his barn a place of welcome and peace. William went over to join the others, noting Grant's neat piles of alphabetically arranged scores and CDs – in anything concerning work, his neatness and efficiency could not be faulted.

Rufus, Bonnie and Grant asked no questions when he reached them. They waited for him to tune his violin, and within moments they launched into Schubert's Quartet in A minor, whose andante always brought William the same solace it did to Grace, though this afternoon he had not dared to believe it would come to him so soon. He scarcely looked at Bonnie. When he did he saw that she was just a bright young girl, an exceptionally talented viola player, a girl he still loved (and supposed he always would, in a way) but whom he had no further inclination either to fantasise about or to pursue. God in His mercy had relieved him of that. From out of darkness once more had come light.

When they broke for tea Grant announced there had been several calls for William.

'Various reporters,' he said. 'Seems it was murder. They heard you were first on the scene.'

'That's right,' said William.

'Phone's switched off now. Anything we can do to help?'

William smiled. 'Don't worry. I'm innocent of murder.' He looked from one to another of them. 'Rather an unbalanced young man, befriended by Grace, stabbed his mother. Of course I ran round to let the police and ambulance men in. Grace followed.'

William saw Bonnie bite her lip. There was a glitter of tears in her eyes. Then one of them overspilled and ran down her cheek, a small thread of tinsel.

'Bloody awful business,' said Rufus.

'Exactly,' said William.

'Brandy, or anything?' asked Grant.

'Perhaps later, thanks.' There was no finer group in the world than these, his players. Their understanding, his love for them, rendered him almost speechless.

'Let's get back to the third movement,' he said. 'Time's getting on.'

When the rehearsal was over, Bonnie came with William out to the car.

'I'm so sorry,' she said.

'It's not your fault.' Dazed, William realised it was now too late and too complicated to correct his answer.

'What d'you mean? You must be in a state of shock.'

'Daresay I am. But I was thinking – well, not about the murder. Anyhow, thanks.'

Bonnie put her arms round him. Her summery smell was intact, but distant as a horizon, no power to affect. She kissed him on the cheek. But she was somehow irrelevant. William felt the chill of her irrelevance wash all over him.

'If there's anything I can do . . .'

William nodded, blindly. A moment later he drove away.

He arrived home to find Grace had been harassed by reporters all afternoon, both on the telephone and at the front door. She had kept up a non-committal front, she said, giving away nothing. But she feared they would distort the few words she had said. She was exhausted, and angered by their persistence. William, furious on her behalf, begged her to leave them to him. If they returned, he said, he'd deal with them in no uncertain terms.

Later that evening two detectives arrived to take statements from William and Grace. The process was long and wearisome, but uncomplicated. Lucien had confessed – apparently with some relish – to the killing of his mother, and was to be charged with murder. It was all pretty straightforward – black and white, really, said the detective, finally switching off his mini-recording machine. Just one of those horrible things in this ugly world. The Handles would, of course, be called as witnesses at the trial, but that was likely not to be for some time. It occurred to Grace to enquire if she could visit Lucien while he was on remand. But then – no, she thought: she could not bring herself to go that far in understanding, even if he was not responsible for his actions due to some quirk of the brain. What she must do now, in order to live with his memory, was – well, she was not yet quite sure. But now that she had had her bout of weeping, and the detectives had gone, life must go on.

'Concert tomorrow, then,' said William. 'I'll be leaving late morning.'

'The Beethoven?'

'The Schubert A minor, too. Went quite well this afternoon. Despite.'

Grace put the guard in front of the fire.

'Would you like me to come?'

'Would I like you to come? Why not, my Ace?' Her presence would not affect him one way or another, and it would please her to feel she was pleasing him.

'I will, then,' said Grace. 'I'll drive you.' This would mean there was no necessity, tomorrow, to start wondering what she should do about her book: follow the advice of a murderer, and finish it, or abandon the whole project with its uncomfortable associations. She needed time to think about how to occupy the clear, fearless days ahead. An evening spent listening to William's inimitable rendering of some of Beethoven's late quartets might inspire ideas. It might also unravel the incredulity within her – Lucien, her friend, a killer: Lobelia, her potential friend, dead.

Grace went to the kitchen to turn out the light. She saw that on the wall calendar she had written LUNCH LOBELIA in capital letters under Friday. The words had been written in such hope. Grace took a red pencil and crossed them out. Then she followed William upstairs. His readjustment of the bed was unusually perfunctory. Grace did not know whether to take this as some sort of sign of future change, or whether the events of the past forty-eight hours had driven him to the kind of exhaustion that blasts all care for the routines of every day.

The telephone rang early.

'Leave it to me,' said William. It was Jack.

'Dad? We see you're famous.'

'What do you mean?' William, with the help of pills, had slept deeply. Yesterday was only just beginning to lumber back into his mind.

'Story in all the papers. This murder. Famous musician rushes to the scene . . . Lucien Watson, close friend of the violinist William Handle – all that sort of thing.'

'Christ,' said William. 'The bastards. Mr Watson was no friend of mine.'

'Must be quite exciting, being in the thick of things, though. What's it all about?'

'Hardly exciting.' Heavens, what a foolish oaf Jack was, apparently jealous of a few moments of disagreeable fame. 'Extremely unpleasant, the whole thing. A neighbour's psychopath son stabbed her to death. As you can imagine, your mother and I had quite a day of it yesterday. We don't want to go over it all again today.'

'No. Well. Quite. Understood.' Jack paused. William sensed there was awe in his son's silence. 'Still, fame at last –'

'Come off it, Jack.' He could see all too easily what Jack was thinking: years of life in the Quartet, and only discreet reviews by way of recognition. Then a neighbour is murdered and suddenly real fame is upon him.

'Can't do you any harm,' Jack blundered on, 'audience-wise. Mark my words, there'll be a rush on tickets for your next concerts. Anyway, I'm sorry, Dad. Wretched thing to be involved in. If you ever feel you want to talk it through—'

'Very unlikely,' snapped William.

'Laurel and I have a good friend who's a counsellor, highly skilled in this sort of thing.'

'*I do not want anything to do with a counsellor, Jack.* Your mother and I, as you should know by now, are perfectly capable of getting through life's occasional unwanted surprises on our own. We're not the sort of wimps who resort to counsellors.'

'Well, then perhaps it's the sort of moment you and Mum should go away somewhere, deal with it all. Go to ground at least till the hubbub's all over. I'm sure Laurel could get you some very good terms – Spain, Greece, whatever. You only have to ask.'

'We'll stick it out at home, thanks. Besides, we've a busy programme. Concerts most weeks almost till Easter.'

Jack gave a small laugh. 'Daresay you'll find yourselves booked up till Christmas, so famous now –'

'Oh shut up, Jack,' said William, and put down the telephone.

A conversation with his son was never a good beginning to a day and William, having briefly felt the benefits of his good night, now found himself in extremely bad humour. The telephone rang constantly: he refused to answer it. A side of smoked salmon, along with a note from a tabloid newspaper offering several thousand pounds for his exclusive story, was pushed through the letterbox. The downside of fame was weighing heavily.

'This is unbearable,' said William, mid-morning to Grace. 'We're off somewhere nice for lunch, my Ace: then we'll drive straight on to Windsor, meet the others there. Here, we're prisoners in our own home.'

Twenty minutes later they left the house in mackintoshes against a light rain. They experienced a tiresome moment as several photographers snapped at them, calling to them to turn this way and that – William paid no attention. Grace was to drive, as she always did when they went out together. But William was stabbed with a sudden moment of vanity. He felt he could not be seen by these rotters from the press to be driven by his wife. There was no chance to convey his change of mind to Grace. Confusion was added to confusion as he pushed her from the driver's door, indicating she should take the passenger seat. Silent eye messages between husband and wife – *What? Why? Do as I say!* – provided further photographic opportunities to the scoundrels jostling against the laurels. Then, deflected by the shouting and the flash-lights, William's exit from his own front door was not the smooth get-away he had hoped for. The maltreated little car juddered into the road, narrowly missing the most provocative of the photographers – the only thing, in a wretched morning, that brought any joy to William's heart.

In the papers next day there were pictures of the Handles in a woebegone state by their car.

'Can that be us?' asked Grace. 'We look so old and dotty. And your *mac*, William. You really must . . .'

But then the story fizzled out. It was a horrendous but straight-forward murder case – no mystery. Nothing further to report, or even speculate about, until the trial.

Grace was one of only three people at Lobelia's funeral, a bleak little occasion in an overheated modern church. As she looked upon the coffin, Grace could only feel the intense pity of it all: an innocent mother whose suffering at her son's hand, both during her life and in her final moments, was too dreadful to imagine. What an end to a sad, puzzled, lonely life. For herself, Grace could not help regretting that the promise of a real friendship had been slain before it had a chance. But she had always been one to count her blessings, and as she walked home she thought of her own good fortune, most especially in her husband of so many agreeable years: William, at this very moment at home, waiting for her.

He greeted her in a dither of barely contained pleasure.

'Stephen has been getting calls all morning for engagements,' he said. 'Where's the diary? The Elmtree, my Ace, is about to experience something of a renaissance.'

Grace was glad of his news. A week had passed since Lobelia's death, and the shock was subsiding. Both Handles were still a little frayed, jumpy, incredulous, but with considerable fortitude were fighting for their own particular misgivings. William still sensed the relief of Grace's escape – something he felt might never leave him. Grace was beginning to accept the idea that Lucien's killing was not her fault. She, too, experienced the headiness of relief: the fact that Lucien would never appear at the kitchen window again was a blessing she appreciated each new morning.

Once the funeral was over, Grace and William shared a feeling that it was time for something cheering to happen. Stephen's telephone call was the turning point. Then, as they knew it would, normal life resumed.

13

To William's annoyance, the story that Lucien was *his* friend, not Grace's, was never corrected. And it was his picture – a very old one he had never bothered to change in programmes, more hair, less wrinkles – that appeared in many papers. William also found it irritating that Jack's prediction had been right. Brief fame, although irrelevant, had brought a surge of musical interest. The diary was more crowded with engagements than it had been for some years. Concerts were full, sold out in advance. To William's disgust, he was even greeted by autograph hunters at many artists' entrances of the concert halls. Although it now seemed the worry of the Elmtree's future could be postponed for the moment, William felt the distaste of the reason: the burst of interest, he assumed, had nothing to do with the quality of their playing, everything to do with prurient audiences. It was sad to reflect that even the followers of chamber music had a baser side: but it was apparently true. William knew that Grant, Bonnie and Rufus joined him in these feelings, though they said nothing. Sometimes he detected, at rehearsals on dark days, a certain grimness in their concentration: a feeling of duty rather than of joy. He could only hope this air would eventually fade, and once the demand for appearances waned again (which, in the natural rhythm of things, William knew it would) the four of them would more frequently return to their old, lighthearted though always punctilious way at rehearsals. Meanwhile, extra engagements meant adding to their repertoire. It was a busy spring.

For Grace, too, there was more work than there had been for many months. After much deliberation she had decided that no matter how evil Lucien's deed, there still existed in him good, and she had witnessed that good. He had encouraged her in her work, which no one else had ever done, and had faith in her. Therefore, in private tribute, she decided to take his advice – stop procrastinating, and get down more seriously to finishing her book. She made the effort, and the discontent with her ability began to diminish. She knew she would never turn into a painter of real talent and inspiration, but her competence was a comfort. She enjoyed her mornings' work.

These days, she did not allow herself to reflect too often on the murder, and her relationship with Lucien that preceded it. In his absence before his final insanity, she had both missed him and feared his return. Now, aware of her own narrow escape, relief that he was safely put away was the overriding sensation. To be stripped of daily fearfulness, having lived with it for so long, is a relief like no other. Grace found her gratitude for safety became almost tangible: and no less rewarding was the appreciation of long-forgotten peace of mind. As for Lobelia . . . Grace was surprised how deeply she mourned a friendship that had been snatched away before it had a chance to begin. She felt the helpless pity for the wretched woman's life, the agony she must have suffered being terrorised by her son. Had she lived, and their friendship grown, they would never have been free of the threat of Lucien. In his paranoia he would have seen them – now friends – as his enemies. So large and troubling complications had been avoided by Lobelia's death. The horror of it all left Grace shaken, but the knowledge that she was freed from a life-draining triangle was some comfort. She believed that a quiet, disciplined life, profoundly rattled, is able to settle back more easily to normal than a life devoid of regular form. Grace felt this process gradually take place. Naturally she kept her sadness, her regrets, and her determination to be less blind in the future to herself. They were not the sort of subjects she and William would ever venture to discuss. Nor did they mention Lucien or Lobelia, characters in a disaster that was now mercifully over. Gratifying work and easy silence returned abundantly. William, for his part, was glad to see that Grace appeared to recover remarkably quickly from the whole horrendous episode, and seemed cheerful and content. He determined to show more interest in her progress, give her some encouragement, just as soon as the extraordinary new pace of the Elmtree died down a little in the months to come.

The day in mid-May, which William was never to forget, was from the beginning full of small signals which he chose to ignore. It was only in recollection he saw them more clearly, wondered why he had not let himself be warned.

The weather was so mild he took off his jacket, which made driving to the rehearsal much easier. Unhampered by tweed sleeves, steering was not a problem and he made less enemies than usual on the way to Grant's barn. This gave him a feeling of rare satisfaction. He began to think everyone on the road shared his benevolent mood, inspired by the purity of the blue sky, and the brightness of the green leaves. William looked forward to the morning playing one of Bartók's more dissonant quartets (which he preferred not to play in winter), and the afternoon when, after a long time, they would return to Haydn's *Sunrise*, which was to be included in a June concert in London.

Beside him, on the passenger seat, Grace had placed a bunch of scarlet tulips for Grant – 'to cheer up the barn,' she said – neither a comment nor a gesture she had ever made before. William did not remark upon this. Since the murder, the abundance of Grace's kindly gestures had increased, and he understood.

William carried the flowers into the barn feeling rather foolish. Their brilliant heads drooped against his Viyella shirt – dependent, neurotic sort of flowers, he thought, casting their coloured shadows. Besides, he had never before, in their entire working life, considered the peculiarity of making a floral gesture to Grant. He had not had the heart to spurn Grace's idea, but the whole matter made him uneasy.

Grant was at the kitchen table studying road maps. He looked up, smiled at the odd sight of the flower-bearing William.

'Rufus has just rung to say he's dealing with a slow puncture. But he'll only be twenty minutes late.'

It was in a way, then, all just as ever. But some invisible feeling in the air alerted William.

'Fine.' William dumped the tulips on the table, pleased to be rid of them. 'Grace sent you these.'

'That's good of her.' Grant looked faintly surprised. 'Please thank her for me. Bonnie'll find a jug.' He was making notes. 'Planning the summer holiday. Not that far off. Complicated round trip – I'm not much good at maps.'

'Oh? Where to?' William asked. He was further unnerved, though could not think why.

'Here and there. Not entirely sure. Decisions, decisions. My head's reeling.' William swallowed. Grant was behaving a touch oddly. He was no planner, and no keen lover of Scotland, as far as William knew.

'Grace and I once had a good time in the Shetland Isles,' he said.

'Probably won't get that far.'

'Lovely little hotel on the edge of a voe, miles from anywhere. I could recommend –'

Bonnie came through the door. She wore a blue shirt that matched a bunch of bluebells she carried in one hand. She looked over Grant's shoulder at William, nodding towards the tulips.

'Did you bring those?'

'Grace sent them.'

'Coincidence.'

William frowned.

'What sort of coincidence?'

Bonnie shrugged.

'I don't know. So many sudden flowers. – I had a lovely walk in the wood. Up in the Chilterns.' This was to Grant.

'Well, I'll be setting up.' William was struck by a sudden need to distance himself from Grant and Bonnie and all the damned flowers.

When he had tuned his instrument, he started to play a passage from Mozart's violin concerto in D major. This he had not planned. The notes had just sprung from his fingers. Beyond them he was vaguely aware that Bonnie was gushing water into jugs, pushing the swan-necked tulips into some form of languorous arrangement. Then she turned her attention to the bluebells, plumping up a fountain of blue heads above a jug whose yellow shone lamp-like down the length of the barn. Through half-closed eyes he saw Rufus at the open door. Rufus paused to listen to the violin music for a few moments, as he regarded his oily hands. He nodded, then moved towards the sink. William stopped playing, mid-phrase.

'Lovely, lovely,' said Bonnie. 'Wish you'd play for us all afternoon.' William's mind flicked to time in the recent past when such words from her would have thrilled his afternoon, reverberated through a wakeful night, strengthened amorphous hope. Now they were merely gratifying, did nothing to endanger stupid fantasy. He could look quite calmly on Bonnie at last. The loathsome event of real murder, beside which his own ridiculous fantasies so appalled him, had stripped Bonnie of her powers. He still loved her, though. God, he loved her, as she might have guessed from his Mozart solo . . .

'Top form,' said Rufus. 'Wish I could play like Handle at his best. – I say, sorry I'm late. Tyre trouble.'

'Let's get on, shall we?' William's playing had done little to dispel his feeling of disquiet. He was impatient to dull the slight edge to the gathering: an edge he could not define precisely, but felt its keenness. The others, aware of his impatience, hurried to their places. The struggle with the unfamiliar Bartók began, and the day was lost in effort, concentration, equal moments of frustration and of joy.

When the rehearsal was over Grant suggested a cup of tea. By now William's inklings of trouble had vanished. He thought only how odd it was for the naturally inhospitable Grant to make such a suggestion at the end of a perfectly normal rehearsal. They sat round the chaos of his table – open maps spread wide, books, gloves, biscuits, full ashtrays – William opposite Bonnie, whose face (a little wary, it occurred to William) was a mosaic of reflections from the bluebells. Beautiful, she was. But how good it was, knowing she could no longer inadvertently torment him. William pulled himself up in his chair, strong in this knowledge. He was enjoying the tranquillity that comes from a still heart. He was enjoying the warm evening air that came through the open door.

Grant, at one end of the table, poured China tea into the usual grim-looking mugs. The thought came to William that the cellist was embuing the simple act with some premeditated lightness of touch, as if acting out a scene which he had judged should be without solemnity. William watched carefully, intrigued. (Later, reliving the tea ceremony, he regretted not observing Grant even more acutely.)

Grant sat.

'Well,' he said, eyes on one of the smaller maps he was attempting to fold, 'I think the time's come to break some good news. Bonnie and I are going to get married.'

In the second before rapid blinking of his eyes began, William saw Bonnie's face, cracked into a thousand pieces by the reflections of the flowers – *celebration flowers*, he now saw – she had clumped in the jug between them. He clasped the loose corduroy stuff of his trousers, felt the fanning of lashes on his eyeballs. Rufus, dear Rufus, thank God, jumped in with the right words of congratulations.

'And what dark horses, if I may say so,' Rufus added. 'William and I never had a clue.'

That was indeed the truth, William reflected, tightening his grip on his trousers.

'Yes: well – surprise. What a surprise. My congratulations, too.' William willed a smile to part his lips and wondered if the hoarseness of his voice was noticeable.

Bonnie was laughing, blushing, exchanging looks with Grant. Grant, to William's relief, made no move from his seat to give some public demonstration of love for his bride-to-be, but went instead to the fridge for a bottle of champagne. Bonnie fetched glasses in a trice. Funny, thought William, he had often wondered how she had always known where to find things in Grant's kitchen. Never had he suspected the reason.

They drank to the future of Grant and Bonnie, and to the future of the Elmtree – the future, now, of the – what would it be? Bonnie's eyes glittered under her dancing fringe, her dimples flashed with a steady rhythm. William could not remember her ever looking more enchanting.

'Amazing, isn't it?' she kept asking.

'Amazing,' agreed William, devoid of new words of his own.

'You're the first to know outside the family.' She smiled, with this bonus piece of information, first to William then to Rufus. 'July tenth is the wedding day, in my aunt's house at Marlow. The garden goes down to the river.'

'Marlow?' Further dismay struck William at this news. He'd always harboured an irrational dislike for Marlow and the Thames valley.

'*Marlow.*' Bonnie was firm. 'Whatever have you got against Marlow, William –?

'Nothing, nothing . . .'

'Here, have some more champagne.' She filled his glass. It would have to be a very slow journey home, he told himself. 'It'll be perfect,' she continued. 'High summer. And you know what we'd like?' She now gave a blatantly flirtatious look, this time first at Rufus, then William. (She'd always been so good at fairly dealing out her winning ways, William remembered.) 'We'd love it if you would play at the reception. I mean . . . would you?'

'Of course,' said Rufus. 'No greater pleasure.'

'Willingly,' agreed William, in barely a whisper.

'And how,' asked Rufus, unusually eager, 'did all this come about? Right under our noses, and we never guessed a thing?'

'Ah,' said Grant.

'I'll tell you,' said Bonnie. 'First day. Very first day. The audition. One look at Grant, and I thought it'd be a miracle if I managed to play at all, I was shaking so much.' *Funny I never noticed that. I could have sworn she was wonderfully calm.* William, pondering, managed a smile. 'All I could think of was, that's the man I've been *expecting*. Corny rubbish, I know, but there it was. I *recognised* Grant as the man for me. By the end of the first concert – you remember? Slough? Rain? – I knew I was in with a pretty good chance . . .'

'And you, Grant?' Rufus was asking all the questions William could not manage.

'I'm not sure I remember with quite Bonnie's pinpoint accuracy. But I suppose by Northampton I felt pretty much the same.'

Northampton: but that was where we drank coffee in the late, empty station after Bonnie missed the train . . . William glanced tightly at Rufus.

'But you never let on – not a sign, not an indication.' Rufus's incredulity reflected William's own, though he had no intention of confessing this.

'Of course not,' said Grant. 'We wanted to make absolutely sure before we chose the right moment to tell you. We couldn't possibly have shared it from the beginning with the two people we work so closely with, see most days. That would have been a terrible imposition, wouldn't have worked.'

'Exactly. It wouldn't have been fair,' added Bonnie. 'We all know the rules. If something's going on between two people in a small group it shouldn't intrude in any way. Just as if one person is affected by another – say my love for Grant hadn't been requited and I'd been miserable – then for the sake of the others it should be kept entirely private.'

'Quite,' said William.

'That's what we believed,' said Bonnie. A flutter of pride, at having behaved as Bonnie would have wanted, passed through William. 'Heaven knows, it was difficult. There were some close shaves.'

'I'll bet,' said Rufus, with some glee. 'All amazing, how you managed it. Iris'll be delighted.'

'We did manage never to lie,' said Grant. 'You pushed me a bit, William, on the way to Bournemouth. But I avoided an untruth.'

William gave a fraction of a smile to acknowledge Grant's skill in that matter. *And in how many hotel rooms did I imagine Bonnie was asleep on her own?* But despite the buzz of shock in his veins, William judged the revelations much easier to deal with than they would have been before the murder.

'I must be on my way,' he said. 'Grace will be so pleased.' He stood up, fingers on the table.

'Course, one of the things that made it easier for us was that you and Rufus are so wonderfully uncurious, unsuspicious, head in the clouds most of the time, hearts and souls in your music whether you're playing or not . . . ' Bonnie petered out, seeing William's face.

'Probably right there,' said Rufus, sparing William the need of a reply. 'Married couple in a quartet . . . How does that strike you, William?'

William paused, searching for words. This was not the time to work out his feelings about such a proposal.

'Don't see why not,' he said at last. Champagne bubbles swarmed through his head, hampering clarity.

'Don't worry,' said Grant. 'We've all sorts of ideas, how things could work out in the future. When we've all got a moment we could discuss . . . Put to you our thoughts.'

William nodded. He shook Grant's hand. Grant and Rufus shook hands, too. Bonnie kissed both William and Rufus on the cheek. Then the group of them, Rufus and William carrying their violins, went to the door. William glanced back for a second before stepping outside. His eyes stopped on the table bright with flowers, then moved on to the small distant semi-circle of music stands. Already the barn looked different. That was the magic of change. The power of news was bound to shift familiar, solid things.

Bonnie put an arm round his shoulders.

'You're the one I should really thank, dear William,' she said. 'You're the one whose decision to take me on counted.'

'Nonsense,' said William, freeing himself gently from her lest her touch, in this vulnerable moment, might work its old magic. 'It was a joint decision.'

'And isn't it all absolutely marvellous?' Now her arm was round Grant's waist. 'Hasn't it turned out amazingly?'

'Perfection,' was the word William used in answer, aware of its steeliness, its precision, its distancing.

On the way home he began to hum the Mozart violin concerto from where he had left off playing earlier. He timed it so skilfully (slowing almost to walking pace round the gentlest of bends) that he reached the last note as he turned into the drive. The accomplishment of this rather minor achievement – perfection on a different scale – gave him such satisfaction that with greater ease than he had supposed possible he went round into the garden, that temperate evening, and broke the news of the engagement to Grace. She, as he had rightly predicted, was full of wonder and delight and observed that, for so well matched a couple, the chances of a happily married life were high.

Bonnie and Grant were married on a day of high summer. Looking back, William was able only to recall fragments of the occasion. He remembered the lusty singing in the church, where the thickness of Norman stone deprived sunblades through roseate windows of their heat. Bonnie: far from clear, she was, in a crown of gypsophila, and her usual long wide sleeves, pure white this time. He remembered the look on Grant's face as he tried to steady his excited wife down the aisle, while a trumpet triumphed through the magnificent Purcell, and the church bells rang out. Then there was the gathering of guests, mostly unknown to William. Their glances snagged on each other as they hesitated across the lawn which ran, as Bonnie had promised, down to the river. The women wore those bright, herbaceous colours that the English deem suitable for weddings. The men, their buttonholes tufted with carnations set in wisps of greenery, seemed unusually interested in the happiness of the bride.

A buffet lunch had been set out in a small marquee. William and Rufus were the first to arrive there. They stuck close together, struck by the powerful smell of lilies and warm canvas. They refused glasses of champagne from wandering trays, lest it affect their performance. Unhungrily they picked at small sandwiches to fortify themselves for their professional role at this summer wedding. William remembered feeling the need for fortification. He remembered noticing his own nervousness reflected in Rufus: they both fingered their silvery ties and worried at their buttonhole carnations. William tried to calm himself with thoughts of thin rain, drowsy bees, crumpets – autumn things. The pictures did little good. He was grateful for the shade and emptiness of the tent, and of the closeness of Rufus.

'You know, I've been thinking quite a bit,' said his old friend. 'When the time comes for you and me to take a final bow, Bonnie and Grant would be a pretty good pair to run the Elmtree. Not much problem finding a couple of violins, I wouldn't have thought. Plenty of young talent about. And they'd carry on in the tradition of the Elmtree, I've no doubt of that.'

'Could be,' agreed William. He could see it all: Bonnie making free with her bows, Grant agreeing to an extravagance of encores. Still, those were minor considerations. Rufus was right. When their present run of luck was over, and they had to face departure, it might well work. But now wasn't the time to think about it.

'What will you be doing this week?' he asked. – There were no concerts arranged until after Bonnie and Grant returned from their honeymoon.

Rufus's hand hovered in a distracted manner between brown and white stuffed rolls. He, like William, was puzzled to discover that even after all these years of performing in public, the idea of playing at the wedding had caused a certain nervous tension.

'Iris and I are going to Norfolk,' he said. (It was William who had recommended the place, years ago, for which he remained particularly grateful since he had become so interested in the plight of birds.) 'We'll take some long walks round those great fields. Corn'll be cut. Hope to come across a few skylarks. – And you?'

'I've no plans,' said William.

When they had finished their sandwiches the two violinists went outside, joined the crowd round Grant and Bonnie. William dreaded his turn to kiss the bride with a kind of empty, dry dread: but it passed off smoothly. He was aware only of a brief zephyr of Bonnie's usual summery smell, her cheeks soft as rose petals, her eyes smiling through the swarm of dot-like white flowers, small as insects. Grant's hand, when William shook it, was damp, and his tie was immodest – he should have come to William for sartorial advice, William reflected: the cellist's taste in clothes had always been on the leeward side of vulgar. But he looked so damned pleased with himself. It was not the moment to voice reservations.

'Back in a moment, I'm going to set up the music,' Grant said to his wife, when he had finished patting Rufus on the shoulder. But Bonnie, her veil tangling with the white clouds above them, did not seem to hear.

Grant led William and Rufus to their chairs, placed with the music stands, in the shade of a small beech tree. They took their time getting out their instruments and placing their scores – hands working automatically, while their eyes flitted across the flutter of the wedding party. There had been several enjoyable evenings when the four members of the Elmtree had had long discussions about just what William and Rufus should play. Bonnie, very definite in her opinions, had been adamant they should include some of the Mozart duos she and William had played that winter morning, despite the fact that they were meant to be for violin and viola. William had found it hard to agree to this, but as there was no protest he could name, he nodded with a gallant show of enthusiasm. In the end, the first and second movements of the Bach Double were decided upon: perhaps, it occurred to William, Bonnie had some idea of how difficult the Mozart duos would have been for him, and was grateful for her change of mind. When they came to the Bach, Bonnie declared, she would leave the wedding guests to come and sit at their feet and listen. – Once the final choice had been made, William and Rufus had further enjoyable evenings, just the two of them, practising.

As they tuned their violins William let his eyes meander more slowly among the guests, their dresses and hats bending and swaying a little in the odd gusts of a warm breeze. He pondered on these strangers – a part of Bonnie's life he knew nothing about. Some of the men were probably of past importance: which ones? Which ones had loved her? And did they still? Were there any hearts beating with a faint, reluctant, bitter-sweetness, like his own?

William's hopeless questions were interrupted by the sight of Jack and Laurel. Even from this distance, William could tell, they were not best pleased. Laurel's offers of any amount of cut-price honeymoons had been politely turned down by Grant and Bonnie, who were bent on a secret destination in Scotland. Laurel had taken their refusal badly. Jack, in a spurt of loyalty, had felt it necessary to make several telephone calls to William, pressing him to persuade the couple to change their minds. William had refused to do any such thing. His obstinacy, as Jack saw it, caused a further rift. There had been no communication between father and son for a couple of weeks. From his unseen position William continued to gaze upon the unappealing couple that Jack and Laurel made. He could see Laurel tugging at Jack's arm, pointing to Bonnie. He could guess what she was saying, and turned his eyes from the pair with a sigh.

William looked now upon Grace and Iris, who kept as closely together as had he and Rufus earlier. They were enjoying themselves, enjoying the view of the river. (Not even on such a day could William's own prejudices about the vicinity of Marlow be overcome. Grace had chided him on the journey to the church, but it had made no difference.) Grace, from this distance, still appeared to be a pleasing-looking girl: her face was freckled with straw-shadows from the brim of her hat, which dipped beneath the weight of a real Louis Odier rose. She smiled her sweet smile about the place, gave William a merry wave. Grace: his dearest Ace. How good she was. She seemed to have got over the murder business surprisingly well: no apparent nightmares, no expressions of continued regret at her own absence on the day of the killing. The whole loathsome episode was not forgotten (never would be, could be). But at least they had managed to cast it aside, and in the continuing of their normal lives some unexpected strength had formed.

William kept fond eyes on his wife, arm now linked to Iris. He saw her move quickly to one side. She, sooner than anyone, realised a path was magically clearing for the bride. Bonnie, William observed, was making her way towards the beech tree. To him and Rufus, no doubt impatient for the music to start. She was almost running, pulling at a backwash of tulle like a small, eager boat. She was smiling, beautiful, happy. Grant, some paces behind her, was hurrying to catch up.

William and Rufus exchanged glances.

After so many years of playing together, there was no need of words between the two founding members of the Elmtree Quartet. They poised their bows, made comfortable their violins on their shoulders. William gave Rufus a nod so brief it would have been imperceptible to any musician less attuned to his friend's economy of gesture.

Bonnie, in all her glorious white, was almost upon them. They began to play.